THE WESTERN LIMIT OF THE WORLD

MASIEL, David

The western limit of the
world

THE WESTERN LIMIT OF THE WORLD

A Novel

DAVID MASIEL

HAMISH HAMILTON
an imprint of
PENGUIN BOOKS

HAMISH HAMILTON

Published by the Penguin Group
Penguin Books Ltd, 80 Strand, London WC2R ORL, England
Penguin Group (USA) Inc., 375 Hudson Street, New York, New York 10014, USA
Penguin Group (Canada), 90 Eglinton Avenue East, Suite 700,
Toronto, Ontario, Canada M4P 2Y3 (a division of Pearson Penguin Canada Inc.)
Penguin Ireland, 25 St Stephen's Green, Dublin 2, Ireland
(a division of Penguin Books Ltd)
Penguin Group (Australia), 250 Camberwell Road,
Camberwell, Victoria 3124, Australia (a division of Pearson Australia Group Pty Ltd)
Penguin Books India Pvt Ltd, 11 Community Centre,
Panchsheel Park, New Delhi – 110 017, India
Penguin Group (NZ), cnr Airborne and Rosedale Roads, Albany,
Auckland 1310, New Zealand (a division of Pearson New Zealand Ltd)
Penguin Books (South Africa) (Pty) Ltd, 24 Sturdee Avenue,
Rosebank, Johannesburg 2196, South Africa

Penguin Books Ltd, Registered Offices: 80 Strand, London WC2R ORL, England

www.penguin.com

First published in the United States of America by Random House 2005
First published in Great Britain by Hamish Hamilton 2006

1

Copyright © David R. Masiel, 2005

and in ... es,
us... ion or are
... cales,
... al.

re[...] ... ystem,
or trans[...] ... nechanical,
ph... ... prior
written permission of both the copyright owner and
the above publisher of this book

Printed in Great Britain by Clays Ltd, St Ives plc

A CIP catalogue record for this book is available from the British Library

HARDBACK
ISBN-13: 978-0-241-14266-0
ISBN-10: 0-241-14266-0

TRADE PAPERBACK
ISBN-13: 978-0-241-14267-7
ISBN-10: 0-241-14267-9

For Dawn and Emily and Jackson
In memory of
Morwenna Louise

PART ONE

THE NAVIGABLE SEMICIRCLE

ONE TREMBLES TO THINK OF
THAT MYSTERIOUS THING IN THE SOUL,
WHICH SEEMS TO ACKNOWLEDGE NO HUMAN
JURISDICTION, BUT IN SPITE OF THE
INDIVIDUAL'S OWN INNOCENT SELF,
WILL STILL DREAM HORRID DREAMS, AND
MUTTER UNMENTIONABLE THOUGHTS.

–HERMAN MELVILLE, *Pierre*

THE BOATSWAIN OF *TARSHISH*

Harold Snow figured he'd seen more dead people than anyone alive, something like 102,000 by his best estimate. Lately his eyeballs played old film, like movie screens showing heinous scenes, the dead queued up before him to shake his shoulders and yell, "Wake up!" But Snow couldn't wake up. The night the new ordinary came aboard, he lay in his bunk being chased by bombs. He was running down the side deck of a fleet oiler in 1942. Then he was in a medical ward at Pearl where a nurse was giving him a sponge bath and a hard-on at the same time. When he finally did awaken it was thirty-eight years later and a voice in his blacked-out room was telling him the ship had been denied entry into San Francisco.

Snow rolled toward the sound wishing he could pretend this was impossible. He wished he could kill the messenger. People underestimated the power of that kind of thing; it was ritualized denial, though in this case he didn't even know who the messenger was. A dream voice, that nurse, flicking his erection as if removing an insect then telling him the Coast Guard was turning the tanker around. Time was muddled. He was ship's boatswain. He hauled himself out of his bunk and across the room wearing boxer shorts, his gray hair sticking straight up off his head. His body was tanned, muscles tightening as he walked, belly round and hard, but his joints clicked. In his private head, he washed his face and combed his hair with Vitalis. By the time he stepped down the passageway from his cabin on the ship's O-2 deck, he wore simple leather work boots, jeans cuffed at the ankles, suspenders, a pinstriped work shirt– blue–and a mackinaw jacket. He descended the internal stair tower and out the companionway to the afterdeck, to a clear winter dusk.

His ship was called *Tarshish,* and she lay at anchor eight miles outside the Golden Gate, just north of the sea buoy and just west of the pilot boat *San Francisco,* its mast lights pitching on a rising southwesterly swell. Beyond, Snow could see the dim hump of the Marin headlands, with the blinking swing of Point Bonita Light defining its seaward side. To the east-southeast, the Golden Gate formed two perfect waves of lighted orange. Along the waterfront, lights began their glimmers, Coit Tower like a glowing fire nozzle, the narrow girded pyramid of the Trans-America building rising before the downtown. The sight of it all, and the prospect that they had just lost five million dollars in cargoes, made a desperate ball form in his chest.

Snow turned up the portside weather deck to find Bracelin, the ship's chief mate, talking with a Coast Guard ensign, leaning toward the man with insistence. "This is cheap screw," he said. Two crewmen listened from above, stretched out over the poop deck railing making motions as if to spit on the coastie's head.

Ostensibly joking, their faces had a grim set, and they looked to be having little fun with it.

The coastie was holding his own, all spit-polish with a voice that lectured. "Some people might be okay with bulk chemicals washing up on Fisherman's Wharf. Me, I have a problem with it. If this were a U.S.-flagged ship, she'd be impounded and towed to dry dock. As is, consider yourselves fortunate."

He sounded like a northeastern boy. One of those yacht guys, a real sailor. Snow had the urge to toss the prick overboard. But the coastie was buff in a thin-waisted way. He could probably tread water for three days. They'd have to knock him one on the head before they gave him the heave-ho, and Snow didn't much care for knocking people on the head. He'd done it before in his life and, truth was, these days he didn't like thinking about it. He didn't like the bad dreams he'd been having. He didn't like the mood of self-judgment, or the way a certain female AB looked at him when he told her things he had done in his life.

He realized now that she'd been the one to rouse him with the bad news. She had told him and run off before he was fully awake.

A crew boat approached along the port side, the coastie checking his watch, then blathering on about two dozen code violations, about illegal soft plug repairs in the pipeline, about a compromised seal on the covered lifeboat. "Mark my words: you try to put to sea in that, you will buy the Ground Port."

Snow wondered what the hell this guy knew about the Ground Port. He couldn't resist chiming in. "Listen here, buddy. First off, that was on our list. So it's clear we ain't trying to hide anything. Second off, we can't address problems if we can't get business done."

The coastie looked skyward in irritation. Then he blanched. The two Malaysian sailors hung over him, lifted their chins at him. "Uhh—" he stammered and looked at Snow. "You're missing the point, bos'n." He looked back up at the sailors and stepped out of their fall line.

"The point," said Bracelin, "is we're working our tails off to make this tub of shit copasetic." He stood a head taller than the coastie. "You got any idea how much money we stand to lose?"

The mate had the ugliest mug Snow had ever seen, like someone had carved a pumpkin only to decide on a different design, and so stuffed all the pieces back in place, the seams showing. As if that wasn't enough dead tissue, he had bead-sized scars all over his cheeks and nose from windblown caustic burns. His arms looked like gnarled tree roots entwined across his chest, and though the temperature wasn't more than 40 degrees F, Bracelin wore short-sleeved coveralls that said WADE on the front patch and CROWN MOVING AND STORAGE on the back. His first name wasn't Wade at all, it was Charlie, but he wore those covies whenever a new man was coming aboard, regardless of climate, so they could see his thick biceps and arcane tattoos and be properly intimidated.

The most obvious tattoo was the analemma on the inside of Bracelin's left forearm. A figure-eight pattern with the approximate proportions of a bowling pin, the analemma showed the variation of the sun's position in the sky, as if you stood on a spot at the equator and took a snapshot of the sun at the same hour of every day for a full year. It bore the markings of the days of the year along with parallels of latitude, while his right forearm showed a series of equations, the stuff of spherical trigonometry. Bracelin's tattoos weren't just ornamental–he could figure his position at sea using only a sextant, a chronometer, a pencil, and his tattoos. Long as nobody cut his arms off, he didn't need star tables.

Now Bracelin's jaw muscles strained as he leaned forward. He looked ready to take a bite out of the guy's neck.

"Just take it easy," said the coastie. "There's nothing I can do for you, gentlemen." He tore off four sheets from his citation book and handed them to Bracelin. "Have a safe trip out of U.S. waters."

With the only good ear he had left, Snow heard a racket from up the deck, where two ABs leaned against the bulwarks holding a fire ax and a length of pipe respectively, hammering the deck with the butts of the tools. Then the crewmen overhead started in to whistle, and before long the crew was crowing and complaining like animals. Snow heard Ali, one of the Malaysians, say "Orang-puteh so stupid one-lah, no get into Frisco no way now!" while above, someone else bemoaned the loss of the Chinese New Year: "Year of the Snake I go Eddy Street get fucky for four dollar. God damn, no go Eddy Street now. No go Eddy Street!"

Snow felt the disappointment too, but he had visions of lost cargoes, lost dollars, lost opportunity–even a lost girl. The coastie looked around at the protesting crew and then stared straight at Bracelin. "Your crew's a bit tense."

"Three months on deep water," said the mate.

"They were hoping to go ashore," Snow added.

The coastie peered around as if seeing the ship for the first time. "Unusual situation you have here. American officers and petty officers, but a foreign crew." He looked to be pondering some life-altering decision. And maybe it was. Snow waited to hear where he was going with this, how far he wanted to push it.

"Ain't so unusual," said Bracelin. "We got a recent sale; we're just seeing out this run."

"Right," said the coastie. He looked around. Then at Bracelin. "What'd you say was wrong with the captain?"

"You saw him. He's sick."

"Never heard of a foreign outfit keeping American officers."

"Listen, bub," Bracelin snarled, "I'm no academy grad. I don't get the plums. I was a raw squid in 'fifty-nine, and the CPO of a nuclear submarine six years later. I been a merchant officer fifteen years. I came up the hawse pipe. I think I understand how things work. My job's running cargo, so I'm gonna go do that. Your job is to wait for your ride and make sure you don't fall overboard."

Bracelin moved topside, taking steps three at a time. Damn him for mentioning the sale, such as it was. The ensign kept watching the crew. Snow wanted them calm—he turned and raised a hand, and they fell quiet. They were a ragged crowd, with Frisco jeans and greased canvas pants and coveralls, faces streaked by sweat and frustration. Not only had they been aboard since Port Kuleng, Malaysia, without break, they'd worked ten hours prepping for this inspection. They didn't give a damn about contracts, all they cared about was sucking down Tsing-tao beers and ushering in the Year of the Monkey in Frisco Chinatown. By Snow's way of thinking, they had reason to be tense.

Ships steamed inbound, a box boat for Oakland and a tanker for Benicia or maybe the Richmond long wharf. Snow watched them with longing, but had to admit that going ashore was a mixed thing, lost cargoes aside. Some ways he itched to head up San Pablo Avenue and have dinner at the Hofbrau and find the Wooden Indian and settle in for drinks just a block from his old house there in El Cerrito, never mind he didn't drink anymore. But he also knew he'd end up walking by the old house, with no one he knew living there after all these years, no wife or son for sure, nothing save a dark hole of lost time. Thinking about that made him want to flee, and in his mind he hopped outbound ships, veering north toward Seattle and Anchorage, or south toward San Pedro, or straight west into the vast black Pacific.

Snow breathed deeply, calmed himself. He said, "I got work," and started forward, took intentionally long strides up toward the midship tankerman's locker. He passed the scowling faces of crewmen. "Time for work, gents!" he said, in a grandfatherly voice, continuing on as if he had something to do out on the bow. But he had nowhere to go. He found himself drifting into the shadows. The weather deck of a chemical tanker was a crowded place, a tangled system of pipelines and bulbous valves and vent stacks rising thirty feet overhead. Snow heard fans running and smelled the gas-freeing of two tanks that once held acrylonitrile. He recognized the peach odor. Made you want to smell it, even though smelling it for long gave you dancing black spots and smelling it long enough left you brain damaged. He wondered if half the crew wasn't already there.

They were known as drugstore ships or parcel tankers. They hauled acids, caustics, chlorinated solvents, aromatic hydrocarbons, in a worldwide trade. Bulk chemicals that ached to react with something: each other, sea water, air, or nothing but themselves. Prior to loading, the crew filled tanks with inert nitrogen gas to keep certain chemicals from spontaneously going off. Right now Snow paced on top of a tank of vinyl chloride monomer, a self-reacting gem. Polymerized, it turned to polyvinylchloride–PVC–the white pipe used in a million sprinkler systems all over America. The crew had to pump chemical inhibitors into the stuff to keep it from turning to plastic right there in its own tanks. Have to tear the ship apart to get it all out, assuming the reaction didn't do it for you.

Snow stretched out his upper torso and dug his fingers up under his right rib as if to extract a rock. A tight pain ran up his chest, like he'd slipped a rib or torn a muscle or something. He pulled his elbows back as far as he could, stretching over and over until they nearly touched behind him, and still the sensation persisted.

He heard some grunting from nearby and weaved through the pipes to find a certain female AB lying on her back, trying to tighten a Dresser coupling with a three-foot-long pipe wrench. Snow watched her face tighten as she yarded on the long end,

punctuating her pulls with sharp exhalations, over the smell of
kerosene-based jet fuel, an oil-only Sorbent pad on her chest to
collect the drippings. Her name was Elisabeth Abudjah.

"You're working hard!"

She started. "Bloody hell, Snow! How about a bit of warning?"
Beth was English on her mom's side and Liberian on her dad's, but
it was her mom taught her to talk.

"One of the ten thousand things I like about you, Bethy.
Hardest-working AB I got. Dress like a boy and work like a man!"

"I quit working, someone might notice me."

"Oh, they notice you all right, you don't have to worry about
that," Snow said, and then a line from a song came to him. Among
other useless talents, Snow did a dead-on impression of Billie
Holiday. He had a high frail voice anyway, and it was a strange
sight, a pot-bellied white man singing like some kind of rare
instrument. Snow stopped crowds when he sang like Billie:

"I got a house and a showplace,
but can't get no place with you. . . ."

"That's a trifle thick when I'm lying here bathed in jet fuel,"
she said.

"I met her once. I tell you that?"

"I know, and shagged her."

"Now, I told you I was kidding about that."

Beth grunted out the last hundredth of an inch on that
coupling before she finally quit. The leak gave one last drip and
stopped. "Listen, Snow, I need to talk to you about Bracelin. The
man won't quit on the crank thing. I've told him a dozen times I
can't get it. I just don't have those kinds of contacts. He's getting
ugly. I need him to stop."

"Well, he's always been ugly," said Snow, "but I'll have a talk with him. What kind of boyfriend would I be if I didn't?"

The watch bell rang before she could answer, and he was glad of that. Red-glowing faces appeared in the bridge glass–Paynor, the second mate; Lucy the Third–and there next to her, the haggard face of Captain McFarland, who hadn't ventured from his cabin in four weeks and now stood staring out like he wasn't sure where the hell he was. Then Bracelin joined them, scowling and mute, staring off with binoculars fixed ashore.

Snow looked along the side deck to where the coastie was talking with Delacroix, the wall-eyed old ordinary who stood with his seabag at his feet prepping to jump ship. The two men were dwarfed by the ship's house, which rose four stories off the stern end, a white monolith of block steel with round portholes like three dozen eyeballs glaring down on him, weeping rust in place of tears. Overhead, the Liberian flag made popping sounds in the onshore breeze and looked eerily like Old Glory: a single star against a blue background, with eleven broad red and white stripes.

Snow was trying to figure out how they could replace five million in cargoes out of Richmond and then another five million out of El Segundo in SoCal. Looking at the coastie now, he wondered how hard it would be compared with explaining to authorities how the body of a Coast Guard ensign happened to wash ashore at Fort Miley with his skull bashed in. Snow felt a kind of narcolepsy wash over him. He wanted to lie down on deck and take a snooze. He wanted to lie down next to the girl and put his head on her belly like a pillow. Then Marty and Ali came along, complaining about not being able to go ashore. "That coastie tight like wire rope, lah," said Ali. "He needs loosen up. I got the wrench to do him aaaah!" and he grabbed Beth's pipe wrench. "Saya mahu membunuh!"

Near as Snow understood, this meant "I want to kill!" in Malay, a desire that needed no translation, since it was etched all over the man's face.

Beth wiped her hands with a rag, then reached out for her wrench. "May I?"

Ali handed it over. "Maybe bos'n want kill coastie!"

"Listen. You'll get shore time in PC and Costa Rica. No sense beating on a dead horse here." The easy voice of Snow relaxed them. "Bow time now, go anchor prep." He nodded but otherwise made no motion to touch them. They nodded—okay, boatswain— and weaved inboard through the pipeline network, then climbed to the fo'c'sle deck with an uncanny instinct for staying invisible to the bridge.

When Snow looked back, Beth was striding away from him with the pipe wrench over her shoulder, and Snow saw the crew boat coming alongside, ferrying the replacement ordinary. Snow knew this kid because he'd hired him. His name was George Maciel. Snow had seen the name on a crew sheet cabled over from the Percell manning agency, called him by ship-to-shore in some shit heel hotel on Howard Street, and learned he was the grandson of Snow's first merchant captain, a man who had pulled the boatswain out of the rubble of war and given him work. Now the kid stood in the stern of the water taxi, bulked up in heavy clothing as if ready for arctic seas, with an orange flotation vest over a thick jacket. Snow wanted to shout, *we're headed for the e-quator!*

The Jacob's ladder unraveled with a clatter down the side shell. The ship heaved in a slow easy rhythm, but the small boat pitched and bucked all over. The kid hefted his navy-blue seabag and tried to keep his balance as the boat thumped and slammed the side of the ship, scraping free a swath of barnacles that flew upward like popcorn. Snow could see the crew-boat skipper going ballistic behind the wheelhouse glass, his face glowing green in the light from his control console, shouting, "Get your ass off my boat and on that ladder!"

The kid was reaching for the ladder. All bundled up the way he was–plus lugging that heavy bag–made him none too nimble. He grabbed and jumped onto the rope ladder. He barely got his boots on the lower rung when the crew boat powered off to avoid a beating, waiting a hundred feet off while the kid dangled. Then a big swell came along and swallowed him to his neck. When it fell away, the sea dragged him off the ladder entirely. He was floating in the swell, getting scraped along the hull with all those barnacles biting into his overcoat. He pushed himself off, keeping one arm hooked through the strap of the seabag. A flailing right hand grabbed hold of the ladder and hung on. As the swell receded, he clung there, tendons lifted and taut.

On deck the crew was screaming *Man overboard!* in five languages. By the time the new man hauled himself up the ladder, he was soaked through. Delacroix helped the kid over the bulwarks and then proceeded to get face-to-face with him, his one eye staring to shore while the other glowed fiercely. "Are you stupid? Is that the problem? You're stupid, aren't you?"

Snow stepped over to rescue the kid. He was standing there dripping, prying himself out of his sopping overcoat. He was somewhere in his twenties, a gangly thing about Snow's height, six-two. But his arms appeared devoid of muscle. "Let him alone now," Snow said.

The kid was blue at the lips, the pale skin of his face and shaved head shining in contrast to his clothes, which were black from collar to boots, and Snow knew at a glance he'd never been to sea in his life.

While the coastie backed down the ladder to board the crew boat, Delacroix's good eye looked over the sopping float vest like he'd never seen a greater affront to a sailor's dignity. "For Christ's goddamned sake, kid."

"Croix," said Snow, "I been listening to your crap for two months. If you worked your arms half as hard as you worked your jaw, you'd be a decent enough ordinary. You might even make AB before you turn sixty."

"Fuck you and your scow, bos'n."

"Just get your ass ashore."

"Poison ship! Poison goddamned bastard ship!" Delacroix swung his leg over the railing, calling out complaints that sounded like warnings and warnings that sounded like complaints. "Nobody speaks any goddamned English! Nobody knows what anybody else is saying!"

The kid showed little reaction to this tirade, like he'd heard his share.

Then, as Delacroix backed down, something flat-out strange happened. His bum eye righted itself an instant and he made full eye contact. Snow felt all squirrelly inside, like he'd been hexed. Delacroix's eyes disappeared down the ladder as he shouted out to the city, "This is what comes from having no union, by God! Flags of convenience! It's the working man takes it up the rear!" His voice faded away.

Snow turned to the kid. "Don't listen to him. We got a first-rate crew."

The kid wavered over his legs, so Snow grabbed his arm and felt someone else take him by the other shoulder–Beth.

"Are you the boatswain?" the kid asked. He said the word the way it looked.

"That'd be me. So's you know, it's pronounced *bos'n*, not *boat-swayne*."

"Leave it to English," said the kid, his lips quivering with cold.

They led him up an external ladder to the poop deck, where

Snow heard a yell and a curse, followed by a splash. Then the sickening crunch. The *man overboard* shouts began again, the crew all dancing like fools save for Marty and Ali, who had come from the bow and were scampering down the Jacob's ladder. The voice of the Coast Guard ensign crackled over the crew boat's loudhailer: *"We have a man overboard! An injured man overboard!"*

Snow turned with Beth and they marched right back down with the kid between them. By the time they hit bottom the kid was moving under his own power, and Snow stepped fast to the bulwark and looked over the side to where the lighted body of Delacroix floated face down in the black water, his arm broken backward at the elbow, his body crushed all down his left side. Snow knew what had happened, knew the sound of a human body getting the quick crunch.

The crew boat idled fifty feet away, spotlight fixed on Delacroix, held off for fear of popping the man a second time. Snow turned to Beth, but before he opened his mouth she was saying, "I'll ride," and moved into the open locker and came out already climbing into a harness while Bracelin called out, "You, Leeds! Boom op!"

Leeds climbed into the open cockpit of the deck crane, pulled the main hydraulic lever and swung the boom out of its cradle and over toward Beth, where Snow snapped the karabiner onto the crane hook. A second later she was in the air, her fatigues bunched up her ass and riding up to show her brown calves as she spun gently in a circle. Leeds swung her out as far as he could and lowered her straight down into the seas, where she floated, still wired up to the crane, and turned Delacroix's floating body over. Snow saw the wet blankness of his face and the bleeding out his eyes and ears, and he thought, that's *one hundred two thousand and one.*

THE WHOLE DAMNED CREW

Inside the passageway, Snow heard competing strains of music filtering through the house as he ushered the kid topside, Indian sitars and wailing Arabic singers and den-den drums going lickety split, and Charlie Parker going off like a mad goose, all to the beat of wet boots squishing behind Snow. The kid dragged that soaked-through seabag with his grandpa's name and address stenciled on it, JOAQUIN J. MACIEL, 610 33RD STREET, RICHMOND, CALIFORNIA 94802, though what he was doing with his gramp's seabag, Snow had no clue.

Beth watched them go as the kid looked back, and something in their traded look made Snow walk faster. The whole scene brought black spots to his eyes. He decided then to do something he hadn't done in fifteen years, not since he'd started sailing boatswain: he'd share his room, bring the kid in to live with him, so he could keep an eye out. Then he felt dread about giving up his privacy. He held out hope that the girl would come to visit him, and listen to Artie Shaw with Billie Holiday and the Count and the Duke, and let him swing her in a circle. But Beth hadn't come in two weeks. She'd sat alone in the crew's mess. She'd brooded, sullen in her tasks.

In the room, the kid dug into his seabag, pulling out wet books and a metal strongbox with a key lock, and finally a black tee shirt that had been stuffed so far down as to escape the seas.

"That girl back there," Snow said, "the one helped you. Just so you know, she's my girlfriend. Hands off that one, you don't mind."

"I wasn't planning on putting my hands on her," the kid said. He had an edge of attitude, like a smart guy, a regular book boy.

Snow wanted to like him. "Just so you know."

The kid's upper body was both frail and severe. His chest was dead flat, fists swollen in a flat ridge across the knuckles. He wore a tattoo on his left upper arm, a blue-ink sign of the cross–simple, just a cross, no fancy parlor job–and a silver earring in his left ear. Snow saw him for the first time all the way around, saw the scars on his backside where he'd been walloping himself a good one. Snow knew a bit about self-abuse, not because he'd ever engaged in any of the painful kind, but because he'd seen plenty who did, in ways countless and varied. One ordinary he knew way back had gone to sea straight from the rainforests of Borneo. Apparently in his tribe you weren't all man until you'd carved two holes under your ribs for the purpose of hanging yourself from a tree. He'd considered it his religious prerogative to hook himself up by chain fall in the fo'c'sle generator room. He hung in there for two hours sometimes, earplugs shoved into his ears, zoned off in religious ecstasy to the tune of a Cat 343 diesel generator set.

The kid pulled the dry black tee shirt on over his head.

"Me, I never saw the point in a tattoo," said Snow. "All them fucking salty dogs with their tattoos turn my stomach. I ain't got even one. I got scars, though, wanna see?"

"Sure," said the kid.

Snow's eyebrows turned up at the end like miniature horns. He tugged his sleeve up to reveal the first dripping shine of burn scars. "Jap Zero blew me thirty feet across deck. Lit my hair on fire. You ever seen a man with his hair on fire? God awful sight." He turned to get a look at himself in the mirror. Snow liked his war scars. "Your granddad was the saltiest bastard I ever sailed with. You don't look even a bit like him."

"I look like my mother, I think." The kid flashed an old black-and-white taken about 1956. She was a tall woman, angular, with a face like Audrey Hepburn. She was holding a baby, presumably young George. Seeing it made Snow think of his own son, the first time he ever saw the boy, an infant no more than four weeks old. Home from sea, first time in his life he'd ever touched a baby. Squeezing the boy's fat little arm, his breath all sweet with that newborn smell you couldn't describe or forget.

The kid looked all morose though, pulling out wet photos and peeling them apart to dab them dry with the tee shirt. He brought more pictures over and laid them out across the tight wool blanket of his upper bunk. Snow caught a glimpse: they were old black-and-white snapshots of riverboats, the old man, and the kid's grandmother—family scenes. Faces smeared and smudged by water damage. Snow recognized the grandmother—he'd met her once, a mousy, pious woman. The kid kept blotting at the photos with the shirt, but only smeared them more. "The guy at the outfitter said this was waterproof."

"Nothing waterproof in the end."

Snow looked over at the portrait of a crew posing on the after-deck of a small river tanker, a boat Snow knew all too well. He could picture stepping aboard it like he'd done so this minute, an old

belching steamer called *San Luis Rey*. Back row stood the grandfather, with black Portagee eyes and bushy brows, in the uniform
of a working captain, a man of the deck. There was the chief engineer too, a man called Van Sickle. In the front row, the scar on
Harold Snow's twenty-five-year-old forehead had only just healed,
his hair just starting to grow back normal, his hands thick and
folded on his lap and the war still playing in his eyes.

The war was ancient history and then some, but heading back out
to work, Snow couldn't get it out of his mind. His career at sea had
begun from war, when he made his way from the mountains of
Washington State to Pearl Harbor on December 5, 1941, lived
through the torpedo bombs two days later, and five months after
that celebrated his twenty-second birthday aboard a fleet oiler in
the Battle of the Coral Sea. He knew well the feel and look of aerial
bombardment, how bombs started round from the underbellies of
Zeros, singing as they fell toward him, then elongating suddenly
and winging past to explode in the water beyond. But one stayed
round all the way, diving straight for his head. He ducked instinctively, felt hot air as the bomb flew three feet over his head and
drove two levels down before detonating. The deck erupted
upward and Snow was blown out of his shoes. His mind tried to
process the reality of being blown from his shoes. He felt his body
turn momentarily to gelatin, and his feet just slipped right out.
When he came down an instant later, a man's shoulder came down
with him, landing on his lap with the arm still attached. He
pitched the thing off, smelled cordite and barbecued flesh, could
hear nothing in either ear, but felt a rush of wind and looked up to
see a Zero fly past and merge silently into the ship's deckhouse.

The kamikaze attack unfolded like a silent film until a wall of
flame blew him laterally thirty feet across the deck. He felt himself
burning, smothering the fire on his head with bare hands, searing

his palms. Out across the deck, amid the pipelines and valves of the oiler, Snow saw a burned lump of coal that a minute before had been one of his shipmates, smoldering now, unrecognizable as anything human save for a high sweet sound, a moan of *Ooooooooooooh-ohhhhhhhhhhh*. Snow was unsure if some life didn't still reside in there, moaning out in hellish pain, or if expanding gas in the lungs was simply activating the larynx. But at least he could hear again, out of one ear anyway.

Sometime later, after the battle, the attackers shot down or driven off, Snow and four others dug down into the wreckage of the engine room and found the kamikaze pilot. They dragged his charred remains out on deck, heaving him over the bulwarks. Weakened by battle, they couldn't heave him far enough, and the body bounced off the outboard edge of the deck and cleaved open. Their cheer was muted by the sight. Fatigued and barely vocal, one sailor said "Hibachi barbecue," and another managed a croaking "Fuck you!" before the body hit *thwap* on the water.

After that he spent a day and a half on a lifeboat next to a burned sailor who kept falling against Snow's blistered arm. Snow would push the man off, saying, "Watch it there, buddy," gentle as he could. They were all in sad shape, no point dwelling on misery, but the man kept leaning against that arm and Snow finally snapped and cursed and shoved him off, only to watch him roll and flop to Snow's lap, face up. Snow stared at his dead eyes for quite a while before he shook him off and watched him roll into the bottom of the boat. Then Snow passed out himself. When he woke up he was on an aircraft carrier, watching Corsairs dive-bomb and sink the ship they'd saved. Then he was in that burn ward at Pearl. "You won the Navy Cross, sailor," the nurse said. "You saved your ship from the Japs."

"And got it bombed by Americans."

"Oh, now, don't you worry a thing about that. Those things happen."

Her angelic face was framed by a starched and folded nurse's cap, like a nun's habit, and even after she flicked his erection and kept on washing like an old pro, he thought, damned if she isn't the prettiest thing. I'll dance with her, he said to himself. I'm gonna dance with this girl. And he did. Two weeks later, after he'd become ambulatory again, he sneaked in a Count Basie record and swung the nurse in circles to the hoots of sailors, their Navy Crosses bouncing, pinned to their bedsheets.

Snow found himself sitting on the side deck next to the boatswain's locker. He was aboard *Tarshish* again. He thought he heard the crackle of fireworks from the city. He stood up and went aft to the fantail. There he found Bracelin reading through the coastie's citation sheets with a look of massive irritation. He folded the papers once and handed them to Snow. "Take care of these." Snow folded them into his back pocket while Bracelin tucked a thick vinyl binder up under his arm, the binder that held all the ship's paperwork, including cargo manifests and inspection papers. The mate stood upright and rigid. "So, this new ordinary. How is it he manages to go overboard before he ever gets on board to begin with? Sounds kinda–paradoxical."

"Now there's a ten-dollar word for you."

"Ten dollars ain't my worry. Ten *million* is my worry."

Snow straightened himself as casually as he could, imposing even at his age. His shoulders felt broad inside the lined macki-naw, and he could ignore now that tight ball under his right rib, not painful so much as knobby. He stared at the chief mate, who stood a couple inches taller than he did, but no thicker. In his time, Snow thought, he might have stood a chance against Charlie Bracelin.

"I don't like you calling manning agencies saying you're me," the mate growled. "It's like you're trying to *usurp* my authority."

Snow just stared at the goateed face, the shining scar tissue looping over his nose. Usurp. For the life of him he couldn't figure out where a pigsticker like Bracelin learned a word like that. "You talk more like a Kings Point captain every day," said Snow. "Keep your eye on the ball, Brace. We'll make up for all this in Mexico."

"Don't *Brace* me."

"I'm just saying, it's all gonna work out. We got a month to get to Freetown."

"And now we're gonna lose two weeks lining up new cargoes, and what do we get for it? We trade n-bute and chlorinated solvents for Pemex gas and ammonia water. We're gonna lose five mil on that trade-off alone."

Snow didn't see the point of all this. If there was anything weak about the mate, that was it: a tendency to go ape shit when things didn't go his way. "Ain't no problem, Mate. Ain't no problem. Trust me on this one."

"Nothing personal, but I don't trust anybody."

"Well, I'm surely glad to know that," said Snow. "Seeing as how we're partners. And since we are partners, there's one more thing, Mate. Don't go harassing Bethy about getting crank for you. In fact, don't go harassing her at all."

Bracelin let out a grunting smirk. "Sure thing, old man."

"I got work," Snow said, and moved around the house and started forward. He saw the crew boat motoring inside the Gate. He heard the clank of the anchor chain rocking up the hawse pipe, and the feeling they were heading to sea again buoyed him. He had no interest in wallowing in the disappointment of Frisco any more than he did the horrors of war. He'd known all along that trying to enter harbor here was a risk. He knew too it could have turned out a lot worse. He'd seen that darkness in the coastie's eye, like the man had a feeling about things. He didn't like the officers or the crew, and if only he could have found something wrong in the paperwork he'd have screwed them to the wall for sure. Maybe somewhere inside, the snotty prick had known the truth, that the ship wasn't called *Tarshish* at all. She had another name, one Snow had purged from his mind like that of an old lover.

The seas were flat calm and warming on their southern track when Snow took Maciel out to the weather deck in shirtsleeves to teach him his knots and splices like a real sailor. He taught the kid timely and necessary knots (bowline, half hitch, sheet bend), as well as some that had gone out of use with the advent of steam, including what Snow fondly regarded as the most useless knot of all: the sheepshank. To him the whole exercise had nothing to do with utility and everything to do with self-image. "A man who knows his craft knows himself," he said, then got the kid going on weaving rope fenders, mending sails, and splicing line, the pinnacle of which was the venerable back splice, better known as a dog prick.

It took half the kid's first watch, but finally they got down to hard labor. Snow had him on hands and knees grinding the deck with a pneumatically driven wire wheel. He was prepping for paint they didn't have aboard, but that didn't matter. The kid didn't flinch, he just worked. "He pushes it, I'll give him that," said Bracelin, as he passed by on his rounds. "For an ordinary semen wiper."

The mate took this appellation from the kid's rating on his Z-card, which was ORDINARY SEAMAN/WIPER, but which Bracelin said in such a way that it invariably sounded like the kid was willing to wipe semen, so long as it wasn't of an extraordinary type.

In Maciel's case he didn't even get that much respect from the rest of the crew. When Snow assigned him to train with Marty and Ali in the finer points of creative repairs, the able seamen waited until Snow had gone and then chased the kid off. "Go work girl," said Ali. "Clean number-three tanks lah."

So the kid went off to "work the girl," a spontaneous reassignment that Snow didn't learn about until after the fact, when he saw Beth and the kid climb out of the tank for a coffee break, the both of them glowing orange with ferruginous dust. When Snow confronted Marty and Ali, they just shrugged and waved and talked in tongues. "What the hell's eating you two?"

"That new man," said Marty. "He's bad news, bos'n. And Delacroix the one has to pay. *Tenía que pagar.*"

"The kid wasn't anywhere near Delacroix," Snow said. "He works hard, give him a chance."

"Work stupid lah," said Ali. "Don't know shit lah."

It had taken Snow a month to figure out Ali's peculiar version of Malay English, a salad of *lah*s and *aaa*s that put pronouns all in a jumble and only made sense if you stopped thinking about it. While it was true the kid didn't know shit, Snow figured what he lacked in knowledge he made up for with basic sense, and what he lacked in sense he made up for with youthful energy. Besides that, off watch he was a good shipmate. All he did was sit on his bunk and read from religious books and write in a small spiral notebook, or listen to a miniature cassette player over small foam headphones that sat lightly on his ears, and out of which Snow could hear something akin to music.

"He can't learn if we don't teach him," Snow insisted.

"Like *syaitan* can't teach nothing him!" said Ali.

"Satan? What the fuck, Ali? He prays like a fucking monk. Reads religious books and writes *reflections* or some such crap."

"*Siapa nama anda?*"

"Name's Maciel. George Maciel."

"What kind name that lah?"

"Sounds Mexican," said Marty. "I know a Mexican named Maciel."

"I believe it's Portagee. His family's from the Azores."

"Maybe we change this one's name lah," said Ali. "Call him *syaitan.*"

Moments like this, Snow understood why Bracelin hated the foreign crew. But Snow couldn't hate them, maddening as they were. He loved their work, the way they could repair leaks in the pipeline on a paper clip and a prayer. They ran better soft plugs than anybody he'd ever seen, covered a breach with a piece of inner tube, ratcheted down an iron screw to make it seal, then covered the whole thing over with epoxy patch compound called Red Hand. Marty and Ali were goddamned artists with the Red Hand, could smooth out an illegal patch job just right. There were a hundred jobs they could do that way, and besides that they didn't care how Snow butchered their languages. Snow was a graduate of what one old French pumpman used to call *le petit nègre* school of languages–the little nigger. The little nigger was never erudite or refined but always hustling, could always communicate his business. That was Snow, the little nigger, and to him it was no racist thing, either, but a title of grudging respect. The crew knew he was no kind to put on airs, was one of their own through and through, and all because of that he carried the chief mate–if not the skipper–right there in his brain, if not his pocket.

Ali shook his head, lamenting the state of affairs now that the new ordinary had come aboard. "Catholics all around now. Ship need more Muslim!"

"Knock that off," Snow said. "I don't give a damn what a man names his god, so long as he does his job. You Ali, quit superstitions. And Martín, next time we got inspectors aboard, don't let Ensign Pulver see you running that soft plug. You see this?" He pulled out the sheaf of citations, still folded up in his pocket. " 'Below-code repairs!' We get *kapal* to port or nobody gets *rhing-rhing* no way," and Snow tore the citations into tiny pieces and tossed them overboard. The crewmen looked at each other and shrugged; they had no idea who the hell Ensign Pulver was anyway.

Snow went down deck to the crew's mess, grabbed a cup of coffee, and looked over at Gino and Katie the Baker. They hung out behind the steam table, white aprons and shirts and round chef's hats to keep their hair from the food, their chubby hands chopping and stirring. A small TV with rabbit ears played news in the background, a reporter going on about the hostage crisis in Iran: Day 89, America Held Hostage. The goofy anchorman looked like someone had troweled his hair in place, but that didn't concern the cooks. They too were still talking about the death in San Francisco, though apparently they weren't sure of the dead man's name, whether Patience or Delacroix.

"It was Delacroix," Snow said, barely able to overcome the din of the galley exhaust fan. "Patience was the one before him. Disembarked two months back."

"Poor wall-eyed sonuvabitch," said Gino. Behind him the TV went all snowy while the Ayatollah Khomeini raised his hand to a crowd in downtown Tehran. "I hear the new guy let go of the ladder on him. I hear it got squashed like a pumpkin on a sidewalk."

"It?" said Katie. "You sound like you're talking about a loaf of bread."

She wiped her wide heavy face with a hand dusted by baking flour, leaving a dash across her forehead. She and Gino spent so much time together they were starting to look like each other, the way an old married couple does, even though both were queer as pocket change at a carnival.

"Come to think of it, he did look kinda like a loaf of bread," said Gino.

Listening to the cooks made Snow think of what Delacroix had told the kid about communication aboard ship. Snow decided then and there it wasn't true: the crew knew what one another was saying, they just never said anything worth knowing.

"Listen up," said Snow. "You gotta set people straight here, be part of the solution instead of part of the problem. I saw the whole thing. The kid was nowhere near the ladder when Delacroix fell. He was up on deck with me."

"That ain't what I heard." said Gino. "Ho no!"

"Well, I'm telling you straight."

"Ain't what I heard either," said Katie.

Snow damned near heard his own synapses firing, making noise out his ears like speakers only he could hear. He took his coffee and climbed out to the weather deck, where he leaned against the railing and breathed the sea air, drank two swigs before he spit a mouthful overboard and tossed what was left, decided his bowels couldn't handle coffee any more than they could handle booze. He wished he could drink alcohol still. The girl liked that, liked to *party,* as she put it. But Snow had quit drinking twelve years before, after a series of drunken blackouts he'd suffered on his way through Nam aboard a dry-cargo ship called *Saigon.* One time they spent a night with a crowd of Marines and Viet bar girls on the roof of the Hotel Da Nang, where they watched the war off in the bush nearby and drank until the girls couldn't stand up. The next morning, back aboard ship, he woke up with blood all over his clothes, hands, and the sheets of his bunk. Scared the piss out of him, frankly. "You look like somebody opened you a new shit locker last night, Snow," said one crewman, and the rest laughed. Truth was, Snow took a shower and found not a scratch on him, which scared him even worse. He hadn't had a spot of alcohol since.

Snow wasn't the only one with a dark past. Turned out Maciel had come to sea direct from a place called the Jesuit School of Theology in Berkeley. High atop a spot called Holy Hill, where they had all manner of denominations and religions competing for ethereal space above the decadent throngs of Radical Land. But Maciel having gone to college didn't bug Snow nearly so much as studying religion for going on fifteen years. He kept wondering why the hell anybody would want to do that and what it meant—literally, how it *looked* to be holed up in a stone sanctuary in a state of spiritual awe. Snow never had much use for Christians or any other of the great religionists. All their monotheistic idealizing boiled down to convincing the world they were the chosen ones. Since the war, he'd felt chosen for very little, if anything. To him, life was a practical matter of survival and sex, and the two had always been tightly linked: he never felt sexless except when his life was in danger, and he never felt truly alive unless he was having sex.

Maciel had no such outlook. He only wished he did. Snow figured him for a weird kind of virgin, like he'd been in fights but never fucked. He was bearing up under the burden of being orphaned. First came losing his mother to cancer when he was nine, alone in the sickness of her green room praying to God for some intervention that never came. Eight months later his father took him on a drunken bawling ride through the streets of Richmond, California, and deposited him on the battleship-gray porch of his grandfather's house on 33rd Street. Without a word he tore off on blistered valves down Macdonald Avenue and never came back. Three nights later the kid was awakened after midnight to the sound of his grandmother wailing in the other room, "Dear God, dear God take my baby boy, take my baby boy," and for a minute the kid thought she meant him, until it became obvious from the hushed presence of police in the front room that the boy's father had managed to drive his Buick nose first into the Montezuma Slough. He buried it to the dashboard in silt mud, and no one ever knew if he meant to do it or was just too drunk to know the difference.

This began the boy's life with his grandparents, his grandma a Catholic girl who went to church three times a week and his grandpa a brawling boatman who might have been to church three times in his whole life. What the kid got from them was every bit as schizoid as Africans in a Christian missionary. He went to church with his grandma, prayed his Our Fathers and Hail Marys, and, with the host still glued to the roof of his mouth, drove with his grandmother to meet up with his grandfather's ship for the last run of the week. The old man worked the Frisco harbor week-on week-off, and the final run was a Sunday ritual, from Richmond to Mission Rock, where the old man would hang with his crew and knock back some drinks at Kelley's, while the boy would wait inside the fogged glass of his grandfather's 1957 Pontiac wagon and watch the sailors stagger out and puke alone or wobble sideways with girls on their arms, pressing to the side of the building with tongues reaching and hands groping at the hems of dresses. He saw things there. Things he couldn't get out of his boy's mind. So he went to church, bathed in the glow and safety, prayed for salvation to the violet smell of his grandma's powdered skin and the droning sound of priests who could read your mind. He went to Catholic schools all the way up to a degree in theology at USF, and then he entered the seminary, only to leave two years later after some vague scandal involving alcohol, a shovel, and his own grandmother's grave. Apparently young Maciel was more fucked up than the ship's average, and that was saying something.

They were making south just outside Mexican waters when Snow climbed topside to find Bracelin eyeing the radar and Paynor finishing up plotting a course at the chart table. "Come to 130 degrees."

"One-three-zero," chimed the helmsman.

Snow got a view of the scope past Bracelin's shoulder and saw a solid band of green clutter lying twenty-five miles south by west. "Looks nasty."

"Tropical storm Eleana," said Bracelin. "A nasty little girl. I think I want to take her from behind."

Snow checked the chart: they angled on a westerly course, the storm's brunt coming on their port side, heading downwind.

"We'll ride her out on the navigable half. It'll take us offshore some."

"We don't want to stress the hull more than we have to."

Snow checked the chart again. With his eyes he drew a circle around the eye of the storm. He ran a line through it, dividing it in half along the storm track. Cyclonic storms cut that way: they had a navigable semicircle and a dangerous one. On the dangerous half, winds blew in the same direction as the storm track. Not only were the winds stronger, but they tended to throw a ship into the path of the storm. On the navigable half you ran downwind, pitched out of the storm's path, and because you ran against the motion of the storm, winds were 15 percent lighter. Still no Sunday breeze. Paynor watched the horizon with binoculars. He was an eastern boy, raised in Jersey or some such place, with a thick head of jet-black hair and a hairy birthmark that looked like a caterpillar clinging to his lip. "Hold on, gentlemen," Paynor said. "Here she comes."

Over the next hour, the ship's motions went from heaving and fluid to thunderous and blunt, and before long they had a report from the bow lookout, Ali, who was just on his way inside when he smelled something very wrong coming from the forepeak. "We got ammonia smell bad!" he said. On his way back in, a wave tore loose a bank of nitrogen bottles stored on the centerline catwalk, and from the bridge they watched them scatter and roll.

"I'll call the ordinary," Snow said. "We'll take care of the nitro bottles."

"Rouse Leeds too, get him down into the forepeak," said Bracelin.

Snow didn't much care for rousing Leeds, who had a nasty tendency to get his awakener in a choke hold before he himself had actually awakened. Fortunately, he'd never done this to Snow, and to Snow's knowledge, he'd never choked anybody out all the way before coming to himself, saying, "Oh, man, I'm sorry, man, I'm so sorry." Which was doubtless little comfort to the man attacked.

The ship was rocking pretty good by the time Snow knocked on the door marked RADIO OFFICER, then pushed through to find Leeds snoring from a single bed set up in the corner. He slept in a fetal position but with his legs out as if running in his sleep, feet pressed to the wooden box frame to keep himself in place. He had pillows stuffed in all around his back and chest too, and looked snug.

Snow shouted as loud as he could from the door. "Leeds! We got ammonia leak forward!"

Leeds sat upright all in one piece. "Got it," he said.

Snow was grateful for no choke holds. Leeds got up out of bed and started pulling on his jeans. He had shocking blond hair, like a surfer boy from SoCal, and silver-blue eyes that radiated light, and a set of choppers that did the same. The whitest fake teeth Snow had ever seen, six of them in a plate that Leeds now shoved into his mouth, smiling like he'd gargled with a gallon of Clorox.

His teeth weren't his only replacement part; Leeds had a steel plate in his skull too, which he claimed expanded and contracted with the weather, making creaking sounds as they steered south into warmer climes. Somehow it didn't surprise Snow that Leeds had something loose topside, but he was a valuable hand all the same, a second engineer who since Malaysia had been the *de facto* chief engineer, not to mention the only qualified welder and riveter on board. Outside of keeping the power plant going, his primary job was to keep the ship's cargoes from enveloping the crew in a toxic cloud. Unfortunately, by the smell of things, he was failing.

Snow hadn't set foot in this room since it belonged to the old

RO, a wispy-thin drug addict who was accidentally left behind in Kiel, West Germany, and never replaced. It was a double setup, with the radio room on the forward side and sleeping quarters on the aft side, with a head in between. On the sleeping side the old RO had made a workbench from wood and Masonite, and behind it glass tubing ran along a wooden shelf bolted into the steel bulkhead. One glass line led to a nitrogen tank strapped into the corner, and another led to the head sink where he had a vacuum branch, so all he had to do was run water past the valve to create suction. On the opposite end, wedged between his bunk and the chemical bench, he had oxygen-acetylene tanks standing upright and leading to a vise, where a torch handle was cinched down to form a Bunsen burner. A corner locker held glass beakers and brown bottles of chemicals.

"What the hell you got going in here?" Snow asked.

"I'm treating my affliction." Leeds held up his hands and flexed them, the knuckles crackling and popping like a wood fire, with pink lesions spread over the knuckle ridge. The chemistry lab was rocking and clanking in the storm, and Snow could hardly imagine the thing surviving much more without collapsing in a pile of shards on the deck.

"Sounds kinda gnarly."

"You got no idea. Psoriatic arthritis. Itches and hurts like a mother."

"It ain't contagious, is it?"

"Naw, man, it's my body eating itself up from the inside out." Leeds sat lacing up his steel-toed work boots, his knuckles curled knobby and scaled pink. "They don't know shit about it. I was on this hard-core chemo agent called methotrexate, but my hair started to fall out and I lost another tooth. Now I'm trying to synthesize my own sulfazine."

"Sounds like a knucklehead notion to me."

Truth was, nothing about Leeds surprised Snow anymore, including how the hell he could clutch a welding rod with fingers that looked like his. Snow left and went down one level to the petty officer deck and into his own room, where he found Maciel spread-eagle with his feet hooked under the metal tube frame of his upper bunk, gripping with white knuckles and eyes wide, tape machine grinding out speed guitars. "Is this a bad storm? It feels like a bad storm."

"There ain't no good storms," said Snow. "Not on this ship. Now shake and bake, we got all hands on deck."

The kid looked at him like *all hands on deck* was a nice way of saying the ship was sinking. He hauled out of bed without hesitation or grumbling, just down in a bound, stumbling and falling all over against the ship's rocking. He dressed one-handed, the other holding to the bunk, and then Snow led him down to the second deck exit forward. The wind beat against the watertight door, and rain swirled. Underfoot came the rhythmic heaving and metallic groaning of the ship. Every time a door opened somewhere you could hear and feel the rush of air through the ship's passage-ways, then the swooping down and thumping as the door shut. Through a porthole adjacent to the door, Snow could see the centerline catwalk stretching forward all the way to the bow. Eight feet over the chaos of the weather deck, Snow saw the entire mass of the ship, two football fields in length, flexing and thumping its way into waves, which came row upon row like alpine ridges.

The kid stood there quiet, bobbing from foot to foot, clutching a door dog with one swollen hand. Snow turned evenly to look straight at him. "You gotta relax, buddy. Gotta go with the flow of the ship. Feel it under you. That's all sea legs is: you get with the ship. Like an extension of your own legs. Then you're free to ply the oceans!"

Maciel gave a nod that looked like a shiver.

"Now see there," Snow said, motioning out the round window. "That's where we're going. And there's two things you gotta understand." He tried to talk over the sound of the storm, but his voice came a little ragged, like he couldn't quite clear his throat. "You stay behind me and you do what I tell you, and beyond that you always take one hand for you and one for the job, got that? There ain't no choice here. You might as well make the best of it."

Maciel breathed and gathered himself. Snow saw him calm, saw his eyes go a little dead. "It's okay," the kid said. "I can do it."

Snow could smell the sleep on his breath. It reminded him of his last days with his wife and son, kissing the little guy in the darkness of midnight before striking off on a ship in '52. From somewhere in some room came the tinny sound of Sinatra singing "The Way You Look Tonight," or maybe that was memory too. He thought now it was—he was hearing things now. He took a good lungful of air, then nudged the kid and pointed out spots to find protection if a rogue broke on top of them. Maciel gazed at all of it as if staring into the abyss, his lips mumbling prayer.

Snow caught some movement out the corner of his eye and looked back to see the old man there—the captain himself—hair stuck up and legs wobbling to the base of the stairs behind where Maciel and Snow stood. He held to the railing, wearing deck shoes and a long raincoat over flannel pajamas. As he hit the base of the staircase, a long thick arm reached from up behind him, turned him without sound, and took him back up.

At first Snow thought he'd hallucinated McFarland there, a queer sight, dressed as he was, there and gone so fast Maciel didn't seem to notice. Snow turned to face the porthole and the storm outside, saying, "First job is to lash those loose nitro tanks, okay?"

"Okay," the kid said, then crossed himself.

Men all genuflecting, or buns-up kneeling toward Mecca, or the animists rubbing at talismans, it didn't much matter; they gave Snow the fantods. He gripped the lever on the watertight door and looked down to see a semi-steady dribble of seawater leaking into a puddle at the door's base. Then he shoved the door open and stepped out and took needle spray to the face. Then came the roar and hiss of wind and rain together. Then the creaking of the ship as it hauled itself over a peak and thumped a trough, burying her bow. His rain suit rippled and billowed like a sail as he moved up the centerline catwalk. The wind gusted and paused and feinted before it whipped back the way it had come and then drove on, like a hard wall shoving against you. With one hand he slid along the railing and a moment later felt the light touch of the kid's hand on his back. Snow paused and let it stay there, feeling the pressure. He liked the feeling–gave him someone to lead through the shit. Maybe that was all he needed. Someone outside himself. He turned and looked at the kid's eyes, saw fear and worry.

A burst of white water fanned up and back in a wedge that smashed over the fo'c'sle deck, tore loose another rack of nitrogen bottles, and sent them scattering aft along the catwalk, like bowling pins come to attack the bowlers. Four or five piled up on one another and two rolled through the railing. One landed with a dim rattle, but the other hit neck down and snapped off at the valve. The bottle flew up like a rocket. Then it turned down and slapped and battered its way through the pipelines and finally erupted out of the entanglement and went end over end overboard in a sweeping shriek. "Ho!" Snow yelled at the kid. "You see that?"

"What? See what?" The kid couldn't see anything but yellow rain suit.

When Snow looked forward, the entire ship shuddered underneath him. The nitrogen bottles weighed one hundred pounds each, and they bounced on the catwalk and chattered against the grating. "You stick here!" Snow said, and scampered down the stairs to the weather deck. He hit the midship square, a small blockhouse structure converted to a tankerman's locker, where he found a spool of yellow polyethylene rope. Back on the catwalk, he grabbed the kid's vest and hauled him toward the bow. Snow saw Leeds on the weather deck forward, at the base of the protected overhang formed by the fo'c'sle deck, shielded from the slamming torrent of white water as he eased himself down through a deck hatch and into the forepeak tank.

Snow pulled off a length of rope, threw a bowline on one end, and strung out twenty feet. He made a loop in one hand and drew his knife blade upward to part the line. He tied a fast overhand knot to keep the end from unraveling, then leaned close and shouted in the kid's ear. "Start gathering them buggers up! Lash them together with this and choke 'em to the railing!"

The kid had happy feet, like he was running in place. But he had strong hands for a skinny guy. They worked ten minutes securing bottles, then moved down to the protected hatch where Leeds had gone down. Snow held the kid by the shoulder and leaned close. "You did good there, buddy. Now you're gonna be welder's helper. You got one job: keep Leeds supplied with rod."

The kid had lost the wash of fear on his face, and Snow figured he'd been through his baptism, and now he'd just have to deal with the confirmation. Toward that end, he puked on his way down to the weather deck, and made his way aft to the midship tanker-man's locker to haul two heavy tin cases of welding rod back for the welder. He tottered and nearly pitched over the railing as he slid along the catwalk with two cases on his right shoulder. They weighed thirty pounds each, but he fought them the whole way and won. Snow met him at the base of the stairs and took the top one, then motioned the kid to follow him to the manhole leading down into the forepeak tank. Snow showed him how to choke the cases with two half hitches, then watched as the kid lowered the first one down hand over hand into the tank. "Climb down after it. I'll lower the next." And with a grim nod, the kid scooted backward down the ladder and Snow lowered the second case, then followed into a world of noxious household ammonia and suffocating weld smoke, odors to assault your nostrils while your ears and brain rang low with the *rooooom-rooooooom* of the bow hitting waves. Leeds had rigged a mist machine, pumped water vapor that condensed and rained down on them to wash the ammonia vapors out of the air and make it possible to weld without blowing them all to hell.

There in the middle of the narrow walk, perched ten feet off the bottom, knelt Leeds. He had stanched the flow of ammonium hydroxide by stuffing sealer compound into the widening split, and now ran a bead to attach a plate-steel doubler that would seal it off completely. The strobe effect dizzied Snow an instant. He couldn't believe Leeds was working down here without a respirator. Maciel carried the heavy case of welding rod by the choked line, scampering along the scaffold. When he reached Leeds he yelled, "Now what?"

"Bust it open!" Leeds yelled up at him.

"How do I do that?"

"Throw it down!" He made a motion with his arms.

The kid hefted the box and threw it onto the heavy planks of the scaffold, hitting along an edge, the weight of the rod inside splitting the box along one seam.

"Peel it open!" Leeds yelled.

The kid reached with his gloved hand, winced as he contacted the jagged edge of the metal box, and pulled his glove off with his teeth to show blood. With his bare fingers he gingerly peeled the lid back, sliding out three thick welding rods. He slapped one into the outstretched hand of Leeds. "That's it!" Leeds said, in his muffled shout. "Now you got it! Keep 'em coming!"

Then the kid sat down. He might have been okay if he'd just kept on his two feet, but then Snow felt the presence of someone behind him. It was Bracelin. The mate threw his rain hood back to reveal his scarred face and long black hair. "Who's dog he been fucking?" said Bracelin.

"He worked hard to get that rod down here," Snow said. "He's doin' good."

"He looks like he's gonna puke all over himself."

"He already done that!" Snow shouted, then coughed as he laughed, then grimaced at the burn in his eyes, and pulled his rain suit hood around to try breathing through that. The welder looked up, his mask robotic, then popped his stinger to life, and began drawing another bead. Bracelin was unfazed by the odor of ammonia, seemed to breathe the stuff in lieu of oxygen. The mate edged past Snow and moved along the narrow catwalk toward where the kid sat, and kicked him in the leg.

"Are you the dip fuck left the door to the second deck open in a gale?"

Maciel looked up like he might throw up again, only this time all over his boss's shoes. "I thought I dogged it."

"Well, you *didn't* dog it, and now we got flooding all down that passageway!"

"Mr. Bracelin–" the kid said.

"Don't Mr. Bracelin me, shitbird. Call me Mate. Ain't you figured that out yet?"

"Mr. Mate–I mean Mate. Mate."

With a quick motion, Snow put a hand to Bracelin's shoulder to stop him.

"Your girlfriend's sick," Bracelin said, heavily into Snow's ear.

Snow replied with a gentle edge. "I got it here, Brace, he's my crew."

"He's a *maroon*."

"He's working his tail off."

"He'd better. Leeds! Good goddamned work!"

Then he climbed out the hole into the rain.

The kid looked green as seawater as he went back down on his haunches. Snow grabbed him by each wrist, lifted him, and for a second thought the kid's arms might tear loose. But he finally got him up and they stood facing each other, the ship heaving around them. Snow held to the kid's wrists, smiled sweetly, and pushed his thumbs deep between the tendons, pressuring the kid's nerves. He felt the kid's body go limp, his arms fanning outward in the pose of crucifixion, like he was trying to flee from his own pulse, backing up his arms, numbing his shoulders, his neck, his whole head. "Harold, wait—ahhhhh, *ahhhhhhh—*"

Snow watched the kid's head roll back and make a wide circle as he groaned, eyeballs doing cartwheels, welding arc flashing. "It's all right now, Georgie."

Snow didn't let go, he pressed harder. The kid's eyes showed white and Snow thought he might faint dead away, and with that he eased off, could see the nausea melt away. Only then did he let him go. The kid's face eased into lightness.

"I learned that from a yogi I met in Calcutta! He taught me the secret ways. There's nerve lines everywhere, you know. Leeds there, he can kill you just by poking you with his index finger. You'd never know it to look at him, but he's got what they call *dim mak.* The Death Touch. He's studied up."

"My whole body—" The kid couldn't put it into words, like he could bound his way to the ladder and fly out. His face lost all that pent-up fear, and Snow could practically see the euphoria swell inside him, washing away everything that came before.

EL JEFE DE SALINA CRUZ

Two days later the storm had broken and Snow went topside to the chart room, where he found the ship six hundred miles off Acapulco, blown as far away as Clipperton Island, a scary craggy rock of an atoll that had once been home to phosphate miners and military men gone mad. He moved forward into the wheelhouse to find Paynor, Lucy the Third, and Beth, who was standing her watch at the helm. Snow stepped up to the glass next to Paynor. "Hey, Second, you manage to contact one of them brokers out of Mexico City?"

"Not yet," Paynor said, and pretended to consult a chart, then looked off and twiddled his thumbs and combed his hair with his fingers. After a decent enough interval–about the time he might claim it was his idea–he took up the ship-to-shore radio and got on the horn with a broker called Muñoz, talking like Tarzan before he finally paused in frustration and blurted out, "Is there *somebody* there who speaks English? That's right, *inglés. Americano.*"

Snow gained eye contact with Paynor and reached a hand for the radio telephone. Paynor glared at Snow with abject hatred. Twin tendrils of hair grew straight down out of his nostrils, black hairs that hung nearly to his upper lip. Snow could barely resist the temptation to reach up and pluck them.

"Hang on," said Paynor, "I got someone here," and Snow took the phone.

Lucy the Third was eyeing the scene with great interest, while still managing to give navigation orders to the helmsman. She consulted their working chart, which lay flat on the chart table set in the starboard aft corner of the wheelhouse.

"*Sí, sí,*" Snow said into the phone. "*Vamos de compras. ¡Tenemos una tarjeta de crédito!*" And he laughed toward Paynor, knowing the man didn't get the joke.

Five minutes later they had contracts for ammonia, gasoline, and aromatic hydrocarbons from a Pemex refinery at Puerto de Salina Cruz, part of it bound for a fertilizer plant at Puerto Caldera, Costa Rica, another part for a chemical plant north of Valparaiso, Chile, and the rest for various ports along the U.S. Gulf Coast. Snow liked the idea of gasoline–with all the uncertainty of international markets, not to say his own contacts in West Africa, gas was a safe bet. People could always use a little base petrol, and they'd always pay for it.

Having proven his superiority in matters of language and business, Snow decided not to push the second mate any further, particularly not in public. The entire scene made Paynor's birthmark twitch twice as fast as normal, like the caterpillar might crawl right off his face. Despite everything Snow hated about Paynor, the guy could flat out navigate a ship, maybe even better than Bracelin, especially when it came to interpolating the screwy variations you got with the SatNav unit and augmenting with celestial when the thing claimed you were somehow steaming through cornfields in Nebraska. He supposed they should keep Paynor around as long as they could, but damned if he wanted to watch him finger that growth on his lip all the way to Sierra Leone.

Smooth as dead-calm seas they made way for Salina Cruz, steaming coastwise south through the warming reach of Mexican waters. Off watch, Snow lay in bed looking through a stack of letters, most of which he'd read several times. On top was a new one from Australia, the return address identifying the sender as Harold Manwaring-Snow, a liquor salesman from Perth who'd sent a half dozen letters over the past year, claiming to be his half brother, not to mention an amateur genealogist whose primary interest was tracking the amorous adventures of Harold Snow, Sr. Snow's father had sailed around the world sixty times in his career and managed to leave behind a child on the average of one per trip. Snow skimmed through and found he had two new siblings, one called Harold Delgado from Chiclayo, Peru, the other Harold Mupete from Dar es Salaam in East Africa. These were added to a host of others: Harold Velji and Hadley Kahn of Karachi, Pakistan, and Harold Sekhon, a Sikh from Punjab. The list went on. Apparently the old man had not only had a stream of kids, he'd somehow managed to get them all named Harold. It was goddamned surreal.

Snow thumbed through the rest of the stack: the last letter he'd received from his son was now eight years old, and one from his exwife now twenty years old. Still, he carried them, along with the rad report from the Feds, and then the one he was looking for, return address Liberia. He held it up before his reading glasses and reread the letter, wondering when the information would be of use to him.

Dear Snow,

Received your note yesterday and can confirm that a miner by the name of Haroun Abudjah does work at the Nimba Mountain facility. Can put you in touch as necessary. As for the other situation, I have to say that the politics here are degrading. Went to your house along the St. Paul and found Yasa safe and sound, though I understand the oldest boy has joined some sort of paramilitary group, an offshoot of a religious organization, from what I can tell. All in all, things are growing ever more tense. Natives are restless, as they say. FUASW.

Sincerely—R. P. Thorson

Snow felt a surge of excitement. He kept thinking of that first time he'd told Beth about his connection to Liberia, and how ever since then he'd wanted to take her there, to a certain house on Goodhouse Creek, a two-story slave colonial he'd built himself. "It's a slice of heaven up there in the mountains!" he told her.

He got out of bed and found the kid's books all stacked and dried and now sitting under chunks of iron plate in the hope of restoring their readable shape. Snow caught their titles, religious tracts all: *The Confessions of St. Augustine*, *The Seven Storey Mountain* by some Trappist named Merton, allegedly an oath-of-silence order, though near as Snow could tell the guy couldn't shut up about himself. Snow sneaked peeks at the stuff. He read where Merton got some broad knocked up in England and had to flee to the monastery to figure out how to forgive himself. Snow wondered if maybe the kid was in the opposite camp—he'd done something in the monastery and now fled to sea in a vain attempt to sleep nights.

Snow looked over at where the kid was doing what he called "spiritual exercises"–real heavy-duty weightlifting by the look of him. "What would you say if I told you I thought this guy was full of shit?" Snow said, holding up the book.

"Merton? He's not full of shit. I find him quite sincere."

"Oh, quite! I'm sure!" Snow flipped through a few more pages. "Problem I see with these Catholic God boys is they're forever using logic to argue their point, logic and evidence this and that. But you get right down to it, they got no argument. They all end up coming back around to faith. I believe in God 'cause I believe in God kind of logic. Circular kind."

"Yeah," said the kid. "I know what you mean."

Then he got down out of his bunk, dressed in his work gear, and went out for his night watch. Snow frowned, watching him go, waiting for some look or some snarl of repudiation, but he got none. He couldn't tell if the kid was toying with him or sincerely understood his point. He lay there in his bunk wondering what the hell George Maciel was doing here anyhow, why a man that close to some godly understanding had come out here, into the bad open sea like his granddaddy. He wondered if it was true what he'd heard, that the kid had wandered into a cemetery with a shovel and started to dig up his own grandmother. Snow felt bad being a snoop, but he went over to the kid's locker anyhow. There in the back, stuffed down behind his shirts, was the butt of something. At first he thought it was a pair of them num chucks that Ali was so fond of, but when he pulled it out he found an old leather flog, a regular cat-o'-nine-tails. Had flecks of blood on it too–a grotesque thing. He chuckled. The western church wouldn't go for that, he knew.

By the start of the morning watch, Paynor had contacted the Vessel Traffic Service and they waited in the outer harbor for the pilot boat to usher the pilot aboard and guide the ship through a breakwater to the inner harbor and the petroleum terminal. Snow went down through the poop deck, curling around the davits there and moving forward alongside the house. Marty and Ali were already out there working a hand wrench to remove a blank at the manifold. The manifold was a giant rack of steel pipes running beam to beam at the midship line, square and strapped and blocked together so all loading and off-loading could be done from the same place. The blanks were the flat plates that sealed the ends of the pipes.

Snow went down to double-check they'd got the right tank line. He counted down and over, methodically, third row, second column. "Okay," Snow said. "We're ready to couple soon as we get inside. We'll be loading number two tanks with ammonia, right straight across."

Marty and Ali waved and nodded. "Okay, bos'n, okay," they said.

All at once a Mexican Coast Guard boat appeared around the stern, came rushing up with a hail from its horn. Snow lowered the Jacob's ladder while Maciel caught the monkey's fist out of midair, arching upward as it did, dragging the heaving line along behind it. The kid hauled the thin line hand over hand and tied it off to the eye of a six-inch mooring line, which they no more needed than they needed a ten-ton anchor. The kid strained like hell pulling it up, the rope biting into his gloved hands and threatening to tear the gloves off. Snow had to laugh, watching him strain so much, his arms popping with tendons like he was all made of wire inside. He let him haul. The kid got her up and shoved the eye through a fairlead mounted in the railing and hooked it around a three-foot deck cleat. Snow liked how he did that—nothing fancy, but he did it.

"Not bad for a Fairy God Boy!" Snow teased.

"My grandfather used to call me that," the kid said.

"I always liked old Joaquin. Now go catch their stern line."

The kid didn't say a word. He just marched aft without wondering or asking whether Snow didn't have somebody else who could yank their arms off hauling up a mooring hawser from a motorboat. Snow watched the Coast Guard officer climbing the Jacob's ladder until he swung up and over the bulwarks and stood next to him. Snow disliked him even before the man said, "I need everybody identification."

The officer had left two enlisted sailors on the boat, one in the wheelhouse and the other standing guard by a machine gun mounted on the bow. He wore the rank of captain—he was no junior prick in training, but the real deal. "I need to speak with the master," he said with halting articulation.

"Master's not available. He's sick."

"With what illness?"

"Nothing contagious," Snow said. "You want the truth? I think the old man picked up a dose of the clap on our way through Bangkok. I keep telling him he's too old for that Thai sandwich he likes so much. You should see his dick!"

The officer straightened himself. "I do not want to see his dick, thank you," he said.

Bracelin emerged out the second deck door to the catwalk above them and stepped down the grated metal staircase to the weather deck, where he grinned big, making his face look weirder than normal, and stepped forward toward the officer. "Charles Bracelin, chief mate," he said. He held the binder tucked under one arm and a leather pouch that looked like a money bag. "We actually met last year, this same vessel."

"It's true? I don't recall," the captain said. "I need to see the master of this vessel."

"He's pretty under the weather, I'd say," Bracelin replied.

"But we can take you to him for a quick authorization. I'll sign the safety paperwork."

"So long as he authorizes burbally."

"Burbally?" Bracelin said.

"*Burbally, burbally,*" the officer said, motioning his hand out his mouth like he was throwing up.

"*Verbally!*" said Bracelin.

"Yes, *burbally*! You do not speak English very well, is that so?" and looked down to where the ABs had unbolted the blank and were swinging the hose coupling from the terminal buoy. "You are not to start discharging until I get the safety papers!"

"We aren't discharging, we're *loading*–ammonia and gasoline," said Bracelin. "Anyway. Skipper's this way."

Snow climbed the internal stairs behind Bracelin and the Mexican officer, then stood at the top and waited. From there he could see both outside to where the gunboat lay alongside and inside up the passageway, a dimly lighted corridor that stretched the entire width of the house, past the chief engineer's and chief mate's cabins. Snow kept to his post, looking down toward the gunboat, where the enlisted men chatted and smoked cigarettes. "Hey Georgie!" Snow shouted. "Tell them two to put the smokes out before they blow us all to Kingdom Come!"

Maciel called down, waving a finger back and forth in front of him. "*¡No pueden fumar! ¡No fumar!*"

The Mexicans looked irritated, flicking their *cigarrillos* over the side, the smokes hissing as they hit water. "*Sí, sí—no fumar.*"

Meantime, down the internal passageway, Bracelin keyed his way into the captain's outer office and ushered the Mexican officer inside. They were in there longer than Snow had expected, and about the time he started to wonder what was going on, Bracelin stuck his arm out and waved him down the passageway. As Snow reached the door to the captain's outer office, the chief mate stepped outside and closed the door behind him, leaving the Mexican officer inside.

Bracelin's face seemed to take on a new set of angles entirely, like he was all set to implode. "We got a problem," said Bracelin.

"That's what you call obvious from the look on your face."

Bracelin leaned close and spoke low. "This fuck wants ten grand. He's calling it a harbor tax."

"For crap's sake."

"Not exactly routine graft. He acts pretty goddamned cocky, you ask me."

"He know something? What'd he say?"

"He just stared at me with them dark Indian eyes and told me the normal amount don't apply."

"Maybe he's just taking a flyer."

"We give him that much dough without a question and *we're* the ones taking a flyer. I say no way—we offer him the normal payoff and let it stand, see if he coughs up something."

Snow's mind snapped with possibilities, and none of them were good, though he had to admit some were a whole lot worse than others. It made no sense—unless the coastie up in Frisco had put them out on the wire. He preferred a lone-nut theory, some Mexican CG officer with suspicion and a shot at a personal bonus. Snow nodded toward the door. "Let's find out what he knows."

They stepped back into the captain's outer office, where the Mexican captain smoked a cigarette and lifted his chin at Snow. *"¿Está el jefe?"* he asked.

Snow didn't reply at first, he just stared past to the door to the captain's bedroom, wondering when the old man would poke his weary head out and fuck the dog complete. *"Sí, sí, estoy el jefe,"* Snow finally said. *"¿Qué es este?"*

The officer was holding a small yellow piece of paper, neatly folded in half. He handed it over to Snow, who gently opened the paper and read it silently:

PETROCHEM MARINER—ROTTERDAM

Snow had almost let himself forget that name, but now it rushed back, and given the hard look of *el capitán* Snow didn't think he'd be able to hold a lie for ten seconds. This was a moment he had refused to let himself think about. He had grown cocky or distracted or something. Or maybe he had always figured it would happen, just not now. If he was being a realist about it–as he was in most things–he should be happy it came here in Mexico instead of someplace stuffed and starched like the Canal Zone, or worse– South Africa. He blinked and wiped his eyes with the back of his hand, then folded the paper back up and handed it to Bracelin, who peeled it open, reading without a trace of confession or emotion, just that cut-up face blank as a granite wall in the mountains. He stared at the CG officer and then at Snow.

"*Cinco mil,*" said Snow, more weakly than he had hoped. If only he could have said it strong. He felt something slip out from under him, as if he were standing on wet ice and the slightest move might send him on his ass.

The officer shook his head. "*Dies mil,*" he said firmly.

Snow looked over at Bracelin and the two held a stare for a long count, and both knew they had no choice.

"Fuck it, let's get this over with," said Bracelin, and pushed into the captain's cabin. For an instant Snow saw the old man sitting on the edge of his bed, letting out a cough that sounded like a one-lung diesel motoring through fog. Then Snow stepped in after him and shut the door. He stared down at the sickly form of McFarland, who looked like he was about a day from death. "What are you two about?" the old man said.

"Just dealing with Mexican authorities," said Snow. "You know how they are, Captain."

"What dealings?" The captain craned his head around stiffly to see Bracelin going into the ship's safe to pull out cash. "How much they squeezing us for?"

Snow felt some pity for the old man. There were two kinds of captains: working skippers and general managers, and he'd known some among the latter who never got out of their slippers for an entire voyage. McFarland was decidedly in that camp. They had used that in their favor. He was the kind of captain Bracelin liked working for, since he had realized sometime back that he might wait fifteen years before he'd ever be master of his own vessel. For some companies a man who'd worked his way up the hawse pipe and never learned how to kiss ass doing it was doomed to a life as a chief mate at best. And of all things Bracelin wanted, he wanted his own ship most of all.

In the absence of his own ship, Bracelin worked for the geriatrics he could control, the ones he could keep happy because Bracelin was the man who took care of business without questions–he was Super-mate. Captain didn't have to think, even if he had been capable, and McFarland wasn't. So when Snow approached Bracelin with his plan, Bracelin bit, not only because he wanted the result–ten million to split three ways–but because he knew that the plan was so audacious as to be unthinkable, particularly for a man like McFarland, who didn't have enough gray matter left to be suspicious.

"Go back to bed, Captain," said Bracelin. "Everything's going to be fine."

"You're the best mate ever worked for me, Charles. You got the con."

"Thank you, Captain. Time for your medication now."

"I'm starting to feel a little rickety again. I wonder when this is going to run its course."

"Hard to tell, Cap," said Snow.

Bracelin popped open a med bottle and slid a blue pill out with a big V carved in the middle of it. "V for Victory," said Bracelin. "You got water there," and the old man washed it down, nodded once, and settled his head.

Back in the outer office, Bracelin came out with a bulging manila envelope and handed it over to the Mexican officer. Then he put one arm behind the man's back and held the other out toward the door, and they followed him back the way they came. Snow watched the captain climb down the Jacob's ladder to the gunboat, yelling "¡Vámonos!" at the deckhands.

"Toss off," Snow called to Maciel, and he pulled the lines free.

"You know," said Beth, "in England they'd think you just told him to masturbate."

"That right? I like that!" He called out again: "Toss off! Let it drop in the water!"

Maciel did as he was told, and the line splashed below, the deckhands looking up and yelling, "¡Chingada! ¡Vago de mierda!"

Marty saw this and called out, "Hey Jonah boy! You learn to heave line!"

"Put a sock in it!" barked Snow.

While the officer yelled in Spanish and swung the boat off in a rush of wheel wash, Maciel gathered in the Jacob's ladder and rolled it on the deck, carrying it over to the storage locker while Bracelin went forward, waving his arm over his head toward Paynor on the bridge, peering out the window. "Let's get this cargo loaded!"

Making their way inside under pilot and tug escort was the most nerve-wracking hour of Snow's life, including the war, since death didn't bother him nearly so much as the thought of rotting in a Mexican prison. They completed the mooring, tying off two lines from bow and stern both, lines sagging toward the dock.

Kairos, the pumpman, oversaw the loading operation while Snow kept to his watch from the bridge wing, eyeing Puerto de Salina Cruz with her tank farm on the north end, and twin radio towers, and outside to the jetty dividing the inner and outer harbors. He hadn't felt this trapped since the Coral Sea. He half expected the gunboat to return, this time with reinforcements. His heart thumped behind his ribs and his mind whirled. Snow was never one to worry unnecessarily, but he knew their situation would depend on one thing: if *el capitán* was working alone for a payday, they'd be safe, but if it was all a setup, then the gig was really and truly up.

Snow kept a silent vigil from the bridge wing with a radio and a pair of binocs and didn't leave his post once in all the time they off-loaded. He watched crewmen come and go, sauntering into the port where they bought fish, and talked with locals in their halting patois. He saw a guy wearing a broad-rimmed Aussie-style hat, chatting it up with Beth and the kid. The scene was as natural as any other port where big ships called—no sign of authorities, no sign of suspicions.

When at last the coupling was broken and the blanks reattached, the pilot came back aboard with a perfunctory nod, and the tugs whirled and worked their way into place at the bow and stern to pull the ship off the dock and out through the break in the jetty to the outer harbor. Snow watched their backside while the tugs released and fell away, and the ship steamed seaward under its own power. He felt almost giddy then, stepping into the wheelhouse to find Paynor and Bracelin bidding *adiós* to the pilot, who scampered down to the pilot boat and was off, and thereafter all Snow saw was the watery western horizon, and for a moment cruising out through the Gulf of Tehuantepec it looked like all would be sound for the trip to Panama.

The illusion didn't last long. Five miles outside, headed south-southwest, they were hit hard by winds known locally as Tehuantepecers, a cloudless norther that lashed in at fifty knots and whipped the seas to a blue foaming frenzy, rocking the vessel in a corkscrewing motion that sent it creaking and popping for the second time in five days. Snow watched the foredeck flex through the seas, thinking she could only stand one or two more like this. He went back to work wearing rain gear, stepped outside to the roar of machinery and the clear evening sky on winds that made your scalp hurt. He kept looking astern toward Salina Cruz, a cold blue reach with whitecaps and surf, the kind of view where you might not see a boat coming for you, not until they were close-on.

HAULING IN

The norther finally died as the ship passed the light station at Puerto Arista, and the night watch came on at eight o'clock to gentle after-swells. The next morning the sun broke upward dead east and blazed a straight path into the noon sky, seas dead calm, and by then a port list was obvious to everybody. On the weather deck Snow found Bracelin moving up the port side with his binder and his steel sounding tape. From the tape's end dangled a stainless steel disk, an emergency signal reflector the mate had permanently borrowed from a survival kit inside the covered life raft. The steel tape was spooled up on a reel with a folding crank on one side, and the mate worked it by popping the ullage cap and lowering the disk down until it slapped the surface of the cargoes. In this way, Bracelin measured tank levels in an attempt to diagnose the source of their portside list, and in the process managed to drag fifteen different chemicals out on deck, including a splash of caustic soda that found his leather work boots and started them to smoking.

Bracelin stood upright and proclaimed Leaks in Australia, which meant Leaks Down Under, and then assigned Snow and Kairos to go down for a look around. Crawling tanks on a healthy vessel was routine work, but on *Tarshish* it was more like a toxic nightmare, and Snow would have assigned himself the task exactly a week from never. He would have put Kairos down under with Maciel, figuring the two would have plenty of Christian things to talk about while wandering in the Underworld. But Bracelin would have none of it. He only said, "I need experienced hands," and then ran aft to douse his shoes with vinegar.

Kairos was a lanky black man of forty, with prematurely white hair and a wide smiling face. He was a war vet, a boonie rat in Nam during the early years, and also a Christian. He was converted while in Ranger School at Fort Benning, Georgia, where he was awestruck and moved to spiritual revelation by the bombing of the 16th Street Baptist Church in Birmingham. The bombed bodies of children riled his hatred while the measured reactions of great leaders made him realize how goodness and righteousness could prevail even in the face of evil. Somehow he managed to learn to turn the other cheek, even as the Army was teaching him how to shoot his enemies in the head.

Snow wiggled his way into a chemical suit and air pack while Kairos went on about his primary obsession: what cargoes they were *really* carrying in their holds. "I'd like one look at that binder," said Kairos, in his booming preacherlike voice. "I have a right to know what we're carrying. A man's got to protect himself!"

The two waddled off down the side deck looking like extras from a biowarfare movie. Snow felt a line of sweat start at his armpit and run down the length of his torso until it snuck into his jeans. "Best thing you can do to protect yourself is work like a dog and stay quiet as a mouse," he said.

"I always worked like a dog, all my life I worked like a dog. When you going to let me see the skipper so I can tell him what Bracelin done to me?"

"See, it ain't really the cargo manifest you're interested in, is it, Stephen?"

"No man got to stand for the disrespect of being called nigger."

"Stephen, you're a big boy, you heard worse in the war, I'm sure. Besides, he apologized for that, I heard him," Snow said.

"All the same, he uses the word *niggerhead* even though I told him time and again it's offensive. He could say *cathead* or *capstan* just as easy and he knows it, he just calls it a *niggerhead* to get my goat. Looks my direction like he's daring me to say something about it. Apology or not, he's got prejudice running in his veins. He don't see men as men. We're the Malay this, the Panny that—he's a bigot, Snow, and I ain't gonna take his cracker-ass shit on the job. I shouldn't have to. I want to talk to the captain."

That was all Snow needed, Kairos talking to the captain. Snow moved past one hatch and saw a white rim of plastic material showing around the rim of two tanks carrying monomers, the self-reactors. With the weather growing hot in the tropics, he made a mental note to check their supply of inhibitors and add more as the temperature rose. He arranged the hood and got set to pull the mask up over his face with a sense of enclosing dread. "I don't know what's going on. He's sick. I don't see him."

"Yeah, I heard that for going on six weeks now. If he's so sick how come he ain't been shipped home?"

"I don't know, Stephen. He's biding his time for his pension," Snow said. "You got a problem, take it up with the union steward."

"The union?" Kairos's face scrunched up in a pinch-faced, angry confusion that Snow swore only a black man could muster. "What union is that?"

"The International Brotherhood of Gripers and Complainers," said Snow, and managed to squeeze a laugh out of the pumpman.

"I like you bos'n, I got no beef with you. But Bracelin's one sick cat, you ask me. And he's got that binder!"

Now he was back on the binder again. Snow was almost glad when they pulled the hoods down over their heads and started breathing bottled air. "Knowledge is power!" Kairos shouted, his voice muffled behind the mask.

Snow carried a portable oxygen sensor and something called an Explosimeter, which measured combustible gas in the atmosphere. He checked levels all the way down, and found the tank clean and gas-freed as they reached bottom. The two men no sooner saw it safe to breathe than they tore their faces free of the confining masks and peeled back the hoods. "Save air this way anyway," said Snow. The tank smelled vaguely of garlic, but they saw no evidence of leaks. With the butt end of a ratchet handle, they tapped along the center bulkhead and then back toward the side along a wall of steel that separated them from what should have been an empty coffer dam. "Check this out, bos'n," said Kairos as he tapped.

Snow went over and put his ear to the steel, tapped once himself, and sure enough he heard none of the vacant reverb you normally got from a void space. A coffer dam had one purpose: to separate tanks of incompatible cargoes and allow you more flexibility in what cargoes you shipped. They worked, by and large, unless you got leaks from two tanks at once, in which case the coffer dam might contain some volatile mixtures. Snow had seen such multiple leaks blow a chemical carrier in half and kill five men in Rodeo, California, in 1971. He furrowed his brow in worry.

Then he tapped again, saw a flake of rust and reached with his thumbnail to pop it loose, and all at once a ten-foot chunk of rusted steel folded down off the wall. Then he was inundated by a flood of bulk liquid chemicals, the constitution of which was unknown but the effect immediate and unavoidable.

Kairos backpedaled against the flow, crying out, "Jesus dear Lord!" before he choked on the vapors. Snow spun and tripped over a longitudinal support beam, falling face forward while the flood of liquid chemicals washed over his back. Then he tried to breathe, gagged instantly, and vomited, disgorging his last meal. Stomach acid hit the fluid at the base of the tank and churned, emitting a chemical smoke just as he yanked his air mask hard onto his face, sucking on the respirator to activate the flow of air. Then he turned for the distant light of the tank hatch, the stair-step ladder seeming too far off. He crawled, scrambled, and finally got himself to his feet and ran for his life.

Kairos was right behind him, yelling the whole way, until he too pulled his respirator mask on and they hit the stairs, climbing. They hauled themselves out to the open deck and peeled off their masks, coughing, eyes burnt to the color of ripe cherries. Next thing they knew they were being tugged at and prodded to crawl their asses toward a decontamination shower set up at midships. Ali was shouting, "They got the dousing!"

The cool water rained down on Snow's head, and by the time he caught his breath he felt his lungs burn with each pull of air.

"Fucking morphodite motherfucking ship," said Kairos. "Fucking morphodite bastard-ass fuckall of a ship!"

Snow lay there, his chest heaving, and saw the boots and legs of Bracelin standing over him. "I think it's safe to say we got leaks down under," said Snow.

"What'd you do?" said Bracelin. "Try to take a bath in it?"

Kairos pulled himself upright, stripped out of the chemical

suit and threw it against the bulkhead. "Mother-fucker! Mother-fucker!" he raged.

"Why don't you calm down, Kairos?" said Bracelin.

"Don't you tell me, Mate!" said Kairos. "This ship got sold three times in the last two years, why don't you tell me what you make of that? Huh?"

"Ain't it obvious?" said Bracelin. "She's making her way *down* the ladder of maritime outfits and the one who owns her now is probably gonna run her until she sinks. You just better hope you ain't aboard when it happens."

"And who is this latest outfit? SeaStar Inc. I ain't never heard of them and I been shipping for fifteen years."

"You trying to make trouble for yourself, keep moving your mouth."

"Ain't no man can demand I shut up."

The two stood face-to-face, Kairos an inch or so taller than Bracelin but only half as wide. Maciel was practically hopping up and down, figuring the two were about to tear into each other. For a few seconds, Snow thought it might get to that. He sat with his back against the bulkhead and peeled his chemical suit down his body and off his legs. Maciel turned to Snow. "You all right, Harold?"

"I'm okay." He looked up, saw that most of the crew had gathered.

Ali stooped down over the boatswain. "Bos'n man! You got something nasty in your eyeballs. *Tst-tst-tst.* What fuck this lah?"

Beth bent over and peered into his eyes, then pulled a bottle of saline solution from a plastic first-aid kit, washing out both eyes until he felt water draining down his neck and into his shorts. "You never looked lovelier," Snow said.

Beth put the saline back into the kit and shut it. "Blurred vision."

Kairos reached into his pocket and came up with a piece of welder's soapstone, then marched long-legged to the coffer dam tank lid and scrawled DNE!! across it–for DO NOT ENTER. He marched over to the tank they'd just come out of, slammed the hatch cover shut and spun the wheel to dog it tight, then wrote the same thing on that. Bracelin scowled, then went over and scraped his boot across the letters, scratching them out. "We got Panama Canal transit," he said. "We won't be advertising this, got it? Nobody open either of them up! Got that?"

"I got that all right, yes!" said Ali, and pushed Maciel in the chest. "We don't need no priest on board for this lah!"

And the crew nodded at that too. Somehow they all managed to blame the kid for this–for Delacroix, for the storm, for the break in the bulkhead down below, maybe for Bracelin too. From then on the Christians, Kairos included, refused to call Maciel by name, preferring Jonah instead and threatening to feed him to a sperm whale if only they could find one.

That night Snow lay in his bunk with his chest tingling and itching, and finally he slept hard straight through the dark hours, his dreams hallucinatory and varied, dreams of bombs falling and sprouting into palm trees that grew from tropical waters. For a while there it was 1945 again, and he was aboard ship at the Bikini atoll H-bomb tests, donning his flimsy atomic sunglasses for a little Operation Sunshine and feeling the bright raging ball of fusion as it rose off the waters of the South Pacific. No palm trees remained. Later he ran the launch boat that ferried scientists back and forth to the island after the blast. He dreamed of sitting in a conference room with the lights low and an overhead projector showing the charts and graphs of all those rads he and the other launch operators had absorbed, tenfold what the others had taken. In the dream he kept pushing his fingertips up under his ribs like he wanted to dig something out of there, like one of those charlatan doctors pulling chicken guts from sick people. He couldn't quite fathom it. He had lived the clean life without booze or smoke these past ten years; it didn't set right to imagine some ball of growth had taken root thanks to nuke tests from thirty-five years back. To make it worse, when he woke up he found it was half past three in the afternoon and he'd slept eleven hours, over twice his norm, and no one, not even Beth, had awakened him.

As ship's boatswain, Snow oversaw multiple watches, so he didn't stand a regular watch himself. He worked 6 A.M. to 6 P.M. so he could manage the day watches comprised of able seamen and ordinaries. He then stood a night watch that straddled those of his crew—spending at least a couple of hours on the bridge between 2200 hours and 0200. The only other person with such a schedule was the chief mate, and the result was simple: they were the only two people aboard who knew what was going on.

But now it was midafternoon, and for the first time since he had sailed boatswain, Snow realized he knew little of what was happening on deck. His brain felt absurdly fuzzy. He shook his head trying to eradicate the ringing in his left ear. The freak of it was, he hadn't heard so much as an inside tapping from that ear in thirty-eight years, when it was damaged on the wings of a 250-kg bomb dropped by the sons of Nippon. He shook his head and tried to think about what they would do next and in what order they'd do it. He thought about Beth. He wanted to find her and have her over to the room. He kept flashing on that first time he'd ever seen Beth, walking up the docks at Rotterdam, striding like she knew where she was going, wearing bell-bottom dungarees and two layers of sweatshirts and carrying two seabags. He had greeted her at the top of the gangway and charmed her into helping with her bags, which were loaded down with a regular commissary. Turned out one way she got along on board ships was to provide minor contraband; anything you couldn't get from the cooks you could get from Beth: every kind of whiskey and smoke on earth, whacky tobaccy, the occasional hashish, prescription drugs, and those weird Indian smokes called *bidis* that tasted like Turkish tobacco and smelled like a chocolate sundae.

They had shared a joint in his room later, and she told him in her strange accent–one part Sierra Leone English and one part London middle class–about the other way she got along aboard ships. "It's quite simple, really. I come aboard, and without their knowing it I interview the crew. I pick the best and most strategic one and take him as a lover. Then the rest leave me alone. It's that simple, really. Men are quite territorial about sex, you know."

Snow did know. "So is this one of those interviews?"

"No, no. First of all, a man must never know he's being interviewed. I've spilled the beans on that one. Second of all–well, you aren't my type."

He didn't ask what was her type; maybe he was afraid to, or maybe he could guess that he was too old and scarred up. "Well, there's always friendship," he said. "Hell, the crew'll probably think we're screwing just 'cause I'm here tonight."

"That could be useful, actually," she said, with a wry smile. "It gets a tad wearing to be constantly doing interviews."

"Sure. You can just tell them you're my girlfriend–that'll keep the wolves away, guaranteed. Around here, Chief Mate is Chief Wolf. We got an understanding."

"Could be complicated."

"Could beat the alternative. But I'm high, so what do I know?"

They had giggled together, even as he reached out and held her hand and said, "Girlfriend."

But all along Snow had been hoping, thinking if he did the right thing and remained a man in her life like no other, someone she could trust, then she might warm to him and see some affection there. Now he didn't know. Or maybe he did.

He tried to make a map of the crew, where they'd be, and what they'd be doing. Leeds would be on his day watch in the engine room. Beth and Maciel would be in the last hour of their afternoon watch. Marty and Ali would be sleeping. The cooks would be making dinner. Paynor and Bracelin would both be on the bridge.

Snow climbed.

He made his way via the internal stair tower, emerging in the chart room, stepping forward into the afternoon light of the wheelhouse, where he found Bracelin and Paynor looking out at the palm shores of the Central American coast. Snow was unsure just where they were, but soon he saw the refinery at Acajutla in El Salvador, and knew they were still a day's sail from Panama.

"Where the fuck you been, old man?" said Bracelin.

"I think there was sleeping pills in them chemicals I run into," said Snow.

"Either that or your days are catching up to you. Got your old body in a jammie twist," said the chief mate. He was scanning the shore with binoculars. Snow didn't feel much like wasting time, so he relieved the helmsman and took the wheel. No sooner were they the only three left on the bridge than Paynor turned and let loose. "If one Mexican CG officer has us made, what makes you think more haven't?"

"Because we bribed his ass," said Bracelin. "If he weren't working alone he wouldn't be extorting us, he'd be arresting us."

"In Mexico? You can guarantee that in Mexico? Give me a break!"

Snow fought through his headache and the ringing in his ear and said, "Let's not miss the real point here, gents. It changes nothing we gotta do, just maybe when we got to do it. We got papers waiting for us in Panama City. The only question is how we run the canal. On that we got two choices: we paint her now and I go ashore in a boat for the papers, and we transit the canal under new flag and new COI. Or we try to run her as is and change her on the other side after Moín, like we planned all along."

"No, no, no." Paynor ran his hand through his thick black hair until it boiled straight up off his head. "There's a third choice. You go ashore, get the papers, and we don't *stop* here. We head straight down the coast, pick up cargo in Valparaiso et cetera, and round the Horn for Freetown."

"Two problems with that," said Snow. "First, that adds two weeks to Freetown, and I ain't sure we can afford two weeks. Second, we need more product. We ain't full yet, and we might get contracts out of Venezuela."

"Not only that," said Bracelin. "But you seriously want to run the Strait of Magellan in this piece of shit? 'Cause personally, that gives me visions of little chunks of rust floating around and not much else."

"I'll take my chances with that over prison in Panama," said Paynor. "I'm serious. I do not want to go to prison in Panama."

Snow could see that choice working on Bracelin, and he understood it: if both fates could be assured they would all rather die going around the Horn than live in a Panamanian prison. But Snow didn't think they would go to prison. He thought they'd make it without trouble, and he said so. "It gets back to whether you believe that Mexican *capitán* put out an alert. I don't think he did. I think he was operating solo and he's gonna take his ten G's and not say a peep. I met the guy. I looked in his eyes. I'll bet my freedom on it."

"I agree with him," said Bracelin.

"Fine," Paynor said. "Fine fine fine. You two make your bet. Goddamn bullshit is what this is. This is stupid goddamned bullshit and I never should have let you two talk me into this."

"We need you, Payne," said Snow.

"Yeah, like fuck you do. First new need you get, you'll dump my ass."

"Guess you better make yourself indispensable," said Bracelin.

"You're our agent," said Snow. "Get us goddamned product to move and we're gonna love you."

"I don't even speak fucking Spanish," said Paynor. "This is insane, Mate, you realize that. I am so far out of my league here. I'm a goddamned navigator, and I'm a goddamned good one. But all this other shit is insane."

"You know the routine," said Bracelin.

"I got me a Berlitz phrase book in my room. I'll drop it by," said Snow, and at that he and Bracelin shared a laugh, Snow's high-pitched and childlike, Bracelin's mechanical and lifeless. Bracelin pulled his binocs back up and started scanning the white beaches of El Salvador.

"Now I got to get out on deck and find out what's going on," said Snow.

Bracelin didn't so much as pull the eyepiece away from his field glasses. "You better start by keeping an eye on that little girl of yours."

Snow stopped just as he was heading out the side door to the bridge wing. "What the hell's that supposed to mean?"

"Don't know. You tell me."

"Mind your own business."

"Yeah yeah, old man, like you ain't my business. Say hi to Lisa for me."

It irritated Snow no end that Bracelin called her Lisa. He hated that name, Lisa. She was Beth or Elisabeth, but not goddamned Lisa. His headache felt like a thousand seeds of pain all sprouting at once inside his brain.

Then he heard the ring of the ship's bell signaling the watch change.

Snow went down the bridge wing and took the external ladder to the poop deck, then down through the internal door to his room, where he stepped in, expecting the kid to be there getting ready for supper. But the room was empty, which was just as well, since Snow had begun to wonder if now wasn't the time for drastic action on the personal front. He pulled open a drawer on the metal writing desk and shuffled through envelopes from that Aussie half brother of his, found a pack of Rolaids, peeled back the foil in a broad strip, and chewed down three.

A big part of him thought Paynor was right; this was all insane. He put himself back in that moment steaming the Strait of Malacca when he'd manned the helm on the midnight watch with Bracelin alone on the bridge, listening to the man's frustrations with Petrochem, how he'd sailed with them for going on ten years, had been by god Supermate. "You know," Snow had said. "There's other options." And he went on to tell him about the people he knew in Port Kuleng, Malaysia, and similar people in Panama City, Panama, who could procure certain documents to turn one ship into another.

"So if we did such a thing–and I ain't saying we should–how we gonna pull that off with McFarland aboard?" Bracelin had said.

"Two choices there," said Snow.

"We kill him or we kill him."

"No, no. That's the beauty of it. We *don't* kill him. We convince him his ship's been sold and the new company wants to keep him on."

Bracelin had snorted so loud Snow thought he might have injured himself. But Snow had it all figured. They actually would start a company, open an account, pay off the crew. They could control the captain just fine—Beth had a two-month supply of Valium to feed the old man's fondness for the stuff and contacts to get more in PC. Bracelin only nodded, muttered, "Hmmm," and went away.

Two days later, with Port Kuleng appearing on their port side, the mate came through the door while Snow was reading in his rack, shut the door behind him and stood there like a steel I-beam set upright. "I been thinking about your idea," he said.

So with a few hundred keystrokes on an old typewriter, fifty gallons of new paint, and some cash exchanged for paperwork in Port Kuleng, the Petrochem *Mariner* out of Rotterdam, Nether-lands, became *Tarshish* out of Monrovia, Liberia. The captain had been retained and the mate stayed in control. The rest of the crew, save for a half dozen, had been fired and sent home, and then along came the Malays and the Panamanians—a motley crew that could barely communicate with one another, much less the officers, a linguistic confusion that suited Snow's purposes to a T. For the first time since he got out of the Navy, Snow felt prospects in the offing.

Now he knelt in front of his locker and dug into the lower drawer and looked at everything he'd stuffed there in the years since he'd been aboard. In place of home, Snow had film. He shuffled through the yellow Kodak boxes, 8mm footage he'd been collecting since the fifties, boxes marked BANGKOK 1952 and INDIA 1958 and so on. Silent footage playing snake charmer along the banks of the River Ganges, guiding for steelhead up the Skykomish, good times with Jill—he wouldn't show anybody *that* one. She'd been just shy of half his age then, and while some thought her damaged and him perverted (or vice versa), he'd had laughs with Jill, laughs and real solid good times. After a particu-larly vigorous night together, she allowed as how she would never again miss the drink or boys her own age. Still, she'd gone off with one, one who could still father a child, and now they lived like a happy family somewhere in the Bitterroots.

On the floor before the box of movies, Snow sat cross-legged, proud he could still do that. He lifted the old Brownie camera with the turret lenses and loaded it up with fresh film—or, rather, blank film, since he'd bought it four years before in bulk and had no idea if it could hold an image. He sat there cranking the windup, thinking if he took film of Beth now he'd have that to retire with, even if she did turn him down. A pathetic thought, complete with visions of a geriatric head case holed up in a moss-bound cabin jerking off to movies of what might have been. He set the camera aside and pulled out the plain box, unmarked by any particular jewelry retailer, containing the diamond propped on a gold mount, a stone he knew personally since he'd practically mined it himself. It was well over two karats, in a setting of white gold, bound to a white gold necklace. Nothing so silly and romantic as an engagement ring, even though in his mind it meant the same thing.

He felt the easy seas beneath him. The sun blasted in a straight cylindrical shot through the porthole. There on the floor, he folded the box closed and lifted himself to his feet, a pain searing up his hip flexors to where he thought he might not be able to walk. Just his luck he'd pull a groin on his way to propose marriage to a girl half his age. He tucked the air mail letter from Thorson into his pocket and figured he'd use that too, if he got desperate, tell her straight out he'd found her long-lost father and was even now in the midst of arranging a meeting, a regular family reunion. It was dicey business, but he knew it might get to that.

He walked carefully down a level to the O-1 deck, to the room Beth shared with Katie the Baker, paused a moment to gather what he thought might be strength, and rapped on the door three times. When she swung the door open, he saw past to where Maciel sat on the floor, cross-legged on the rug Snow had made for her, smoking a cigarette and listening to music, that same garbage the kid listened to in his bunk. Near as Snow could tell the kid's music was to real music what a root canal was to glorious sex, but Beth seemed to like it.

"Well, my my, if it isn't Harold Hardrada," she said, and something in her manner struck him, that she was talking to him but flirting with the kid.

"Hey there," said Snow, but he felt his mouth hanging a bit—an odd sense of déjà vu, like walking into his own nightmare, and it damned well showed.

Then something inside him clicked over, maybe something about keeping your friends close and your adversaries closer, or maybe just because in truth he liked the two of them, and knew full well that acting all jealous would do nothing for his cause. He had to suck this one up, there was no other way. "Hey—I am sorry to interrupt," he said. He felt the cardboard box in his pocket and smiled genuine now, his own presence tall and strong as he stepped inside like it was his room after all. "Just wondered if anybody was up for a party!" he said. "Thinking on one of them bottles of single malt you got stashed in your footlocker."

"But you don't drink, Harold." She eyed him. "You haven't been tapping off my stores, have you?"

"I wouldn't pilfer. I told you I'd let you stash it in my room. I'm just feeling festive!" he said, sitting on the lower bunk as if he'd sat there often enough to call it his own chair, elbows on his knees. Maciel sat on the floor below. "Either that or we could smoke a little whacky tobaccy—more my style."

"You know the rule," Beth said. "No pay no play."

"Sure. I'll pay." He fished into his pocket and brought out a twenty. "How much for this?"

"That'll get you two joints," she said, and she went into the locker beneath her bunk, her head practically between his legs amid all the items of her business, and pulled out two rolled ones.

"That's all? My day that'd get you four joints and a blow job!"

"Be good, Harold," and she handed it up to him and took the money at the same time. She got up and moved across the floor with the frayed bottoms of her pants sliding along the deck below dusty bare feet. She was goddamned cool, dragging on one of those Indian smokes of hers, squinting and holding it in her lips as she turned the music up—some heavy guitar concoction or another. To Snow it all sounded the same, like a collision on the London underground set to a reggae beat.

"God, I love this song!" she cried, and set the smoke in an ashtray and started to dance all frantic—like her limbs might fly off, or her clothes. He enjoyed the dark skin of her hips just above the waist of her green fatigues, worn like hip-huggers to where he could see just barely the band of her underwear and wish for more. He enjoyed the tight hair of her head, bristly as a scrub brush, making her look like a boy. That's what she meant to do, divorce herself from her very gender, not realizing that half the crew of half the ships she'd ever been on would like her better that way.

He wished he could someday at least see her nude, touch the firm tight skin at the base of her back, where fine black hair grew like grass up hollow valley land, and where her body flared to her rounded bottom. But these were rare sights here, and he wondered if they weren't for the kid's benefit anyway.

Snow knew where to find sex anywhere in the world, and had. But to actually make love one last time before he died—he didn't imagine he'd ever wish for something like that, something he'd had with his first wife just after the war, something he had lost while working the river because he'd screwed everything he could get his hands on. Inside, deep where the hot metal of the kamikaze had burned into him, he knew he would throw himself in front of a crane hook for Beth.

He watched the two now, trading smiling glances as they drew on their exotic smokes, moved like wild banshees to a music that left him behind, like they knew already what would happen later, after the old guy left. But they didn't see the danger, didn't fully understand that, as far as the crew thought, Beth belonged to Snow. If they thought of him as her father or her brother or her protective uncle, they'd try to move him aside, because those relations didn't have the power of sex and sexual possession. He guessed it some strange and primal respect paid to a man of sixty who still inspired a kind of awe, or maybe just the outmoded stupidity of men who regarded women as property. Snow wondered if Beth got that at all, wondered if she had any idea how the tribe really worked.

He took out the Brownie and let the motor fly–"Smile for the camera!"–and then held the joint up with his other hand, saying, "Let's fire this puppy up!"

Maybe it was the three Dixie cups of Glenfiddich combined with the joint, or maybe the music that raked through Snow's skull like a road grader, but soon the ghetto blaster zoned from the Clash into Pink Floyd, and Snow was right back in a room in Da Nang with a bar girl in 1968, the Year of the Monkey, the eve of Tet and the Tet offensive, listening to the Doors and smoking dope. Only that was just memory, and bad memory at that, since now he wasn't with a bar girl, he was watching these two, knowing exactly why Beth had failed to awaken him. Suddenly he hated everything that came from the kid's mouth, a pouty little mouth at that. Beth and Maciel sat facing each other in the middle of Snow's rug smoking *bidis* as if he weren't there. And it wasn't as if Snow didn't want to hear about the death of the grandfather. He was curious to know how old Joaquin had gone in the end. He settled in and tried to listen. It turned out they were hard days, the worst kind of days in the shit, as the old-timers would say. Days in the shite, as Beth would say. Old Joaquin appeared there for Snow, right there in his eyeballs: batting his hands like a swarm of bees was trying to fly up his nose, lost in storms at sea–U-boats! U-boats!–attacks that ended with the old man trying to abandon ship by climbing out the window into his vegetable garden. He refused all that last-rites-and-unction nonsense, fighting some unseen menace on his own only to crap his pants while his grandson tried to help him make it to the john. He groaned *For God's sake, Georgie, for God's sake,* and as George cleaned him up he mumbled *Dear God I never thought it would come to this.* It was much later, well into the final vigil, that all the old man could say was *Van Sickle.* He must have said that name a hundred times. And it stuck at the kid then, wondering who this *Van Sickle* was.

Snow knew. He saw the man as clear as if he'd stepped aboard the *San Luis Rey* this second, a rowdy boiling red-bearded man with grease permanently pressed into the cracks of his calluses. Dutch Van. Chief engineer and third in a drinking triumvirate that included Snow because Snow was a war veteran and had the scars to prove it. Snow liked that–he liked the end to the formalities of deep water, the hierarchy of the military. He warmed fast to the inland boatmen, the river men, who on water never ventured more than a stone's throw from land, who never got quite so crazy–he thought.

But all men everywhere got crazy, got old and scary. Young Maciel had never seen a man die before, never seen a man dive off down the spiritual storm drain dragged by ghosts and dead men. Old Joaquin was convinced of his fate, just as Snow was somehow grudgingly convinced of his own. There were things you did in your life that you couldn't duck. Old Joaquin wanted one thing: to be buried next to his wife of fifty-four years, his beloved Marie. He pressed the kid to use contacts the kid didn't have, pressed him to make a direct appeal to the bishop, as if anybody would let him, a lowly seminarian, a Jesuit at that. The monsignor crossed his sausage fingers over his fat robe and said, "You could always move her." The thought alone was repellant. Buried six years before, after a life of good works, after a life of humility and suffering, a Christly life, Marie de la Rosa Maciel died and went to heaven and was buried in the hallowed ground of the archdiocese. To give his grandfather his last wish, George would have deprived his grandmother of hers.

Joaquin lay in a hospital bed they'd rolled into his room, shades drawn and tubes up his nose, the kid unable to understand how the old man could profess not to believe in God yet believe so completely in Hell and the Devil. He clung to his desire, that the church might step aside and let him be laid to rest on their sacred turf. Worm food! Worm food anyhow! The old man clung to the matter of burial as if it meant something to the spirit world, as if it meant everything to this world.

Snow looked at the girl. His head started bobbing around like he didn't know whether to nod his head or shake it. She was right there in it, into the kid, leaning into him and into the story because *isn't it so sad and romantic* to imagine two people who *loved each other so much* they could forgive their differences and live together over five decades only to die separately and in such despair. A tragic love story expanded to the afterlife. *In nomine Patris, et Filii, et Spiritus Sancti. Amen.* Snow wanted to blow chow. How could these people expect more? Knowing what had happened in the war alone stripped away all expectations of intervention. No Elysian Fields or Valhalla for Joaquin Maciel—or for Harold Snow either, war veterans or not. A pair bound for Hades if there ever was, while life slips past like fodder for ghosts, and whiskey slides straight down your throat to explode in your stomach and bounce back to a throbbing head. It was all chemicals on chemicals.

Snow knew about death, and old Joaquin, and the kid, how he'd fled to that church and how he'd censored the grandpa half, how he'd cut out that gene, or tried to, sat on it, whatever. The dangerous semicircle of his own corkscrewing DNA, with a strange upbringing throwing in a kink or two. The kid ran from his own bad self for twenty-five years. Now he was here. At sea. Asea. Snow hated him for it. Wanted to slap him for it. Wanted to tell him about real death, about the truth behind death and how it came for everybody and none of them were special. He wished others could have seen what he'd seen. He wished they could see the humped charcoal bodies. He wished they could see Tet 1968 in Da Nang. Viet bar girls. Jarheads without a conscience. Why the fuck *did* he have someone else's blood all over his body? But none of that was anything compared with the Bay of Bengal in 1970. That was it, you wanted to see the absurdity of death you only had to be there aboard a dry-cargo ship on the dangerous semicircle fifty miles from Chittagong, in East Pakistan, being blown aground on 140-knot winds and a sea surge.

As that storm got going, Snow had climbed topside to begin his standard watch on the helm, on a ship where the stair tower was set off the bridge deck, connected by a fifteen-foot catwalk of grated steel mesh and steel handrails. Rain flew across at 90 degrees, pulsing as the crests of waves were torn off at the top, lashing at the ship with spume and rain mixed like a thousand fire nozzles. Snow knew he'd be a wet rat by the time he crossed over, so he took off all his clothes, tucked them in a ball under his belly, and ran like a naked fullback through rain that felt like ten thousand needles piercing his skin. When he got to the other side he had dry clothes, and a good thing too, since he was the last man to make that run for the next twelve hours. He stood the wheel, steered the ship into a blunt force blast of wind and water, blowing them into the wall of the eye, where they hove to and put out two anchors and turned full ahead into the teeth of it and still got blown backward twelve and two-tenths miles. Up into the Ganges plume, where Snow watched the silt waters scour the ship. When they woke up the next day and walked out on deck they found the entire windward side sand-blasted. Shined like silver. Made you want to paint it. But that wasn't all, that was just a vision of possibility, of life, because the reality was darker than silver; the reality came in that sea surge that ran up-delta and drowned a quarter million—*a quarter million*—men, women, and children. Half were Hindus, too many to cremate, so they said words over bodies and dropped live coals in their mouths to symbolize cremation and dumped them in the river to wash out to sea. Next morning, along with a silver ship, that dry-cargo ship called *Nineveh,* there floated a hundred thousand of the dead all around them, their black Indian hair waving in the water like seaweed and their mouths burned out like somebody had taken a blowtorch to them. All that night lying in his bunk he heard the sharks crunching on human flesh and bone, and that was horrible to hear, but there was no guilt. He'd had nothing to do with making tropical cyclones in the Bay of Bengal. But guilt came from other places, the old man's wheezing refrain: *Goddamn you Van Sickle you get the hell from my house you get the hell from my house!*

Snow held out a cup for Beth to pour a little scotch, and she frowned but did it anyway. He watched her long black fingers where they held the bottle, nails worn to the nub, the ends blunt and rounded by callus, and her forearms scarred by work. And he saw the way the kid looked at her, and all at once it just flooded from him, how could the kid not see it was all just Catholic guilt come to take a man in the end, just that, fucking brainwashed by his pious good girl for fifty-odd years and you too by the look of you. And how the kid looked at Snow. Like right at him. I don't think you know anything about my grandmother. His deep-set eyes incapable of concealing malice. He wanted to lunge at the old man, he wanted to strike out and kill him, thrash him. "Lemme tell you something about your gramps," Snow said. "Truth is, he was an angry fuck. Great boat operator, shitty skipper. The master of the single screw." Then it melted and spread between the two of them, expressions played out to acid rock, and the two staring through a veil of smoke and hatred. They both hated him now. Didn't bother or surprise the kid that his old gramps was a bastard, just so long as he wasn't an incompetent one. "See, your gramps had a little problem with needing a whipping boy."

"I don't think I want to hear this."

"Too bad, I got some good stories. I can tell you all about Dutch Van Sickle too, if you want."

Maciel's face rotated upward in fear. He stammered, " 'Course I want to know. Why do you think I'm here? He never mentioned Van Sickle until the end."

"Guess that makes sense. He died in 1948. I know 'cause I saw him die. Stood there on the afterdeck of the *San Luis* and watched your gramps beat him to death with a marlin spike, then dump his body in the river up near Decker Island. So I guess I can see where old Joaquin might have been a little *overcome* by memories of Van Sickle."

Snow enjoyed watching the kid's face, enjoyed making him look like a little boy before Beth, stammering with his tiny little mouth, trying to find something to say about the kind of man his grandfather was.

"I wouldn't take it too hard, Georgie. There's a little killer in all of us."

The both of them turned to Snow, Beth's eyes like dead lumps of ash, pink tongue licking chapped lips. The kid's eyes turned to slivers on his face the more pissed off he got, and then he stood up and walked out. Beth stood up after him–said calmly, "What the bloody fuck was that about?"–and left Snow in her room to stew in the juices of conflict and an altered mind.

When it was clear no one was about to return, Snow climbed his way up one deck to his own cabin and opened the lower left drawer of his desk to pull out a map of the world. Every man needed a map of the world. To know its limits, where the earth ends and something else begins. Snow spread the oversized sheet out on the flat carpeted deck and then lifted it whole to the steel bulkhead, fumbling with the awkward size of it but finally stretching it to cover the mirror there. In the glass, he caught glimpses of his own scary hair and squinted eyes, all cut up by the movement of paper, which he taped and brushed flat with the back of his hand.

Once he'd hung it on the wall, he pulled out a sheet of round stickers in two colors, blue and red, and went over the various letters from Australia, putting blue dots for males and red dots for females. He figured there was a story behind each dot. He remembered when his father had first admitted he might have "one or two bastards" floating around. Snow wondered, given the names–all those Harolds–if maybe all of them hadn't thought of themselves as first families. He'd never had more than one child with any woman, near as Snow could tell. Snow took a ballpoint pen and clicked it open, and in a careful script he wrote the names of every one of them. Manwaring-Snow had tracked thirty-seven of the sixty. Harold Sr. had scattered his seed on the seven seas and let it drift ashore. Thirty-seven. They were the only family Snow had left, yet he didn't know a single one of them.

Then the kid came in and Snow drew the deepest breath he could, shoving his belly out to accommodate the air, and stood upright. "Hey there, buddy." His brain spun from the sauce.

"Do me a favor and quit calling me that."

"Come on now. Life's too short to dwell on moods. At sea you're stuck with each other."

"That's obvious." The kid looked around darkly, then went to his locker and shoved some clothes around, like he might actually have planned on changing his shirt or something. He was rummaging around in there for quite a while when Snow pointed at the map of the world. "See there, what I put up."

Maciel pushed around inside his locker as if putting something back in place, then looked over at the map. "Yeah? What is it?"

"Those dots—well, I guess you could say they're my family. This half brother I got, he sent along this list. Seems my old man not only had a woman in every port, he had a kid to go with her! Now me? I got my nuts clipped after one. Got me a son by my ex-wife."

The kid stared at the map a moment. Snow couldn't tell if he was still pissed off at him or just brooding over his grandpa being a killer. "Are you Mormon or something?" the kid asked.

Snow laughed. "Do I look like a Mormon to you? I'm more like an old Greek Pagan. I like all them gods whoring around and living like people do."

Snow nodded at the map. A cluster of red dots around Panama City and one blue in Colón, and on up to Puerto Limón in Costa Rica; two sisters up there. "This Digger's a real resourceful guy. Why, I got half sibs spread out all over the frigging world. African, Indian, Vietnamese, Burmese, Pakistani—Jesus Christ, you name it: white, black, brown, yellow—I got it all. My family's like a walking UN." He paused an instant as the image settled. "Lucky bastard!"

He stopped and just looked at the kid. "Listen, I'm sorry about all that in Bethy's room. Truth is, I got jealous. See, I told you Bethy was my girlfriend and—well, it rankled me that you was there."

"Nothing was happening."

"Oh, now, don't say that. A whole lot was happening. I can see; I got two eyes and one good ear left."

"We were just listening to music and having a smoke. Besides, she told me she isn't your girlfriend."

Snow heard the clicking and popping in his bad ear again.

Maciel went over to the map as if to physically change the subject. He looked it over from one end to the other, then turned around and said, "Bracelin gave me what he called a contract job. Paint prep. He wants me to do it with Lisa."

"With *Lisa*! Is that right? I don't like that name much."

"It's how she introduced herself to me."

"She hates when I call her Lisa." Snow went to put another sticker up on the map, but for the life of him he couldn't get the dot peeled off. "Contract job you do on your own time, off watch. You'll have till Panama City to get her done. Bethy's good aloft. You'll be doing the funnel."

"What's the funnel?"

"The housing around the exhaust stacks. You get to hang down from the top like a rock climber. Wash and chip and grind. Then paint. Hope you don't mind heights."

"I think I can manage."

"Well, whatever you do, don't look up. They always say don't look down, but I say don't look up. World spins out from underneath you. Don't want your thoughts too high in the sky, Georgie. And another thing: don't do what Bethy does, that girl has no fear."

"I don't get it," said the kid. "It looks like it was just painted."

"Ship's been sold, what I heard. We'll do the stack and the names."

Snow remembered the last repainting. Beth did the contract job solo that time, hanging in the boatswain's chair, running sideways like a real climber, dusting her brown knees with the oxidized white paint, and dripping sweat in the afternoon sun.

Snow moved over to the writing desk and picked up the letters. He started to tell the kid something about them, but anything significant seemed to evaporate from his head. He felt a blank where his anonymous half siblings were concerned. He tried to conjure some image of them, but all he could manage was versions of himself in color. In his mind, even the sisters looked like him.

CLEFT

Along the palm shores of the isthmus country, *Tarshish* ran coastwise, steaming east into the Gulf of Panama, past the light at
Punta Mala, which sat amid a few clustered buildings on a steep,
rocky point, a low sweep reaching north, past a series of river
mouths to a tongue of sandstone called Punta Lisa. All the way
along, the crew worked feverishly, dangling over the side to scrape
the hull free of barnacles, and on the weather deck to stem the flow
of vapors and liquids. Snow anticipated an on-board inspection to
gain entry to the Canal Zone. Marty and Ali put down fifty-three
soft plugs and used ten gallons of Red Hand to cover the patches,
and then the entire crew attacked the pipeline and weather deck
with the only paint they had aboard: deck red. By the time they
took their place in line for the canal, the ship looked pristine in

the pipeline and like a burn victim on the exterior of the funnel, where the kids had done their contract job with admirable zest.

But the good news about Panama was *radio practique.* For reasons known only to Canal Zone authorities, the ship was cleared via radio and informed that no inspector would come aboard. Snow rejoiced–he felt his luck turning. They were halfway over their final transit hurdle, and now he could legally go ashore in a boat, do his business, and take an evening out with Beth in Panama City, work and play at the Rojo y Negro. They had planned it way back, pre-Frisco, but now when he was set to go in, he couldn't find her anywhere. He searched all over, found Katie the Baker sleeping, found Leeds brewing up something of a chemical type, and finally on the bridge Paynor said Beth had signed out a Zodiac and gone into PC about an hour earlier–with Maciel. Snow's head twitched in response.

Carrying fifty grand in large bills, his Z-card, and his reading glasses, Snow caught a water taxi into the old quarter, pulling away from the ship to the sound of Frank Zappa singing from an upstairs porthole: *My ship of love, my ship of love, is ready to attack.*

The Rojo y Negro lay at the end of a blind street off Calle 4, where a mix of battered Fords and sparkling Mercedes-Benzes bunched up on the cobbles outside the stone facades of the old quarter. Inside, Snow surveyed the early late crowd, the half dozen or so languid dancers weaving and grinding to a Latin beat, the swerve of lights, the long bar to the left with a cascade of glass and gold liquids behind, where a bartender stood leaning over the bar. Snow nodded. *"Necesito hablar a Quirarte."*

The bartender stretched his arm out and pointed toward a staircase, with a cigarette dangling at the end of two fingers. The music's beat pulsed inside Snow's skin as he climbed along a staircase that overlooked the dance floor and disappeared into a dark hallway, where he came to a room marked OFICINA. He knocked once, cocking his good ear toward a door painted gloss black, and still heard only the thump of music from the disco below, until he cupped his good ear and heard a distinctly impatient *"¡Pasale!"* Snow pushed in to find the man seated behind a broad wooden desk, as neat and orderly as an accountant's.

"I'm from the ship."

"Of course, please sit–" Quirarte was a lithe little man, with childlike hands, the left bearing a tattoo arching over the back in the shape of an octopus clinging to his wrist. He reached into his desk with the same hand, and for just an instant Snow thought he'd miscalculated, that he'd been caught napping and now would pay a big tab as the man pulled a badge or a weapon or both.

Instead he came up with a Tyvek envelope, white and unsealed. Snow took it, pulled the papers up slightly, and saw the Certificate of Inspection and the registry papers, signed off by a Venezuelan classification society. "Do you want to buy a flag also?" said the manager.

"We got that, thanks."

"The name is as you requested," he said. "You'll note the paperwork is all in order. There are blank records dating back, for you to fill in. Did you need cargo manifests?"

"No, we have them also, thanks."

"Bueno. Ahora." He paused, regarding Snow with his eyebrows lifted, as if Snow should know what he was about to say. *"Tiene que pagar."*

"Right. Truer words never spoken," and Snow straightened his legs out and lifted up on his haunches to slide the billfold from his front pocket. "The ol' tango *que pagar.*" He laughed at his own joke, then felt the bone of his hip sticking out–focused for a second on lost weight. He pulled a wad of bills from the pocket, an inch thick at least, folded once and tied by a rubber band. He tossed it to the desk and watched the octopus hand creep over it, withdrawing like a sea predator.

"Would have preferred to do that by wire, you understand," Snow said.

"All ships carry cash; this is nothing. I don't like records of certain transactions. I'm sure you understand."

"It's all very discreet when you know who you're dealing with."

"Well, that is just it. I do not know you from anybody. It is only because of our Malaysian friend that I am even doing this now."

Snow clutched the Tyvek envelope, stood up, and turned for the door. He thought as he reached the handle he should have offered his hand to shake, but by the time he decided it was never too late for politeness, it in fact was: the door had closed unceremoniously behind him. As he made his way down the hallway, the music reverberated in the confines and opened out as he hit the top of the stairs. He felt a spooky kind of mistrust lurking behind him like dangerous fog, and it felt good to be going down the stairs again into the open room.

As he made his way down the steps he clutched the Tyvek envelope and wished he'd been more thorough in checking through it, thinking Bracelin would have him for lunch if Quirarte had screwed something up. He thought he'd hit the head right off, do a double-check on the documents, but then, halfway down, he caught sight of Beth on the dance floor and felt his heart sink just as blood rushed his groin, and he stopped for fear he might trip and fall head first to the base of the stairs.

He had never seen her dressed for a club. She wore skin-tight blue jeans, unbuttoned on top to reveal her bare tummy and the top of white panties, and though this was apparently a style in the Rojo, he confessed it was enough to make his entire lower half go into fits of spasm. A black light shone from the corner, and though other light competed to reveal the truth of the dance floor, this light dominated her, made everything white on her glow like moonlight, made everything dark on her appear like velvet. She danced close with Maciel, too close for Snow to watch, astride his thigh and moving in circles with her hips. Snow turned and made for the head, a clean modern facility that told you how much money they brought through here.

He stepped into the first toilet stall, turned and sat on the open industrial toilet seat, and felt his ass sag downward toward the water. He peeled open the white envelope and withdrew the papers, studied them carefully, and found nothing amiss. They were first rate, not forged photocopies of documents but the actual documents themselves, and the raised seal of the Venezuelans appeared authentic in every detail. He kept staring at the name of the vessel, a name he had chosen out of some romantic brain snap, what felt like a grand idea at the time, but now seemed useless and even dangerous. *Elisabeth.* A ship called *Elisabeth.* Then he heard someone step through the bathroom door, causing him to hold his breath as footsteps drew near and the door rattled in front of him.

"Está occupado," he said.

"I can hear that," said the voice of Bracelin. "The question is, bos'n, what are you *occupado* doing?"

Snow slid the papers back into the envelope and turned as he stood off the pot, shoving his left foot against the flush lever, causing the toilet to explode with a sucking sound of rushing water. "What the hell you doing here?" Snow said.

"I asked first."

Snow pushed out and faced him. Bracelin was with some Panamanian, some coifed nancy-boy staring at himself in the mirror. Snow had no clue what these two were about, and part of him didn't want to know.

"What's shaking, Popeye?" Bracelin said.

"Just taking care of business," said Snow.

"Everything in order?"

"Looks good. They do good work out of here."

"They should, for all we paid for it."

Snow leaned over to the cloth roll of towel and pulled down sharply, drying his face and hands against the rough fabric. He glanced back at the mirror and caught the Panamanian eyeing him by reflection, then standing straight, slicking his hair back. Snow resisted the urge to hide the envelope and, instead, stood upright and turned to face Bracelin, whose head rose above the stall's upper rim, smiling over toward Snow, his piss stream sounding more like a horse than a human. "Ahhhh," Bracelin said. "Feels good to finally get some of that Panny beer outa my system. Now you being from Panama got no sense of how crappy your beer really is."

"I am proud to be Panamanian," he said, still eyeing himself in the mirror but glancing over at Snow. *"Roberto Duran viene de Panama."*

"¿Quién es más macho?" said Bracelin, with a surprisingly passable Spanish accent. *"¿Roberto Duran? ¿Harold Snow? ¿O Jorge Maciel?"*

"How long you been here? I didn't see you when I came in," said Snow.

"Just got here. We knocked back a few at Lu-Lu's, and I thought I'd come to cover your backside just in case."

"Well, no just-in-case required," said Snow. "What the hell you doing at that place anyhow?"

"Just seeing how the other half lives. I saw your kids out there on the floor when I come in. I don't believe I ever seen Lisa looking quite like she looks tonight."

"I picked them jeans out." Jesus, he felt like an ass.

"Oh, I'm just sure you did. Looks to me like you're losing your seat on the old horse, Snow. That is, if you ever had a seat."

"If you got something to say, maybe you should just say it."

"Well, I got this feeling come over me, a kind of idea that got stuck in my head that she ain't been fucking you at all. Like not even once."

Snow let out a long slow breath, glanced at the Panamanian guy, tried to figure his age–late teens, maybe early twenties. "You can think what you want, Brace, don't make a difference to anything like reality."

"Reality's a funny thing. You just can't tell what's what sometimes."

"Amen to that." Snow pulled the door open, glancing back over his shoulder where he caught the Panamanian man staring at him in the mirror.

"*¡Los griegos!*" The guy shook his head. "*¡Son muy fácil!*"

He heard Bracelin say, "Facile? Facile? That what you think? Huh?" and then laughing, and a struggling growl, followed by the younger man saying, "Stop, stop–" and then words Snow couldn't make out, and then scuffling and the muffled voice of the Panamanian, as if someone had a hand over the guy's mouth. Snow thought he might go back inside, but he wanted nothing to do with Bracelin's sideshow, whatever the hell it was about.

In the dim hallway, cigarette smoke wafted out of the bar and up through the ventilation system. When he broke free of the hall and saw the dancers again, he caught sight of the kids, dancing belly to belly to a fast song called "American Girl," their movements like hard and furious fucking, and he thought, well, that was one thing Beth wasn't.

He slid his way onto a bar stool and ordered a gin and tonic, sat watching the kids dance until he noticed a burly-shouldered guy at the end of the bar doing the same. Snow caught a glance in the mirror, an Aussie ordering a Foster's lager, dressed like an AB with a belt knife and a thick gold shipwreck earring, staring at the kids like he wanted to move in himself. When the song ended and the dancers took a break, the kid moved off for the head. The Aussie looked at the bar keep, said, "Where's your loo?" And while the bartender motioned to the hall, the Aussie was talking about Arenal, saying, "I hear you got a volcano going off up-country." Then he moved down the corridor where Maciel had gone not thirty seconds before. But Snow was distracted by Beth, moving toward him with a sweating smile and a deep breath, fanning herself with her face tilted down, eyes looking up from underneath toward Snow. He was transfixed even as a local boy took her and turned her into a new dance, and she was gone in a smiling shrug.

Between the encounter with Bracelin and his little friend, and the sight of Beth now, Snow felt a finger to his chest, prodding the aching underside, as if it might flick him with a middle finger and stop his heart dead in a beat. He had meant to check in with Beth, had meant for this night to be a lot of things it wasn't about to be. He made his way along the bar and out the front door into the soft Panamanian night, that Tyvek envelope tucked tight up under his arm.

A low mist hovered at daylight, sun glow spreading up east over the canal as Snow stepped to the bridge wing, watching the pilot boat make up alongside their starboard stern. The ship lay west of the Bridge of the Americas, the steel structure arching before them like a giant clasp holding two continents together. The Miraflores Locks sat dead ahead, open and ready to receive them, escort tugs swinging into place, heaving lines arching through the morning air.

Snow's hair was combed, work clothes clean, new suspenders, shirt tucked in. He looked fit, healthy, robust, and hoped that anyone would say the same about the ship. But looking around now he thought it might have been an error to grind and prime the ship too soon. Normally he was not one to dwell on people imagining the worst, but for some reason he thought *Tarshish* looked suspicious, as if anyone with half a wit would see that primed funnel and know a name change was in the offing. But damned if the pipeline didn't look fine. Snow leaned out over the railing to spy where the pilot had already exited the boat's wheelhouse and now climbed the Jacob's ladder. Snow straightened himself and watched the man stride up the external stairs–all business, all-American, his eyes casting about the ship as he made his way topside toward the bridge and past Snow with a perfunctory nod, then inside to the helm. "A fine day for transiting," he said, and settled in to make radio contact with the escort tugs.

It wasn't until they were approaching Miraflores, and the shoreside line handlers were gearing up the "mules"–small locomotive engines that would pull them through the actual locks–that the pilot stepped outside for a look over the side and then nodded toward Snow. "You bos'n? I'm Captain Davies."

He stuck out his hand for a real squeezer of a shake. For some reason, Snow didn't want to say his own name. "I'm bos'n."

This Davies had wandering eyes but an appreciative air. "You look like you're working hard on this ship," he finally said. "That's a good sign–compliments on keeping an old scow together like a real crew."

"Thank you, sir. We been working hard on her."

"She's a T-2, converted. Class of '45, that right? Rare breed these days."

"Aren't we all," said Snow.

"I figured you were too. Where'd you serve?"

"South Pacific. Fleet oiler *Puget Sound.*"

"I know that ship. You've been in it then."

Then the pilot focused on nothing save his job of piloting the vessel to Colón, and his job had nothing to do with worrying over the ship's identity or even talking to the old boatswain, even if he did know all about what happened thirty-eight years before. Snow felt optimism rise inside him, like a bubble swelling. They were three for three in Panama, and for the first time since Salina Cruz he began to believe that all would work out for them in the end, and he kept saying to himself what a big ocean lay out there to the east, beyond the Caribbean, and how maybe he could learn to not hate the kid so bad, like he did when he saw the two of them out there on the bow huddled forward of the anchor windlass as if no one could see them.

Snow decided to keep his mind on something useful, so he went below to the captain's quarters, where he peeked in on the old man to find him sleeping, then sat down at the desk in the outer office and opened the Tyvek envelope to slide out the new registry papers. He laid them all out and, with a blank stack of cargo manifests, began filling in false dates and false cargoes dating back ten years. The work was laborious, and he would get Paynor and Bracelin to do their share as well, if only so the records weren't all in the same hand. It took forty-five minutes, but he filled in two dozen or more, using old forms and new forms both, tracing a ship's history as if writing his own story. He played games with it, imagined transatlantic journeys and Far Eastern runs, carrying exotic chemicals that he knew by heart: chloroacetic acid, chlorosulfonic acid, phosphoric acid, known variously as the nasties, the hat tricks, the triple 4's–the last in honor of their 4-4-4 rating–the highest on the health hazard scale according to the *Chemical Data Guide*. If they didn't burn you up or choke you out, they'd be sure to give you cancer down the road. After that he wrote in some standard bulk chems just so he wouldn't appear *too* exotic.

When he finally finished his first batch, he stacked all the papers in a single pile with the COI on top, the name *Elisabeth* there written out in a plain type. His chest tickled him, beset by the beating wings of a thousand moths. He wondered how Beth would react to the naming, and when he thought about that the moths all died in a pile somewhere in his belly, wing dust turned to mud.

Snow needed air, figured now was a good time for a tour of the deck, see where the kids were and make sure no line handlers had robbed them blind. First he went to look for Leeds but found him in the midship tankerman's locker applying a wooden ax handle to a metal grinder. Oddly enough the grinder spat a steady stream of metal sparks onto Leeds's work boots, a paradoxical sight to be sure, and when he looked up, Snow could see he wasn't wearing his teeth. "What the hell happened to your choppers?"

"Oh, man. I've lost weight, you know? They rattle around in there, drives me whacko." He held out the ax handle then. "How's that there. One nimble little bludgeon."

Snow looked the ax handle over. It was maybe a foot long, and Leeds had drilled out the center and filled it with molten lead. Snow wondered what anyone needed with a bludgeon–nimble or not–when he had *dim mak*. Then Leeds took off his welder's glove and Snow saw the pink lesions of psoriatic arthritis again, flexing his knuckles in a way that made Snow's neck twitch. Snow decided not to dwell on any of it, not even to chastise Leeds for stealing lead sinkers out of his tackle box.

For now he hightailed it to the bow, where Maciel refused to look at him, all guilty about moving in on his turf, maybe, but nervous too, in a way that got under Snow's skin. They were already in the midst of some plan or another to head inland during the loading at Moín, and Snow was reeling trying to figure out what to do, reeling for most of the transit trying to figure out how he could take control of this little trip the kids had planned, how he could keep them from going off together for all to see. When Maciel did finally start looking at him, his eyes held a new kind of suspicion, like he had a road map to all Snow's dark places, knew all about ulterior motives in love and maybe a whole lot more than that. Snow felt his neck twitch.

He stayed out there on the bow feeling like a third wheel as the ship passed into the Gaillard Cut, what had once been called the Culebra Cut. The high earthen walls sloped fast down to the water as the ship steamed past a dredger and then a cruise ship, people bouncing off a high dive on the ship's top deck. Snow stood alone with the kids, thinking of all the workers who had died building the canal, particularly the first time around, when the French had tried back in the 1800s, when thousands died of malaria and yellow fever, their corpses sold and stuffed into drums filled with formaldehyde and shipped to medical schools and research labs all over Europe. He thought of all those poor-ass Indians curled up in preservatives. Nobody liked to talk about that, but that was the truth of the canal, the truth of linking East and West, the truth of the profession he'd chosen back in '42.

At Gatún Lake the ship navigated through clouds of mosquitoes, pushing along the earthen dam, and Snow thought of places they could go to get off the ship together so he could manage some control. Friends close, he thought, enemies closer, though in truth he couldn't tell which were which around here. The kid kept up with his furtive glances, dark brows, and a half-trembling, half-snarling upper lip like he'd never mistrusted anybody so much in his life, like some accusation might be forming there in his righteous mouth. "What's got into you?" Snow said.

"Nothing's got into me," he said, and looked away.

After the hyacinth patrols motored past, small boats with giant hedge clippers lowered down off the bow end, to cut back the flowering water weeds that forever threatened to overcome the man-made lake and tie up the screws of the big ships that ran through. Around here, trees cropped up out of the water. In the midst of the upper branches people had built tree houses, had laundry hanging out and boats tied off at the base of a ladder at the water's surface. Snow waved to a child dangling a foot over the side. Beth said how she'd die to be sitting there right now; even a tree over water would beat where she was.

"I got an idea," Snow said. "How'd you two like to see a volcano go off? It's a bit of a hike, but we could do it out of Moín."

"I could go for a little volcanism," Beth said, and pushed against Maciel's shoulder in a suggestive way that made Snow remember that time after Okinawa, when she'd put her hand on his leg in the bar and then kissed him a soft gentle good night to the mouth. Memories of light touch and earthen scent boiled through him in the tropical heat. He couldn't look at the kids now, so he just stared at the Gatún Locks. They appeared like stair steps, a liquid escalator to the Caribbean.

Two days after the pilot descended the ladder in Colón, the ship docked at the long wharf of the Moín refinery, where they had contracted for av gas, petroleum solvents, and turpentine. As the loading process went on, Beth and Maciel finished tank cleaning to free them for their trip inland, and Snow ventured topside to the bridge, where he watched the kids emerge from an expansion trunk hatch looking hot and dusted white by the dry chem residue they'd been sweeping from the base of the tank. Snow found Bracelin in the midst of filling out his share of bogus cargo manifests. Snow studied the equations on his right forearm. They read:

$$HA = L - alpha + 180 + 15 \times UT + LONG\ ALT\ [degrees]$$

and on and on, more than Snow had a clue about.

"Just to let you know, we're heading inland this afternoon," Snow said.

"Inland? What the fuck's inland?"

"Going to go see Arenal light off. I heard in PC it's happening."

"Who the hell is *we*?"

"Me and the kids," Snow said.

Bracelin squinted at him, his face doing a flex thing that Snow had seen before. "We're at a critical point here, Snow. Seems to me your mind ain't in it."

"My mind's in it. All's in order. You got Kairos and Marty and Ali for the loading. She wants to see Arenal. I want to show her Arenal."

"And you can't have her going off alone with the ordinary. So fine, I'll tell the kid he has to stay. Or I'll tell them both they have to stay."

"Sure you will. You been doing nothing but throw them together on jobs since he come aboard."

Bracelin grinned, and Snow couldn't help noticing how whenever he smiled his eyes took on a blank look, like a man looking a thousand miles off. "I'm fucking with your head, old man."

"Like I need more of that."

"Forget about her, Snow. She's just another piece of black ass. You've had plenty. I admit she's a beautiful woman, but you've had them too."

"Not lately."

Bracelin stood there like he had an iron post for a spine and a four-by-twelve header board for a pair of shoulders, and Snow saw the whole thing flash on him like a flood. "You old grizzle dick. You *ain't* had her. All this since the Med has been one fucking bullshit pose. I figured it, I figured it when we were in Okinawa! In that bar, when she had no reason to, I could tell she was giving you blue balls. She's a fucking tease, ain't she? There ain't nothing I hate more than a fucking tease."

"She ain't a tease, believe me." Which was true.

Bracelin just eyed him. "Sure thing, old-timer. Don't matter. How about I kill him for you? How about you start cleaning the toilets instead of him?"

"We're a crew for now, and he's a good kid."

"I don't give a shit you knew his gramps. Means nothing to me."

"Well, it means something to me. Joaquin Maciel did stuff for me nobody else ever did. I was one fucked-up dude after the war, and he set me on the right path and gave me more than a second chance."

"The right path? You call the last thirty years of your life the *right path*? You slay me. You must hate the kid. I'd hate him. I'd kill him. I'd kill her too, while I was at it. But not before I fucked her in every hole she had."

"Well, that's the difference between us, I guess."

"I know you, don't give me that line of shit, save it for Lisa."

"Quit calling her that."

"What the fuck you going to do about it?"

"How about I call West Africa?"

Snow didn't want to have to remind Bracelin that they needed his contacts in the W.A. It seemed to imply that Bracelin couldn't figure it out on his own, or that he was half inclined not to care. Snow might have been screwed in the head about some things, but he had enough presence left to understand Bracelin. All life on ship was a ruse, not just the kid's faith or the girl's love but trust too, and Snow thought maybe he should take him up on that offer to keep them both close to home. Then he thought it might just make it worse and somehow more public. If they had to fuck, maybe they could do it someplace off ship, where they could get it out of their system and Snow could figure a way to keep it under control. Like the volcano, these things had a way of burning a path through the woods all their own.

•

To the sound of Delta blues on a crappy old radio, they caught a bus from Moín to Puerto Limón, and there on the edge of Calle 6 on the outskirts of town they waited for a transfer up into the mountains. Somewhere south they heard a baseball game rising up and out of a semipro ballpark, the crack of a bat, and the humming of the crowd erupting into a wide and solid roar. The road before them was broken asphalt, the ground beneath seeming liquid where it dropped and split in rounded dips like broken eggshells, sections made worse by any traffic that happened by, most of which were Ford Pintos and AMC crap cars, Gremlins and Pacers, and VW Things. The buses that passed were all bound for San José to the west, and they wanted the northerly route to La Fortuna.

They waited on that bench for two hours before anything resembling a regional bus showed up. Snow cried out *"¡La pura vida!"* as he climbed the steps and made his way through a crowded sleeping bus. Up front sat a Jesuit priest traveling alone, reading a book by the dim light of a portable reading lamp. Maciel paused alongside the padre, letting Beth catch up to Snow, who had found three seats, two on one side and one on the other. Snow felt magnanimous somehow and decided he'd let them sit together, so he took a seat alone and watched Maciel as the bus lurched forward. He knelt next to the priest, who leaned his head toward the young man and spoke to him in tones drowned out by the grind of diesel, the engine vibrating behind and below the back seats. "Looks like Georgie's getting his confession heard," said Snow.

"I suppose we all need to unburden ourselves."

"That's right. We do. I got one. Feels like a train wreck in my gut, but the truth is—I love you. It ain't just ruse. I love you and I want you. I don't want you for him, I want you for me. And it made me jealous back there in Salina Cruz. I said things just to hurt. Some not even truthful things, and I'm sorry about that."

"Perhaps it's you who needs to have his confession heard, Snow."

"Well, I'm more like the kid's gramps that way. Screw confession and unction. I don't need a priest to absolve me, I'll handle that myself."

She turned forward then, as if the whole thing had been settled, though for the life of him Snow couldn't see that it had. He watched her face flashing in the dull, intermittent street light as they headed out of Limón. Her eyes glowed yellow and pulled him out of his false bravado, and he leaned his head back, wishing he had a cold beer to wash away the metallic taste in his mouth and trying hard as he could to find fault in her–in her beauty, her character, her remoteness, her heat–but he couldn't. The bus stopped on the outskirts of town, long enough to duck into a roadside market and buy a case of Pilsen beer, which Snow lugged back to his seat on his shoulder, just ahead of two young Americans, early twenties frat boys on a solo spring break, eschewing Cabo for the minor adventure of the most peaceful country in Central America.

Snow befriended two coffee farmers on their way back home from a bender in San José, and before long he was trading cold bottles of beer for slugs off a bottle of some local firewater called *guaro,* which tasted like cheap rum and made his face glow and his belly rumble–he wondered if it cured dysentery or caused it.

"*¡La pura vida!*" Snow yelled, and hoisted the *guaro* bottle like a moonshiner. "*¡La pura vida!*"

"*Sí, sí, pura vida,*" said the coffee farmer, and patted Snow on the back.

Up two rows some locals felt bad for the two young Americans and one of them offered up his seat to the kid with the backpack. Two hours later they were still riding the range and the local asked for his seat back, but the American was asleep, his head bouncing left and right. "Pardon me," the local said in English. But he got no response, only a death curl on a bouncing seat. "Pardon me, excuse me," and finally the American woke up, bleary-eyed and looking like he had a hangover.

"Yeah? What?"

"I have my seat back," the local said.

"No way, dude, you gave it up," said the American, and half rolled in his seat, turning his back to the local, who straightened up and was promptly knocked to the floor by the thump of a chuck-hole beneath them. He ended up sprawled out over two women three rows forward, and by the time he pulled himself up and toward the frat boy, he was looking around for allies. By now most of the bus was asleep; even the driver seemed to catch a few winks in between turns in the road.

"Excuse me," the local said again, his English halting. "Excuse me, Mr. American." He tapped the kid on the shoulder.

The kid shrugged him off with a complaining groan. "Dude, get *out*!"

When the local was about to tap again, Snow stood up, said, *"Lo siento mucho para mi paisano,"* and grabbed the kid by both shoulders, hoisting him kicking and flailing while he tossed him forward a good six feet, where he landed face first in the aisle. Snow felt the pinch at his chest, like he'd dislocated a rib in the process.

"Dude, like what the *fuck*? Mind your own fucking business!"

"That's just it, bub, I gotta do business in this country, and *norteño* assholes like you don't help. Now sit your dumb ass on the boards and shut your piehole."

As Snow came walking back he saw Beth staring at him with eyes wide open. "Good show, Harold," she said.

When Snow turned back to the American kid, he saw him

stretching out on the aisle with his backpack under his head. "He *gave* me his fucking seat," he said.

All occupants of the two rows directly in front of the conflict had awakened, and now they clapped their hands in appreciation before going back to sleep. A warm rush came to Snow's chest. The priest turned, mildly interested. Beth patted Snow's arm, and George smiled after three days being downcast, looked at Snow with something like affection for the first time since PC, an image corrupted only by the fact that he was holding Beth's hand at the time. Even the driver grinned in the rearview, right before he hit a pothole going fifty miles per, and four people fell out of their seats and thumped the deck like sacks of corn.

At La Fortuna, on the mid-mountain shores of Laguna de Arenal, they found a cab to take them to see lava flows. The cabbie was a playful, thin character in his thirties named Cayetano. Snow offered him a cold beer and an extra hundred dollars, so Cayetano said he'd take them to the best spot for viewing lava flows and sitting in hot water. "Talk of hot water!" he said. "Fifty feet from you it boils!"

"*¡Pura vida!*" Snow said, and chugged another beer, his eyes catching the glint of lights, bouncing off a sign reading CURVO PELIGROSO. He glanced into the backseat, where he caught a glimpse of Beth, and though he didn't linger on them, he saw them pressed tight to each other in the back and felt a surge inside him, half aroused by the sight of her and half jealous of the sight of him, wanting to reach a hand back there like a dance chaperone and push between them. He reached back with beers instead, levered open a third for himself, and offered one to the cabbie. "I do not drink while driving," he said. "But when we stop and it is hot in the pool, a cold beer would be most welcome."

"They ain't so cold anymore," Snow said.

Just then, they rocked up a dark road, off the paved path, and upward along a two-lane dirt road through the trees of a sparse forest, cresting the hill before the glow of fire. At one bounce, Snow glanced back and saw the pair kissing. He turned his head forward and stared at the floorboards, his feet there, flat on the deck, anchored. He slugged back more of the beer. He imagined her tongue, searching. He imagined her pressing body, thought he heard a gentle moan escape the backseat, but refused to turn to it. Any arousal at playing the voyeur had evaporated, but he kept telling himself it had to be, they had to get through this, though still it made him angry. He knew he'd be better for her, knew he'd make her feel things she could never feel with a neophyte. But there were other feelings: she'd feel all his desire, his tenderness, his need to cradle her, to love her forever. Jesus–love!–it near flattened him to the seat to think she might actually be falling in love with the kid.

The headlights picked their way along the ridge and the driver pulled off the side at a wide spot, braking abruptly to send the backseat pair into a scattered clutching of each other, hands to the back of the front seat. Snow looked out toward a trail that led to the river. He could see the glow of lava through the trees, and the sound of howler monkeys out there, or maybe a jag or two. He'd never seen a jaguar in the wild, and was sure he didn't want to, not at night near a pool, anyway. He checked his knife, wished he'd brought a gun, pushed open the passenger-side door, and grabbed the beer. "Let's hit the hot pool," he said into the back, and saw the two sitting facing each other, not quite able to see in the darkness but then catching sight of her finger inside the kid's mouth.

He slammed the door and started down the trail.

The cabbie followed. "Keep an eye out for a wooden wall, we will turn right at it. Will those two find their way?"

"Never can tell," said Snow. "I think they're groping for it right now."

But their groping and Snow's groping went in two different directions, and they didn't follow, not right away. Snow and the cabbie found a flat rock overlooking a pool in the river, a back eddy swirling inside, feeding warm water there, in a space protected by rocks.

Snow imagined her liquor-soaked tongue in his mouth letting hot liquid pour into him, his neck aching in dull throbbing bands like fingers there to choke him out. Then he felt the night air against his face, cooler than down on the coast, and heard the kids finally, back behind him, running, calling his name. "Here!" Snow barked, and sensed their turning; they'd lost the trail and were pushing through underbrush, giggling in tipsy ecstasy, while Snow focused on the opposite bank of the river, the smell of burning tinder, the smoking mass of lava as it curled into the river and fell like an orange tongue that steamed and hissed as it hit water, turning to black piles of stone. The cabbie was right: river water boiled along the far bank.

As they stood there prepared to take the plunge, Snow could feel the warmth against his face, and from the trees heard the screech of some wild animal or another, until Snow looked up and saw the wide eyes of a howler monkey. "Territory," he said. "You got to respect territory!"

"What is that?" said the cabbie, drinking his beer now. "I am going to take my clothes off," he said. And stood up.

The kids were behind him then. Snow eyed them for some sign of what had gone on in the cab after he'd left. "Go that way twenty yards and you'll be boiled alive, Georgie!" cried Snow. "Stick to the downstream hole!" Then he stood up, stripped out of his jeans and boxers, pulled his shirt off over his head, and with an open beer in one hand plunged straight off the flat rock and into the river, his bronze upper torso like a shadow over a moon-white ass, his arm raised, hand clutching the beer. *Pura vida,* he thought, the Costa

Rican national motto. He felt the cold water at his feet, rising in gradations to his torso, until at the top it felt warm and steamy.

"Ahhhhh!" he said, bursting from the water to shake his hair. "Watch out for jaguars—they swim like fish and this might be their turf."

"Howler monkey are more worry," said the driver, behind him to take the hot plunge, water splashing up and over Snow's face and head and into his eyes.

Then came Beth, who in the dark stripped fast to nakedness and flew into the water, swirling downstream in inebriated silence, Snow letting out whooping spirited calls of joy into the dark steaming waters of the volcanic river.

Beth turned, beads of water glistening moonlight over her tight black hair. She drew the kid's clothing off as if by magic, ignored the eyes of an arboreal creature only fifteen feet away, unnerving Snow with its watchful eyes, until he dipped backward and let his feet rise out of the water, the skin of his ankles burning in the night water, and a lizard flashed past him, scampering like a demon across the water. It startled him, sent a chill through him. A Jesus lizard, so-called for obvious reasons. He heard the sounds of the jungle then—as if the lizard had tuned him in to the submerged humming of the forest, the night birds and buzzing insects, and the pale glowing eyes of animals—and he wondered again if a jaguar was among them. The *guaro* still burned at the back of his throat, and he felt rain begin to patter out of the night sky.

"Look." Snow pointed, and Maciel turned to see lava seeping into the far end of the pool, the water sliding over a short fall and steaming, and the steam enveloped them. Snow could feel fish nibbling at his legs, while he watched through wafting bands of steam, rain-steam on lava, obscuring and revealing, alternating as the kids began a passionate tongue kiss, slinking off into the far end. She clutched tight to him, her legs wrapped around him underwater, Snow figured, and he kept wondering if he was inside her now, if her lips had flared in the water's heat, or her own heat, opening to fold over his head and draw him into her.

Snow's mouth ached for her. Bracelin was right, he hated the kid now and half thought to let the mate kill him. He would have Beth to himself if he let something like that happen, except that another part of him knew that it was just such thoughts that kept him from her. The crunching crackling sound of lava burning wood filled his ears, and he watched the face of the cabbie and the arching neck and buzz cut of Beth, dark and matted, glistening in the fire glow, merging and nuzzling to the kid's head as his own lips fell forward to her neck. Their eyes glowed like baboons, the smell of burned wood from a tree fire smoldering as a bank of molten rock urged past, and the hot sliding feel of her body strad-dling someone else. Snow turned away then, his own eyes rolling to see the wide-eyed face of a monkey, big and dangling like a human boy, and the boy inside Maciel, coming out all wild and passionate and adoring. Then Snow was over to them without even realizing it, his body making firm strong crawl strokes to propel him there, to reach his hand between them, aroused in spite of himself, aroused to the point of wanting to press himself to her bare body and urge himself into her. "What the hell you doing!"

He saw in their faces the same question of him. "Oh, Jesus!" she said, and slithered off then, away from them both, and swam away, left the old boatswain there grasping at black water, the kid staring at him in stunned silence, his eyes glowing to the shrieks of howler monkeys, gaggling their warnings behind the wall of night.

Maciel hauled himself out of the pool and onto the bank, where he sat naked with weeds growing up between his legs. Snow turned to see Beth rise naked out the far end and put her clothes on and move off toward the cab. Snow hoisted himself and followed. "Get your clothes," Snow said to the kid, as he was already sliding into his own, looking at the kid lift up and move like a jackknife through the orange dark.

Snow caught up to Beth as she got into the front passenger seat of the cab, dimly backlit by the overhead. Snow put out his hand to stop the door from closing, and she immediately swung her legs out the door but stayed seated, as if ready to get back in or run off, depending. "You got to understand how this makes me feel, here, Bethy."

"This has nothing to do with you, Harold."

"You in love with him or something?"

She rolled her head, half shaking it, half nodding it. "I don't want to have this conversation with you."

The kid and the cabbie were far back now, and Snow half hoped they'd been swallowed by lava or a hungry jag. "You of all people ought to understand. I got this here, I got for you–" and he dug into his pocket, his heart racing, and gave her the box. She looked up at him but didn't take it. "What is it?"

"Go ahead–open it. It's for you."

She looked up at him, as if she could see what it was, see right through his eyes to what it was. "I can't accept that."

He let his arm drop, holding the boxed diamond down at his side. "It don't have to be defined any way you know. It can be what-ever you want it to be. As long as we're together, I don't care."

"What if she wants to be with me?" the kid said from behind.

Snow turned to see him standing there in blue jeans and wet short hair with that cross tattoo peeking out from under his black shirtsleeve. "This don't concern you, George. So why don't you put your fingers in your ears and hum the 'Star-Spangled Banner' for a spell."

"But it does concern me."

"No it don't!" Snow shouted, and the kid flinched.

"Harold. I'm thirty next month," Beth said. "I'm thirty and no one will tell me who I can and cannot fuck."

Snow stood upright, ran his hand through his hair and felt how thin and long it had gotten, and let out an exasperated breath. Then he leaned down close and talked in a hushed voice. "So okay, okay, so you gotta fuck him, fuck him. Just come away with me when you're through."

"Harold." She looked at him. "Don't you see? I already am fucking him"

Snow was frozen a count. He felt his nostrils itch, then the burning. In an instant he could have pushed it straight into his eyeballs where it would come out as tears. "When?"

"Panama City."

"Ah, Jesus–Jesus–" He was taken by how it surprised him.

"I love her," said the kid. "It's true. Say what you want. It's true."

Snow let his arm droop from the roof of the cab. He stepped back and leaned against the door. The girl just stared at the kid from her place on the seat, but Snow couldn't tell what she was thinking, if that wasn't the weirdest way for someone to inform you he was in love with you, or if she shared it, or was afraid of it, or hated and mistrusted it. Whatever it was lay thick between them. "You two got to understand what position this puts me in with the mate."

"I understand you need me to appear to be yours. I'm not sure I see how it's in my interest."

Snow couldn't imagine how anybody would see the world so differently than he did. "If this puts me in a position with the mate, it puts you in a position with the mate. And you?" he pointed at the kid. "You better steel yourself, buddy."

Maciel's face hardened, turned into his grandpa before Snow's eyes. Snow remembered that look on the heels of some insult to the dignity of a woman. Old Joaquin was such a prude deep down. That was the reason the old man could kick ass; he fought for honor, or for love, or ideals—and all as if his life were at stake. For a man who had no God, Joaquin Maciel fought his own private Holy War.

"You got your granddad in you, I see that."

"So what if I do? Some bad old man he was, huh? What about you, Harold? What about the things *you've* done?"

"I ain't done shit."

"Yeah? You sure about that? You sure there isn't something back there that *you* did? Never mind my grandfather. What about you? What judgment's out there for you, Harold?"

"What the fuck you talking about? You got some God vision, you think? See the first and the last and all that crap, George?"

"What about Vietnam, what happened there? Merchant ships during the war years, wasn't that it?"

"Oh, now, I know you been talking to someone. I never told you anything about Vietnam."

The kid's mouth froze, hung open slightly. He looked at Beth.

"Who you been talking to?" Snow asked.

Maciel closed his mouth. He stared at Snow like he'd just been pulled over half drunk and was gearing his mind for a roadside sobriety test. "Nobody. I have ears. I listen."

"Well you're listening to the wrong people, George, and you better start listening to me or it's all going to bite you in your skinny ass."

"You think I'm going to leave her to you and yours? You think that, you're crazy. I don't know what you've got going on this ship, I don't even care. But I'm not going to leave her to you."

"Go be noble somewhere else. She got along fine without you."

"I can get along without you too, Harold." Beth sat looking at her shoes, like she couldn't say a thing like that and hold eye contact at the same time. "I don't need any of this shit."

Snow felt like two clammy hands had just crept around his neck from behind. "And what about Bracelin?" he choked out, the words garbled. He tried to clear his throat. "There's only one way to get along with Charlie Bracelin! You prepared for that? Is *he*?" He jerked his thumb at the kid.

Beth rotated her face up toward him, her eyes honest and dark, her voice softer than he'd expected, softer than he could have managed just then. "Let's drop it, Harold. Just drop it."

Snow wished he could drop himself, give himself the old hook from backstage. He wished the cabbie would hurry his ass. They should get back to the ship now. Out of the blue he thought how didn't he have a sister or something in Puerto Limón, some Harolda or Hally or another? How damned weird that would be to show up at her door and ask for safe harbor, like you could ever bank anything on blood relations. He wished he could gather all them lost siblings together in one place right now and take Beth there, so she could see them all in one place. So she could see he had people. For the life of him, though, the only family he felt he had, painful as it was, stood before him now. The kid, with all his moral judgments and looks and suspicions, and who the hell was he talking to anyway? Was this what he got for sticking in the kid's corner? For feeling something beyond just shipmates? He couldn't hate him much as he tried, it was too late for that. And the girl with her cold remoteness, her dead soul turned toward Snow now. Truth was, he felt sorry for the kid. The Christians had it wrong. God wasn't love, he couldn't be. All Snow's experience led to the opposite conclusion. Love was hell.

NATAL

Snow returned to the ship frantic to put to sea and get back to running his crew, working six to six plus his midnight bridge watch, and knowing what the hell was going on for a change. *Tarshish* steamed east, down coast through Venezuela and Guyana and into Brazil. They took on whatever cargoes they could find, paused at tank farms with piers angling into five-fathom water. They loaded liquid urea, an organic fertilizer that smelled like old piss mixed with kitchen ammonia. Snow had crewed on tugs to Alaska towing urea barges, what Puget Sound towboaters called the "diarrhea run." Snow didn't even know that anybody made liquid urea, it seemed a foul thing to put such a chemical into a *more* volatile state, and the stench permeated the ship for three days after the loading. They sealed the tank, which was closed save for the vent stack thirty feet up, but on a tail wind even that didn't help.

Then came the freshwater effluent of the Amazon.

While they put down anchor in the silt bottom, Snow stood at the porthole in his room and watched Beth and the kid doing stevedore work out there in the stink. A small rig tender delivered stores. The kids unhooked crane loads of shrink-wrapped pallets of food. He could sense their recklessness building, the way they worked touching hips even when they didn't have to, the way they traded looks from underneath when they thought no one would notice. But people did notice. They were there in full view of the bridge. Snow watched them laughing as they walked aft to the fantail, and he made his way down in time to see them plunge overboard into the freshwater of the Amazon.

The crew gathered to watch, drifting over there on smoke breaks to lean over the railing and stare. Beth disappointed nearly everyone by going over with all her clothes on, minus only her steel-toed boots. Somehow, being fully dressed made her all the more the focus of their attention, as if they had to look extra hard for fear they might miss something.

Maciel had found a pair of old swim trunks in the boatswain's locker, World War II–vintage tight black trunks like Burt Lancaster in *From Here to Eternity*. He took the warm plunge feet first, and there below him, Snow imagined the smells of their cargo disappearing on airs. Above, Snow stood among all those staring males, their hard-ons poking their jeans outward.

Snow wondered if he oughtn't strip down to his skivvies and join in. There'd been threesome rumors that he'd heard in the whispered Spanish of the Panamanians. But Snow was caught above. He might have been able to pull it off with sufficient gusto, but somehow he lacked the energy. They'd all know it wasn't his scene. Maciel righted himself and began to tread water, his feet reaching for hers underneath. "Freshwater, this is amazing!" he cried. "I can't even see land!"

"You're swimming in the Amazon, George!" Beth cried.

Her oiled skin gave off a slick all her own, vague rainbows trailing behind her where she swam. Maciel slipped his feet up the skin of her legs, reaching his toes up inside the billowing underwater fabric of her fatigue cutoffs, and from above, the scene was obvious to all. Lining the aft railing, the crew smoked and watched in silence save for a few grunts and groans when they saw Beth's ass arch out of the water and dive.

The crew laughed then, leering and hooting, glancing at one another for affirmation that they'd all seen the same thing, sharing the momentary fantasy. Marty snarled and lit a cigarette. *"Cubiche,"* he said, meaning Maciel.

"Puto y puta," said another, and everybody laughed.

"Makes you wonder just who's fucking who, doesn't it?" said Paynor, who along with Snow and Bracelin stood on the poop deck overlooking the show.

Bracelin remained silent on the subject of fucking, but said, "That's *whom,* not who. You fucking academy grads really crack me up. You can't even fucking spell, but sure as shit, you're the ones always get the ships!"

"Poor guy, Brace. What's it matter to you now?"

"Matters 'cause I could out-skipper anybody in this fleet, academy or not."

"Don't lose sight," said Snow, "of the fundamental realities."

Snow liked that term; he'd read it in a magazine, an article on military history.

Bracelin snarled. "Don't fucking give me a lecture on realities when you got your dick in your hand and your *heart* squirreling around on some fucking cloud."

Snow didn't know what the hell to say, so he went below and lowered the Jacob's ladder for the kids to climb back aboard, motioning to Beth with an insistent nodding of his head, like an impotent dad goading his daughter out of some boy's car. They were no sooner up than the crew was hooting down at them from the poop deck, leaning out over the railing. They were laughing and passing it off as teasing good humor, but it wasn't that. Someone spit, a long hard hock job that went over everybody's head, but wasn't lost on a soul. Beth looked up and made a gesture with her hand, then called out, *"Oi! Sibodoh! Anak haram!"*

"Pelacur!" one shouted back, calling her a whore, and *"Berapa?"* wanting to know how much she charged. The Malays laughed their asses off and flicked their cigarette ashes over the railing, some of it trailing into Snow's eye.

"Goddamn you fucks! Work!" Snow rubbed at his eye.

Their laughter faded and they just stared at Snow with malice he'd never felt from his crew. Up ahead, Maciel moved toward the external stairs, climbing in his swim trunks right into the crowd instead of taking the internal stair tower to the room. The crew stepped aside on the stairs and made kissing sounds, and someone grabbed his ass. When he slapped at their hands, and jumped and turned and walked on, dark-faced, they were reduced to riotous laughter, slapping their knees and snapping their fingers.

"You see what's happening here?" Snow asked.

"I see it."

"So maybe you should start thinking about wise choices."

She blew a droplet of water off her upper lip with a huff. "Well . . . there's always Bracelin. He could be my new best friend."

He felt a chill, not just what she was suggesting but how her voice held it, like she was flat-shoveling roadkill off the pavement and taking it home for dinner. But she was naïve too. She operated under the belief that all men were seduceable, but she didn't know Charlie Bracelin. Snow had made sure of that.

"You think you invented me, Snow? How do you think I've gotten along, really? You fancy it's all reefers and Count Basie."

"Don't forget Billie!" He tried for a teasing smile and it fell flat.

"Billie's a trifle closer to the mark, I'm afraid."

"Hey there–this is me now. You don't gotta play me."

"*Play* you? Who plays you, Snow? Aren't you the one doing the playing?"

He focused on the beads of water clinging to her hair. He surveyed her features and tried to find a flaw somewhere, maybe her nose was a little too wide, or her lips too round and full, or her eyes too vacant black. Most people got ugly when they got angry. Not Beth. Bracelin's new best friend? Maybe she was just beautiful and wily enough to manage that without losing limbs in the process. Somehow, Snow couldn't see it.

She went off wet, her green fatigue shorts clinging to her ass and showing her panties, Snow all the while unable to think of anything but how it would feel to have her naked on his lap, how it would feel to look her in the eyes and slide up inside her with his hands floating over the turn of her waist to grip her round hard bottom. Beth wisely ducked inside and took the stair tower up to avoid the crew. She knew that much.

"Ohhh, bos'n on the outs lah–no get play-play from girl AB no more!" said Ali.

Snow looked up to see the man dangling down from the railing with a smoke in his fingers. "You're just jealous you ain't fucked her," Snow snapped. Then he felt shame ripple through him, not only because of the lie but because maybe Beth was right. He never *had* thought about anybody but himself, at least not for very long.

They were steaming toward Natal, Brazil, when Snow went up to stand the bridge watch and ran into the captain on the stairwell, wearing an old officer's cap with his leaves on and about ready to fall down. He looked like a fleet admiral in a bathrobe. "You, son. I been meaning to talk to you."

Snow wondered if McFarland recognized him, wondered what the hell he could possibly be seeing to call Snow son. The captain had five years on him at most. "How you feeling, Captain?"

"I need help, boy, I need help!"

"What you need help with, Captain?"

The old man leaned forward and reached for Snow's arm, but he missed and stumbled downward, nearly bowling Snow over as they both grabbed the stair railing to keep from going ass over teakettle. The old man's breath smelled like gum disease, right there in Snow's face. "That Bracelin's trying to bugger me! And I don't mean maybe. It's too late for me but you gotta take this, you gotta take this and take the right action when the time comes. You got me? The right course, you gotta decide the right course, and I can't help you with that 'cause I'm not gonna be around."

Snow felt that quivering in his vertebrae again and wished the old guy would let him go. He had a scary strength in his old bony hands, and he gripped Snow's arm like a crab. "Sure, Cap, I gotcha," Snow said, then felt the old man press an envelope into his hand, a long business-size envelope folded over once.

Just then Bracelin appeared at the top of the flight. "Captain, come on now," he said in the closest he could come to a soothing voice. "Room's this way, let me help you up."

"Sure you want to help me," said the captain. "You're trying to bugger me, admit it for all to hear! For once in your goddamned life admit what you got going!"

Bracelin reached down and tugged gently on the old man's arm, then came down another step and put his arm around him and led him up, turning at the first landing to cast a flat-eyed glance at Snow.

Up on the bridge, Snow stood before the radar and the engine room gauges and the wheel itself. In the red light of the chart table, he unfolded the envelope to see block printing in the captain's hand, OPEN IN CASE OF EMERGENCY.

Snow figured you could never tell about emergencies, sometimes you were in one and didn't know it and this might be one of those times. He tore open the envelope and pulled out a sheet of yellow paper, again with the captain's handwriting, a note that read *Port Left, Starboard Right* across the middle of the page, as if stating some profound truth. On the other hand, there was a simple elegance in it. Came times when the shit rained down so hard you really did have to be reminded of your left and your right. He knew it too as they departed Natal on a fine moonlit night, Snow on the bridge wing, and Maciel standing lookout on the bow, and Beth weaving her way through the pipeline to join him. Snow couldn't help it. He imagined her on her knees in front of him, blocked from view.

The next day Bracelin stepped into the crew's mess and announced that the captain had died quietly in his sleep. He said the ship had been sold and renamed and he himself had been made skipper. The crew murmured and whispered until Bracelin left, and then erupted in loud talk in countless patois. Most of it centered on the belief that they'd never be paid.

"Say, bos'n man, we gonna get nothing for all our work lah, that's how this one is gonna go!" said Ali.

"You'll get your dough. I'll see to it."

"How about you give it to us now, then?" said Kairos. "You want some good faith, how about you walk us up there to the ship's safe and settle up the SeaStar side of the payroll? While you're at it, maybe we can get some pay from Petrochem too! You remember Petrochem, don't you?"

Ten faces turned toward Snow. They all voiced their agreement with Kairos, whatever the language. Marty and Ali stared out from behind crossed arms.

"Why the hell you looking at me anyhow?" Snow said. "I get my money from the same till you do."

"We all know about you and the mate," said Marty. "You don't play dumb with us."

Snow felt fairly certain that what they thought they knew had little to do with the truth, but that didn't mean their worries weren't dangerous. "Listen, I'll see what I can do. I ain't in the know." That much was true; if Bracelin was making a move, this was the first Snow knew of it. "I'll talk to the mate about pay." And he got up to bus his dishes. The dishwasher was back there working amid the steam, and though Snow could only see his midsection through the silverware slot, he could hear his Malay voice plainly. "Who is the *kapal*? Who is the *kapal*?"

The question of who the ship was struck Snow as ludicrous, some kind of metaphysical statement rather than a practical one. Snow prided himself on the practical, on looking forward, reassessing, and not dwelling on what might have been. There was just one thing to do now: hold off an insurrection by getting their money and, come Freetown, set about dismantling the crew.

Outside, Snow went topside and tried to convince Bracelin to give them a payday, or at least settle up the SeaStar accounts, but Bracelin wouldn't have it. "They get paid when the voyage is through," he said. "End of story." Snow walked forward then, out the catwalk, where he found the kids dangling ass over the bow, stencil-painting the new name as they steamed across the mid-Atlantic, throwing porpoises out ahead of them, writing in white across each bow: ELISABETH . . . ELISABETH. And across the stern, yet again: ELISABETH. His romantic idiocy was now emblazoned across the ship for all to see. He could hear them already, *Orang-*

puteh so stupid one lah! Bos'n no play-play with AB no more, all lovesick buddy!

In the calms of open sea, the heat rising up around them, Snow went topside to do a postmortem sanitary on the captain's quarters. He found sheets stripped from the bed and smelled the musty, closed odor of death. Death had its own smell. He didn't find it repulsive, exactly; it was ill defined, as elusive as the newborn smell on his tiny son. Maybe there was something in that, some distinct aroma to birth and death, the one fresh and uncorrupted, the other stale in decay. Snow started by emptying the garbage, a small cylindrical trash can with tissues spilling out the top. Then he opened the portholes to let a hot moist breeze inside.

When Bracelin nixed the idea of early pay, it was Snow who felt the mutinous ripples. That night the crew again crowded around him in the mess hall. Even Leeds was there, albeit an officer, stoking the crew's paranoia. "What are they going to do with his body?" he wanted to know. "I want an autopsy."

"I heard his last wish was to be buried at sea," Snow said.

"I don't know about that. I think his last wish was they not kill him."

Snow wondered who Leeds imagined this sweeping *they* to be. He wondered if he wasn't considered a part of it. He shook his head emphatically before the pressing faces of the crew. "Listen, I got no information you don't. When I learn something, you'll be the first to know." Leeds shook his toothless mug and walked out, Snow following with all eyes on his back. He figured Leeds was the de facto leader of some rapidly unifying movement toward mutiny. As he ducked into his room, Snow knocked crisply on the door and stepped inside to all the chem equipment. "I need your help, Leeds, not you making matters worse."

"I just don't like this business with the captain," Leeds said.

"I need your help, and I'll pay for it. You hang with me and don't ask too much, I'll be sure you get a bonus when the time comes."

"I'm not stupid, I know you got some side action, bos'n. Frankly I don't want to know more than that, but you better keep that Bracelin away from me. I got enough to think about trying to keep this ship afloat."

"Done." Snow looked over the chem lab and now saw a new feature: a ragged piece of tissue in a jar, pale, with a plastic luminosity, save for human hairs sprouting out one side. "What the hell is that?"

"Don't freak out, it ain't what you think."

"What do I think?"

"You think I carved a chunk out of the captain's leg for some nefarious purpose. But I'm testing for fat soluble compounds. I'm talking poison. We need to know."

"Sure thing, Leeds." Snow decided what he needed most was to get the hell away from Leeds and stay there. He was about to go out when he heard something from the radio room, behind the closed door on the opposite side of the head. He stopped and for a strange jealous instant he imagined Beth hiding in there, imagined that Beth was secretly doing Leeds too. "Who you got in there?"

"Oh that's probably just the ordinary."

"That right? What the fuck he doing in the radio room?"

"He likes to listen to the radios. He comes in all the time. Boy's a pugilist, he tell you that? You ever look at his knuckle ridge? I showed him some things."

"How long this radio thing been going on?"

"Week or so, something like that."

"Since Panama City." Snow looked at the door and couldn't hear anything then. "You sure he just listens?"

"I don't ever hear him talking any. He's got some radio fetish or something. Into listening in at night when the world's asleep and only work boats are moving."

"That right." Snow reached for the railing by the door and steadied himself, thinking he felt some seas beneath them for a minute, then grasped the door handle and went out, shutting the door behind him and staring down the passageway to the radio room door. Somehow it came off too silent in there, like the kid was hiding behind the bank of dials and frequency bands. Snow guessed it was possible he had a night obsession with voices on waves, but he didn't like it much.

He went down a level to his room where he sat in front of the trucker's fan and read about the invasion of Guadalcanal, all blood, fear, and Marines crapping their pants. Between the fan stirring hot air and the book stirring bad memories, Snow thought he might boil alive. He went for the coolest place on board, the walk-in reefer just off the galley at the first deck below. There Snow stood in the blow of cool air for two or three minutes before he noticed, on the deck tucked under a shelf, the captain, wrapped in Visqueen, the outline of his old dead body like a ghost behind the translucent plastic. It made the cool reefer feel like a dark tomb. He couldn't help but look at the captain's leg to see if a chunk was missing, and sure enough, there it was on his right thigh. Three days later, the heat drove Snow into the cold-storage walk-in yet again, only this time he found the captain's body gone. He stood there in the cold, wondering what Bracelin had done with him. He imagined overboard, adrift and naked, with a hole in his thigh.

Up in the room that night, he found the kid doing push-ups, punctuating each thrust like he was delivering a hard body blow. Then he started playing with his knife, oiling the hinge so he could flick it open fast, the way Leeds had taught him. "Them things cut both ways," said Snow, and got ready for bed.

"My grandfather taught me how to take care of myself."

"I figured."

With his half-glasses on and a book propped on his chest, Snow tried to forget about the kid's preparations and paranoia. He read about how old Homer dug into his symmetry-craving soul and mapped out a River of Ocean that flowed all around the flat disk of the earth with Olympus at its center. At the western limit lay the Fortunate Isles, there at the gateway to the Underworld. Beyond that lay the land of the dead. Snow supposed you'd cross the River Styx there and pay the ferryman and go right into the Elysian Fields or left into Hades, and only the Fates decided which way you'd go. Odysseus sailed there with his men and performed blood sacrifice to conjure and communicate with the dead, to help him make his way home.

That night Snow couldn't sleep at all. He heard whispers among the crew and muffled stories inside the clicking hollow of his deaf ear. The voices said things like *you're doomed,* and *watch out,* and *port left, starboard right.*

MEFLOQUINE DREAMS

As if they needed paranoia fuel, five days out of West Africa, Lucy the Third issued malaria meds, mefloquine that caught dreams in a jar and fed them to you all through the next day until you couldn't tell dreams from memories. Snow refused to use the stuff. He was haunted enough by the things that really had happened. But halfway across the Atlantic, mosquitoes appeared, hovering in the passageways around the engine room and galley. Snow ran into a regular cloud of them on his way to chow one night, and though he had no idea where the hell they came from, he did what he always did in the tropics: wore long-sleeved shirts, endured the sweat, and smeared 90 percent DEET solution on every exposed patch of skin, and then on his clothes for good measure.

Ten minutes later he broke into a bubbling red rash every-where he'd swiped his hands, including two hand prints where he'd tried to slap some on his upper back. Lucy the Third stated the obvious—it was some kind of allergic reaction. "Maybe your body can't take any more chemicals," she suggested.

The mosquitoes on board could take that and more. Leeds's theory was simple. These mosquitoes constituted a shipboard subspecies. For countless mosquito generations they'd been breeding and hatching and feeding in the engine room of a ship awash in toxic chemicals, much of which resided in the blood they sucked from the necks of engineers and oilers. As far as Snow knew, nothing came from Leeds's experiments with human flesh, but he was hell-bent to figure out something useful about insects. "They're super skeeters, immune to the base chemicals," said Leeds, and swept a jar through the passageway air to capture five, which he promptly carried off to his room for further experimentation.

Snow figured the real culprits were two banana plants and a lemon bush that Gino had brought aboard back in Puerto Limón to save the crew from scurvy, or so he said. Regardless, DEET did nothing to deter the beasts, did nothing save turn Snow's skin into a blistered welt.

He was only mildly concerned about going without protection. He had been semi-immune to malaria since '59, when he'd contracted *P. vivax* and *P. falciparum* strains in the same six-month voyage. He was sick for over a year, during which time doctors treated him with quinine, and he finally beat them both, but quinine didn't work anymore. Among all the ingenious ways the Brits had screwed the Third World, one of the more insidious was the practice of treating "a touch of malaria" with quinine water. There wasn't a finer drink in the world than Bombay gin and Schweppes Indian Tonic Water, but a small dose at a time left *Plasmodium falciparum* bathing in the stuff to no consequence. Pharmaceutical companies had been chasing their parasitic tails ever since. Now, the only thing that worked was mefloquine, aka Larium, and unfortunately it worked a little too well in directions you'd rather avoid.

Given his newfound sensitivity to DEET and his hatred of psychotic nightmares, Snow found an old rusty can of Off! spray and figured he'd use that. But the kid did as directed, started the weekly Larium regimen by washing down the white pill with a bottle of rust water. Two days later Snow was reading in his rack when Maciel came in from watch looking rattled and fidgety, like his skin was trying to crawl right off his frame. He went into the head and leaned on the sink, bending over to splash water on his face. Snow could see him reflected in the mirror as he rolled and jerked his head around. His hair had grown out to a short dark stubble. He ran his hand over it like he was trying to rub his hair off, and then he fingered his earring. Someone walked past outside and he started, his hand flinching toward his face.

Snow asked about his dreams. "Having any weird ones?"

"I don't know," said the kid. He shook his head and glared at Snow as if to say *don't pretend to be my friend.* Then he went into his locker and started fishing around in there until he seemed to get a grip of something, which he held on to but didn't pull out.

"What the hell you doing in there? You stroking the flog?" Snow asked.

Maciel blanched and pulled both his hands out. "You been going through my things? Is that how it is?"

Snow shook his head evenly, peering out over half-glasses. "You think I ain't seen your scars? I know a self-abuser when I see one. Besides that, you look sorta unnerved. Why I asked about the dreams."

"What do my dreams have to do with anything?"

"Gotta watch for that Larium, there, buddy. Makes your night world real, some ways. Think about all these chems you got running around in your blood too. Chicken noodle soup around here tastes like ether. Toss this psychoactive fucker drug on top of it, and you got a demon pot. When Larium first came out, I took one dose and dreamed I had homosexual congress with the master of the vessel. I believed it was true. Took me two weeks to look the man in the eye again."

Snow could laugh at it now, but the kid barely registered the story. He refused to disclose anything about his dreams or his life. Not about Beth, or voluntary radio watch, or Panama City. Snow got the worst feeling that the kid knew everything about him, all the bad shit, every ounce of it, like he could see through the years. How could he know anything when Snow himself didn't? To him the past was unknowable. All the same, he felt the weight of judgment, like he had with Beth, from the first he'd known her, like they could see it all and didn't approve. Made Snow feel weak and squirrelly. Like he gave a shit. Like he wanted the kid to love him or something.

George closed the locker and vaulted up into his bunk with his clothes on, stripped down to his boxers up there, and put on his headphones, went for the wall-of-sound method of eradicating dreams. He listened to Lou Reed at full volume. Then he lit a smoke. Snow wondered about the kid's panic–the mefloquine maybe, dreams of the crew preying on him, cannibalizing him, heaving his ass overboard on a midnight crossing halfway to the Old World. To see the mother ship steam away from you. To wake up for your next watch in your rack, with the only salt water soaking your clothes being that of your own sweat. From there, mistrust lay like a seed in soil, with tropical heat and psychoactive fertilizers to help it grow.

After a few minutes of unrestrained guitar frenzy, the kid got down out of his bunk, went into his locker, and pulled out the leather flog, not looking at Snow once, not caring fuck-all what Snow or anybody else thought of him, and in that act he gained a measure. He took it up into his bunk with his headphones, caressing the thing in his lap like a pet. Snow put his glasses and book aside on his shelf, turned out his light, and listened to the ship's engines. Next he knew he had awakened to the sound of slapping coming from up there. And over the ventilation hum, barely, he heard the whimpering groans of the kid against the snap of leather tails.

Aberdeen, Sierra Leone, lay like a cluster of brown buildings on a green wedge, shaped like the forward half of a ship turned upside down and beached to form Cape Sierra Leone. From Snow's watch on the bridge wing, it loomed as the only rising promontory against an otherwise bright band of green vegetation. Africa lay like a green and orange mystery to the east. With the pilot aboard, the closer they came to the oil terminal at the port of Kissy, the more Snow smelled burning wood mixed with trash. It had a sour edge to an otherwise pleasant smell that reminded him of burn days as a boy, in his uncle's backyard at the old incinerator, the smoldering scent of food on paper, of meat on wood. A haze hung over Freetown and extended offshore, a haze of whited sand fog blown from the inland Sahara on Harmattan winds.

After the mooring operation was finished, Snow came around the corner of the tankerman's locker and saw Ali had cornered Maciel, saying, "Oh boy you got the worry look, you got the scared look lah. Jump ship you. Jump ship now lah."

"I'm not jumping ship," said Maciel.

Ali licked his lips and leaned even closer to the kid. "You got be sure what you doing lah. Try help you. This serious business. That mate no kind of man to trust. We leave—all of us leave. And that girl she never leave old bos'n no way."

"Never know," said Maciel.

"Ahh, you all lovesick puppy, just like bos'n. Girl AB got salt in her. No love nobody. She hard but she ain't leave old bos'n lah. They got bond like Red Hand. He like *bahpah,* she like *anak.*"

Snow got a queasy feeling and retreated back around the pipeline. He stepped toward the gangway, could see out the corner of his eye how Ali leaned close, like he was offering earnest counsel. *Bahpah* and *anak:* father and daughter. Snow moved down the gangway and met the pumpman making his way back up.

"What the hell's matter with you, bos'n?" said Kairos. "You look like you're about to upchuck!"

Snow looked back at the two, still standing up by the midship square, Maciel staring over the Malay's shoulder toward the bos'n like he was taking that father-daughter talk literally. He heard the grind of trucks then, and a line of tankers came driving up through the terminal and parked at the midship line in preparation for off-loading. "Gonna take a week to off-load all this," said Kairos.

"They might get more trucks running," said Snow.

"You sure you all right?"

"I guess I'm gonna have to be," said Snow, holding to the railing. "You got a big payday coming for sticking this out, Kairos."

"I better, hanging with this scrub-ass crew. That rookie's balling your girl, ain't he?"

Snow couldn't reply, nothing made sense to say. His girl. Your girl. She was gone, he had to get used to that now. Didn't matter what Ali had to say about it, he knew she'd go, and then they *would* be left with a scrub-ass crew. He could only hope that when the day came to make jetsam of the scrubs, Snow himself wouldn't be mistaken for one, or worse yet, actually be one.

•

The bush taxi for Freetown was an open jeep frosted over with a layer of red dust, plates semi-obscured but legible so that Snow knew it had just come from the mountain country to the east and south. They gathered at the gate to the Kissy marine terminal before an oppressive line of diesel trucks. Wet heat drew sweat from their bodies, soaked into clothes, and beaded on skin.

"This place stinks," said Leeds. "Worse than Nam ever thought of stinking."

"Smells like life," said Snow. "Opposite of that ship." He looked at the driver and addressed him with a friendly smile. *"Kou shay."*

The driver lifted his chin without returning the smile. *"Eh bo."* One hand rested on the vibrating stick shift of the jeep, just inches from the stock of a weapon, half concealed there between the seat and the hump in the floorboard. Snow caught it all—saw the sedate hostility in the driver's eyes, saw the mud-spattered gun, wondered what this one had been doing up-country.

"Ow mus Freetown?" Snow asked.

"Tin U.S."

The driver eyed Beth suspiciously as the crew piled in: Snow in front, Bracelin, Leeds, and Beth crowding across the backseat, with Maciel folded into the cargo compartment at the back. The kid gripped the roll bar to keep from being pitched out by a chuckhole, and when Snow looked back he saw his face inches from Beth's back. Snow kept his eyes on the road between Kissy and Freetown. It rounded north of Mount Aureol, then curved along the waterfront.

In the back, Beth sat on his right smoking hand-rolled Drum cigarettes, while Leeds sat in the middle talking about how much he missed the war, his fingertips sliding along Beth's bare leg in a covert way. "Best time of my life."

Beth turned to him, exhaled cigarette smoke, and looked down as if Leeds's hand were a cockroach crawling up someone else's leg.

Leeds laughed–toothless again–and pulled his hand away.

"You can *have* the war, all I care," said Snow.

Snow leaned his head out an inch or two, and in the sideview mirror he could see Beth bouncing in her seat, Maciel back there with his nose practically in her neck. Snow could tell–he was smelling her. He wondered what she smelled like. All he could smell now was the dust of the road boiling up around them and settling into their hair in a reddish glaze.

Then he heard automatic weapons fire slap from out of the trees in the mountains to the southeast, then a thud followed by a hissing rush. "Recoilless rifle," said Leeds, nodding uphill.

"Ten miles, maybe," Snow said. "Back southeast of Bunce."

The explosion sounded metallic, a deep-down rush of hot steel. Snow didn't like it much, nor the sound of the AKs, which came off metallic and cold, like real machine guns, not the toylike popping of an M-16.

"Damn, I miss the war," said Leeds. "I mention that?"

"You mentioned that, Leeds," said Bracelin, glaring back up the mountains toward Bunce. "Now why don't you shut the fuck up about it?"

"Don't you too, though? A little bit? Miss night patrols?"

"I do, Leeds, I admit it," said Bracelin. "I miss being six-four and sneaking up on those little rice burners and dragging my knife across their squeaker before they knew what hit 'em." Then he paused. "I was chief petty officer on a nuclear submarine, Leeds. I never *went* on night patrols."

"Yeah. Squids," said Leeds. "I was in the Corps."

"Fuck Marines. I eat Marines for lunch," said Bracelin.

"Sounds tasty," said Beth.

Red-dirt alleys ran off the main road, dry as summer tinder, last season's runnels etched into them and filled over by the powder of iron dirt, the afternoon air thick with the smell of smoke and laterite dust, the air glowing orange. Snow heard blues riffs, saw movies of old foot-stompin' John Lee Hooker howling at the night, remembered the soft hand of Billie when they shook hands and she said, "Pleased to meet you, Mr. Snowman," and how he missed his chance to ask if she wouldn't sing that for him once, that Funny Little Snowman song.

Freetown was still two kilometers to the west, and a sign displayed the Sierra Leonean coat of arms. It stood painted on a wooden frame, the outline of a lion and the regal ribbons that displayed the country's motto: UNITY, FREEDOM, JUSTICE.

"It should be their motto," said Snow. "It's the three things they ain't got."

The bush taxi cut up past an enormous cottonwood tree, turned at a sign that read Free Street, and dropped them at a corner cab stand where two other four-wheelers waited, muddied from up-country journeys. Standing on the dirt street, Bracelin nudged Snow to indicate one of the drivers, a narrow-faced young man, Somali or maybe Mauritanian by the look of him, his face black as night and his features fine and angular. He wore a machete tucked into his belt, and stood there staring at Snow, and finally lifted his chin in some kind of distant recognition. Snow smiled back, gave a discreet wave, then mumbled toward Bracelin. "I know that guy," he said. "He gets near me, you kill his ass."

"Quietly," Bracelin said.

From there they set out on foot. Government soldiers, awkward in their tiger suits and steel helmets, toted AKs and wore aviator glasses. The crew was stopped by two military policemen asking for papers. Snow talked, and they passed their Z-cards to the military men. Snow caught the look on Beth's face, like it always looked when she had to present her fake card, which looked damned good, well laminated by a forger in London. Snow sensed the soldiers glaring from behind shades, like highway patrolmen on a routine traffic stop, bored and inhuman, but a little excited too, to be stopping white Americans, to eye Beth and sense their kinship with her, though as always there was that lurking question of what she was doing with a pack of white men.

"Shoulda brought Kairos," was all Snow said.

"How else we gonna get use out of the worthless old nigger?" said Bracelin quietly.

"Why don't you shut your idiotic mouth?" Beth said.

The cop eyed Beth and Bracelin with rising interest.

Bracelin turned to her without a word. Then he leaned close. Snow could hear him, in a voice just above a whisper: "You little cunt. I want to talk, I talk. I want to bend your black ass over an H-bitt, I'll bend your black ass over an H-bitt."

Beth didn't flinch. She turned and eyed the mate, who touched the bare skin of her arm with his finger.

Leeds's gnarled hand came to a rest on Bracelin's tattooed forearm. Bracelin jerked his arm away. "Get that shit off me!" he barked.

Leeds smiled, his gums pink and wide. "Maybe we all gotta keep our hands to ourselves," he said.

Snow kept his face trained on the cop, like all this was just banter and nothing he should concern himself with, but he could hear Beth breathing heavily.

The cop nudged his partner and nodded toward the conflict.

"We're moored over at Kissy," he said to the cop in English. "Discharging base chemicals, and we got just a few hours for a drink. Been a long time since we had a drink shoreside. Been since Panama."

"Not so good time to be out tonight, we got curfew, think about that," the tall one said. "SLPP backers come around nights, try to make trouble for OAU."

"I'm gonna guess you for Nigerian," Snow said. "Ogoni?"

The cop eyed Snow, taken aback. "That is right. How you know Ogoni?"

"Ran rig tenders for Shell operations down in the delta. I got people down there too, at Brass Island."

"I know Brass Island."

"So how is Shagari's government setting with people down delta?"

"Shagari is all right," he said, diplomatically.

"I got a half brother at Brass Island. Name of Saro."

"Not Saro-Wiwa," said the cop. "The writer?"

"Naw, not Saro-Wiwa. I know his books–fiction, right? Me, I like history."

The cop seemed to like this answer. He nodded. "You be careful Freetown."

"We'll head back before dark," said Snow.

When the soldiers waved them on, they walked in a line down a dirt road that jutted past a series of dusty shanties, an aspect of sadness and excitement all at once–the vacant faces of parents completely belying the joy in the children as they looked out and followed the strange group with their eyes.

They went down the hill until they hit Circular Road, into Victoria Park, where Beth walked spinning circles, looking at landmarks. It was a place she used to play. Lived nearby. A small white house along Garrison Street. "It's all changed so much," she said. She pointed to a house. She used to run away from the boys by climbing onto its roof. "They thought it great sport to reach inside my shirt and pants. But I could always outclimb them."

They walked past the multistoried houses showing painted

walls chipped down to ancient coats of colonial whitewash. Once-regal balconies and wraparound porches clinging to facades. Freetown soaked itself in heat and humanity. Cooking smoke fluttered out of an old house, pouring from an upstairs window where somebody had built a fire in what had once been a bedroom. A three-story blockhouse structure stuck up, walls leaning in four directions, all of them inward, a dark brown wood weathered by rain and leaching back into the ground it had arisen from. Snow heard the echo of prayer, in Krio:

Papa God we de na evin
mek olman respekt yu oli nem
mek yu rul kam
mek wetin yu want bi na dis wol
leke aw i de bi na evin

He heard it drifting up over the park and saw the wonder on the kid's face trying to place it, wondering why the familiarity, why the rhythm and cadence made young Maciel's face flush with something lost–until Snow told him. "Don't you know what that is? Hell, even I know what that is. That's the Lord's Prayer. *Our father who art in heaven, hallowed be thy name* and all that crap."

Maciel's ears searched the air for the incantation of prayer, but instead saw only poster boards advertising King Blue Washing Powder, Crown Mayonnaise, and Reynolds Ball Point Pens. Beneath them sat a young man, holding crutches tight to his chest, his amputated leg reaching barely to the end of the bus stop bench. Farther on, a girl sat on a street corner where a dirt road intersected a paved one, alongside a Mercedes sedan that looked like a giant creature had thrown a medicine ball through the hood. The girl wore gauze wraps on each of her wrists where her hands had once been, her face wide and disconsolate in the afternoon dust that ringed her eyes.

"Some sick tribal shit going down around here," said Bracelin.

Snow led the group down a narrow paved street, hugging close by a concrete retaining wall that oozed water. They came to a stairway that led upward toward a structure sitting upon the hill, which Snow first took to be a hotel of some sort but soon realized was a Catholic church. As they cut through the grounds, he saw Maciel pause. "I'm gonna go in here for a minute," he said.

"Like fuck you're gonna stop here," said Bracelin.

"I am," said the kid, and marched up the stone steps and pulled on the large oaken door–heavy, by the strain in his arm– and disappeared inside.

"What the fuck is this?" said Bracelin.

"Let him be," said Snow.

"I ain't waiting for him."

"Well, I am. You go on if you want, save me a seat."

Snow could see this work on Bracelin. Hardcore as the man was, there wasn't freshwater's chance on a lifeboat he'd be going alone to the Snap Trap. "I been to some sore-ass shit lockers in the world, Snow. But this place takes the red-eye award. A-*freak*-ah."

Snow was glad for the kid's moxie. He even wondered what the hell he was doing in there. So he climbed up the steps and pulled open the door himself and stepped inside. It was cool inside the church, and he found the kid kneeling before a statue of the Blessed Virgin, lighting one of them candles with his old Zippo, burning his fingers in the process. He rubbed his fingers and got the candle going, then settled in to pray. Snow could see his mouth moving. Snow couldn't take his eyes from the scene. The kid was gone from everything then–everything earthly, anyhow–and even as Snow felt the warm air from the door behind him, and caught the smell of the girl as she moved up alongside, a strange sensation overcame him. He felt his face flush. He wanted to laugh or cry—he wasn't sure which. It was both. They were alone in there, just the three of them. The kid crossed himself, moved to the center of the church and genuflected before the altar of the grand crucifix. Snow wanted more than anything to know what he'd been praying about, but on the stone steps outside, the kid had a half grin on his face and said nothing at all when Snow asked. He'd been praying for dead relatives to come rescue his ass, Snow figured, or for the Good Lord to bring him a bountiful harvest in the flesh of a girl.

PART TWO

THE DANGEROUS SEMICIRCLE

For as this appalling ocean
surrounds the verdant land,
so in the soul of men there
lies one insular Tahiti, full of
peace and joy, but encompassed
by all the horrors of
the half known life.

—Herman Melville, *Moby Dick*

SNAP TRAP

The bar called Snap Trap was housed in an old hospital, built by the British before the war, and had a wide concrete veranda and tall windows that once held glass. But no longer; the room was open to the street with only shutters to keep out the weather. The building had been damaged by apparent street fighting that left behind not only bullet holes but the occasional chuckhole brought on by something more explosive. What it didn't have was a sign, yet it was known by anybody who'd spent half a day in Freetown.

The smell of chicken simmering in pepper sauce lingered in the hazy air, and the bar brimmed with its own brand of home brews: palm wine and distilled spirits called boiled wine, or *omor-lay*, and a local beer called Star, served warm with cassava and yam roll-ups, or flat bread baked in pit ovens dug from the ground out back. Overhead a ceiling fan turned slowly, creaking from a bent fan blade that scraped the wilting plaster overhead, digging out a circular trough.

The eyes of locals cast toward the five as they entered and found a table on the far left wall, as far from the bar as they could get. Right off, Snow saw Favor seated with his back turned to the room. Snow made no move to greet him, though he knew Favor had seen him enter. Snow moved past tables to the bar and ordered drinks for the table, bottles of Star and homemade palm wine brought up from plastic petrol cans behind the bar to refill quart-size Pepsi bottles, the spiral ribbed glass like a swirling ribbon.

"Best is two hour ol'," said the bartender, whose brow glowed with the sweat of afternoon labor indoors without air-conditioning.

Bracelin moved up next to Snow. "Just covering your backside, old man."

"Keep it calm," said Snow.

The beer was served about five degrees below room temp, which wasn't even slightly cool. Somebody put on Otis Redding singing "Dock of the Bay," and Snow felt a ringing in his bad ear, then knocked back a cup of boiled wine like an old veteran, the sweet easy vocal running through him like cool water.

Bracelin slugged down a cup and made a face. "Jesus." He spat out a mosquito and wiped his tongue with his shirt.

"Better you eating them than them eating you."

The ceiling fan fell without warning like a whirling chopper blade, crashing half onto a table and clipping a soldier on the side of the head before it landed on the floor. The soldier turned around and shot it once with his pistol. The entire room went dead quiet for about a half count, hands to their weapons, gazing at the crippled fan. Then they went back to their drinking.

Snow checked down the bar, four bodies down, where he spied the arms of Buck Favor clutching a pair of brews. "Gimme six more just like that one," Snow said to the bartender.

"*Omorlay,*" said the bartender. "Dis kick like de bucking mule bronco," and he pointed at his own tee shirt, which bore pictures of two football helmets butting together, one the Denver Broncos, the other the Dallas Cowboys. Underneath it read SUPER BOWL XII.

"Cowboys won that game," said Bracelin.

The bartender paused from his pouring. "Yah? Dat is right ah? Member too: *inch no in masta, kabasloht no in misis.* Dat tree quid." And he pointed at the drinks.

Bracelin paid the three quid with five American dollars, which further irritated the man, though he accepted them grudgingly, waving the mate back to the tables as if shooing a fly. Snow looked down and saw four dead gnats floating in his own cup. "Protein!" he said, as soldiers eyed them all the way across the room, even after they pulled up chairs to join the others.

"This is one rank-ass bar," said Bracelin.

"I like it," said Leeds. "Reminds me of the war."

"Not this again for chrissakes."

"It's the W.A.," said Snow. "Like they say, if you don't want a monkey's tail to touch you, don't go to a monkey dance."

Bracelin glared around like he was waiting for somebody to give him a reason to tear their head off. "They'd know, bunch of fucking monkeys."

Omorlay definitely managed its "boiled wine" moniker without boiling out any of the alcohol; it made Snow's face burn and the back of his neck itch. He kept his eyes moving around the room, to see if anybody was watching Favor, anybody who had the dull stupid glare of a cop. He eyed two men at the bar wearing revolvers on their belts, and one old black two stools down had a bolt action Remington .306, a goddamned deer rifle, leaning between his legs. A fourth had an Israeli Desert Eagle semi-auto .357 in one hand and a cup of boiled wine in the other. From the bar's end, he heard the easy lilt of an Aussie accent–New South

Wales by the sound of it–though he didn't see which man it was coming from and wasn't even sure he heard correctly, what with all the chatter in five languages and the popping inside his bad ear.

"We got something like mercenary central here," Leeds said.

"Fuck 'em, what I say," Bracelin chimed in. "Kinda faggots need a gun to fuck with you. Get me naked with one of them in the hold of a tank ship, and I'll have him sucking ammonium disulfide in about ten seconds."

"That what comes outa your pole, mate? Ammonium disulfide?"

"Fuck off."

Snow finally stood up and moved again through the room, around chairs where smoking soldiers turned to peer up at him with a dull, muted violence. He moved past the ceiling fan lying on the floor with bullet holes in its carcass, and came to the bar again, nodding for another boiled wine, then turning toward Favor. "Hey, Bucky. What's shakin'."

"Your dick from the look of you, you old bastard!" Favor reached out for a hard handshake, his fist red, white, and freckled. "I seen you over there checking things out. You ain't changed that way." Favor was a round-faced jowly man with a boil of red hair growing off his head, and twin shocks of it coming out his ears. "So we set for up-country?"

"Be on Goodhouse Hill in two days."

Snow looked to the end of the bar, down the faces of Anglo security guns. The guy on the last stool, his voice rising, that Aussie voice. Just then the guy glanced toward Snow and got up to move out the back toward the head. The turn and set of his jaw rang familiar, not to say the twin humps of his trapezius muscles, taut and defined like ten-inch hawsers between his neck and shoulders. He wore a green military tee shirt soaked through with sweat; as he turned, Snow caught sight of an earring hole in his right lobe. Not scarred over, but open and clean like he'd been wearing an earring just yesterday. Then Snow remembered him, from the Rojo in Panama City–the Aussie at the bar.

He shook his head as if to ward off the boiled wine and turned back to Favor.

Somehow he knew that the last thing he needed was more drink, but he knocked back another cup of boiled wine anyway, bad old days in Vietnam brought into close focus seeing Favor, so close Snow could touch and smell the time. Then his mind snapped to the present, out there in the back with that Aussie, wondering what the hell he was up to and what the raw chance was of seeing the same man on opposite ends of the ocean in less than two weeks' time. A minute later, the kid made his way semi-wobbly toward the bar and then past, out the back toward the head. Snow waited while Roberta Flack sang "Killing Me Softly" over the house hi-fi, and Buck Favor droned on about the Lebs and how he was sure to frag the man he worked for if he fucked with him even one more time.

"You know this Aussie was sitting down here on the end a bit ago?" Snow said. "You ever seen him before?"

"Aussies are criminals and drunks," said Favor, gulping back half a beer. "I avoid them."

When the kid came back into the bar, Snow watched his face for a hint of something, saw his dark eyes roam the bar like he was surveying some great risk. He lit on Beth, held held his gaze for a long count. Snow moved over to the bar to pick up four drinks for the table. "How's it going, Georgie?"

"Going okay, Harold. You?"

"Going okay. So tell me, George, you happen to see that dude there at the end of the bar earlier?"

He looked down the end. "That guy?"

"No, guy from earlier. He went out back just ahead of you."

"I didn't see him." The kid shook his head while Snow stared him down. Drunk as he was, Snow could read the lie like he could read a woman's face and know if she did or didn't want him. Some things a man just knew.

"George Maciel, Buck Favor, old comrade in arms thereabouts Vietnam—he fought and I fucked. Heh! This here's the grandson of Joaquin Maciel."

"Who the fuck's that?" Favor stuck out a meaty paw, lifted his chin. "I don't know grandpa from Adam, but good to meet ya, kid."

Snow excused himself to go to the head, stepping to the rear entrance. Eyes followed him, and he thought he might kick-start a chain reaction just by walking past. He glanced back once to see the kid talking to Favor. In the alley, he paused to wait for the toilet to open up, at first thinking himself alone. Then he saw a sober-faced African man standing down the alley a ways, in tribal dress, like he was shot in from the bush. Snow closed his eyes, and felt the instant swirl of his brain around a spinning earth. Pagan stuff, but he could feel it.

When he opened his eyes the man was gone. Snow wasn't quite sure he'd been there to begin with. He could see down an alley to the back of a residence, where a chicken ran past followed by a small child, naked and notable primarily because he still had all his limbs intact. The air back here had the strong odor of sewage mixed with baking bread. Inside, the Turkish toilet functioned mercifully well. No shit piled up inside the hole, at least. "Turkish tobacco and Turkish toilets," Snow said aloud, as he stood on the foot pads and peed.

He blinked back the burning at his eyes, the wood smoke and the booze, and the salted sweat of people. Above the sink hung a discolored mirror, its backing paint flaked off, blotting his image as if by skin cancer.

Snow staggered out into the alley, where he saw the Aussie making his way into the bar again. He hurried to follow, came through the swinging screen door into the bar to find him just exiting the front balcony and stepping down to the street, headed east. Along the bar he found Maciel standing before Favor, getting an earful of the old days, which at that moment meant claiming status as one of Snow's oldest friends. Buck had a cheekful of Red Man chewing tobacco and drank from two beers held in one hand, the longneck bottles laced in his fingers as if they were permanently woven into his knuckles. He called Sierra Leone "Salone" and tipped both bottles up, swallowed down the double shot, then spat tobacco juice on the floor, drawing a shout from the bartender. "Spit juice outside!"

"Gotcha, Gid," he said to the bartender, hoisting his brews as if making a toast, then immediately spitting again on the broken concrete floor. He called all Africans *Gid,* short for *gidda-gidda*– a term used in Arab North Africa to refer to all sub-Saharan Africans. Simply translated, it meant nigger. "White man can have his way in this land if he knows what he's about, ain't that right, Snow?"

Favor slapped him hard on the back. Snow winced. Favor was fifteen years Snow's junior. He had always worn a crazy recklessness that Snow had once found useful if not amusing. Now it set him on edge. Come to think of it, everything in the Snap Trap set him on edge. He stared hard at the kid, who kept his attention on Favor. Snow guessed it was easier that way.

"This here's the greatest bear hunter in the entire Pacific rim," Favor announced, clapping Snow on the back yet again.

"Truth is, Bucky, that goddamned hurts when you do that."

"Hah! Harold Snow hurt!"

Favor launched into a story about how Snow once killed a black bear with his own hands. It was a true story, but to hear Favor tell it

you'd have thought he was making it up as he went. Snow had shot
the thing and put it down over a creek bed, hiked across river rocks
and bent over with a skinning knife, set to put it to the bear, when
the thing rose up like a brush fire and slammed him into the stream.
Favor told the story with great animation and drunken glee. In the
story, Snow rolled into the water and came up with a river rock and
bashed the bear on the side of the head. The sensation was something like hitting a rock with another rock. Then the bear bit into
his left shoulder. Favor said he heard the cracking and crunching
as he ran down off the hillside and started screaming, and still the
bear was working his teeth into Snow's shoulder. Finally the old
man came up with his boot knife and opened up the bear's neck
with it. Snow knew if he pulled away the bear would take a chunk
of his shoulder with him, so he hugged the animal tight to keep
him from working those teeth around until he bled out.

Now Snow caught sight of Beth over at the table. She had a
worried look. She motioned with her eyes outside—the sun was
going down.

"That's pretty wild," said the kid.

"Wild! You got no idea, kid. This old fuck has lived through
shit that you only imagine in nightmares. Hell, he's *done* shit
that'd curdle your blood."

Snow stared at Favor now, frowning down his nose. "I ain't
done nothing, what are you talking about? Had shit done to me. I
absorbed twenty times the radiation of anybody at Bikini."

"Yeah, you're a victim all right. Maybe you'll bank with them
lawsuits."

"Ah, fuck that. I don't collect no unemployment and I don't
suck off no lawsuits. I'm sixty in about two weeks and I could out-
hike and out-hunt any man in here. All these pussies who survived
the war come to find out it killed them after all. So what if it did?

Fuck 'em, they're lucky they had the forty years. I seen kids eighteen get their heads blown off and land on my goddamned lap."

"It's bound to have an impact on you," said the kid.

"Sure. Shit like that changes a man," Favor said, downing yet
another foaming gulp of Star beer.

"Didn't have no effect on me at all. I think all that's just bullshit excuses. It's prissy shit, complaining all the time."

"No effect my eye," said Favor. "I ain't judging, I'm just saying."

Maciel downed a cup of firewater, then stared into the cup as if
reading tea leaves. "Is there room for God?"

Favor looked at the kid like he'd just crapped on his boot. "You
got God worries? That your thing?"

"He's definitely got God worries." Snow looked at him. "You
do."

"Get Snow to tell you about his drinking days in Nam. You can
get by that, you won't ever have a God worry again in your life."

Favor knocked down both beers, then reached back to rap the
empties on the bar and nod for two more. " 'Member that one little
Viet chippie, what was her name? Mi Lang? Snow loved them Viet
girls. You should have heard him: *They got the tiniest little pussies,
just the tiniest little pussies.*' He's got movies of all his girls, you
should get him to show you. Skin flicks from back in the fifties!"

Snow had never wished for a man to shut up more. Now he was
the one avoiding eye contact with the kid, sensing the judgment
in his gaze and somehow the twisted betrayal of Favor's story-
telling, masquerading as wild nostalgia but feeling a whole lot
more like a mind-fuck. Snow glanced toward the table where Beth
sat with Leeds and Bracelin and wished he could fly off on one of
the science-fiction jet packs, just lift right off and fly away to sea.

"So what about that night in Saigon? When you come home
with all that blood on you not remembering nothing? What about

that? I ever tell you I had a CID man coming around asking me questions about that night?"

"No."

"You cut up that hooker, didn't you? Just to see what it's like to play God, I'm gonna bet. Or'd you just get outa hand with the rough stuff?"

Snow felt the back of his neck tighten. He felt the kid's eyes on him. He was glad Beth wasn't in earshot. "Outside of war, I never killed nobody, that's bullshit. For one thing I didn't have that blackout in Saigon, I had it in Da Nang, aboard the steamship *Saigon.* So get your story straight if you're gonna tell stories."

Favor held up his hands, and the bartender thrust two beers at them. "You're the one can't remember what happened. You're the one's gotta live with it. Crawling around the world searching for snatch."

"Well, if it ain't Buck the Fuck. Haven't seen you in years. This is what booze does to a man, Georgie. Why I quit drinking ten years ago."

Favor chuckled as he downed another swallow. "Yeah, you look like you quit drinking! You keep going like you are and you'll be needing old Buck the Fuck to bail your ancient ass out of the Negro sling. Hey, kid, why don't you ask him why he can't go back to Index, Washington? Get him to tell you about the little retarded girl he was fucking before her uncle found out about it!" Favor let out a drunken laugh.

Snow set a bill down on the bar, nodded to the bartender. "I got some business to take care of. Now shut your trap and get to work. No more bullshit."

"I gotta hit the head," said Buck. "See you up Nimba county in a few days."

"I need water," the kid said, after Favor had gone. "A glass of cold fresh water."

"Don't listen to that guy."

Maciel nodded unconvincingly, his gaze falling and holding to Snow's eyes until the old man saw movies playing there, regular skin flicks and horror stories. Snow took him by the arm, harder than he meant to. "Don't look at me like that."

"Like what?" The kid spoke it firm, even hard, like his gramps. He had that moral judge in him. Snow could feel it. He hated a goddamned moralist.

"Like you believe that cocksucker."

The kid tried to roll his arm free and Snow felt himself resist it, like if he let him go he'd never get to say something he wanted to say—except he didn't want to say anything. He didn't want anybody to. He wanted quiet.

"I don't know Buck Favor from anybody," the kid said then. "He seems like an asshole to me."

"He's a racist prick is what he is. He thinks he knows what I'm about, but he don't know shit. Just 'cause we do business with each other, he thinks I'm like him. Well I ain't. Hell, during the times he's talking about, the VC were coming out of the woodwork in Da Nang, and who the hell knows whose blood was all over me anyhow? Who the hell knows? I could have saved five lives for all anybody knows—and here, well, here these people been screwed by one group or another, missionaries and capitalists and you name it—first the Christians here to save their bacon from the Devil and then the Muslims with their Koran-or-the-sword business—Favor's just another in line."

The kid eyed Snow evenly. "You know it doesn't matter what I think. It doesn't matter what Buck Favor thinks, Harold." The kid looked calmly at him, wobbled slightly to show he was drunk. "He's right, though. You're the one has to live with yourself. It only matters what *you* think."

"Jesus Christ." Snow wished he could have felt better about

that. "I gotta go see a guy. Tell Bracelin to wait a half hour, then get a cab and meet me at the corner of George and Boston Lightfoot." Then he stepped out through the front door into the glowing, muggy dusk. He wished he knew why it mattered what the kid thought of his life, but there were practical matters here, like why the lie about the Aussie, if it was a lie. Snow tried to focus on that, tried to understand the here and now and not to care what the kid knew about Index, or what he himself remembered about Da Nang and Viet bar girls.

Evening was settling with no cooling of smoky air as he turned down Howe Street, past the street vendors closing up shop, a stooped man gathering cassava, and a fat girl of twenty wearing a flowered dress selling the last pieces of grilled fish and chicken from an open barbecue. Within two hundred yards there stood five dozen men who would as soon kill Snow as let him pass, but let him pass they did, for despite his age he knew where he was going and carried himself as such. He ticked through his mental list: get the contracts into Churchill's hands, hope the unscrupulous bastard didn't fuck him over completely, and set sail.

He longed for something simple. He wished to God he could go back to the Cascades, felt tightness in his chest when he remembered the clean air of the mountains, the cool-aired mist of home in Washington. And the girl from Index. He quickened his pace, as if getting to Churchill to nail everything down would somehow stave her off; Favor had a way of dredging up the shit. Snow hated when people called her retarded. For his taste in younger women, he pled guilty. There was something about youthful womanhood, how it never censored or angled but flung itself headlong into life and love and bed with a complete lack of guile, got its heart broken, swirled, and ached for its loss. Women were complicated, girls were simple. Like he was simple.

He had never been with anybody who gave herself so completely to him as Carly. *Carly.* He had tried a long time not to think of her name and how he'd say it while they were together, urging her, inside her, staring at that twisted ecstatic face. He tried to blot out how utterly she craved him, and the ways she came to him, stealing away to scratch at his door after midnight. He hadn't used her. He cared for her, showed her affection. He never thought of himself as a user. He wanted to protect her. But then the endgame hovered and goaded him. They sent her to some home. Some "managed care facility" or whatever they called it. Twelve years ago now. She'd be twenty-nine and still a girl in her mind. For him there was only the banishing. If he believed in confession he would have to admit this was the gravest pain of all. He could still remember how they descended on his house, Elks Club elders, men he'd played cards with, chased women with, hunted with, sitting him down and leaning into him, stern and clear: *We all got our vices, but you have crossed a line. There are two kinds of people in this world and you are the wrong kind, Snow. You are the wrong kind.*

Snow walked in short quick steps. In a strange way he wished for a sterner reprisal, wished the girl's uncle had hit him in the jaw, wished he could have pulled himself up off the ground to explain instead of being driven off like a wild animal. He couldn't have lived with prison, but he craved the judgment of a day in court. Let his accusers face him. Let them cry and strike out and maim him. Now he wished he could run right out of his body. He doubled his fists, brought his knuckles to his temples, and began to rub. The pain ran into his skull and lodged there. He kept hearing that Krio Lord's Prayer. He looked around wondering where the hell it was coming from, his dead ear ringing and popping like gunfire.

Two men on a bus stop bench eyed him as he rounded the

corner up past a big gray mansion off Boston Lightfoot, and for
ten steps he thought they might be cops, and he sensed his backside, waiting for them to follow. But they didn't follow. He found
himself looking for the Australian, wondering, really, how was it
you could see the same man in PC and Freetown on the same trip
without assuming he was following you? He turned up George
Street, making him think of the kid and all his understated moralizing. He walked past St. George's Cathedral, where he saw a
priest standing at the door, a black man in a black robe, one of
those Jesuits. He felt his pace slow. He stared as he walked along,
jamming his toe on a rise in the concrete walk and stumbling
forward. He regained his balance and stopped there, wondered
what he might say to such a man if he were to walk up those steps,
something like *fuck me father for I have sinned it's been fifty years
since my last confession so how about you order up a bolt from Zeus
and get it all over with?* He stared slack-jawed at the priest,
lowered his head and let out a tiny whining sound, like a small two-
stroke motor climbing a hill. He threw off confession worries and
started moving again, shaking out his hands, feeling his steps
down inside his boots. A block later he climbed the front steps of
the wooden cop house.

Inside he went to a counter enclosed by glass two inches thick.
He put his mouth to the rounded vent. "I need to see Mr.
Churchill," he said. "He's expecting me." And he sat back to wait.
A long-necked man stuck his head out the door and waved him in,
drawing looks from others, and he was led down a short, warped-
wood hallway to the end office, where Churchill came out from
behind his desk with a big smile and his hand stuck out. He wasn't
alone, though. There on the settee by the window overlooking the
garden sat a strangely familiar guy, damned near Snow's own age,
with speckled white hair. He couldn't place him, and got no help
from Churchill, who didn't bother with introductions.

"I got the paperwork here," Snow said.

"I think that we are not going to worry about paperwork," said Churchill.

Churchill had round massive eyes with languid lids, and a tight, knurled scar that interrupted his left eyebrow where some cop had whacked him back in '67, before he became a cop himself and started doing the whacking.

Snow turned to the older man, trying to place him. "We met? Name's Harold Snow."

"Excuse me," said Churchill. "This is Mr. Johnson."

"I do believe we've met," said Snow. "You're from Lofa county, Liberia, that right?"

"You have a good memory."

"I tried to buy some land up there. Tried to set myself up in business in Lofa county."

"I gather it did not work out."

"No, sir. Own a small piece up in the mountains."

"Near the border."

"That's right." Snow paused and looked over at Churchill, his head bobbing a bit as he turned back to Mr. Johnson. "Now how is it you know that?"

"It is the preferable location. A deduction."

"What is it that you Americans say about real estate?" said Churchill. "Location location location! Three locations!"

Snow felt unnerved. He gave a casual glance to the door. He felt a sudden need to get to Goodhouse Creek. He stared over at Mr. Johnson. Snow had a nearly photographic memory for people. This one eluded him still, in part because the man gave nothing away, not about Lofa county, or the Mandingoes Snow had known there, or their ties to the military down in Liberia.

He put the contracts on the desk.

"We both know how you have acquired these cargoes,"

Churchill said. "It is obvious to everybody." He held up his hand. "Don't worry, we won't be exercising legal authority over you. But it does change the reality of our arrangement."

"We got contracts here for bulk chemicals," Snow said. "My assumption is you still want to do business. So I don't see how reality's changed."

"It is a matter of options and aspects," Churchill said. His police uniform looked two sizes too small. He'd been a tough man in his time, but he was growing fat here.

"Options and aspects? What the hell's that supposed to mean?"

"We need part of the cargo to be delivered to Monrovia, so we will only be able to off-load half of your shipment of chemicals here. First aspect, then, is that we have no capacity, you have already seen that our tank farm is filled to capacity and we are running trucks into downtown storage facilities."

"Yeah, I saw."

"The second aspect is that there are some people of Mr. Johnson's who need transportation to the Liberian capital."

"Transportation? Like a ride to the airport, or what?"

"To Monrovia. Aboard your ship."

"Ahhh—I ain't into that game anymore."

"It is no game. They are laborers, but not the kind you think."

Snow stood up. He wanted to jam his fist into Churchill's smug bureaucratic face. He could feel the hard shove into a tight corner. "What about our agreed sum? We got five-six million in cargoes on that ship."

"We rather doubt that sum. And owing to the new situation, we will wire a percentage now, and then the balance after delivery in Monrovia."

"What the hell does my cargo got to do with Monrovia?"

"That is not your concern."

"It is if I got to deliver it!" His voice strained forward aggressively. He took a breath and set his feet flat on the floor.

"We are all West Africans together here, which is something that Americans do not seem to understand. The colonial boundaries are what you would call capricious. And we have need of petrol in Monrovia."

It smelled like a line of shit, like a big web of shit out there, stretching south across the border—who knew how far and how big? But these were no simple corrupt officials like some Mexican *capitán.* They had their long arms out, and Snow could feel them curling around his backside, corraling him. His brain ground to a halt. He stared in turn at the two men, their faces mute, stolid, needing him a lot less than he needed them. He felt a black hole spinning inside his brain. Jesus! He managed a nod. "All right," Snow said, his voice coming out like a twelve-year-old boy with a sore throat. "But we'll be looking for that deposit, and if something snags we'll have to bypass Monrovia and sell in Lagos."

"I understand," said Churchill. "But there will be no need. You are right, we do want to do business with you, it is just that the realities of the market are apparent to us now. My chemist has already contacted me. He has tested your cargoes. Unfortunately, a fair number appear to be off specifications."

"Wait a minute. Which is it, our cargoes are off spec or you're in need of it elsewhere?"

Churchill twisted a pencil in his fingertips. "It is both. Must it be one or the other? It is both!" And he let out a wide laugh. "As I told you when we first spoke, we have no need of these base monomers. Styrene and the like—we have no plastics industry. For these reasons the earlier sum seems overstated. We will give you the equivalent of two point five million American dollars."

Snow felt stomach acid churning. He had no choice here,

because the truth was he didn't want to sell in Lagos or anywhere else. Nigeria would be nothing but a bureaucratic nightmare of paperwork and suspicion. His contacts were here; and they were in process of bending him over a table.

Outside, his face burned from the heat of confrontation, and Snow found the cab motoring in the street. Night had fallen, which felt eerie enough, but now the streets were devoid of people, save for his crew, looking half passed out from boiled wine. Maciel sat curled up in back, his head propped against the roll bar. Beth smoked in front of him, casting her eyes about warily, and Bracelin was so torched he didn't even care that Leeds had passed out with his head on his shoulder.

Snow opened the cab door and swung his trailing leg up with the help of his right hand, firmly cupped under his thigh. "Kissy oil terminal. Like right now. You think there's a chance Paynor didn't get rid of the crew?"

The cabbie took off driving.

"What the fuck happened?" Bracelin said.

"They want to split the cargoes between here and Monro," said Snow, slapping at his neck, then scratching the spot without a second thought.

"What the *fuck*?" said Bracelin.

He grabbed the roll bar and shook the bush taxi on its springs until the jeep was bounding up and down, causing the driver to swerve and shout "Hey dere now!" and Leeds to jump awake like he was looking for somebody to choke.

Bracelin leaned up between the seats and let fly at Snow with a torrent of abuses and profane references to Snow's mother. Fortunately for Snow it happened to be his bad ear, so he didn't so much hear the haranguing as he felt it in the form of a saliva bath that he kept wiping away in the hope Bracelin would get the picture and quit spitting all over him without being told. "Shit happens."

Bracelin let out an exasperated breath, sat back and scanned the streets as they drove toward the port. "The fuck I let you talk me into, old man. Would you look at this place!"

"You wanted into this!" Snow erupted, his brow sharp and flaring. He eased off grudgingly. To a grim scowl. "How about you take just a smidgen of responsibility."

"I don't know these people from fuck-all. They ain't my people."

"And who is, Charlie?" Snow said with dull irritation. "Who the hell is?"

Bracelin just eyed him, jaw muscles flexing like a man chewing on his own teeth, not because it mattered to him that he was alone in the world, but because he was politic enough to know that everybody else would think him an asshole if he admitted it. By the time the cab pulled into Kissy, they found Paynor alone in the wheelhouse, and the ship vacant save for Kairos. "Where the hell is everybody?" said Snow.

"Jumped ship," said Paynor, his face as vacant as the tanker. "I was all set to dispatch the ones you said when that Ali character and two of his buddies cornered me and demanded pay for everyone. Afterward they all left. They're gone. Even the cooks. Lucy's out too. She told me to tell you 'fuck you' from her."

"That's great, Payne," said Bracelin. "Thanks for passing it along."

"She said you'd know what she meant. What'd you do to her, anyway?"

"Shut up, Paynor."

Snow looked out at the empty deck and watched their cargoes being trucked off under armed guard. There wasn't a thing in the world he could do about it, not any of it, not what people thought of him, or how hard they worked for him, or even who worked for him. Out over the lights of the deck he could see the mosquitoes gather, like they were all set to fly up his nose, and he imagined himself there on his last bed, swatting at them like old Joaquin.

THE ROAD TO NIMBA MOUNTAIN

A few miles out of Freetown harbor heading south, Snow lay in his bunk with a warm mist surrounding him. Though his eyes were closed he dreamed he could see through his lids like an amphibian. He was not asleep at all but living a lucid nightmare: floating in brown water with blood clouding, cyclone victims in the Bay of Bengal, dead bodies suspended around him, entangling him in their long arms, black hair, and burned mouths. Dutch Van Sickle appeared, red-haired and obvious, looking open-eyed at him, holding a marlin spike in one hand with blood all over the thing, coming for him with Joaquin Maciel rising up behind like a bulldog–

He awakened sometime late in the night to realize the propellers had stopped their churning, the engines turned back to idle. This was his cue. He rose quietly only to find the kid gone from his bunk. Snow dressed, staring at the unmade bed, then went down the passageway, wondering about what Ali had said about Beth never leaving him. Snow hoped it was true, even if he didn't want to be her *bahpah.* The ship was empty, the only noises the constant drone of idling engines and the ship's ventilation system. He stepped outside to the poop and found the deck completely dark save for a single stern light and the red and green glow of their running lights. The ship was just where he figured—a cove in southern Sierra Leone. Overhead the stars were shrouded by haze, a faint overcast of Harmattan dust.

No fires or electricity pulsed from shore, while west over dark ocean a distant lightning storm erupted along the horizon, crackling the reach of coast with dry lightning flashes that rippled toward them. From shore, a longboat heaved its way over light surf and paddled out toward the ship. Snow watched the paddlers swing alongside their port bow just as he reached the Jacob's ladder, where Bracelin stood by himself. "You didn't wake me," Snow said.

"I didn't want to interrupt a wet dream."

"Jesus, you got no idea."

"That right? Well, good for you, least you got something to jack off to."

"Naw, I mean wet like blood. I'm dreaming about blood."

"Not mine, I hope. Don't go dreaming about my blood. I don't want that shit on me."

Together they leaned over and watched the first one come up, a stocky black man in his twenties, nodding but saying nothing as he stepped aboard carrying a bag. There were eight of them in all—and below in the longboat was a wooden crate.

"We have to put you in the fo'c'sle," said Snow. "It's not luxury accommodations, but it's the only way to get you through border controls at Freeport."

"Show me," said the first one, who was evidently the leader. He had wild hair rising off his head like metal springs, and he wore street clothes—jeans and sneakers and a black tee shirt emblazoned with a single white star set dead center on his chest.

"We'll be in Monrovia in a few hours," said Bracelin, as Snow led them in single file to the fo'c'sle, the men hoisting their wooden crate as well as a long massive seabag made of waterproof lined canvas and zipped closed on top. It had the knobby look of rifle butts inside.

In the paint room, Snow pushed aside five-gallon buckets of marine enamel and swung open a door leading into a small cramped crew's quarters. "You bring your own food and water?" he asked.

"We have water, but that is all."

"If all goes right, you won't be aboard long enough to need food."

Snow ushered them inside with a bad feeling about these eight. They had a sullen professionalism about them—talked to no one, took care of their own gear, stowing it inside the prow-shaped quarters as Snow flicked on the dim light to reveal bulkheads painted light green, and four bunks with mattresses and nothing else. A toilet was set directly forward. Then he backed out, pulled the door closed and dogged it, while Bracelin stepped over and set the padlock.

"Hey! Hey!" said a voice from inside. "You lock us in!"

Bracelin could scarcely suppress a grin. "Got to, bub. Not taking chances with unknowns! We'll let you out when it's time to disembark. We'll be in Monro in three hours."

"He lock in?" came another voice.

"I hear him," said another.

"What we go do?"

"We go sleep. Work soon."

Snow put all the paint buckets back in place, stacking roller
extensions and gear up around the door until it was completely
concealed. Then he backed out of the paint room, dogged the
door, and found Bracelin under the fo'c'sle overhang.

"They got enough ventilation in there?" the mate asked.

"Sure. It was built for this. No one will ever know they're in
there."

"I just don't want eight suffocated men in that hold when we
hit Monrovia. Last thing we need is a boatload of dead niggers."

"They'll be okay. I moved plenty of people in there." They had
been Cambodians and Sri Lankans, refugees typically, desperate,
bound for wherever they could go and however they could get
there. For a while in the mid-seventies she'd been a tramp tanker
more ways than one; even her cargoes were tramps of a sort.
"What do you think these are about?"

"I don't know, Snow. You're the one arranged it."

"I didn't arrange it. It got arranged on me. No fucking choice."

"Man's always got choices, Snow. Just sometimes neither of
'em is any good."

Snow climbed up the forward stairs that led down on both sides
of the centerline catwalk. At the top he looked forward across the
arrow-shaped fo'c'sle deck to the sight of two beady eyeballs staring at him from deck level. He about jumped out of his skin before
he realized the eyes belonged to Leeds, who lay on his stomach, his
blond hair shining in the moon and his teeth back in. "What the
fuck you doing, Tim? You scared the shit outa me."

"Used to be you didn't scare so easy, bos'n," said Leeds, and
Snow could hear his fists crackling like he was there in the dark on
his belly on the fo'c'sle, doubling them up, playing commando.
"Used to be you could laugh at this fucked-up world."

"You know, goddamnit, you're right," said Snow. "I just don't see a goddamned funny thing anywhere around me. You included! How's that for a laugh? How's that engine room doing?"

"Not looking so good. Got no engine crew. Ain't been wiped since Brazil."

"I'll have the kid pull some wiper OT and be sure to avoid the engine room personally." Snow stepped down the centerline catwalk aft, hearing it creak and rattle all the way along, until he saw them—two men talking against the manifold, well concealed from view at nearly every angle. Snow paused and stepped back to the port railing. He could barely make them out, only occasional movement in the shadows of the work lights. Then a thickly built man wearing deck covies and a work vest stepped out of the shadow and moved outboard, disappearing aft. Snow didn't recognize him from his silhouette, so he pushed down the catwalk as Paynor got the engines churning to full ahead and the ship smoothed out. When Snow broke on the other side of the midship square, he saw no one aft, wondered if the figure hadn't ducked down into one of the empty tanks, wondered if he could even rely on his own perceptions to be sure there really was a man. He couldn't bring himself to go on some gameless hunt, had no energy for that.

He was in the room on his back for ten minutes when the kid came in, smelling of the engine room.

"What you been up to?"

Maciel was pulling off his shirt and making for a shower. "You probably don't want to know."

"How about you tell me anyway."

"I was with Lisa. She has her room to herself now."

"*Lisa*," said Snow, and rolled toward the wall. "Christ." He wallowed in that sickly pain for a minute or more; then his brain turned and he thought about what a good cover story it made, knowing how it would gnaw at him to think of it, to imagine them together doing what he ached to do. Snow felt pain radiating up out of his abdomen, his thoughts frazzled even without the mefloquine. He shivered once, felt hot in the room despite the open portholes, and stared at the kid's form depressing the upper bunk. "Who was that you were talking to in the pipeline when I was coming in from the bow? I didn't recognize him."

Snow was taking a flyer, but in the silence that followed, he wished he'd asked the question in broad daylight, where he could see the kid's eyes and know if he was lying. Now all he got was a cloister voice in darkness, a voice trained and measured and calm. "That wasn't a he. That was Lisa."

"Quit fucking calling her that, goddamnit!"

That name and the image of the two coupled hung there like a big foil balloon. Snow couldn't tell what was true, couldn't settle on a thought long enough to know anything one way or the other. He only knew the kid was cocky now and on top of it somehow, like he'd settled into the Larium and knew just what was what. He pressed PLAY on the ghetto blaster and out blared Bobby Darin wailing on "Mack the Knife." Snow closed his eyes and felt his nerves crackle, felt a fever coming on.

What caused the hang-up getting into port at Monrovia, Snow had no idea, but next day, after his morning watch, they were hanging offshore in the company of a U.S. Navy vessel when the fever hit Snow full on and drove him to bed. Through an overheated brain, he tried hypnotizing himself on the springs under Maciel's mattress. Pain ran through his nerves like mice in a maze. He tried staying motionless, practiced his belly breathing. Even his skin ached. Covering himself with blankets, he stared straight up and vowed to break the fever by force of will, drinking from a plastic gallon jug of rust-tinted water and staying bundled until he fell asleep.

Sometime in the night he came to consciousness with the kid next to him on a milk crate gripping his hand while Snow's face flamed and he vaguely heard the echoes of his own voice in his ears, and he knew he'd been talking. Then he felt a cool wet cloth to his head and opened his eyes barely to see the face of the kid saying *stay calm Harold stay calm* while that cool compress patted him lightly. He closed his eyes again, felt the hand there squeezing, all calloused now, squeezing even if Snow couldn't grip back.

When he next awakened the kid was gone and his sheets were soaked through in the shape of his body, his forehead cool to the touch. He stumbled into the head feeling like he'd dodged one. He felt only general weakness in the aftermath of fever, but besides the knob up under the ribs, and a dull headache, he felt surprisingly pain free. Climbing two flights topside took no small exertion of limited energy. He was practically on his knees by the time he made the chart room, pulling himself into a bright wave of light as he entered the bridge. A pale yellow glow was all around where Bracelin stood beating the radio microphone on the control console like he was trying to wake somebody up, muttering through gritted teeth, "Fuck me! Fuck me!"

"Don't want to," said Snow, holding himself as tall as he could and moving his head in a pose of alertness. He stepped up alongside the mate, one hand gripping the wheel for balance.

"You feeling better?"

"Broke that fever anyway. So what's going on?"

"I called that pilot office four times to get a boat out here so we could enter the harbor, and there's no boat yet. You said Monrovia was a lock."

Snow looked out across the morning reach. To the west he saw the U.S. Navy ship, a guided-missile frigate by her silhouette, offshore at twelve miles.

On the bridge, before the helm, engine controls, and navigation gear, Bracelin paced and worried out loud about Churchill's men in the forepeak and about the harbor pilot who couldn't seem to get his black ass out to guide them in. "We oughtta just go in ourselves; who needs a fucking pilot and an escort tug at this shit-heel port? Liberia! It ain't quite the Congo, I guess, but fucking-A."

Snow assured him Monrovia was an open town and they had nothing to worry about with the pilot, let alone inspectors. They'll rubber-stamp us, he thought, feeling his brain clatter to a raucous standstill. Voices pattered at his inner ear. Then he noticed Bracelin giving him a long look, with no small level of menace. Suddenly the mate seemed speedy. He had the look of it, his big black pupils taking over his eyeballs, the darting looks. Snow would have bet he hadn't slept since they'd arrived in Sierra Leone two days before. He was standing no watches at all, since he was always on watch. It only made sense—he'd found his crank.

Then the radio crackled. Finally, the pilot boat. Bracelin answered the call saying, "It's about time!" into the mike, then shoved the throttle forward, activating a bell and sending a read-out to the engine room, where Leeds or maybe Kairos or maybe Beth would push the throttle to half ahead. The ship powered forward to where the pilot boat came alongside.

"There's one more thing, Brace," he said. "I'm thinking we should delay our discharge here. I gotta be honest. I think Churchill's gonna fuck us all the way on this. He just wants delivery here because that's where *he's* resold the cargoes. Plus whatever shit those men in the forepeak are here for."

"So why stop here at all? Let's kill the fucks in the forepeak and dump them in the Gulf on our way to Lagos. Let's sell this shit in Lagos."

"I gotta go up-country, I told you that."

"For your rocks."

"That's right. Plus I want to find Yasa. Churchill and this guy there, they were talking like they knew my house. Plus I got something I need to do for Beth."

Bracelin let out a snort and shook his head–pathetic. "She don't love you, Snow. You're doing all this love shit, and she's not into fucking geriatric cases."

"Oh, why don't you just fuck off."

Bracelin let out a hissing snake-laugh, through his teeth. "I'll ride up-country with you for half of what you get from Favor."

Snow stared. "A third. I gotta pay off Paynor too."

"Fine, a third then."

"We'll know by the time we get back if Churchill's gonna renege. If the first half of the wire transfer ain't gone through by then, we just go. If it has, we finish the deal here."

"So we gotta delay the agents here in Monro," Bracelin said, his mind in it now. "Tell them we're short on crew and we have to wait to off-load."

"We'll take Kairos with us. No pump operation without the pumpman. I'll take the skiff in and hit Congotown for an up-country vehicle."

"Okay," said Bracelin, and slapped him on the shoulder, a friendly slap that only hurt a little bit. Snow moved down the inner ladder, holding tight to the railing, careful not to slip.

As he launched the skiff off the seaward side of the ship, Snow felt like he'd been on the short end of a fight with a man fond of low blows. The pain felt like it might be in his back, except that he couldn't get comfortable, no matter how he shifted. He ran the skiff in to the port, tied it up alongside the quay, and removed the spark plug. Riding a cab toward Congotown, he imagined letting

the impulse ferry him through Monrovia and Congotown toward
Roberts airport, wondering how much energy it would really take
to lean forward and say *Robertsfield,* where he'd catch a plane for
Abidjan, Lagos, and London–with thirty grand in his backpack–
just go, even if he didn't know where in the end. He sensed that
need, to let it all go–the money, dreams of the girl, realities of
the life.

He tried to put his worries about Churchill out of his head. The
bridge tracked over the southeast end of Providence Island, where
American slaves had first landed 150 years ago. The cabbie swung
north up Water Street past the Waterside Market, where the good
smells of barbecue rose up off the waterfront and a swarm of
people crowded the stalls to buy hot peppers, yams, fish, and
cassava. He watched the vegetable vendors selling sweet potato
greens and bitter tomatoes.

He took UN Drive around the loop, past the U.S. Embassy and
Papa Dee's, feeding into the coast road, past the executive
mansion, which Tubman had built back in the sixties. It looked
like a multi-deck parking garage, with deep recesses and over-
hangs, giving it a gloomy, paranoid facade. The Temple of Justice
was just as bad, like a cheap concrete high-rise hotel. On the broad
upright section it read TEMPLE OF JUSTICE: LET JUSTICE BE DONE
TO ALL MEN.

Snow had always liked that one–justice being done *to* people
rather than *for* them or *with* them, like Justice was a stick somebody was hitting you with. Since Tolbert that's the direction things
had gone. Snow had made his contacts in '69, visited three times
that year on dry-cargo freighters, met Yasa at Papa Dee's, got
addicted–to the woman, to the cool air up-country. In '74 he built
the house on Goodhouse Creek, lured Yasa away from a longshore-
man she'd taken up with out of Freeport, moved her into the

house with her kids, and only then did he realize how far things had gone with Tolbert's crew.

One of the reasons he'd built out there was the influence of the iron mine at Nimba Mountain, which was operated by a Swedish outfit with their own security force and promised protection. But that turned on him, when the head security prick grew a snake up his ass for a white man with a black mistress, and got some locals into the act, and the harassments started. Like everything else in his life he'd figured the politics too late. Now he thought maybe the only thing separating him from disaster was a single bag of uncut stones buried under that two-story slave colonial on Goodhouse Creek–and maybe a miner at Nimba Mountain, an old miner to shake Bethy's tree.

He felt his heart race just thinking about that, spinning off until he felt it leaping out his throat. He realized he was slipping in the seat some, lifting his chest, pain now radiating upward from his lower abdomen. The cabbie was watching him. "You sure you want hire car?" the cabbie said, eyeing the rearview. "You no look good, friend. I can take you where you want go."

"I'm just having what you call a heart attack," said Snow, and laughed.

"Dat no good. You want to go JFK?" he asked, meaning the hospital.

"No thanks," Snow said. "Hotel Congo."

"Dat all the way Congotown."

"I told you, I want go Congotown."

"Ah right, my friend. But you look like you go die."

"I not go die," he said. "I ain't having a heart attack, I'm having a frigging gas attack."

"You mean de mustard gas?" And he laughed.

"Never mind," Snow said, and the cabbie mercifully shut his

mouth all the way to Congotown, probably figuring Snow was more trouble than he was worth. He pulled the car in front of the Hotel Congo.

Snow tossed the guy a five, then pushed out of the cab and went in through the weathered swinging doors. Standing at the front desk, waiting to hire a car, Snow watched the white suits hang loosely on the Liberian waiters moving past, oversized gloves with trays perched in delivery to the two dozen tables. The place looked like something out of *Casablanca,* except that every inch of it, lath and plaster and wood-frame construction, was melting away in the heat. He'd heard that Said, the Lebanese owner, was floating the hotel for sale, had heard a lot of that kind of activity going on, like those in the know were anticipating wholesale change of a different type.

Snow rented a big old bush cab, a Toyota Land Cruiser with mud on the fenders and dents in the doors, driving it back up through the hot dry streets of Monrovia until he located a truck driver who could handle the trek up-country with some drums of fuel for the return trip. He drove around the downtown until he found one, paid him half now, promised half on delivery, and told him where to pick up six drums of gasoline and where to meet him in Nimba county.

Liberia had enjoyed 136 years as America's only African colony, and while in the postmortem of true colonialism, the place was run by a dozen or so families, all of them descendants of the freed American slaves who had landed here in 1822 and promptly set about enslaving the locals as best they could. The tribal people of Liberia were nominal monotheists, Muslims and Christians to the tune of 70 percent, but you never had to explore far before you saw the fetishes or heard the *juju* or the invocation of ancestral spirits good and bad. They were good pagans here, like Snow aspired to on some level, something down and human about paganism. Animists wandering the land of the Forest Devil. And among the people, the family divisions and the clans and the tribal underscoring. Tribalism ruled the world, Snow thought.

At Freeport he found the crew waiting, the ship behind them sitting high, with Paynor looking on from the bridge deck. Kairos stood with Bracelin, Beth, and Maciel on the wooden dock. "Did you have any idea there was men in our forward hold?" Kairos said. "I saw them myself. They marched out of here ten minutes after we arrived."

"Who were they?" Snow asked. As if any of them knew.

"They were some shifty-looking characters."

"Let's go for a little R and R, Stephen. You've earned it."

"You're right, bos'n." He grinned. "I have too. I damned well have."

Getting Kairos off the ship was only one reason Snow wanted him along. Having a black man up-country couldn't be a bad thing, even if he was from East St. Louis. At least they wouldn't look like a pack of wild white men kidnapping Beth and hauling her into the forest.

A canopied military truck sat idling on the opposite side of the dock area, up the hill some, and inside were two government soldiers. Snow could only assume that more men sat there in the covered bed, concealed. He kept his eye on the truck as he ground gears out of the parking area, giving a wave to the men in green and heading back toward town. "What you know about these soldiers?" Kairos asked.

"I know they got guns," said Snow.

Snow angled over and ushered Beth into the front seat where she could ride unmolested, despite Bracelin's protest that he should ride shotgun. They looped south of the city and headed east up the coal tar between Monrovia and Ganta. Into the night Snow saw a fire erupt down through a valley in upper Bong county, reaching toward Nimba county, in the clan of Ganta, and after that came more fires, flickering behind the forest canopy and up between the thatched roofs of roundhouses and the corrugated angular roofs of concrete construction. He heard it then, the even rhythm of rolling drums, like giant heartbeats in the night. If they were bonfires of celebration or acts of arson, Snow couldn't quite tell.

"Tell me it's some holiday I ain't heard of," Bracelin said from behind him, and only then did Snow realize that somebody besides himself was awake.

"No holiday I know of," Snow said.

At Ganta they saw four military trucks rush past headed west, toward Monrovia. The soldiers wore green tiger suits and helmets and held their M-16s upright, their jaws set and their cheeks jiggling in the flashing lights of the roadway. These were the only vehicles they'd passed, and Snow felt mild surprise that they'd not been stopped, but the trucks seemed in a hurry. Through the town, dawn felt half a lifetime away, and Bracelin wondered out loud where the hell they were going, as the road went from coal tar to red dirt and on into the dry scars of a distant rainfall, flickering in the headlights of the Land Cruiser. They came to a bridge over a wash, made of a dozen round logs with the bark all worn off, stretched from dirt to dirt. Snow pulled forward slowly until he was confident he'd lined up the tires to the logs; then all at once he punched it hard and bounded and powered over the bridge.

"You taking the long way for a reason?" Bracelin asked.

"Told you I got me a surprise for Bethy."

"You're so fucked up, Snow."

Snow cast a long look to where Beth lay asleep with her head bouncing on the window. She shifted her position, then opened her eyes and sat up. "I need a cigarette," she said, and searched the leg pocket of her fatigues before bringing out a bag of Drum.

As they bounced along, she rolled one. "By the way"–she touched a match to the end of the hand-rolled smoke–"I truly loathe surprises."

In the cool period before dawn they pushed on four-wheel drive out of the rainforest of the western slopes, the roadsides choked by bamboo tracts and mahogany trees, ironwood and raffia palm giving way to the sparse canopy of the elevated plateau. Snow had always felt at home here, from his first visit back in '69, and now once again he drove straight east toward Nimba Mountain, a monolithic cone of iron ore that jutted dark blue in the moonlight. Snow pulled slowly down the gravel and cinder road of the mining operation, checking a letter he held in one hand, finally matching it to a house number, and pulled in alongside a boxy-tall Land Rover.

They had decent digs up here at the mines. The neat, orderly rows of rectangular concrete houses, interspersed with shade trees, and cars parked out front–all of it made him feel like this was some corporate colonial town, not even Africa: the mountains, the calm cool air, mining for iron with Swedes in charge. He'd only been here on two other occasions and hadn't seen Thorson since early '77; now, when the man answered the door, wearing his canvas pants and a work shirt, he held a cup of tea and peered out the cracked door. "Thorson. It's Harold Snow. Long time no see."

"What in hell you doing here so early?" He had a rolling Swedish voice that reminded Snow of his maternal grandfather.

"Just drove up from Monro."

"Who is that with you?" he asked, glancing past to the vehicle.

"My crew. They're okay."

"Park the vehicle parallel to mine and bring them inside. We can't attract any attention, not now."

Snow stepped back to the Land Cruiser, which he'd pulled off the side of the road, and climbed in behind the wheel. Only Beth was awake, still smoking in the front passenger seat. In the back, Bracelin had finally fallen asleep, along with the other two, whose heads were tipped back with their mouths wide open.

"Thorson's got a little spooky," Snow said.

"Spooky about what?" she said, hunkered down now, looking moody and sleepy and puffing away on her smoke. "My surprise?"

"No, no, he ain't your surprise, he just knows where to find it."

She glanced toward the front of the house, where a dim light glowed in the window. "Listen, Harold. I've been meaning to talk to you about this surprise and all that." Snow started the motor, not sure he wanted to hear this. He worked the Land Cruiser in parallel to Thorson's Rover. "I don't want you doing anything like give me a big sack of rocks, okay? I really really don't want into that business. And I definitely don't want to end up playing somebody's mule."

Snow felt something like air go out of his belly, and he thought for a second he'd lost control of his bladder. "Mule's a sexless creature," Snow said, forcing out a laugh. He thought he'd shown her more of himself than that. "Anyway, I got a sack of rocks all right, but it ain't for you! You should know by now I got a girlfriend in these parts. I been seeing her coming on six years now." He turned and stared, serious now. "The world don't revolve around you."

She let out a short little breath, like half a snort. "I know that."

"Let's get inside before Thorson has a fit."

Inside, Thorson had a fit anyway. He wanted to know why in hell everybody didn't come inside as he'd asked. "I'd have had you park out back if I knew they were going to stay in the vehicle," he said, checking through the curtains.

"What the hell's the matter with you, Thorson? This area's secure."

"What is the matter with *me*? How about what is the matter with this country? It is many things, but secure is not one of them." He sipped from his teacup two or three times, fast. "It has been all over the radio the last half of an hour," he said. "There has been a coup. They found Tolbert this morning. He was disemboweled, Snow. In his bed."

Snow felt a strange swirl come to his head, dizzy for a split second, like maybe his fever had returned, or was about to return. He thought of the soldiers at the dock, and the trucks they'd passed in Gomba City. "We saw fires all the way up," he said.

"Dear God," said Thorson. He went over to a cabinet and pulled open the door, brought out a bottle of vodka, and poured some into his teacup.

"Mind if I have some of that?" said Beth.

Thorson pulled open a different cabinet and came out with two more teacups, handing one to Beth and one to Snow, then poured them each a cup, said "Skoal," and downed his own in a single shot. "They are sure to be coming through here this morning, I would guess," he said. "The new county administration. I have heard the coup is well executed, very surgical. Word by radio was that they 'executed' ninety last night. Traitors, of course."

"Ninety?" Snow was surprised.

"I suppose we will just keep on. There is ore to mine, correct? They will want to keep the mine going, one would think."

"There's a lot to mine. The government's gone for at least a few days–how are people reacting?"

"Those fires you saw, probably celebrating. But you know how celebrations can go. Sometimes it is happy fire from five miles off that crowns you."

The thought of happy fire and all that went with it, cane juice and revolutionary euphoria, gave Snow a sudden need to get to

Yasa's house. He imagined driving outside of Likepa toward the Guinea border, the rise of Goodhouse Hill. Suddenly he remembered he'd arranged for the trucker to meet him in Likepa, so they could drive the last ten clicks together.

The vodka burned in his stomach and seemed to spread into an acid-induced bellyache that made a beeline for that spot under his ribs.

"So you got that information we talked about?"

"One moment," he said, and went into the living room, opened a rolltop desk, and brought over a folded paper. "Here is the one. He is up at Nimba Road number four. Just one crossroad beyond."

"Got it."

"You tried to sell your house three years back?"

"Never tried to sell. I wanted Yasa to have it."

Beth looked at him in a queer way then, and he hoped she'd see his goodness in that, and part of him hoped she'd be just a little jealous.

"Let us pray they don't decide to kill white people around here. From what I understand, Likepa is for the coup," Thorson said. "Might not be a bad place for you. On the other hand, it could be worse."

"*I* ain't against the coup."

"Even if you can't tell what is better or worse?"

"Who can say about that? All depends which team you're on," said Snow, and with that, he figured he'd said enough. He shook Thorson's hand. His bony little fingers gripped like clothespins.

TRIAL BY ORDEAL

Out at the car, Snow slid behind the wheel and just sat there a minute, Beth climbing in on the passenger side. "Now what?" she said.

"I gotta go see a guy." He backed out, turning left up the gravel drive of Nimba Road and counted up four houses before he turned into the empty drive. "Why don't you come on in?"

Snow glanced back at the sleeping trio. They looked almost innocent save for the tattoos and earrings, the white hair and twenty-inch biceps. The two got out and walked up the front steps toward the house, where a light shone dimly around the edges of a thick curtain. Snow knocked three times hard and stood back to wait. Beth looked toward a narrow gap in the curtain, Snow staring at her wide eyes before he realized someone was looking out at them through the front window, drape held aside covertly. "Who is this guy?" she asked.

"Miner."

Her brown eyes shifted toward Snow, and he didn't know what he saw there–fear or anger or some look in between. But he had to believe she sensed something here, maybe even recognized the man peering past the drapes. The door swung open and there he stood dressed in overalls, dirt-dusted, ready to go to work. And the thing was, Snow knew the man. Not by name but by face. He'd worked for Thorson a long time, he was sure of that. He'd been to Goodhouse Creek once with a group of Dan elders, ate kola and drank palm wine with him on the porch with Yasa. Three years back. Haroun. They hadn't talked more than five minutes. Snow kept wondering what Haroun meant in Arabic, or whatever language it was borrowed from.

"Yay?" the man said, looking at the girl.

"Bethy, this here–" Snow paused, the gears grinding. "This here's Haroun Abudjah. I believe he's your father. You're Haroun Abudjah, ain't that right?"

The man nodded. "Abudjah, that is right. I am also running late for work."

She had his face, top to bottom.

"This here is your daughter, Elisabeth Farrah," Snow said.

"Yah, I heard you say. How have you been?"

Beth's face underwent something akin to spontaneous polymerization. She looked down even as she spoke. Her words seemed to come from nowhere and everywhere at the same time. "They told me you were dead."

"Your mother's family, yes. A man cannot worry over what is lost."

She kept looking down, like she was staring at the man's feet. Snow had never seen her do that. He wondered if she'd ever stop now. He wondered if she hadn't been doing it some other way all this time.

"Would you like coffee? I have some prepared."

"Sure," said Snow. "Love a cup."

Beth followed as if struck on the head.

Inside, the house was an exact replica of Thorson's, except three ebony-wood masks were lined up along a coffee table shoved against a concrete wall. The gray walls were exposed cinder block, gray, without images of Swedish tundra and Norski fjords. Two narrow masks hung there on concrete nails, one Senegalese by the look of it, the other Hausa.

Abudjah poured two half cups of coffee and left them on the counter. Snow slugged his back, hoping it would counteract Thorson's vodka. Beth held hers by the rim and sipped it off one side and stared at her father. The three stood there, mute. Snow kept thinking about something Beth had told him about traveling to London with her mother. They made only one trip there, by train, to stare silently at her grandmother and aunt over tea until her grandmother said to the girl, "Your father–your father must be very dark," between bites of tea cake and sips of Earl Grey. Her mother's family had known of her existence but not her race. Her mother had played her for shock value. A marker of the mother's independence, a black stone in a game of Go. On the ferry crossing from Dover, with the salt air in their faces and the Channel sweeping Beth's mind into the North Sea, her mother had turned and said, "Did you hear her, after all? 'Your father must be very dark.' Indeed! Now you see the people you spring from, my dear. Of course, there's no point in dwelling on such matters." She lit a cigarette. "They're rather bitches." Rather.

Snow had bad feelings rising in him, that somehow he'd done the same thing in reverse, that he had used her father against her. For his shock value. To knock a death ship off course. But somehow the familiarity of the man's face–Snow stared too now–maybe it went beyond the resemblance to Elisabeth. For one thing he wasn't dark at all; he looked half European. And the more Snow looked at him the more other faces came into his, a swirl of people, familiar and familial, and all at once Snow shot down the rest of the coffee and felt it scald his tonsils and burn down into his stomach. His mind tumbled. He shook his head unconsciously, and when next he looked at him he thought maybe Abudjah wasn't familiar at all, just some stranger he knew because he saw Beth's face in him, and her face was somehow stuck in with his own. The man came at him like that ink drawing Youth/Old Age where you blinked once and saw the craggy old woman, blinked again and saw the lithe beauty.

"You mind I ask where your mother's from?"

Abudjah looked grateful for something to draw him away from Beth's relentless stare. "She is from Freetown."

"Freetown? That right. What year you born?"

"I was born in 1930. Why do you come asking questions of me?"

Snow waved his hand: never mind, sorry, never mind. Had his father been to West Africa in '29? He looked at Elisabeth. "You want some time alone?"

"All right," she said.

"I really must be going soon," said Abudjah.

"It won't take long," she said.

Snow went outside and stood on the concrete step, listening to the halting murmur of their voices, thinking she was almost certainly questioning him, like why did you leave us? Why did you fuck my mother and leave us? He was glad he couldn't make out the words, and wished to hell he'd never come here. He went back to the car and sat behind the wheel, watching the three sleeping in back, their heads tilted and their mouths open. Kairos lay like a snow-haired ghost with his head against the window. Bracelin slept with his arms crossed. Maciel fought a continual battle. His head bobbed around in a state of semi-sleep, reaching the end of its range only to bound back up and shift again in an endless unconscious attempt to find rest.

And rest lay in balance.

When Beth came back out, the old man was right behind her, turning to lock his door and striding off in his miner's covies with his lunch bucket and his hard hat with the lamp attached. He moved toward the mine without once looking at her. She came to the car and pulled open the door, got in and started rolling a cigarette. "Some things are better left undone," she said, staring mutely forward as she licked the paper and held the smoke lightly in her fingertips. "The worst of it is you, Harold. I have this feeling you did it for your own pervy reasons."

Snow gripped the wheel. She flicked at a lighter over and over to try to light her smoke, but got only sparks, no flame. She held her head down, leaning forward, her body bouncing with the road under their tires, and Snow wished he could stop looking over at her. He drove with only one hand on the wheel, could tell she wanted out, to jump and flee the car. Sea-foam, she'd done nothing but carve sea-foam, just like him. Salt water parted in front of you and closed off behind.

"I thought you'd want to see your father," he finally said.

She turned to him. "You really are off on your own planet."

His nostrils flared and started in to burn. He looked forward, both hands on the wheel, and steered along a lumpy section of road. He kept seeing the face of Abudjah. He looked at her face and saw his father there too. Snow rubbed his own face, felt the friction of his clammy hand burn his nose and cheeks. "Family's important," he heard himself saying. "I know 'cause I ain't got one. I think it's best to make peace with people while you can."

"You haven't any idea what he tried to do to me."

Well, shit, when she put it that way Snow couldn't help but imagine the most heinous things. Somewhere inside it titillated him too. He chided himself. What was missing in him? He wanted to know. He thought maybe he was incapable of feeling. He felt consumed by scar tissue sometimes, or like his nerve endings were all burned up and curled like the delicate trailing of ash at the end of a candlewick.

"You know what they do to girls around here when they're of age, don't you?"

So it was that. They'd cut her. She'd been cut and cleansed in a twisted-up way. Scoured out. Sewn up. Snow thought he might puke. He could see it, the scraping, the scars left behind there, and all so a woman would not want to fuck. The ultimate in use, a man's use, saying your pleasure don't matter. For all he loved this place, he hated this about it. He could think of Beth in no way now, no way but there, hurt and small and innocent, and for the first time since he'd known her, he saw her as a little girl.

She peered at him with her head cast down, looking up under her brows. "They woke me up and told me to come with them. We lived on Garrison Street. We walked right by that house in Freetown. My father was no bloody tribesman. He was a city boy."

Snow wanted to feel it, feel himself in the legs of her girlhood, vibrating against the back bench seat of her father's car. Surely it had meaning inside him. In his mind he tried to put himself there. He imagined what she would have seen. He wanted to feel it, feel something besides himself. She rode quietly in the back of that car, she was just a girl after all, stared ahead and saw the sign in the headlights: Mile 91, didn't recognize the clan village, so far removed from their city lives, from her English mother and their house on Garrison Street. But the girl knew what it meant, being there. Her father and her uncle whispered at her in the darkness, to remain calm, saying it was best, that it was said, that it was more ancient than Allah.

And she said *but Daddy, we aren't even Mende.*

They pulled into the village. Stepped past roundhouses. *Stepped past roundhouses.* To the only angular concrete construction in the small cluster. *And there: the darkness of the enclosure, the lights from yellow lanterns in the living area, weak and pitched downward by shades and flickering in a way that caused everybody to bounce and quiver. The room had a raised wooden floor that shook when you walked on it, and a medical table bought used from the Connaught hospital in Freetown. Iron stirrups swung out from the table's end and glowed in the soft light. Rusted so completely over, their surface had the lustrous look of fur.*

She had known girls who ran from these rituals rather than be cut, to be scraped out and scarred forever, who fled into the mountains and were tracked and caught and returned and "cleansed" anyway. If she could get to her mother, she thought. If she could find her way back to the city. Beneath a yellow light, one man sat, a man in a physician's surgical mask, off-white—they took her hand as if to shake it, then pulled her toward the table. No conscious decision, nothing realized but simply acted on: she ran. Shook their hands free and ran directly through the stunned faces of elders—

Their arms flailed, but she was beyond their reach and gone into the night. She ran and fell and ran, and hit a tree with her right shoulder, and slipped on something soft and fell to her bottom, sliding down a muddy embankment toward a river. She had kept moving during the first part of that night, when she could still see by the moon filtering down through the canopy, and hear the voices back behind her calling *Elisabeth! Elisaaaaaaabeth!* When the moon glow finally faded, leaving only blackness, she backed herself into an ancient teak tree, cleared away spiderwebs and spiders, and staked her ground, huddled inside the massive arched roots. In the deep night, she could not adjust her eyes no matter how she blinked and tried to accommodate the complete lack of light. Unable to move, she cowered and cried in a hole, the iron-red ground all around her.

Now through the thumps and pits in the road toward Likepa, Snow couldn't keep from looking over at her. In her round face he could feel how alone she was. He couldn't see her now without seeing the little girl. Feeling the bench seat beneath her legs. As the sun rose over the Nimba Mountains east, the Land Cruiser rocked through the high country, the roads empty of car traffic, though it still took most of the next day to reach Likepa, requiring slow navigation and good luck on the log bridges.

In Likepa, the road through the village narrowed to a single track, and Snow stopped and climbed out before a woman selling greens and yams, cassava and cracked wheat and hot peppers, bought two bags of food and climbed back behind the wheel. He put the groceries on the front floorboard and waited for the driver coming up from Monrovia. His eyes darted to the rear- and side-view mirrors, his fingers tapping on the wheel. Beth feigned sleep with her head on the window. Snow rested his hands in the ten and two position.

"Wonder when the rains are coming," he said. "People just get up-frigging-tight around here until the rain starts—eases everybody's minds. Old days we used to serve cane juice at the house and the elders would come for twenty miles and sit on my porch and drink my booze and eat kola just to get through it."

But maybe that wasn't where he'd seen Abudjah. Maybe that wasn't why his face seemed familiar. Beth leaned forward, put a cigarette in her mouth, and cupped her hands around it, flicking her lighter.

"You and your fucking cigarettes," said Bracelin. "Put it out."

Beth got out of the car and leaned against the door smoking, staring down at the ground. While they waited, a crowd gathered amid some roundhouses just off the main road through town, an open area that seemed like some kind of town square. A girl of maybe seventeen, pretty and dignified and tall, stood in colorful head wrap and cotton dress, tight to her hips. A raggedy old guy, two feet shorter than her, stood in front of a clay pot containing hot coals, shoving a machete down into the hot coals, working it in and out and mixing the coals with the blade. He wore a peacoat and shorts and went barefoot despite a stocking cap on his head.

Snow knew what it was: a trial by ordeal, the small man the "healer." Beth knew what it was too. "Oh, what a crock of shit," she said, from outside the open window. "These people need a bloody fucking lobotomy."

The healer was there to divine truth. This particular healer had a five-day beard–gray, like silver frosting spread lightly and evenly over his face. He kept mixing the coals using the machete, not looking at the young woman. She stood some twenty feet away. Beth couldn't take her eyes off her: she was tall, angular, slumping, turned half away from the healer, her eyes and mouth tight and worried. The healer stood up and moved to a bucket of fresh water and herbs–a kind of spiritual soup–and shoved the blade in, the hissing of steam rising up around his face. He caught the girl's gaze and held it, his eyes someplace else. She held out her hand to him, and the healer pressed the machete to the back of the girl's hand, held her tightly when she tried to pull away. The healer locked on her gaze, held her in place as much with his eyes as his grip.

Beth threw her smoke to the ground, crushed it out with the

heel of her boot, and took off walking toward the circle. "I wouldn't go there, Bethy!" Snow called, but her attention was fixed on the healer as he pulled the blade away, looked at the girl's skin, looked at her eyes. The healer stood back, glared at her. Beth was making tracks toward them. Then Maciel was out of the car too, going after her. A godawful superstition, Snow thought, right up there with throwing witches into a river to see if they'd float, right up there with cutting little girls to cleanse their sex for some future man bound by virginal need. Never mind a woman might know how to fucking swim, never mind a woman might want her own pleasure in life. Never mind that the skin can't withstand the coals and the herbs and the hot blade of the machete. Daddy gods pissed him off.

"I once heard the best healers didn't just look for burned skin, but a flinching heart," he said.

"It's still some creepy-ass shit," said Kairos.

"Brace, go get them, goddamnit."

"Fuck her, you get 'em. What the hell I care she gets her hand chopped off."

Beth was just making the edge of the crowd, turning her shoulder sideways to squeeze past only to find Maciel there behind her, his hand on her hand. "I said don't touch me!" she said, shaking her hand free, but then the kid angled around in front of her, holding her back with every bit the intensity of the healer.

"Don't get involved."

"Bit tardy on that one."

Snow came up just as she slipped the kid, his hands around her waist. Then Snow moved in front of her, stretching his arms to corral them back toward the car. "Sorry for the interruption, folks!" said Snow to the crowd, then eyed Beth.

The three stood on the outside of the circle then, as the old healer called out "Innocent!" and the crowd suppressed a little shout of joy, quickly falling into a secret murmur, after which the girl's friends came to her, looked at her hand intently, and spirited her away for treatment. Beth's shoulders relaxed. She shook them free and marched back toward the Land Cruiser, where she sat down abruptly on the ground and leaned back against the front tire. She held her head in her hands, elbows on her knees.

Snow saw a local man staring at Beth like she was some kind of an alien. "What that girl on trial for?" Snow asked.

"She accused adultery," said the local. "She go with married man. What trouble with that one?" He pointed at Beth.

Beth muttered and threw stones across the open area, then turned to climb back into the Land Cruiser. "Men really should be killed."

"She's all right," said Snow, but the local man seemed unconvinced.

"She got the *juju* on her, maybe."

Snow decided it might be best to wait on the outside of town to the east, where they parked in the shade for thirty minutes before a flatbed Toyota pickup four-by-four came chugging around the corner from the western road, carrying six 55-gallon drums of gasoline lashed to the back bed. At least now they'd be able to get back down the mountain to Monrovia. "I hope nothing's happened to the ship with all this coup business," he said. "You know we can't expect anything."

"Great, Snow," said Bracelin. "You're on the job, that's for fucking sure."

"You can expect madness, is what you can expect," said Kairos.

Snow started the Land Cruiser, and with an easy wave of his hand, as if nothing at all had happened there, he lurched onto the red-dirt road, powering north in four-wheel-drive low, the big engine groaning as it bore them along a road marked by rivulet scars that hadn't seen water for months.

•

They drove slowly toward a wood-and-wire automobile gate, swung open and half broken. When Snow saw the broken gate, he said, "Tolbert's people," and turned in quickly, waving the truck to follow. There they came to a two-story house, with a shuttered balcony on the top floor and a wide porch stretching across the bottom. It looked old and broken, several shutters hanging from a single hinge, and the corrugated roof peeled back where winds had caught it.

"Ah, Jesus," said Snow, his voice cracking as he pulled forward. "What the hell's happened here?"

Both vehicles swung up around to the front of the house and parked, the truck bearing the fuel drums pulling up behind. The driver stepped out and up to Snow, shaking his head, laughing. "Yu bra elephant!" He laughed with nervous energy. "I thought I no make Gomba City, forget here! You hear what happen night last? They kill go'ment! They cut Bill Tolbert gut out. All the way up, people go mad, say they overthrow Americos. *Overthrow True Whig Party! Kill the Americos!*"

It meant kill the Americo-Liberians, but somehow Snow felt it sounded a little too close to killing him. He immediately started pulling out money, specifically American dollars in tens and twenties. "This here's the real deal for your time," he said, snapping a twenty-dollar bill in the driver's hand.

The guy took the cash and looked at one corner of the house, where a fire scar licked out the window like a giant tongue of black, as if someone had built a campfire in the living room. "Dat go'ment right there. Dat Bill Tolbert. Bill Tolbert gutless!"

More ways than one, Snow thought.

The drums served a dual purpose: fuel for the Land Cruiser on the return trip to Monrovia and bribe materials for same. But the number of possible problems had skyrocketed. Snow had seen it before. A top-down coup in a precarious state brought out the clan boundaries. In a normal day you might pass through fifteen clan villages, all wanting to know who you were and why you were here before they'd let you pass–for a fee. It was like hoofing it through gang turf in the barrio.

Snow promised the cabbie food and drink and a bonus if he'd stay over. Then he leaned toward Maciel. "I want him to lead our butts outa here," he said in a whisper, then spoke up to the cabbie. "If we go somewhere else, we can negotiate the fee then, how's that?"

"Well, that sound okay," said the driver, looking up at the afternoon light. "Lest now, anyways. I go stay."

Bracelin frowned. "Which is it? Go or stay?"

"Go stay," said the driver, nodding to settle the matter.

Bracelin's mouth curled in disgust, and he looked around as if for help. "Don't fuck with me, bub, or I'll cut your black heart out."

The driver flinched and stepped backward. He looked over at Snow with a stark-eyed fear fluttering over his face, like he knew of such things, and didn't take such threats casually at all, certainly not as casually as Bracelin had offered it.

"You go fuck you," he said. "Get him de way away from me," he said to Snow.

"Charlie," said Snow. "Don't go threatening things like that. Not here."

"No fucking threat, *promise*!" Bracelin boomed, barking at the driver, who flinched as Bracelin managed to spit all over the place.

"Just leave him alone!"

"Suck my pole, old man," said Bracelin.

"He means he *will* stay!"

"Then why don't he just say so?"

"What the fuck you on?"

"Not enough of anything, too much of the stuff that don't help," Bracelin said.

"You look cranky to me. You got Leeds brewing up crank for you?"

Bracelin grinned. "He couldn't make speed if his life depended on it. Lisa got me some bennies in PC. Flash from the past, good old cross tops."

"That's just great, Brace. And you say *my* mind's not in it."

As they turned, two young men stepped from the house and nodded toward Snow, while Bracelin reached inside his pants for whatever small weapon he carried there.

"Them are Yasa's cousins," Snow said, waving Bracelin off. "You guard house? Where go Yasa and family?"

"They go refugee Bo Waterside. Soldiers come take house."

"How long?"

"Three months. Yesterday soldiers run back to Monro. We hear some bad shit happen there."

Snow turned a circle and let out a grunt that sounded like he was passing a kidney stone. "Three months! Son of a bitch. She go okay you hear?"

"No hear nothing," said the first cousin. "Go'ment not like this area much. Don't know what it be now."

Both young men had fetishes around their necks—monkey-figure talismans—and one wore a crucifix underneath the wooden charm. Maciel was staring at them: the monkey with its mouth wide, threatening; the Christ figure, neck tilted in crucified death. An unsettled sensation ran through Snow. Then the kid reached into his pants pocket and came up with a set of black rosary beads and started playing with them in his fingers. He could just imagine the kid's grandmother that way, beads wrapped around her wrist as she worked her way through the rosary saying all those Our Fathers and Hail Marys until it sounded like an ancient chant.

They were all just rituals, he thought, rainforest rituals, idols dangling from leather necklaces, the beads of ancestral spirits, forces in the world with gods to match. The kid reached out and handed the rosary to one of the cousins. He took it, lifted his chin to acknowledge the gift, and stuffed it into his pocket.

Up-country Liberia had a tense stillness about it—until they all took the seven dilapidated steps into the house. As they did, Kairos tapped Maciel on the arm, lifted his chin to him. "You don't give up your God here, son," he said. "Keep your head."

Maciel gave a little nod, smiling up at the taller Kairos. "Don't worry about me. I'll be okay."

Inside, the part of the house that wasn't burned made Snow nearly break down and fall to his knees. A broken vision of his past, a step backward in time, half burned by war and abandoned by people.

"No go live here, people say it cursed," said one of the guards.

"It is cursed," Snow said, feeling his eyeballs burn. "And I cursed it."

He looked around, waiting for someone to burst from the bush and attack them, and already he was looking for escape routes. Then he took the crew through the grand entrance like a defeated tour guide. A wood-constructed house, it was built from red ironwood and teak. Built solid, but a wooden castle nonetheless. The house both inside and out showed the effects of humidity and weathering, inside paint peeling, the smells of mildew and mold mixing with the burnt-out smell of old fire. The staircase led upward dead center, and on both sides the foyer opened to sitting rooms, and behind on the left, the kitchen, and to the right a room with empty bookshelves and a pile of a hundred or more African masks jumbled about the center of the room. "I used to have them hanging on the walls," Snow said.

He had one for every conceivable ritual. He even had a World War I gas mask. Maciel moved over and put on a dark sliver-eyed mask of polished ebony wood that glistened and smelled of the forest. "Dan masks," Snow said. "That one there represents female fertility."

Snow ran his fingers over the burnished wood—hard black and gemlike to the touch. Maciel held it up to his face again and moved slowly, turning his face with an unreal, dreamy silence. The boy guards came into the room then, pausing to look at the kid wearing the mask.

Beth frowned, watching him. "That's mad," she said. "Stop."

Maciel put the mask back down on the pile and picked up another one.

This one had leather straps across the back and wide-open eyes. It represented initiation into manhood and the cult of a warrior god.

"These Dan masks aren't just about hiding yourself, they're considered like gods themselves, you know, and some of them tell the history of the village, and some you gotta consult before you do anything important," Snow said. "Like them oracles in ancient Greece."

The guards lifted their brows and fondled their necklaces, then marched on through the house to the back, where they started drinking from a wood pitcher without benefit of glasses.

Kairos put a different mask on, one with a tied leather chin strap. "Hmmm." Then he took it off and frowned at the mask, tossing it back onto the pile looking disgusted with himself. "That's some sick paganism," he said.

"You can't judge these people," said Snow. "Not from your world. Besides, I don't see how all that Father, Son, Holy Ghost stuff is any different."

"I just thought of something," Kairos said, staring at the pile of masks. "These people sold my ancestors into slavery."

"Oh, Christ, not this again. So fucking what?" Bracelin said. "We all got pain. My ancestors were sold into slavery by the fucking Romans."

"Just pointing it out—makes you think," said Kairos. "How much family history floats in our veins, you know?"

"I've thought a lot about that too," said Maciel.

"So point it out, but what are you complaining about?" Bracelin said. "Let's face facts. Slavery's the best thing ever happened to you. Weren't for your ancestors takin' it up the ass, you'd be living in some West African hellhole with plates in your lips."

"That's one way to think about it. Other way is maybe I could use a little plate in my lips."

"Yeah? What the fuck *for*?"

Kairos paused, just stared Bracelin in the face. "The Lord's work is a mystery, Charles. You can't tell how the flesh might respond to such manipulation."

"I can bet it fucking hurts," said Snow. "You'd know about that, right, Georgie?"

"In a weird way, it feels good. You go beyond pain and then nothing can hurt you."

"You're a fucking perv," said Bracelin.

They stepped out the rear, through wooden French-style doors made from ironwood, to the torn and battered screened porch with a swinging door dead center that led down stairs to a series of wooden terraces that overlooked the creek bed. The boys were tipping up the wood pitcher and grinning wildly. "This is not good cane juice," they said, and laughed.

"See that there?" said Snow. "On the other bank of that creek is Guinea. Nothing between you and freedom but puff adders and black mambas!'"

Truth was, as Churchill and Mr. Johnson had suggested, the house was built precisely for its proximity to the border. In the middle of up-country forestland, any need to flee offered two countries within twenty miles.

"How about we think about getting out of here," said Maciel.

"Used to be I had plans for this house," said Snow, glancing over at Beth and feeling more morose than ever. He didn't much care for the feeling. He wished Maciel would stop looking at him.

Beth looked away, toward the drinking guards, and shook her head—she saw oppression in every glance, he thought, and it occurred to him that she lived on a different plane from all of them, where words were not only unnecessary but an outright misdirection of truth. Nothing could express her connection to this place.

Just then a white face stepped up the creek trail, followed by a dozen Africans, all wearing jungle fatigues and looking well-funded if not well-fed. "Looking for the Snowman!" called the white man.

"That Buck the Fuck?" Snow called back.

The soldiers following Buck Favor eyed the scene warily, staring toward the boy caretakers, who traded sensible if semi-drunken looks, realizing they were outgunned. These were Buck Favor's own trained soldiers, who had traded tribal loyalties for more lucrative ones. They scanned the perimeter with discipline, wearing tiger suits and holding their Kalashnikovs at the ready.

Favor climbed the last few steps up from the stream and reached out to shake hands vigorously. Somehow they felt like the best of old friends now. It was like hearing the "Star-Spangled Banner" at home and finding it the most awkward national anthem on the planet. But hear it on a foreign shore—by God you couldn't hold the shivers back.

"Let's do this fast, I got a rendezvous down the mountain in four hours," Favor said.

"You hear what happened to Tolbert?" Snow said.

"We just crossed overland, haven't heard anything."

"They assassinated him last night. We saw fires all the way up the Ganta Road coming here. Couldn't tell what they were about. Now we hear the army's taken over."

"I guess it was coming," said Favor. "You're getting out just in time."

Snow glanced back into the house to where Bracelin had gone. He stepped left and saw through a dirty window into the library, and through the front room and out an equally dirty front window to where Bracelin was carrying the nylon knapsack up the front steps. As he hit the porch, he pulled from the pack a semi-automatic handgun, flat black, and a Tyvek envelope. He pulled the slide back to cock it, then stuffed it into his jeans. Maciel saw it all too, looking like he was about ready to flee into the woods and never come out again. Buck Favor—he wore fatigues and carried a short-barreled machine gun with a looping wire stock.

"Let's get down to business," said Favor.

In a strange way, Snow wished business could wait. He somehow wanted to pretend he'd managed some exotic post-colonial retirement, that his screened porch in the midst of mountain-jungle Liberia was actually safe. But this would never happen, and he motioned Buck Favor through the house toward Bracelin on the other side. Favor paused long enough to bark at his troops in Krio to get their black asses around the house and not track mud inside—what'd they think this was, some mud-floor shanty in Salone?

His troops eyed him oddly, blinking at the insult, as the boy caretakers followed them around the side of the house to the front.

Snow stood in the back room, waiting for the kids to follow, then saw that one of Favor's men had stayed behind and moved up to Maciel like he might take out his frustration toward Buck Favor on the kid personally, if only because he was this innocuous-looking white male maybe, or perhaps because he was standing with Beth. Ever since that mefloquine horror flick, Snow thought, he'd shoved himself right up to the edge of it, and Maciel had a hair trigger now. The soldier smiled and threw a quick glance toward Favor, who marched through the mask room and out the front door to where Bracelin stood with the knapsack.

"That de cane juice?" the soldier pointed at the wood pitcher sitting on a little end table.

"That's what the other guy said," Maciel told him.

The guy picked it up, sniffed it and recoiled slightly, then tasted. "Bad," he said, shaking his head. Then he tasted some more. Sweat glistened off his face. "Good cane juice get you going," he said, gazing at Beth. "Favor no go live tomorrow." He pulled a small bag out of his pocket and produced a kola nut.

"Why is that?" Beth asked.

" 'Cause I go kill him." He popped a pod into his mouth and chewed, then put the rest back in the pouch. "I kid," he said, and winked unconvincingly.

Snow wasn't sure if he meant he was kidding or if he was a kid, a child.

In the living room, Buck Favor took possession of the Tyvek envelope full of cash and in exchange gave Snow a dark-blue athletic bag. Snow shook his hand, firm, and they nodded like they might actually miss each other. Then Favor struck out, down the drive and out across the road, climbed a red embankment, and disappeared overland with the mercenaries close behind. The mercenaries had somehow induced the two boys to join them, perhaps for promise of better weapons, and together they angled up the dirt road and followed Favor off into the bush like a trail of army ants.

"We'll stay the night here," Snow said. "Go down-mountain in the morning." He stepped through the living room, surveying the house. Kairos came up alongside him and together they walked to the back screened porch. "You get the feeling you're being watched?" Kairos asked.

Beth took another shot of cane juice. "Try a nip, that feeling goes."

"Not sure I want it to go. You catch my meaning?"

"Of course. Two nips, that feeling goes as well."

Kairos reached over for the pitcher, took a shot, and nearly lost his breath. "Holy firewater," he said. He caught his breath and tried another. "Savages."

Beth blinked her eyes rapidly, as if gnats had flown into them. "We have to get the hell out of here."

"We will," said Snow. "But tomorrow. I'm not going to try traveling down-mountain at night. It's too risky."

"Why?" said Maciel. "People are sleeping; it seems riskier in the day."

"Because the people we got to worry about work at night."

Beth looked straight at Snow and now he saw himself reflected in her eyes, like he was the ultimate shadowy kind of evil, like he'd manipulated this whole thing from start to finish. He frightened her, and her fear knifed at him. He smiled gently, and reached out a hand, and just as he touched her shoulder she turned and walked down the wooden steps to the back path, moving slowly at first until she hit the trail, where her pace quickened.

"Where are you going?" the kid called.

"You better go get her," Snow said. "I would, but I'm afraid she'd outpace me even on a good day, and I ain't having a good day."

"Beth!" The kid called after her, but his words seemed to drive straight down into her feet like fuel, and her steps grew faster. Then she was running, her work boots hitting red dirt methodically down the natural staircase to the streambed, sprinting now, strong-legged, like she knew where she was going, down the hill from where Favor had come. She could cross the river and be in Guinea and just keep going, without a pause or a glance back. She stepped into a wet spot on the creek's edge, sinking to mid calf in river mud. Only after the kid caught up to her did Snow relax some, even as he saw them start back toward the house, holding each other close through a flurry of mosquitoes.

On the porch, Kairos reached for the wooden jug and tipped it up to his lips. "It grows on you after a couple," he said. "I think I'm gonna pass out, bos'n."

"Me too," said Snow, watching the kids make their way up the earthen path, staring Snow's way, like they thought he was as much the enemy as the night forest, like even if they were coming back, it was no bargain.

FLINCHING HEART

When Snow heard the fate of William Tolbert, erstwhile president of the Republic of Liberia, he couldn't keep from imagining how it would feel to have your guts pulled out. He imagined a sharp bowel pain like a knife in the lower abdomen, and then the emptying. He couldn't get that kamikaze pilot out of his mind either, how he'd broken up as he hit the ship's edge, his bowels spilling out, the smell of barbecued flesh like funeral day in India. An old Hindu woman once told him of the irony that weighed on cremation: that first a body smelled bad as it decayed but then, once set atop the coals along the holy river for a slow burn, it smelled good, like barbecue that would go unconsumed except by fire itself.

After the others had gone to sleep, curling in their clothes on the high ground, incapacitated by cane juice cocktails, Snow swore he heard the upstairs bed doing the fuck squeak. He couldn't not see them in his mind, how it would look. On the main floor he opened the warped wooden door that hung askew on its hinges, descended the basement stairs to the soft red earth below, pointed his flashlight toward the northeast corner, and saw two giant millipedes engaged in their curling writhing sex. They were each about eight inches long and big around as nickels. Snow nudged them aside with the muzzle of his flashlight, but in their passion they barely noticed. Then he dug in the soft red earth until he came to the bag he'd buried three years before.

Sweating, his gut feeling like he'd swallowed a sack of diamonds rather than dug them up, Snow sat breathing the dank air under the house and opened the nylon bag to slip his fingers into the raw ragged stones. Almost a quarter million on the wholesale market, he figured. Along with Favor's bag he had twice that. If Churchill really and truly fucked them over, he'd at least have something—all he'd have to do is figure a way to keep Bracelin from demanding the whole thing.

He climbed out of the basement to the first floor, pushed through the door, and there a flashlight shone on his face an instant, then pointed down to reveal the black outline of Bracelin, wearing only his boxer shorts, his knife at the ready and the flashlight showing his white hairy legs. "What you doing down there?" he asked, flicking the light at the door.

"Just getting these," Snow said, holding up the bag. But he was thinking about Yasa, the taste of her skin, the memory of it glistening beneath his white hand. "I'm thinking I need to go to Bo Waterside."

"Oh, fuck that, Snow. Don't go all fucking sentimental on me now. You leave them for three-year stretches, shit's bound to happen."

"Yasa was always special. I built her this house. She's family."

"I doubt anybody ever said you *had* to leave them here."

"This was her home. She loved this house. Having me here made it harder on her. That's why I left."

"Anybody calls this place home deserves what they get."

Snow ignored this too, as if anybody had a goddamned choice of where they were born and where they called home. It just happened; home just happened to you. If you were lucky. "If we left now we could make Bo Waterside and still have time to get to the ship before our customers have a shit fit."

"You fucking with me?" Bracelin asked, with suspicion in his voice.

"I ain't fucking with anybody. I ain't got the energy to fuck with anybody. I just need to find Yasa."

"Yasa? You're feeling bad because of *Yasa*? You're feeling bad 'cause of this one." Bracelin nodded his head upstairs. "I heard them up there. He's dicking her right now. Fuck her, forget her."

"That's what I was trying to do."

"Oh, yeah, I know. You're in fucking *love.* Love never did much for me."

"Just let it be. Keep our eye on the ball."

"Keeping our eye on the ball means traveling light and alone, and you got all these goddamned side treks lined up. And why? 'Cause of women. Women are your fucking undoing, Snow."

Snow leaned toward Bracelin. He wanted to explain to him. Why in hell he wanted to explain to Bracelin was beyond him, and he almost whispered it. "The thing is–her old man. I kept looking at him, thinking if maybe I hadn't seen him somewhere. Maybe he used to come out to the house with some locals. But then I kept looking at him and damned if he didn't start looking like *my* old man. But he looked just like Beth, just the spittin' image. I don't know now. Every time I think of him he changes in my mind. For all I know, my mind just conjured it."

"Yeah," Bracelin said, nodding in a rare moment of compassion.

"It's almost like you're fucking out of your mind. Who knows and who cares if he looks like your old man?"

Snow stared at the shadow of the door, slashing across the broken room where you could look up through the burned half of a roof and see the canopy and even a star if you moved around enough. "Time was, I just figured I'd go to hell."

"*Go* to hell? You're *in* hell. Now we gotta figure our way out, and it don't involve Bo Waterside. I say we go straight to Monro at first light and pay off militias as much as we have to, and we get our sweet asses out of country. You got what, an extra half mil in rocks? We got five times that on the ship, Snow. We can still pull this off, but you gotta think real."

When Snow thought real he kept seeing that figure talking to Maciel in the pipeline. He knew how Beth looked in covies and a work vest now. With time and distance from the ship, his mind felt clearer, and he just didn't think it was her. He kept seeing that reflection of the Aussie in the mirror at the Rojo and then his broad Oz accent in the Snap Trap, and that neck, those god-awful trapezius muscles as he moved away toward the head. And then Maciel following. Snow knew he ought to tell Bracelin what he thought he saw in the pipeline. He wondered if he could tell him without getting the kid killed. He kept thinking how this deal—his deal—might just manage to get a whole lot of people killed.

"Listen. Brace. I think we might have a security problem."

Bracelin stared straight ahead and worked his lips in a bitter way like he'd just eaten kola. "What kind of security problem?"

"I don't know yet. I saw a guy at the Rojo and then in the Snap Trap. Same guy, I'm sure of it. I've put my skull around it every which way and I just can't imagine it being a coincidence."

"What'd he look like?"

"Aussie. Five-ten. Two hundred pounds, wrestler build. Brown hair cut short. His dress was different. PC he looked like a sailor, Freetown he looked like a merc."

"You see him in Monro?"

"No." Snow left out what he thought about the kid, and about the pipeline. He didn't need Bracelin going off on the kid. He couldn't stomach the thought.

"You think he's got something to do with this Churchill cat?"

"I don't know. If I had to guess I'd say private security. Could work for Petrochem. Outfits specialize in the maritime angle; could be that."

"Well, we gotta find out. We can't just cower from it, Snow. We'll head down-mountain first light."

"Okay." Snow rolled his neck around as if to work out a kink.

"Why the hell didn't you tell me this sooner?"

"I wasn't sure. I don't know. That fever, fucked with my head."

"You got a boatload fucking with your head, Snow." Bracelin stood tall and scanned around. "Goddamned fucking place gives me the creeps. Whatever else happens, you better not ever let any of them tribesmen get ahold of me, or I swear I'll get my revenge on the lot of you. To your dying day, Snow, I'll haunt your ass from the spirit world."

Snow didn't believe in the spirit world, but somehow like old Joaquin he feared it, feared he might be wrong about it after all. Back on the second story he heard only snoring now–Kairos, he thought–but pausing at the door to the kids' room, half opened to allow a little air movement through the house, he saw them lying together. He stepped toward the far bedroom, the one he'd once shared with Yasa, using a penlight to find the backpack, too paranoid to use anything bigger in case somebody was watching the house.

Jesus, he hated thinking somebody was watching the house.

He imagined rousting everybody and getting their asses safely down the mountain and back aboard ship, but he thought they'd do better in daylight–not even whacked-out revolutionaries were as far gone first thing in the morning. He lay on the bed for a half hour listening to the night, and somewhere in all of it, like a miracle, he slept, dreamed he had a regular family and lived in the mountains, kiddos running around like muskrats, getting into everything, and laughing.

Sometime beyond midnight Snow awakened to the sound of rain slapping on the corrugated metal roof, and the moisture of rain over his arms as the entire house came alive in wetness. He turned over on the bed, still wearing his clothes. The room was too dark to make out anything, no moonlight or starlight to give even a haze of gray outline. Absent vision, he came to sound: the drumming of rain, the rattle of wind on the window shutters across the house's front balcony, the humming trickle of water feeding down toward the St. Paul River in Bong county, the rhythm of her breath, slow and even next to him, drifting toward dreams. But she wasn't next to him, she was sleeping with the kid now. But he could smell: her skin, her hair, her breath. He shook his head, tried to gain his bearings.

He climbed out of bed, clicked on a flashlight, and shined it briefly through the open door to his room, and then down the hallway. Stepping down the main stairs, he scanned left into the front room where water was dripping along a broken ragged line of the roof, and the wind blew into the house and made the loose boards overhead creak. And there, in the front room, just out of the rain, sat a man in a wicker chair.

Snow stopped cold, his limbs heavy. He felt in his pants for his knife and pulled it out, ready to flick it open if he had to. The man sat upright, fully clothed in a plain gray shirt, short-sleeved, and loose slacks–the driver of the truck. "Whatcha doing there?" Snow asked.

The man didn't answer. He was wearing a mask. In the bounced light of the broad flashlight beam, Snow saw his eyes move behind the dark holes of the ebony wood, wide and open, mouth a round hole. The driver sat with his arms on the armrests of an overstuffed chair. He waited there as if waiting for Snow to move, and Snow felt a sudden need to pee. He went down and out the back door with the hair on his neck itching. He stepped down the rickety wooden steps to the forest path behind. He listened to the beating of rainfall on the metal roof behind and added his own water to the downpour of the forest.

When he went back inside, the man was gone, the chair empty. Snow blinked and rubbed his eyes like he might come into focus and reappear. Snow felt like somebody or something was curling around his feet. He shined his light down, but there was nothing, not a snake as he suspected, not even a bug. He ran his flashlight around the room, then out the back. Still nothing. Snow climbed the stairs as quietly as he could. In the big bedroom up front, he looked through the window to the balcony. Then came the sudden eruption of the truck outside–the flatbed, he thought, turning over and over and finally starting. The beam from the headlights disturbed no sleep but crept out, slowly in the rain, onto the river road.

Snow had no memory of lying back down; his entire body simply gave in to the enormous fatigue, and when he next awakened it was not to rain but to its absence. Vague drippings, then silence. Then silence shattered: the sudden rise of fighting as it rolled down the mountainside and echoed along the banks of the creek. Cries came on the heels of gunfire, bursts terrific and sudden and short-lived, and then the inexplicable sound of hysteria, of laughter rocking the forest.

The crew gathered in the main foyer, flashlights bouncing off the buckled floorboards of a rain-rotted house, careful not to shine in faces, leaving eyes peering out from the shadows of cheekbones. The sounds and shouts from outside came again, the smatter of automatic weapons, and instinctively the flashlights flicked off. Snow popped his own light on for just an instant and checked the drive, where he saw that the truck was gone. He'd not been hearing things, at any rate.

"Any idea who they are?" Kairos said.

"Nope."

"We have any weapons?" Kairos's mind was kicking into a different mode. A resignation to violence, maybe. He'd been here before, in the jungle at night, facing battle.

"I got a 9 mm semi-auto," said Bracelin.

"Just stay calm, gents. The two of you, no jumping the gun–I mean it. They're gonna be way more armed than we are."

Snow stood watching from the porch as they all reflexively followed him, milled their way as a group to the exterior, which had cooled in the night, and now in the rainless dark all five could hear the bluntness of hand-to-hand fighting, then again the cries, the horrible sounds of pain and desire and hatred all mixing in a mass.

"Bloody shite," said Beth. "Let's get out of here."

"Wait–*wait,*" said Snow.

They waited, in the same way one rides out an electrical storm while exposed to the elements: counting time between flashes and sounds. Estimating distance, flicking a light to give an image of the driveway before the forest swallowed the afterglow and left nothing.

"A click southeast, maybe two," Kairos said.

Snow flicked his light into the forest, then off again. "Wish them two boys hadn't joined up with Favor."

"Where's our driver?" Bracelin asked.

"He run out in the middle of the night," Snow said. "He took our extra gas, or most of it."

Flick. Snow saw Kairos grip a blade in his cupped right hand, running back up behind his wrist. Snow felt a simmering in his chest and his eyes fought to adjust to the darkness, to find a patch of sky with at least a few stars.

"Should we try in the Land Cruiser?" Bracelin asked.

"I ain't gassed it. I took two drums off before dark. We maybe could make Ganta or a little beyond, but that's it."

"So whatta we do?"

"Hunker down, stay quiet," Snow said. "Be ready. We don't want to overreact." He whispered now. "Remember, mostly this area's been hit hard by Tolbert, so these are probably celebrating locals, nothing more. But if they think we got ties to the government, we're gonna be in for a fight."

A metallic click came from his right, and the buzzes and clicks of insects fell silent. Snow smelled Bracelin, heard the slide of the ambidextrous safety on the 9mm.

"I may know these people–I may not–been three years," Snow said. "Harsh truth–probably not."

Snow wished they could stay unseen in the night, just let this crew pass on by, but he figured they'd know of the house and its being abandoned. Sometimes your best hope was facing it. "Beth and George stay here–no lights. Kairos and Brace, you come with me."

And he went off into the black. As he stepped down the cinder drive, he heard Beth's voice in a desperate whisper, "I told you we should have left."

"We're better off with Snow."

"What, stay and fight it out?" she whispered. "Remember the Alamo and all that? I don't think we ought to stay in the house. They know we're here, Harold–"

Her voice begged Snow, but Snow was twenty feet away now, in the darkness of the drive. He didn't look back but instead flicked his own light, catching glimpses of Bracelin and Kairos on either side of him as the fighting rose up and over the hill to the south and seemed now to be across the road, perhaps two hundred yards over the hillside.

The flare of flames rose up over the trees, wrapping them in the silhouetted glow of a fire that had broken out beyond the river road. They could hear running, the panting and shouts of those being caught, the clacking of rifles and machetes. On the drive, Snow flicked his flashlight on and off and saw the woods and drive light up, then blacken, leaving only the afterimage. The three men stepped another fifty feet closer to the road, and the images of five or six men came over the hill, carrying flashlights of their own, duct-taped to the barrels of their weapons, and flying down the road to join them came a green Toyota pickup truck with two men in back, the headlights bouncing and lighting the under foliage.

When Snow turned his light on this time, it brought a chorus of shouts in an African language, and the ramming cocking of automatic weapons. Their words came like a barrage. Snow flicked the light off–then offered them smokes from a red pack of Marlboros, flicking his lighter to light their smokes, talking gently to them in his easy voice, a voice that could soothe strangers. "I just live here, this is my home," he said. Their faces reflected in the bobbing incandescence of the Bic.

"Home here?" came a voice, flashing through a cloud of Marlboro smoke. "You stupid white man."

And everybody laughed.

"Way things are going, I couldn't agree more," Snow said, which brought out another laugh, this one a little less tense than the previous.

Only then did he light his own cigarette.

Snow had no personal knowledge of these men–they were boys, really–Krahn tribesmen, the oldest one maybe eighteen. One of them called himself the Colonel, and he held in his left hand the lower half of a human arm, held it as if he'd been shaking some guy's hand and somehow managed to pull his arm off at the elbow. Snow couldn't help noticing it was the arm of a white man, and even in the dim scattered light of periodic flashlights and lanterns, he knew the red freckles and boiling red hair of that arm.

Snow stood there thinking the only reason they didn't kill him on the spot was that they were coming down off of whatever chemical had driven them into the fight to begin with–ganja plus cane juice. And now, maybe, they'd been stunned to superstitious silence to see a white man stumble out of the darkness. Snow remembered one religious group from back in '77 that called themselves the Cherubim and Seraphim Society, with a military arm known as the Army of God's Peace. He knew how it flew around here–the awkward twists of religion and war. Liberia was known for its secret societies, and mostly they did a lot of good, but he could imagine that same impulse carrying people into a whacked-out realm of redemption and violence: the PRC– People's Redemption Council. He didn't know the individuals here, but he recognized their wide-pupiled attention to the night, the nervous flutter of satisfaction after battle. If this was redemption, they'd all pay a steep price for it.

"I've got fuel," Snow said. "For your truck. Two drums around side. More down-mountain, bush taxi."

He felt a tension building on either side of him. Bracelin and Kairos stood there like twins of opposite stripe, poised and all too ready to fight–one for the pleasure of it, the other for the simple necessity.

The one they called the Colonel, the senior officer at eighteen, motioned for two of his fighters to follow Snow around the side and load up the only two drums left. Snow wondered what he would do now to make it back to Monrovia. They might have to walk the ten miles to Ganta and catch a bush taxi from there. He should have filled the Land Cruiser when they arrived–should have taken care of practical matters first. He felt mentally deficient, sloppy, and weak. Awkwardly the two militia boys tried to lift the drums over, but couldn't manage it, so they shoved it over on its side and rolled it to the back of the Toyota pickup. Then they couldn't get it back upright, at which point Bracelin snorted and said, "You want me to get that for you?"

The Colonel stared, apparently uncertain what to say. He finally nodded almost imperceptibly, and the mate walked over to the truck, licked his fingers, and grabbed the steel lip of the 55-gallon drum. He put one foot on the base and stood up, throwing his free leg backward. The thing popped upright. Bracelin wore a white tee shirt that showed every inch of his arms, and his curling tattoos, that analemma now sideways and looking like the symbol for infinity as he bear-hugged the drum and lifted it up to the tail-gate. He shoved it straight back into the bed, alongside some gear covered by a tarp. Then he went for the second drum and did the same thing, with no noticeable strain whatever.

Bracelin held the Colonel's gaze and stepped back over to Kairos and Snow. Every man in the Army of God's Peace stared at the mate as if he were a god himself, or a night devil, and Snow thought they might kill him on the spot, out of fear, or just to prove he wasn't anything but human.

Then Snow saw inside the truck bed, noticing that the tarp had been dragged backward as Bracelin had pushed the drums in, and beneath the tarp was obviously the body of a man, a man in name only for his arms and legs had been cut off, sharply by machete, and aside from the one held by the Colonel, lay in a pile atop the body's chest and stomach. As the Army of God's Peace climbed back aboard, a flashlight illuminated the truck bed in flashing angles of light and shadow. Snow saw that the hacked man's face was that of Buck Favor. He absorbed the sight without reaction; it only confirmed what he already knew.

The Colonel looked up at the house and swung his flashlight up there, his weapon trained, and there on the porch Beth and Maciel stood like two mannequins. The Colonel looked at Snow and lifted his chin as if making an accusation. "You got women!" he said.

"One woman," he said. "Wife."

The Colonel stared at Snow then, hard and long. No laughter verged now. Snow's face remained like ancient stone, with Bracelin to his left, dead as ever, Kairos to his right. Some unspoken territoriality hovered between the lot of them, as if some contest were being played out on an otherworldly plane and the men inhabiting these bodies were simply waiting to find out the result. Snow himself felt it. He wondered about that world. He wondered about how it would fit with the world he knew now. Finally, the Colonel looked away, defeated. He was a boy, and he glanced then at Kairos, and perhaps because he'd retreated from a battle with Snow, he latched onto Kairos as if to a new mark, and the fact that he was black somehow made it easier. As he climbed into the rear bed of the four-by-four pickup and thumped the side to signal it was time to go, the Colonel watched Kairos. They accelerated away down the night road; their flashlights swept sideways and illuminated trees and people–the face of Kairos. The weapon tapped, bullet snapping past, streaking in the flashlight and tearing into Kairos at the chest. He fell like a sack. Snow and Bracelin dropped to their bellies alongside, Snow reaching toward the lanky form of the fallen man.

Against the whine of the disappearing Toyota motor, the red lights streaked down the road, the stoned howling of its occupants receding behind the canopy of the night forest.

"Fuck!" said Bracelin, when it was apparent they weren't going to shoot anybody else. "I swear to Christ I'm gonna get one of those fuckers by the time we're out of here. I swear to Christ, Snow, I'm gonna kill me two or three of them junked-out tar babies."

Snow rose up and shined his flashlight onto the blank face of Kairos, his eyes black, pupils wide and fixed.

Snow turned and said, "Let's go. Time to get out of here."

He felt his own heartbeat high in his throat, could feel a pulse against his own thumb, watched as Beth and Maciel came into the light of his flashlight, and he saw Beth there, holding both hands on her head and saying, "Oh, goddamn you, I told you, I told you damnit!" And he got the idea that she was talking to the kid, and strangely enough it made Snow want to hold her, his face close to her mouth, wanted to breathe her breath like oxygen, staring down toward where Kairos lay motionless on the dark drive.

Snow tried to clear his mind. He realized now that he could make no trip to Bo Waterside, that he'd have to leave Yasa and her children to whatever fate awaited them since fleeing Nimba county. Snow thought of his father, how this was precisely what he had done, dodging fidelity, evading family, and never once missing his ship as it sailed off. In the end he had passed on genes and little else.

It began to rain again as they wrapped Kairos's body in a bedsheet and loaded it into the back of the Land Cruiser. Snow took a last look at the house–remembered its raising with a palpable yearning and a hopeless sense of loss. In the last flashes of light they pulled out, slogging on four wheels down the wet mountainside with a bag of diamonds, leaving behind a mad romantic dream, the ghosts of Yasa and her children, whatever they looked like now, and that house of unreality, a mansion in the rainforest, half burned and leaching into the soil, prey to throngs of ganja-mad boys gone berserk with machine guns. And Beth alongside him, brooding and silent and wanting nothing more than to get back to sea. Beth who so obviously hated him now, for giving her back to her father, for somehow violating her with the insinuation of ancestry.

His thoughts drifted on the wheels of the Land Cruiser, the road sliding and flooding out from under him, like a boat on a waterfall. They hit a turn ten clicks east of Ganta and saw, flickering in the headlights, the bush taxi stopped, the cabbie lying face down on the roadside with an AK-47 at the back of his head, and the faces of men turning toward him, shining an instant in his headlights before he flicked them off, their gunmetal arms flashing toward him in the rain.

He turned right, off-road, instinct driving him into the depths. The road fell away and he tried powering down it, the embankment falling, sliding in a mud torrent into the streambed below, a tree there between them and the bottom. He debated in an instant whether he wanted to run headlong into that tree in hopes it would stop them–knowing then he'd have to face the men back up the road–and he powered past to take his chances in the gully below.

"Ah, God!" cried Maciel from the backseat.

And their voices and breaths all drew inward, their own death-fear that Snow felt only distantly, vicariously, for others. Snow did what instinct and experience told him to do: he punched the gas.

They hit hard in a shuddering slam he thought must have exploded all their tires on river rocks. The impact bolted through all of them, and for a moment Snow thought he'd been driven into unconsciousness. Then he felt the four wheels bite into the creek bed, powering on, his body rippling in his seat, not unlike that moment in the Coral Sea when he was blown from his shoes. He kept seeing the face of that healer when he pressed the hot machete to the hand of the girl, even as his own head hit the roof for the third time. He winced and looked to his right, wondering about Beth in the seat beside him, her body jerking and her head flopping at the impact on stones, and the grinding of their bottom until he felt sure he'd tear the engine from its mounts. Then a wizened African man sat there between them, wearing a monkey fetish that looked to be holding a crucifix. Snow turned back to the road and saw the creek bed unfolding before him, as if his own foot pressing the gas was hardly connected to his brain. He was only vaguely aware of the choice he'd made to press on. Snow was not one to consider suffering. He had never responded to images of the nailed Christ. But from the lips of the old man, dried by dirt and dirty water, came an incantation, that Lord's prayer in Krio: *Papa God we de na evin, mek olmen respekt yu oli nem—*

"Get the hell away from me," Snow said.

He smelled the scent of violet and cut-stone church walls. He felt for the kid back there in the rear of the Land Cruiser, that boy left behind on the porch, abandoned by his father. That lost boy. Floating, flying along the river bottom, riding a crested wave to the sea.

Snow drove down the mountain on logging roads, his foot pressing as hard as he dared on his way to the coast, bounding over log bridges, not pausing for the possibility of being stuck in the mud or stopped by men with guns. Along the Monrovia road they found a boy of ten with a 55-gallon drum of gas and Snow paid him a hundred dollars for ten gallons of it, standing in the rain looking forlorn and weak under the hood of his rain suit, rain pouring down all around him as he watched the gauge and Maciel worked the barrel pump. "You're damned good at that business."

"I think a chimp could probably do this business." His arms strained, and Snow laughed and clapped him on the back.

"But you're a smart chimp!" Snow looked up and through the raindrops where they fell straight down and clung in droplets to the tip of his nose.

"I don't want to be on board that ship anymore," Maciel said.

"Ain't obvious from the way you work, buddy."

"I'll do my job, but I gotta get out of here, Harold."

"We all do," Snow said, and dug down into his pocket, his hand appearing from the sleeve of his rain suit. "You ever seen a raw diamond?" He pressed his palm into Maciel's, passing on the lumpy round stone with crystalline edges. "Now you don't want to be showing that around. Fetch you a grand in Lagos."

Snow went to the back, took the athletic bag of diamonds where he'd stuffed it alongside the stiffened form of Kairos, and pulled the thin nylon sack out, stuffing it down the front of his pants. When he turned around there was the kid, finished with his pumping and staring there through the wet air at Kairos. He could see the heartbreak in the kid, the limp muscles and fixed eyeballs. You could see it all play out there: about his granddad and his dad and priests who could read minds.

"It's the nature of the place," Snow said. "Things happen here."

"He was a good man," said Maciel. "Whatever you got going here killed him, Harold. You gotta face that."

"Now wait a second–that's bullshit, what that is."

"We'll see about that."

"Don't get all fucking sanctimonious on me. You think I don't know he was a good man or that I ain't sorry he got hit by that hopped-out freak? Of course I know; of course I'm sorry it happened. You think I didn't like him? You think you got a corner on feelings for others?"

"Sometimes I get that feeling, yeah." He said it sad, though, not like sanctimonious, and Snow shut the rear gate.

"You think I'm some kinda evil guy, like I've done all this evil shit in my life. Well maybe I haven't been Padre Pure, but I'll say one thing. I never rat-fucked a friend of mine. Not ever. You gotta start thinking about who you're listening to and who you're talking to, George. 'Cause the thing is, I don't think I was hallucinating when I saw you on the bow. I think you're telling me you were with Beth because you knew I'd choke on that one alone. Best lie is closest to the truth, Georgie. You selling me down the river? That what you're doing?"

"No, Harold. I wouldn't do that."

"I hope not, Georgie. I surely hope not. You wouldn't happen to know if we can expect company when we return to that ship, would you?"

"How am I supposed to know that? Of course I don't know that."

Snow stared at him. Damned if he couldn't tell. Damned if he couldn't quite be sure one way or the other where the kid stood. He hadn't just become a better seaman, he'd become a better liar too.

Snow moved back around to the driver's side. "We gotta go."

"I think you knew he'd be the one to draw the fire," said the kid. "That's why you wanted him along."

"Get over your goddamned self why don't you? I didn't know any such thing. Jesus Christ!"

But back in the driver's seat, he did know it. With gears grinding and engine rising, Snow's thick hands gripped the wheel, his mind spinning through retribution and responsibility, concepts he hated and mistrusted. "This here is what I call fundamental realities." But he couldn't shake the hellishness of goading guilt, no matter how high he wound the engine to drown his thoughts.

Bracelin groaned. "You and your goddamned fundamental realities."

•

Down the mountain, the air warmed toward the muggy seaside of dry-season Monrovia, and Snow knew they had experienced little more than mountain showers up-country. The air lay still despite the threat of showers to the ocean side, and Snow felt all those diamonds stuffed around his balls growing hotter and sweatier the closer they got. Diverting north to cruise an empty dirt road along the St. John's River, they dropped down through the flats along the lower gathering of water and saw the Monrovia Peninsula like a multicolored finger sliding through orange alpenglow.

The tanker now called *Elisabeth* lay alongside the number-two berth, and immediately Snow saw she was sitting higher in the water than when they'd left. He let out a crackling groan, his throat raspy, as Bracelin burst out, "I'm gonna kill that second's ass!"

Paynor paced the bridge wing as the crew approached and mounted the gangway, leaving the Land Cruiser there in the asphalt parking area. Three Liberian men stood along the railing at the weather deck, eyeing the crew as they came aboard bearing Kairos's body.

"Who are you?" boomed Bracelin.

"We are the sailors," said one. "He is the cook."

They stood with seabags at their feet and obviously had only just arrived on board themselves. "Good time to get the hell from here," said the cook.

"Stay the fuck out of my way and don't unpack your bags." Bracelin mounted the steps two at a time toward the bridge. They could hear him up there, demanding from Paynor what happened, and even below they got the story of soldiers with M-16s and a middle-aged man who was said to be a chemical engineer who oversaw the off-loading.

"I told them to be careful, that some of them would blow up if they mixed them. They went ahead anyway. I couldn't stop them."

The chemical engineer had tested each tank and off-loaded all the gasoline, av gas, and benzene, leaving behind a tank of chlorinated solvent, one of sulfuric acid, and the monomers. Six tanks left.

"There was something else," Paynor said then. "A guy showed up here. I don't know where he came from, but all the sudden he's on board. Right after the Liberians showed up. He starts claiming he represents the ship's owners. This Liberian army guy is in my face; he's in my face; he's in the Liberian's face. Soldiers finally ran him off, sent him to the maritime authority. But all we heard all night was fighting from over on the peninsula. I haven't seen him since."

"Was he Aussie?"

"Might have been. Maybe South African, I don't know. They all sound alike to me."

Snow looked over at Bracelin and traded heavy glares. "At least that coup was good for something," Bracelin said. "Maybe they arrested his ass."

"Maybe," said Snow.

The afternoon sun, muted through the red-brown haze, played on the surface of the deckhouse and pipeline network, flickering in orange tones that might have meant something romantic, save for the olfactory reality that the ship empty didn't smell any better than the ship full. In fact, to Snow it smelled worse, perhaps because he hadn't smelled it in a day and a half, like a rancid piss pot, the mugging hard ammonia smell of liquid urea lingering despite being long gone. All the same, Snow reached into his pants and came up with the sack of diamonds, wanting little more than to get to sea as soon as possible.

They weighed anchor thirty minutes later, swinging the bow

out on their own, not waiting for an escort tug. The going was slow, with Bracelin at the helm, steering the ship manually out of the harbor like a very big boat and somehow managing to do it without running into anything. They steamed out of Monrovia just as the sky flashed with lightning in the languid dusk, with flashing tracers and shouts rising off the beach. Their work done for now, Snow and the rest of the crew lined the port railing, watching the Monrovia peninsula slide past, the two Liberian sailors, Maciel, and Beth standing on the side deck, watching the commotion along the ocean side of the city, hearing gunfire crackling from the beach.

"Now what the hell are we going to do?" Beth said.

"How about getting ashore at the first civilized port?" said Maciel.

"Only one problem. There *are* no civilized ports."

"There's bound to be one. And from there we head home."

"Don't have one of those."

"You can come with me to mine."

"You're mad."

"I have my grandfather's house in Richmond."

Snow could just see it, the two of them all set up and domestic.

The Liberians let out a choral "Ooooohhh!" and pointed toward a skirmish of firearms that snapped from a cluster of homes on a knobby rise of Capitol Hill. Then a crowd flowed out past the Old Executive Mansion and streamed onto the beach, a mix of civilians and green-clad military pushing prisoners ahead of them. The prisoners were lined up along the beach, their backs to the sea, as automatic weapons fire flew from the soldiers and scattered past the prisoners, wild and helpless, rifling and slapping the Atlantic Ocean. The soldiers stepped up point-blank then, so they couldn't miss, and the bodies of prisoners fell in a teetering heap and lay haphazardly on the sand.

"Oh, praising Jesus! Praising Jesus we got the hell from there!" said one of the Liberians, whose name nobody had bothered to learn.

"Fucking cannibals," said Bracelin. Then he barked at the Liberians to go clean their rooms.

"Clean rooms?" they said. "We ain't been in 'em."

"Then go clean the toilets," said Bracelin. "Just get doing something if you want to go praising Jesus!"

The kid stepped over and held out his hand. "I'm George. This is Lisa."

"Me, I am Jimmy. This my brother Danny."

Jimmy and Danny were twins who had lived in Monrovia all their lives, had worked five years running forklifts on the docks, but had no experience at sea. To them it was a grand adventure and a timely departure rolled into one.

"Let's go, scoot it!" said Bracelin. "Snow, find them a room."

Snow didn't pay any attention to Bracelin. He kept staring at the beach, alternating with glances at Beth, thinking this was it for her: she'd be gone first chance she got.

Jimmy and Danny went off, scowling back behind them. Bracelin sidled up next to Beth and pulled a can of Copenhagen from his pocket and dipped his tongue into a mound of fine-grain tobacco, licking a thick wad of it and stuffing it into his lower lip until it bulged like some kind of Ubangi. "Isn't that attractive," said Beth.

The beach was a random jumble of bodies flopped over one another just beyond the line of surf. As the ship steamed toward open sea, the dry season ended for real. Rain and dust congealed into thick drops of mud that spattered out of the sky. The kid reached his hand along the deck and felt it between his thumb and finger; rolled it; brought it to his nose and smelled it. "That's what they found in my father's lungs," he said. "When he drove into the slough."

Snow took a deep breath. He shook his head to clear his thoughts of asphyxiation, imagining a man's last heaving breath of river mud. To clear his mind of faces. To fill it with the job ahead. Then he went topside, to the bridge to plan for Nigeria, then into the dayroom where a wool blanket was stretched. He lay down there, motionless for a long time, hypnotized by the sounds of the ship's bridge–radio chatter and instructions to the helm.

THE BIGHT OF BENIN

They made coastwise past Buchanan and Harper and finally rounded the rocky peninsula of Cape Palmas and into the coastal waters of Ivory Coast, but instead of turning east directly they headed straight out for two hundred miles into the Gulf of Guinea, in a big looping arc bound for Nigeria. Snow awakened stiff-kneed, and hobbled below to prepare the body of Kairos for burial at sea. In the walk-in reefer he heard Momo clanging pots and pans and wondering if it was right to do such a thing as carry a body in a refrigerator that carried food as well. Momo was an old-fashioned man, a Liberian of indeterminate age, somewhere between fifty and seventy, diminutive and unshaven, but he knew his way around the galley of a merchant ship. Momo had shipped out since he was fourteen, as a steward aboard Liberian-flagged ships from here to Canada. He also had a morbid fear of cannibalism and was convinced he'd somehow mistake Kairos for meat and wind up serving the man for dinner.

"What kind business you got on this scow?" he said.

"Nothing kind about our business!" Snow said. "Just trying to sell our last cargoes in Lagos. Nothing more than that."

"Ahhh. I hear that Nigerians are our brothers."

Snow went into the reefer to prepare Kairos, tightening the sheet that wrapped his long black body. Snow saw the blue-black lividity, where blood had pooled in the low spots within his body cavity. He fingered the lone bullet wound, now dried and blackened around its cornice. It's nothing new around here, he thought, waiting for Bracelin to join him for the muscle end of the operation. Out the starboard side exit from the galley, they mounted the steep stairs to the weather deck, carrying the body by the knotted sheet.

"You're just going to dump him overboard?" Beth said.

"Nothing else to do," said Snow. "Momo's all bugged out. We can't have Momo bugged out about a body in the reefer."

"I ain't dealing with the questions when we get to Lagos," said Bracelin.

"It's all a trial by ordeal," said Snow. "Life's like that."

"We could at least say a few words," said Maciel.

"That's what we just did," said Bracelin. "Those were a few words."

"If you want to, say some different words," said Snow. "Just go light on the Christ thing. It offends us pagans."

"He was a Christian," said Maciel. "How am I supposed to go light on the Christ thing?"

"Just see if you can," said Snow. "Like Father, Son, Holy Ghost. Think of it like the Holy Ghost part."

Maciel stared at Snow for a long count. "Let me get his Bible, all right? The man should have a passage read for him."

"Fuck that," said Bracelin. "You ought to have some memo-rized."

"I got one," said Snow. "*'Make thee an ark of gopher wood!'*"

"Good one," said Bracelin. "Now you."

Maciel stood there with his lips moving, giving it some thought. His hair had grown out enough to bend in four directions. "*'Remember this day, in which ye came out from Egypt, out of the house of bondage.'*"

"Works for me," said Snow.

"And you never mentioned ol' Jesus Christ once," said Bracelin. "Amen." And they gave Kairos the heave, leaning out to watch the body fall, all four of them, watching the long form tight and wide at the shoulders, striking water.

The body scooted aft, skirting the thick deep prop wash, where it bobbed and rolled over, face down, the head and arms tight within the white sheet. Maciel stood there watching, staring overboard to where the sheeted body of Kairos receded on their stern wake, rolling in the waves somewhere in the Gulf of Guinea.

Even before he was out of sight, the ship turned east, then northeast, headed for Lagos, where they could sell off the six tanks of cargo they had remaining, as well as Snow's diamonds. Snow dreaded Lagos. You could buy and sell anything in Lagos, but that didn't make it easy. "It's the worst city on earth," he told Maciel. "Even Nigerians hate it."

But he needed it—that was the worst part of the worst city.

Snow went topside to find Paynor and Bracelin steering their course northeast toward the Bight of Benin and the entrance to the harbor channel beyond, Bracelin claiming he'd as soon take entry on the run. "I don't like anchoring off Lagos. I been on ships that got boarded by pirates while waiting for the pilot to come aboard," he said. "So we'll hang back at the twenty-mile mark until they're ready for us."

Snow barely contemplated the irony of their getting boarded by pirates at this stage, particularly since they had no weapons save an assortment of knives and bludgeons and one 9mm handgun that Bracelin now wore stuffed into the back of his pants. He got on the horn to the Nigerian Ports Authority, knowing the routine of entry was enough to frustrate him on a good day. The rules for entering the harbor here were a full page in the port guide, a vestige of the Brits, who had only given up their colonial hold on Nigeria in the last twenty years. Right off, the NPA agent told them they had to call seven days before ETA, then again at four, three, two, and one day out, but Snow explained as easily as he could that *Elisabeth* was a tramp chemical tanker with a recent contract to sell base chemicals to a plastics company in Lagos. "We got a schedule to keep in Cabinda in less than a week," he said.

"What I know about Cabinda?" said the agent, and proceeded to keep Snow on the radio telephone for a good twenty minutes while he said no chance, well maybe, there'd be extra fees, etc. Bracelin was sighing and running his hands through his hair saying, "This isn't going to work, it's not going to work. . . ."

Then the agent left the phone for five minutes, during which time Bracelin stood over a sheet of paper calculating the value of their cargoes and the value of the ship itself if sold as scrap. "We can haul in a mil-point-five now," he said, looking up. "Not including the rocks from up-country."

"A mil-five to split three ways?" said Paynor. "That is not what you two told me when you sucked me into this mess!"

"Well, things change," said Bracelin. "Deal with it. That fuck still got you on hold?"

Snow was about to answer when the agent came back on to say it would quite simply not be possible to enter Nigerian port unless the vessel had registered with port authority two months prior to ETA in order to obtain a Ship Entry Notice. "But your own rules say that isn't necessary for a vessel carrying bulk petroleum products!" Snow said.

"What's that about petroleum?" said the NPA agent.

"A SEN isn't necessary for petroleum products in bulk."

"What's that you are saying? Send what?"

"S–E–N, Ship Entry Notice!" Snow said.

"Ahhhh, SEN–no, it is true, you do not need SEN for petroleum. You are carrying petroleum?"

"Bulk liquid chemicals," said Snow. "Petroleum products, yes."

"You should have said that from the first," said the man on the phone. "Call back when you are one day out. You will proceed then to off-load at Ijora Wharf."

"What is your name?" Snow asked.

"I am Albert Warri. Like the city."

Then he signed off.

Snow tried not to focus on the fact that he *had* told the guy they were a tank ship from the start. Snow found Nigerians in general to be a disagreeable people. He had never been to a place where the line between normal discourse and violent confrontation was so thin and unpredictable. He had spent only a few nasty, hot, polluted nights in Lagos, during which time he'd usually run into a dead body on the side of the road somewhere with people stepping around it like it was a chuckhole, and ending in someone trying to rob him on the street outside his hotel. Still, he got his opinions less from personal experience than from the experience of his Liberian friends, who regarded Nigerians as the armed bullies on the West African block. And all this piled onto the fact that he had his own armed bully to contend with: Bracelin. Near as Snow could tell the man hadn't slept in three days. Snow thought he should probably call back to tell the NPA they were already a day's sail out, but the thought of talking to Albert Warri again made his scalp hurt.

Down two levels, he slipped into the room to wash up for dinner and found Maciel in there playing with his seaman's knife. He snapped it open, gripped the handle in his fist with the blade facing down, and let loose with a flurry of fast boxing combinations.

"Why do you keep doing that?"

The kid was grunting and shadowboxing, and improvising with the knife. "Leeds showed me this," he said. "He has a ton of knives. And he knows how to use them." He threw three fast jabs, then a right and a slashing back fist that would have buried the blade in somebody's carotid artery.

"Yeah, but why are you doing it?"

He closed the knife, locked it, put it in his belt holster and pulled it fast, snapped it open with a flick of his wrist, and went through the whole barrage again.

"Never know," the kid said, breathing hard, "when you might need your knife fast."

"George. Don't get yourself on a hair trigger here."

"You never know," he said. "You have to be ready, don't you?"

"Well, yeah, sure, but–"

"No buts, Harold. You can't trust anybody. You just have to be ready to do what's necessary. I'm starting to get it–I'm not leaving. I'm not leaving Beth here. I don't care what Ali said or Bracelin says. Or even what you say."

He sounded like Leeds with his ax handles. Between pirates and the Nigerian Ports Authority and Bracelin and Beth–and now the kid, acting ready to open somebody's veins—Snow felt like the dike boy with leaks all around, far more than he could plug with ten thick fingers.

He knelt down before his locker, keyed open the padlock to the lower drawer, and hauled out the rocks. He sifted through them, his hand hot and sweaty as he rolled the rough-edged stones and weighed them in his mind. "Won't get so much for these in Lagos," he said. He rolled the bag into a sausage shape and taped it closed, then stuffed it into a money belt and tied it around his lower abdomen. He pulled his shirt down over them and tucked it in, looking now like he had two potbellies instead of one. He went to his own drawer and took out the boning knife his son gave him the last time they saw each other ten years before.

Watching the kid get himself all geared for a fight left Snow with a goading desire to protect him, even if he didn't need it, even if he was the most dangerous man aboard somehow, even if he had taken the word of Favor, or some unknown Aussie trailing the play. No sooner would he think of his own son, and any sort of danger at all, than he thought of the kid. He thought of the girl too, and then, as if he'd conjured her, she stepped inside the room and let the door fall closed behind her. She looked at the kid with a pensive look, like they both had something to say.

"You two up for a party?" said Snow, as if there was any chance of that.

"Afraid not, Harold. Listen." Her voice had a tone that told Snow his entire day was about to go down the toilet. "George and I have been thinking about it, and we've decided we're going ashore in Lagos. I know what you're going to say, that it's a shit hole and no place to jump ship. I won't disagree, but we're going just the same."

"That right?" Snow turned to the kid for confirmation.

"That's right, Harold. We're not staying around to the end just to say we stuck it out. It's insane. This ship is insane. You know that, right?"

Snow felt something ugly rise up inside his throat, all that vomit and acid right there on the cusp, until some of it got into his mouth, and his lips recoiled from it and he stood there snarling. He looked over at all those religious books. He wished he could absorb some kind of Christian response to this thing, but the thought of Beth leaving him just hung there in front of his nose.

He thought of home, the clear cool of the Cascades, the northern air, out of the swamp to take off gliding on snowshoes on a flat stretch of glacier, or cresting a granite divide in midsummer to the crash of a waterfall and the smell of cedar and Doug fir, and climbing, always climbing, even when going downhill, effortless climbing down into the sky.

"There ain't nothing I can do to stop you," he said.

"No. There really isn't," said Maciel.

"But you'll need money to get home."

"We'll manage."

"But you know—I could go with you. Maybe we could all go together, you know? I ain't trying to mess with your thing here, I just—I've got half a million in rocks here—"

They just stared at him. He sounded so goddamned desperate.

He could see that too, the reflection of his own pathetic countenance in the chemical glaze of their eyes. "Fine then. Fine."

"This ship is going down, Harold," the kid said. "I'm not going with it."

Beth stepped toward him, her hand out and lighting on his shoulder. She leaned into his ear, spoke softly—just between them. "You know it's right, Harold. Time to leave this."

"But you're the whole point of it! Don't you get that? I only did this whole thing for you."

"Did what whole thing, Harold?"

Snow frowned at her. So the kid hadn't told her either. He sure was a secret shit. Snow figured it for a Catholic thing, discipline of the secret and all that. He didn't answer her, though. He looked at the kid instead. "Why don't you tell me who that guy is. The Aussie. You at least owe me that. I've seen him. I know you been talking to him."

The kid straightened, went dead a little, his mouth downcast and not even grim, just past caring. "His name is Slaney."

As much as Snow knew he was right, the confirmation hit at him. "Slaney." He elongated the word, as if it were somehow synonymous with eating bird shit. "Who's he work for?"

"Some private security agency."

"Like I thought—Petrochem's the client."

"Insurance. I think Lloyd's is the client."

Snow appreciated the honesty. Just like that he felt the kid had come back to him somehow, though he guessed that in the face of Bracelin, it only made sense. The kid was playing his angles like everybody else.

"What'd he come at you with?"

"Accessory to everything."

"I don't want to know anything about this," said Beth. "What do you know about this?"

"Only what he told me. That the ship's owners have filed a loss claim."

"What'd he want from you?"

"Two things. A position report and a destination. I radioed to him before Freetown. I told him we'd be there."

"Fuck. Fuck." Snow couldn't stop saying fuck. He must have said it ten times, under his breath, out loud, inside his head. He didn't know the difference anymore anyway, words aloud didn't do any goddamned good. Fuck. It was the only word that made sense anymore. As in *I am fucked. You are fucked. We are fucked.* The declension of a fundamental reality.

"Time was I'd have tossed your ass over." He just looked at the kid with profound disappointment, tears straining at his eyeballs. What was the point of it–the point of anything now. "The thing is, it don't surprise me. I knew it all along. I knew it from PC on. So you can jump ship here. Just know I trusted you. Protecting you two was always on my mind. Both of you."

"Harold," Beth said, making a half step toward him before stopping.

"There was nothing I could do," said Maciel.

"Oh crap. Look inside your head, scrape out all them church cobwebs and mush talk and be at least in your head honest with yourself. You coulda come to me."

"He said you killed someone. He showed me the photographs. Some girl in Da Nang. It was pretty fucking grisly."

Snow shook his head in long swings of his neck. "No, no. No. That ain't true. That's bullshit pinning that rap on me."

"Well, then it's your turn to be intellectually honest."

"Intellectual! Don't give me no fucking intellectual. All mind puzzles and rules and regulations and garbage. It's all wishful goddamned thinking–living in clouds, man, see the ground!"

He felt his head go light, and before he registered anything else he was lying on his bunk with the two looking down at him. Like watching a movie that got spliced together and left something out.

"What happened?" Snow said.

"You passed out."

"I don't pass out."

"You just did," said Maciel. "Let me get you some water."

And while the kid went into the head, Snow reached for Beth's hand. "I don't think I can take you leaving me," he said.

"I'm afraid you'll have to, Harold."

"So just go then," he said. "Just go ahead and go."

She stood up then, and the two towered over him, all lithe and

young. He heard his knees crackle as he pulled himself to a standing position, one hand to the bunk. "I gotta write a letter," he said,
and stumbled across the room to the desk, where he fell into the
chair. The kid came over and held out a cup of water.

"You want some help, Harold?"

"I don't want your help, no sir."

The two went out and left him. He heard the heavy metal door
swing open, the *whoosh* of air from a draft somewhere down the
passageway, and then it thumped closed and he was alone in
there. He had no clue what he might write, or to whom. He only
knew he had to do something, but all he could think was black and
vast, and all he could feel was the diamonds there at his gut, biting
at him.

By the time they were in the pilot zone for Lagos, Snow hadn't seen
the kids anywhere for over two hours and figured them for down in
Beth's room getting their things together. He tried to think of some
way either to keep them aboard or else go ashore with them. He
ought to do the right thing and help them get ashore. Help them
get away from him and Bracelin both, let them live a life together
like young people needed, quit his messing with their lives.

Walking stiff from the diamond bulge, Snow hiked topside to
the bridge, where he stood the helm for Paynor, steering north by
west toward the entrance to Lagos harbor, where a pilot boat
approached. Paynor made radio contact. "You can come along our
starboard quarter, we'll have a ladder for you there," Paynor said
into the mike.

"Excellent, *Elisabeth,*" said the pilot in a heavy Brit accent. He
was white, Snow was sure of that. There were a few of them roam-
ing around still in Lagos, old-timer holdovers. "*Elisabeth,* I'm one
hundred meters off and yet to see the ladder you're referring to.
Over."

"Just tell him it'll be there by the time he comes alongside," Snow said toward Paynor.

"She'll be there by the time you come alongside," repeated Paynor.

"All right, then, see you on the bridge in five," said the pilot.

As the pilot boat twin-screwed to a stop, turning a circle a hundred feet off their starboard side, Snow knew it didn't matter what the kids were going to do, he had to try to go with them. The thought of following them like some stray dog was enough to sicken him, but he couldn't imagine himself doing anything else.

The skies to the north in the Bight of Benin had what local boatmen called the Smokes, more of the dust sky you got from Harmattans, obscuring the land to where you couldn't even tell there was a continent there. To the south, Snow saw squall lines, the seas from these periodic storms causing a swell that heaved the vessel as she approached the sea buoy.

He went below to tell Maciel and Beth they'd be free to go ashore after they'd helped with off-loading the monomers. Give her half the diamonds, he thought, leave her with that anyway.

Down to the third deck and into the passageway toward the room, he stepped inside to find it empty and well kept as always. He rolled his shoulders and shivered. He went into the head and found a clean white towel, soaked it through with cold water, then rolled it up and wrapped it around his neck, stuffing it down into his shirt to secure it, feeling the cool moisture seep into his neck and head. It did nothing to ease the pain, but the coolness distracted him. He knelt and dug into his drawer and came up with the undeveloped film box marked ELISABETH 1980. He pocketed it, reached into his pants and unclasped the money belt full of rocks, and stuffed it into a knapsack along with some underwear, socks, and a change of clothes. Then he slung the pack onto his back and went out to greet the pilot boat.

Stepping down the outboard ladder, he watched the kid come along the side deck toward Bracelin and moved to intercept, pulling him into the galley door off the weather deck.

"Listen, Harold, you okay?"

"I've felt better. But I been thinking. I know you probably need me around like you need a poke in the eye with a marlin spike, but I decided I'm gonna be jumping ship here too. Bracelin and me— we got things that go back deep, and I got no plan to stick around until he's figured out he don't need me anymore. So you just got to play it cool for now. Help me with the Jake's ladder for this pilot. We can't get into harbor without him."

"Why don't we just take a skiff in?"

" 'Cause we got cargoes to off-load. This is the last shot for the cargoes. We got stiffed in the W.A., flat out. Bracelin needs these cargoes sold. Besides all that, I got rocks on my back. Lone skiff off a tanker not cleared for entry is gonna bring the Nigerian CG sure as shit."

"What's the matter, Harold?"

"Ah, for crap's sake, don't ask me that. You ain't got time for the answer. Honest truth, I just want Bethy to be safe."

"She thinks you're working an angle."

"Maybe I have been. I don't know."

His headache rose to a dull throbbing, and pain spread from his lower gut until it ran up and down his spine.

"It's okay, Harold—okay." The kid put a hand to his shoulder and looked at him like he was some old man who couldn't make it to the toilet.

Snow shook him off and moved down the side deck and watched the pilot boat swing south of the ship as Paynor powered back to dead slow and the boat came alongside. While Maciel and Beth manned the ladder, Snow's brain tried to figure just how to word this new plan to Bracelin, what on earth he could do to convince the mate of the need for all three to get ashore here alone. Every possibility rang hollow, save the truth that he couldn't live without her. His body felt crumbly, like old dry cake.

He guessed the kids were in love or something. He guessed they'd go to London together, or New York, or San Francisco and Richmond together, live in the old man's house, become parents and grandparents and die sixty years from now, older than he. They stood at the top of the ladder and watched the starched Brit pilot heave himself over the bulwark. Snow moved to usher him up. When they got to the second deck, Snow nodded topside. "We're kinda short of crew, so I got some tankerman work to do. You'll find the chief mate up there. He's got the con."

"And where might be the captain?" said the pilot.

"Sorry, I meant the captain. He's topside. Name of Charles Bracelin."

The pilot frowned, then rubbed his nose, looked up the side of the house, and said, "Actually, I believe I know this ship."

"That right?"

"Yes. This is one of those T-2s that Petrochem converted to the chemical trades back in the late sixties. They cut off the upper deck of the midship square and turned it into a pumpman's house."

"Lotta outfits did that," Snow said. "Hell, I sailed a T-2 in WWII–I know these boats."

"Then you know what I'm talking about. Others cut out the midship square altogether, but these were converted."

Snow watched the pilot's motor racing. He wasn't entirely certain how to respond.

The pilot looked around. He spoke the King's English. A real upper cruster, though how he had ended up in Lagos was beyond Snow. "These were all retrofit jobs." He cast his eyes about like a man with suspicions he was looking to confirm.

"This is the only one still floating, I'd say," Snow said.

"Petrochem runs a few others as well. I can tell because of that flare in the flying bridge, that contour. Some foreman had an attack of the cutsies, they say. Amusing, actually." He pointed up at the rounded underside to the windows. Minuscule, Snow thought, but come to think of it, he'd never seen it on any other tanker either.

Snow turned to the guy. He had the look of someone who thought he was better than a mere boatswain. Snow knew that look, and it made his own stubbornness flare. "I know those ships," he said. "And this ain't one."

The pilot looked around, frowning, glanced at Snow an instant, then back down to where the Jacob's ladder dangled off the side. "How many crew you have aboard this vessel?"

"We got the usual complement," Snow replied.

"I thought you said you were short?"

"Well, we're short with the usual complement."

"Then where might they be?"

"Oh, they're out and about." Snow nodded to where Beth and Maciel had moved forward to prepare mooring lines. Something in the pilot's demeanor told Snow they'd been made, had been all along, maybe. The pilot's eyes darted toward the ship's bridge and then down to his own boat, and he said, "So sorry, seem to have forgotten my log book."

"What's that there?" Snow said, tapping at the bag he had under his arm.

"Papers and such, but I left the log on the console of the pilot boat," he said. "Won't take but a minute."

The pilot moved back down the stairs, stepping quickly, his soft-soled shoes noiseless even on the metal stairs and deck leading down.

Snow muttered under his breath and moved for the railing, still thinking maybe the guy really had left his log book. But when he looked over the side and saw down to the pilot boat, the wheelhouse glass held the broad band of reflected black that was the ship's hull, rising up at distorted angles to reveal the ship's house on top. Tiny in the wide-angle image, a robotic pinhead peering down. There in a blank spot in the boat glass, as if staring out of the reflected porthole itself, Snow saw that face. He couldn't even say he was surprised, since he figured what had gone down in Monro, could imagine the guy caught in the same chaos they were. How he banked on Lagos could have been deduction, or monitored radio traffic, or getting more info from the kid along the way. Slaney was his name, or he guessed so, anyway. He could just imagine how the Nigerians would have dealt with him. Have to get the ear of a sympathetic man of the crown, that pilot aboard to get their evidence so they could walk her into waiting authorities. He knew then how it would all transpire, though there were alternate realities to be sure. He could still affect things.

While the pilot scampered down the internal stairway, Snow moved to the port-side railing and motioned down a deck to Bracelin, shaking his head emphatically and pointing the opposite way. Bracelin dropped everything, and disappeared into the ship's house. By the time Snow got back to the seaward side of the ship, he saw the pilot boat down below, and he was glad that *Elisabeth* had a skeletal crew. It wouldn't do anybody's health any good to see Bracelin intercept the pilot, ushering him inside before he'd have to force the issue, so that nobody on the pilot boat could see. Snow saw, though. He watched the door until finally Bracelin came out a few minutes later to climb down the Jacob's ladder into the pilot boat. The Aussie must have seen him coming. He stepped from the wheelhouse in all his short wide bulk, and Snow thought him formidable, except Bracelin was on him so fast, reversing him into a choke hold and jerking his neck, which even with all its muscles gave way and the man's head flopped sideways, his body limp. The boat operator had no clue what was about to tumble onto him. Bracelin pulled open the aft door to the wheelhouse and disappeared inside. Any sounds of protest were swallowed by the din of the ship's main engines.

When Bracelin finished with his business there, he went belowdecks, opened the pilot boat's sea valve, and released the lines before he climbed topside ahead of the inflow of water, stepping to the Jacob's ladder just ahead of her scuttling.

Still making eight knots toward Lagos, *Elisabeth* ran nearly parallel to the coast when Snow went topside and ordered Paynor to steer as inconspicuously as he could to the south-southeast, to come to full ahead, the bells ringing below in the engine room. Snow knew none of them would be going ashore now, and he hated Lagos enough to feel okay about that, except for the minor fact that he had no idea where they'd go now.

He stood there wearing his knapsack loaded full, feeling like a tourist who'd just missed his bus. He felt a fog press onto him from above. He scanned the horizon and wondered how long it would be before the pilot master caught on that his boat was missing. He rubbed his face. Jesus, he thought. *Jesus.* The Smokes left nothing ashore but a muddy sky, and he was glad for that. As they turned south the squall line closed down.

Down below, Bracelin gave the bad news to Maciel and Beth, and Snow watched from the bridge wing as Beth motioned to shore and then pulled her arms in and crossed them, looked down, and went to work tightening down the canvas covers over the raft davits.

Smoke billowed from the stacks, and the massive main engines rumbled up from underneath as the vessel changed headings toward the south, out of the Bight of Benin into the Gulf of Guinea and beyond that for the vast open ocean of the south Atlantic. Night was already falling, and the sky glowed a deep purple toward the east, falling toward black, even as the remnants of sun clung to life in the west. The winds started then, rising at a clip you couldn't imagine except from a line squall. They'd be into the storm soon, and beyond it soon after. A squall wouldn't last long, and it would be good cover, he thought. Cover to keep the Nigerians from hauling ass after them until the ship was good and gone toward Ilha do Príncipe.

Snow stood inside the bridge scanning aft with binoculars, still with his backpack on, as it had been since the pilot came aboard. His heart migrated upward as he watched, waiting for the end to come down on him, wondering if he could have handled things any other way.

"They'll call first," said Bracelin.

"Probably," Snow replied.

The ship had been steaming south for just under an hour, the seas lifting and heaving the ship, when the call from the pilot dispatch office came, wondering what had happened with the ship coming into port and where the pilot boat was. "Ah, yeah, no pilot came aboard here. Over," said Bracelin.

"Our records show that you called and requested a pilot," said the dispatcher.

"Yeah, roger that," said Bracelin. "I'm afraid we had a miscommunication with our second mate. He called."

Snow turned forward from his binocular vigil aft, noting Bracelin and feeling the pilot incident settling into him now. He felt some great force out there, all around wherever he looked, pressing toward him. He kept seeing that line of hunting buddies in the Elks Club—you've crossed a line here, Snow, you've crossed a line. Maybe he'd go to hell. Maybe he was in hell. Come to West Africa like the ancients, to find the real limit of your life.

"The pilot reported he was going aboard," said the dispatcher. "That was at 1635 hours. Over."

"Negative," said Bracelin. "He came alongside. He was about

to come aboard, but we explained the miscommunication and the pilot boat peeled off. We ordered no escort tug. Over."

"Roger, that confirms what Victoria Towing has told us. Problem is we have not seen the pilot boat since. Over."

"Nor have we," said Bracelin. "Over."

"Very well. Update as information warrants, *Elisabeth*. Lagos Pilots, over and out."

Snow felt little relief. He wished he could catch his breath. "So what do you think?" he said.

"Plan B," said Bracelin. "We try to sell in South or East Africa, and we run the ship aground in Bangladesh."

"You think she'll make it?" Snow asked.

"Maybe not."

"I know a scrapyard near Dar," said Snow. "We could sell monomers in South Africa and head to Dar. Avoid crossing the Indian that way. Get what we can for the ship."

"That might work. But we'll need to pick up crew in Luanda or Cape Town–half dozen warm bodies at least."

"Okay, so that's the plan. First stop, Luanda."

"Another fucking shit hole. I should kill your ass for bringing me to this part of the world, Snow."

He said it as a joke, but Snow knew it wasn't far off the mark for Bracelin. He thought about all the times he was convinced he'd die and didn't, and about being cornered and what he was capable of, and how maybe living a moral life was about not getting cornered, because deep inside you knew how you'd come out, if you had it in you to kill a man.

He felt bad about the pilot, worse than he'd ever felt about business like that. He supposed he could blame the kid for ushering that Slaney along, even if it was only to Freetown. He felt an odd lack of anger toward the kid, even knowing the man couldn't have tracked the ship without his help. Now they'd all pay for it. He guessed it was how it ought to be, except that there were still innocents he wanted to protect, still Beth, even if she didn't want his help. It was all such sickening business, he wanted to know how he could stop it, he begged to know how. *Please tell me how, please.* He had no idea to whom he was even begging. The image of Van Sickle came at him now, that marlin spike concealed up behind his wrist. What if there really were spirits out there? What if Van Sickle really had come for Joaquin on his deathbed, what would that mean for him? Who would come for him? A shiver wracked his body and he wriggled out of it, did what he always did at moments like this. He tried not to think. Let Bracelin do that, let Bracelin think of the pilot and what he did to him and where he put him when he was finished. Maybe Slaney was still out there floating or treading water and coming for them. Maybe you couldn't stop a man like that, couldn't really break a neck like that. Through the door to the dayroom, Snow could see Paynor sleeping in there, his lips pursed as he let out air, like he was kissing some lover in his dreams.

Snow left Bracelin on the bridge. On the way out he checked the anemometer, saw that winds were pushing fifteen knots now, with the barometer on a free fall. Stepping out to the bridge wing, Snow felt the fresh wind blow at his hair, a cooling wind at least, though up ahead rising cumulonimbus clouds vaulted to the strato-sphere and flattened off into anvil heads. Snow felt small all of a sudden, hunkered down. He looked out the long foredeck, and even now, with the waves rising to ten feet, he could see the hull flexing, sagging amidships as they moved into the trough, a motion he felt in his own belly, like the both of them would bust a gut down deep. He'd look for the kids to start a ballast operation, get the ship trimmed up. They should have done it sooner, he thought, as he started down the outside stairs from the bridge wing to the poop deck, where to his own surprise he found himself hoping, really hoping, there was no God.

HORSE LATITUDES

He couldn't hope long. Descending the ladder from the poop deck, Snow felt a glowing and crackling sensation, rolling up his face and over his head and down his back like electric flickers of truth. The ringing in his left ear had graduated from a popping sound to where he now heard voices. He heard old Joaquin grumble, felt somebody shaking his foot to wake up saying *time to turn-to now, Snowman, time to turn-to and stand your watch, you're on lookout!*

Awake was the last thing Snow felt. He walked in baby steps, as if one stride of his long legs would throw him out of control and he'd somehow walk right overboard. As he stepped out the center-line catwalk, he looked up to the bridge where the face of Bracelin loomed behind the glass, his eyes picking up Snow's movement, and glaring.

Snow went searching for the kid, walked the decks in a kind of daze. He saw people out there—a ton of people, people of the past. They were all around now, stepping out from behind stanchions and vent stacks, curling around valve stems and pipelines. A Viet bar girl in a miniskirt. A thousand Hindus naked, black mouths, wild salt-caked hair. He couldn't find the kid anywhere. He searched for Beth, but couldn't find her either. He searched for Leeds—he'd be in the engine room standing at the control panels with his *dim mak* and useless hands. Old Joaquin kept up, with his hand there shaking his foot, saying *time to turn-to, Snowman, time-to, turn-to.* Snow could hear him in both ears.

In the here and now, the crew had evaporated. A six-hundred-foot tanker and they were all gone from sight, and he figured it could go that way now, one by one, until he never saw any of them again. If he were Bracelin what would he be thinking? If he were Bracelin he'd need the crew as long as the crew was useful.

Stepping down the catwalk he felt it flex and creak as the ship labored over rising waves. As the pilot had noted, this was a T-2, a rare breed because most of the rest had been turned into Chevrolets. Like Liberty ships they were all welded, disposable tin cans that broke in half often as not until they took to riveting straps along the side shell fore to aft. Rivets that creaked inside his own skull, like popping in a deaf ear. The catwalk chattered and the wind pulled at his hair as if someone had grabbed a fistful to haul him around deck like a slave. The pain spread down and through his skull. He stood in the wind at the midship line, just over the manifold, and heard a deluge of sounds that transformed in his brain to scrapes and groans, pops and clicks. People shouted at him. They crowded out of nowhere talking in tongues, mumbling Sanskrit and Latin and ancient Greek, Chinese and Malay. Riveted straps or not, Snow felt *Elisabeth* ready to break open down under. She'd founder before anybody knew what had happened. "That strap goes, she'll unzip like a whore's skirt," he said aloud to no one, but heard Joaquin answer in his deathbed rasp, *Goddamn you anyhow, Snow—except for you I'd a made heaven!*

Snow thought of maybe calling Leeds to get his take, but that would mean nobody to man the engine room. Maybe the new Liberian was down there—Danny. No, Jimmy was his name. The other one was Danny. Danny was on the helm with Bracelin and Paynor. Then he saw Joaquin Maciel striding the deck stowing work gear, holding monkey wrenches in his fists and a marlin spike tucked up behind his rain gear until it turned into the kid, turned into George.

George was a worker now, nose to the grindstone, don't look up, don't notice, don't be noticed. He moved past, grim, a downcast look on his face, and Snow thought right then the kid was capable of killing a man. He wondered how far he'd thought it through. He wondered if the kid really understood and was already mapping it out. He wondered if something horrible weren't happening before his eyes, that lost boy on a porch, how that must have felt, how that must have felt to hear Grandma wailing the news of your father's demise.

Around the forward side of the midship square stood Beth, strategically out of view of the bridge and looking like somebody had been chasing her or was about to start. "Harold," she said. "I went down to open internals and found the midship wing tank full of water."

"We already ballasted it?"

"Not to my knowledge."

"Where's the kid?"

"He just walked right past you."

"Yeah–" Snow peered past the midship square and up to the bridge, saw Bracelin still, then down the other way, forward up the pipeline. "That's right–but where the hell is he?"

"In the pump room setting ballast pumps. Mate's orders."

They went down to the weather deck, and Snow paused to put his left hand to his hip while his right hand held the railing. The ship rolled all around him. He felt the steel pipe of the railing quiver up from its base on the weather deck below. Beth moved down ahead of him and then looked back up the stairs and waited, waves and wind engulfing the scene behind her. He made his way slowly down to the weather deck, holding tight to the railing and not sure he could even stay aboard. Like the whole ship, the whole ocean was shaking its back to rid itself of him, to toss him off.

He faced five easy steps to the watertight door of the tankerman's locker. He gathered himself and stepped toward the door, counting inside his head as he made his way into the room ahead of Beth, who followed up and dogged the door shut against the waves that washed the weather deck. A steady dribble leaked at the base, no matter how you dogged it; bent steel was bent steel and the whole ship was askew, not a square door in the thing.

"You look like you got something," she said.

"I got that rad poisoning thirty-five years late."

Down on the main deck now, Snow felt the sagging action worse than he had above. Water in the wing was a problem because they couldn't get to any damaged framing to repair it, and the only conclusion he could draw was that they had a side shell split below waterline. They needed to get all available ballast pumps running on those wings, he thought. He had to get Leeds up here. He himself could stand a watch in the engine room.

"We can't do what we need to do in this weather," he said. "Squall should be past in an hour."

"Hour can be a long time."

"For an old bag of bones like this ship," Snow said, and even as he talked he felt the whole ship bloat out into the sky, but as soon as he felt the ship rising he realized he was up above it all alone, the ship below him, stretching out. One hour was a long time when six hundred feet of steel flexed and twisted and quivered through every trough and crest. Lightning cracked and exploded all around. Then he was grounded all at once, down inside the tanker-man's locker with Beth holding his hand. He turned to look at her and knew he'd been afraid to look since Nimba Mountain for fear of seeing the father in her eyes, but now he looked and she was just Beth and both their hands were wet and warm. Until he said, "Listen, I got a feeling I know what Bracelin's going to do. We gotta keep an eye out. If he thinks this ship won't make it, we're all gonna have a common problem."

She nodded without a word, her lips set and round. Then the door opened in a rush of water and rain, fat droplets flying side-ways and splattering over the workbench, and the kid stepped inside fast and slammed the door shut. He tried like hell to dog that door so it wouldn't leak, but after he'd resigned himself to fail-ure, he turned to Snow. "I got the ballast pumps going. We're putting water into the number-two tanks all the way across."

"Good work," Snow said.

The kid stared at him like there was a badge on Snow's forehead saying PUT ME OUT OF MY MISERY. "You feeling okay, Harold?"

"Jesus Christ leave me alone," said Snow, and pulled in a deep breath. "Now we gotta get ballast *out* of the wings. Get sub-mersible pumps coming out of every hole that tank's got. Stuff 3-M pads to seal up the gaps where the hose comes out the hole, any way you can, so we don't take on as much as we pump out."

As Maciel stepped out, Snow could see he was packing one of them ax handles as well as his locking knife, which he wore in an open sheath. Snow figured him for one other knife, a smaller locking one in the front pocket of his Friscos. He guessed maybe the kid would need all that, he guessed he felt bad now for snapping at him.

"Hey, George," he said. "I know that insurance guy pushed you. I know how that feels. I don't blame you. You're a helluva good hand. You can be on my crew any day."

The kid looked at him. "Thanks, Harold." Then he was out.

When the squall ended, it ended fast. By dusk, the doldrums were upon them. Night settled, cool from the passing storm, and on the bridge, the mates glowed red in the chart light. Below, the deck crew, led by a slow-moving Snow, went about their work. They steamed south now into a flat-calm sea, water spewing from hoses wired off to the cable railing, like a half dozen fire hoses emptying the wing tanks of water.

Snow smelled fresh diesel. His nose drew him aft, where he peered over the side to see a flat stream of fuel two feet wide spurting from the side shell. He keyed his mike and called for the engineer and the chief mate both. "She's got a side-shell crack at the port diesel tank," he said into the radio. "And likely another at the midship wing."

The ship came to all stop and everybody gathered, including the Liberians, the crew standing there watching the fuel escape. Vapors drifted on airs. The plume of a rainbow slick spread through the water in the glow of work lights, which drew dolphin fish in a school that swung past and glittered like gold knives in black water. There for the taking, Snow thought, if only he had any sinkers left. Then he looked up and saw the mate striding toward him in those gold coveralls, radio around his chest.

"Lucky it's night," said Leeds.

"Why's that?" said Maciel.

" 'Cause welding that sucker up on a hot day would be a risk."

"Welding it up?" the kid said, incredulous. "You're going to *weld* a tank full of fuel?"

Bracelin looked over at the kid like who the fuck was this guy anyhow. "You know, you really do need to learn to shut your fucking trap."

"There's only one way to shut that spigot off," said Leeds. "And that's to hang down there on a bos'n's chair and weld the sucker. So, like I say, we're lucky it's night. Tanks full, theoretically we should be okay."

Something in Leeds made you wonder if the steel in his head was riveted in place or if it wasn't just free-floating on the surface of his brain. Beth went for the harness and helped Leeds strap it on, all the while Leeds saying, "I never knew you cared, Liz, I never knew you cared."

"We're losing fifteen gallons of fuel a minute," Bracelin said. "So whatever you do, do it now." Then he went forward with a sounding tape to check first the midship de-ballasting, followed by the number 2 tank ballasting operation. As soon as Bracelin was out of earshot, Maciel said, "There's got to be another way."

"It'll probably be all right," said Leeds, and winked.

"How about we pump the contents into another tank, gas-free this one, and *then* weld it?" said the kid.

Leeds sat with his legs dangling over the side. He frowned like he had some trouble with the idea, but he couldn't quite put a name to it. "That'll take too long," he finally said. "Just string my leads and get a case of jet rod. There's a portable machine in that aft boatswain's locker."

"And you're sure it won't blow up?"

"You can never be completely sure of a thing like that," said Leeds.

Maciel threw up his hands. "I hope you know what you're doing!" he said, and went for the boatswain's locker.

"I know what I'm doing," said Leeds. "That don't mean I know what's going to happen."

Snow couldn't even engage the debate in his own mind. He moved over and leaned his back against the house and slid down to his ass and sat there. Sparklers appeared, little fireflies swirling past his field of vision. He felt blood coursing into his head. He sat there smelling the ship until Maciel arrived, lugging the small welding machine. He set it on deck and lit it off, the engine sputtering and then gathering steam. Thirty seconds later it was zipping along clear and high. Snow shoved himself off the deck and went to help Beth rig the harness to lower Leeds over the side. They tied the line off to the nearest cleat and Leeds rappelled over and waited next to the stream of diesel, while Maciel lowered his stinger down, saying, "There's no way I can talk you out of this?"

"You could run like hell if you're inclined."

"That's what I do, by God!" said Jimmy, leaning out to watch the flow of diesel. "I run to the goddamned bow!" And he did just that.

But Maciel didn't run, and Snow couldn't have run in any case. Along with Beth and Momo, they hung out over the side, wanting to see what happened, or maybe wanting it to end fast if it did. In the din of the welding machine, Snow heard more voices. They started doubling up on themselves, voices he recognized and could even put faces to. One of them sounded like Snow himself, yelling off in some far corner of the ship, words he couldn't understand.

"Okay!" Leeds yelled from over the side. "Here I go!"

Then he touched the stinger and the flat stream caught fire in a burst, at which point Momo hightailed it out of there. Flames jetted and hissed three feet, shooting out of the ship's side like a flat-edged flamethrower. Maciel moved off to the boatswain's locker and retrieved a welder's mask, handing it to Snow so he could watch the progress. Snow stared through the thick welder's glass. The eerie phosphor-green glow, the dancing bead of white molten steel, and the leaping flames like cool negatives—there was no sense of the danger until Snow removed the hood and watched Leeds down there dangling by a nylon line, flames pouring past his hand as if the ship carried a cargo of fire.

It took twenty minutes to weld the split. As he neared the end and closed the leak off, the flow of fuel ended, and the flames sputtered out. Leeds tipped his mask back and looked up at Maciel. "Told ya so, naysayer!"

When Bracelin came back, he peered down over the side. "You are one balls-out motherfucker."

"I noticed you were nowhere to be found," said Leeds, climbing back over the bulwarks.

"Only an idiot goes to the beach to watch a tsunami. You note the Liberians vacated."

"That's 'cause they have sense," said Snow.

"So what's your take on this split," Bracelin asked. "We got more?"

"Probably," said Leeds. "If not now, then soon."

"How many of them line squalls can she survive? What about rounding the Cape?"

"Who knows? All depends. We hit some bad shit—probably not."

Snow watched as Bracelin snarled and gazed around ship. The tanks were coming up slowly, he said. Too slowly. "My bet we got bulkhead breaks down under and we're ballasting more than just the number-two line. Snow, send the chick down to find out."

Snow knew where Bracelin's mind was going. He was already moving past Plan B and formulating Plan C, whatever it was. He'd probably lift it off his arm tattoos. "What the fuck you carrying in that pack, old man?" Bracelin asked, and slapped at it.

Snow was wearing the pack around without thinking about it,

and now his irritation at the mate simply emerged from his mouth. "Well that's none a your business, Mate."

Bracelin's lips went angular then, just as flat and shut as a smile on a clamshell. He turned and marched up the outer stairs toward the bridge, where he moved over the bullet raft, pitched there on an incline, and leaned over to inspect the door seal. He dug at it with his thumbnail and out came a chunk of old rubber. He flicked the piece aside, and moved topside.

The calms held out through that night, when they passed Ilha do Príncipe under a moon that backlit the rugged southern end of the island. Viewed from the west, it took on fantastic shapes, a series of gnarled hillocks and obelisks that took human form—an old man there at the top on Pico Príncipe, and by his side a boy, and off left, a woman, shrouded in greenery like a shawl—like God, Jesus, and Mary. Looking out to sea where the ship steamed through flat water, Snow hoped the seas ahead would stay that way—he welcomed the calms.

Flat water held into the next day, the boiled sun rising, steam drifting from the still-wet decks. The crew worked until noon ballasting the forward tanks, and the ship leveled out like the beauty she wasn't. They pumped the last barrel of inhibitor into the midship tanks of monomer, but in the equatorial heat, plastic formed around the mouths of the expansion trunks and bubbled up through a crack in the ship's deck. The ship swelled and creaked as they made south into the horse latitudes. It fit Snow's mood to imagine their naming, picturing old Spanish horse traders, sailing on dead and dying airs to jettison their horses rather than compete with their own cargoes for fresh water. The seas over the Angola Basin were as desolate as anywhere, islandless from Annobón to the Cape of Good Hope, and now took on the green-gray reflection of boiling sky.

Snow practically crawled topside to stand a wheel watch, thinking he'd do better to stay close to Bracelin just now. On the bridge, the mate was silent and scanning, and Snow held to the wheel just to keep from falling over, even on flat water. He kept imagining those Spaniards heaving their horses off the poop deck of some old merchant galleon. Snow could see the scene as if he'd filmed it with his Brownie, how the horses plunged with their stick legs pumping, eyes wide and white in terror, noses up, reaching for air and sky until only their flared nostrils were left, huffing and snorting until they finally drew under. He never liked the name horse latitudes, preferred the softer Calms of Capricorn, and he never could understand why the Spaniards hadn't just eaten the horses instead of pitching them.

Snow held to the lathed round knobs of the wooden wheel while the afternoon sun swung dead overhead and boiled the waters, his eyes watering incessantly. He took to wiping them on his shirt, already dripping in the heat. Bracelin trained his binoculars aft for some time, but it was all Snow could do to stare at the gyro. Then the mate went forward and started playing with the radio, tuning to different channels, then checking the Sailing Directions and tuning to Channel 71 VHS and 1785 kilohertz on the sideband. Snow finally turned around and saw the ship.

"How long that been there?" he asked.

"Six hours. She's not gaining on us."

"Just a ship? Any radio traffic?"

"Nothing. I got it tuned to Nigerian Navy work channels."

"You think there's any chance that private dick survived that?"

"Survived having his neck broken? Be a pretty tall miracle." Bracelin nodded toward the radio. "You hear anything, let me know." Then he went down the internal stairs.

Paynor awakened soon after, and Snow pointed out the ship

just as Danny came back on the bridge to stand the wheel. "You're telling me you got no idea who that is?" said Paynor.

"None."

"You try to hail them?"

"No response."

"Well fuck if I like that business. Who the hell could it be?"

"Nigerians, probably. We need another storm to lose them. On the other hand, if it were a speed vessel they'd have caught us by now. I don't know, Payne. Could be anybody."

Paynor looked aft with binoculars then shook his head. "I'll keep a lookout."

Snow took the chance to hit the medicine cabinet, see if they had some Sudafed left over from the time they actually had a medic on board. As he passed through the stair tower he looked out a porthole to see Leeds crawling into the wing tank, which had apparently been emptied sufficiently to find something worth welding on.

On the main deck sick bay, Snow popped three Sudafeds chased by metallic water. He was walking topside when the Sudafed kicked in, cleared up his watering eyes and nose, but then wired him, made him shaky. He gripped the railing on the stairway but felt little strength in his hands. His choice to hit his bunk was an easy one. He took his own sweet time up the stair tower to the second deck, pausing at every other step. Down the muggy internal passageway, he entered his room and lay back on the lower bunk with the little trucker's fan going full blast. The room still smelled vaguely of urea, ether, and rotten eggs. He thought maybe it was his birthday today, he'd forgotten to notice. In 1942 he had spent his birthday on a lifeboat with third-degree burns over half his body.

Then Bracelin was pounding on his door. "I need you down under, old man. We got something sour in the number-three cofferdam."

"I ain't going into no cofferdam," Snow called back. "Just keep it battened down and forget about it. We ain't got a way to fix things down there."

"We got a problem that throws them cargoes off spec, and we won't get squat for them." Bracelin pushed through the door. "What the hell's the matter with you?"

"I ain't feeling well. Picked up a head cold or something there in that storm."

"You dying on me?"

"Just give me a minute."

Bracelin stood in the room's middle and gazed over at Snow with complete disinterest, then turned and started eyeing the old man's locker, glancing down as if scoping a broad on a dock in Rio.

"We gotta take advantage of flat water while we got it. I'll give you one minute. Then I'll have the ordinary crawl tanks. Keep the girl with me, that way I can keep an eye on her."

"You know you're gonna be a lot better off to just keep your eye on the ball."

"What'd you do with the rocks?"

"I got them in a safe place. Why, you want to divvy now?"

Bracelin narrowed his eyes, like he figured he was being played but didn't know how. "Naw, we'll do that when the time comes."

Snow figured as much. Bracelin didn't want to look selfish or paranoid. He was playing it calm. Not a care in the world. Not a care save the worry of ships following them—real and imagined—and the fact that when the time came there'd be no divvying.

"Meantime we got a shitload to do. You seen the girl?"

"No, I ain't seen anything but the inside of my eyelids."

"I got Leeds welding a strap inside that port wing, and Maciel's been setting ballast pumps, but I ain't seen the girl. You and the girl are the only ones fucking the dog."

"I'm sick, goddamnit!" Snow found something in his voice. "We all work hard here, so why you gotta say crap like that?"

" 'Cause I don't like their little thing. It just fucking *bugs* me to think of him getting her and not me. You know? Don't it just get under your skin, Snow?"

"What say you give me that minute?"

After Bracelin finally left, Snow closed his eyes and kept seeing those bygone horses. He could imagine just how it felt, the ocean closing over them. The sea here was desolate and hot—he hated the south Atlantic almost as much as he hated the south Indian. Ugly oceans. And no place to swim if the chief mate decided to jettison you. No place to run if a following ship turned out to be the law. He tried hard—unpleasant as it was—to stuff himself into Bracelin's tall Red Wing lace-ups. Only one thought cycled inside: the mate's mood was way too good for the circumstance.

He pulled himself out of his bunk and went to the locker, where he changed his underwear to a pair of tight whites and then pulled the diamond sack from his backpack, dumped half out, and stuffed it back into his pants, running silver tape there to keep it from moving around and chafing him. He strapped his money belt on with all the cash he had plus the other half of the diamonds. Subdivide, he thought. Subdivide and conquer. He tucked his boot knife into the top of his boot, all the while wondering why the hell he couldn't just give up.

With considerable effort he hauled himself out to the passageway, water dripping off his brow. He wanted to shower. His body sweated a chemical odor, and he tasted lead in his mouth. He took two steps along the railing, paused, breathed, and wondered where Beth was. He could use her arm. Straight ahead lay a door leading out to a Texas deck catwalk that led inboard to the centerline catwalk, and outboard to a corner platform and then up the third deck to another door, and then farther, to the bridge wing. Snow tried to place everybody aboard, but his mind couldn't seem to work toward it. He stalled out on the barbs of a rising headache. He kept seeing Beth's face in his mind. Her head tipped down, eyes looking at him on that night in Okinawa. When he felt her lips and thought maybe, just maybe.

He went out the door, turned right along the balcony and then up the catwalk past the stairs to the poop deck. As he stepped from the grated catwalk to the solid metal deck of the poop, he saw Bracelin hunched over the door of the bullet raft with a knife, prying up and pulling out the dried cracked seal, which came out in a cloud of decayed rubber. Then he came up with a fresh seal and ran a bead of glue and started running the black rubber into the slot with a narrow roller.

Snow paused a moment and watched him, and wondered if he shouldn't just kill him now. Wondered if he shouldn't just see where everything would head. It reminded him of his father, who once said that the man who wins a fight is the first to realize he's in one. He knew he was in one. He withdrew back behind the corner of the ship's house and onto the catwalk balcony and pressed himself backward against the steel house and felt for his locking knife, down deep in the pocket of his jeans, gripping and regripping, thinking it would be no small matter to step up there right now. Step up there and drive the tip of that Buck knife between the man's shoulder blades, past the bone of his vertebrae and into his beating heart.

He had no real understanding of what stopped him. Fear of failure, or a dark pathetic judgment weighing on him. The coming of the surrogates. The girl, the boy. He had never seen himself a man before. It only now occurred to him, he'd never really been responsible to anybody, even as a parent. Snow came back into the sun, beating down, with a sea rising. The ship began rocking through the soft round swells, and Snow thought about Bracelin and how he'd want the cover of storm. The following ship held position astern, maybe fifteen miles. Snow held the knife and resolved to step around the house. He'd go to hell anyway, if there was a hell. Maybe in the end he could do something to save some-one. You slept with men like Bracelin, and you sealed yourself into a dank poison box. Little pieces of the man sloughed off, like scales of dry skin breathed deep into the lungs of anyone who occupied space with him. Snow clutched the knife and started to move around the corner with a ball of fear choking off his throat, and looked to the aft railing and the bullet raft there alone, door shut tight and locked, and Bracelin nowhere in sight.

Just as well. He didn't think he could have done it anyway. He moved back along the side and around the forward corner of the house and looked out over the foredeck. Clouds rose like columns of smoke on some invisible burning horizon. At first they were all haze and white, but even as he stood there he felt the cooling as the sun slipped behind the thunderheads, and then darker, until lightning crackled the air and a line of waterspouts appeared, first scattered dead ahead, then all around the ship in clusters of threes and fours.

The seas lifted the ship and brought her down with a rolling shudder. Wind pulled at his scruff of hair, and the rain spattered in thick drops across the weather deck. With added ballast, the ship now sat down to her load lines, and Snow could feel her hunkering in for the shit. He made his way forward along the catwalk, pulling himself along and listening to the ship creak and rattle. Spray hit him from the bow, first a wisp of spume and then the thump of a real trough, and white water cascaded through the bulwarks and up and over the railing, fanning up and back over the fo'c'sle deck like hard surf on a rocky shore. From the midship tankerman's locker, up on the catwalk, Snow thought he saw someone out there on the bow, was thinking they ought to come in before it got too much rougher. Bracelin wanted them separated. One at a time, Snow thought, he'd come one at a time.

Busy workers, easy marks.

Rain flooded the pipeline network, waves sheeting off the deck as the ship rolled through the squall, a wave breaking over the bow and tearing through the pipeline thrashing chaotic around valves, hitting an obstruction to pop skyward and then rush toward gravity. A wave tore loose the padding around one hole and ran past the hose and down into the tank in a swirl, the hoses continuing to emit their paltry ballast. Snow felt the tingling wash over him again, beginning at his head, paralyzing him. He stood holding the railing, looking toward the bow for signs of anyone, for life, but he saw no one. He turned back. There was nothing he could do out here. The railing vibrated under his hand. Someone shouted in his ear in Hindi. At least he thought it was Hindi, it sounded like Hindi. He caught movement out the corner of his eye and turned to find nothing. Saw something back the other way, sensed someone behind him, but no matter how fast he turned he caught nary a glimpse. The catwalk stretched a long way aft, seemed longer now than coming out. The ship slammed a trough and seemed to thud to a standstill. He stood up as the bow lifted, and ambled aft as fast he could, one hand sliding along the railing, going downhill, his feet trying to adjust to the heeling of the vessel as it swung through the waves. He could see that the ship was no longer sagging, but hogging. The hunched back of the weather deck was pronounced, and he could hear fatigued steel.

He waited for a trough to pass and then stepped down slowly to the weather deck and turned into the midship locker to find Maciel in there pulling on an air pack with its sealed mask respirator. "What you got going?" Snow asked.

"Do any of these tanks have air left in them?"

"Not to my knowledge. Listen, Georgie." He tried to form the words first, so they'd come out right. "There's things you don't understand. Things between me and Bracelin that go way back. Not only that, but this ship."

Maciel strapped the buckle across the front of the shoulder straps and then stared at Snow. "Well, thanks for telling me, but Leeds nailed that one somewhere around the Amazon."

"We got a ship on our stern end for better part of two days. The thing you gotta know is, the more Bracelin feels cornered the more you want to watch your backside."

Maciel let out an exasperated breath and breathed into his hands as if praying, or blowing on lucky dice. Then he looked up. "So let's kill him," he said. "Let's get Leeds and we'll kill him."

Snow shook his head. They were thinking on similar lines anyway. "You got no clue about him, George. He ain't your average guy."

"Fuck it, there comes a moment, Harold. It isn't a matter of right and wrong anymore."

Snow's lips parted, but he couldn't quite express to the kid how slippery that killing slope was, even if you did have a pretty good idea where the conflict would all end up. He saw the face of Dutch Van, saw his body like a knife edge moving toward him with that marlin spike tucked back up. He saw Joaquin Maciel emerge from the house to the afterdeck. He saw the marlin spike striking human flesh, the meat and bone giving way under the force of blows, something brutal and immediate about the closeness of it. Snow reached back behind himself to steady against the workbench. "I can't help you. I'm too fucking sick. What you do, and when you do it–that's your choice, George. I'm here to tell you if you stick him in the back out of nowhere, it ain't gonna feel like self-defense. You'll have to live with it. And if you believe in your God, you'll have to die with it too."

Snow felt the pain rising up from the center of his skull. All this talk of guilt was wearing him out. He leaned back against the bulkhead and tried to roll with the seas. "I gotta get to my rack. Help me up."

Maciel gave him a hand and Snow stood up, holding to the chemical suits hanging from their hooks. He waited for a wave to pass, then went out, leaving the kid behind, and grasped along the handrail through the rolling sea as he went up the stairs to the catwalk, then started aft as a new wave roared up and over the bow. He didn't think about where the kid was now, back behind him somewhere. Off to do his deed. Off to take control, maybe, off to dive like all the others he'd known into the abyss of the killing sea. He found himself in a stumbling run, a futile sense coursing through him, as his right hand caught on something as the ship hogged over another wave. He stopped, felt it pinch, jerked his hand away without thought and felt the flesh tear. He looked down to see the catwalk railing popped open at a weld, flexing open and closed with the movement of the ship.

When the bow rose upward, making for a downward slope leading aft, his feet moved on automatic, and he held to the railing with his left hand now, dodging bottles of nitrogen, and felt the ship roll sideways some. Once to the house, he went down the stair tower to the sick bay, where he pulled off his glove to find a chunk of flesh missing from the meaty part of his right hand, just below the baby finger. The blood was unbelievably dark, almost black, as it oozed from the hole there. He shivered at the sight of it, rummaged through medicine drawers until he found a thick wide Band-Aid to cover the cut on his hand, then set about hauling himself topside for the room. When he got there, the room was empty, his locker door clanging open and closed and the contents strewn about the deck. He knew Bracelin was into it now, knew the fight had begun. The kid knew that too, Snow hoped, since he himself had missed his chance. That's just what moralizing did for you, drew you off the practical side. He lay flat on his back. The mattress of his bunk had never felt so pointed and hard, like a bed of nails.

He remembered dancing with his wife when she was still his nurse, remembered the rattle of war medals and the shimmer of ribbons and his mother playing that song on the piano in the front room of their house in Bremerton: "Funny Little Snowman." The tinkling sound of keys, and her voice, pure and slow, matching the piano note for note as she gazed at him and smiled, a song just for him, just for her boy. How old had he been? Five? Eight? He remembered summers in the Cascades as a teenager following his uncle into the woods, on a USGS crew while his old man was off at sea. He remembered the year he left Index, that sinking feeling as he rode the poop deck all the way out the Strait of Juan de Fuca. Life was all memory in the end. What did it matter what anybody knew about the things he'd done. Even Beth; what did it matter how she judged him or even *if* she judged him. He wished she'd come see him now. *Come see me,* he thought. *Come see me.*

Even then he felt a cold inside his shoulders. His breathing grew ragged as he felt the ship rise and heave and whistle with the stress of a real storm. He closed his eyes, and when he opened them again, there she was, like a spirit he'd conjured.

"Elisabeth," he said.

"Are you all right?"

"I ain't all right." He strained to sit upright.

"Hold it there, Harold, lie back down." She leaned close to him and put her hand to his forehead. Her hand was cold, cold, sent a shiver through him. "You know what's wrong?"

"There's so much wrong now, there's no counting," he said. "I'm sorry about your old man. I'm sorry about that—I was being selfish."

"Never mind it now," she said.

He stared at her and his eyes turned watery, not even sure they were tears because his eyes watered pretty near all the time now, but whatever the source he felt sad, and water flooded his eyes, and he wanted more than anything to be able to keep from crying, but the water just came. He could feel his body failing out from under him. "I met my first wife in a burn ward. I tell you that?"

"No, you never did."

"She was the prettiest nurse there. No one believed I could get her. We were so goddamned in love it was almost painful. After I fucked my way out of my marriage, I hoped I'd never have that feeling again. Now I don't wanna live without it."

"You don't have to live without, Harold."

"I do, though–I do. 'Cause she loved me too. She loved me better than I loved her in the end. But not you, Bethy. Not you. You're my comeuppance. It's all goddamned clear to me now. There is a God, and I'm screwed."

She held her lips tight and brought her hands to her mouth, together like prayer. "Harold–" Her eyes were earnest, glowing. "Don't you see that I do love you? Granted, not in the way you want. But it's so. I love you."

He let out a laugh, or tried to–he felt his eyes burning and he wasn't sure if any sound came out his mouth. "That's what they call small consolation."

She sat there next to his bunk, sitting on an overturned milk crate gripping the base of the bunk with one hand and with the other holding his forehead, her hand warming under the heat of his brow. Equilibrating. Transfer of heat. As the ship rocked, the locker door clanged open and shut, beating against the drawer, where the yellow movie boxes lay piled under the padlock he'd used to secure them. All them bloody movies, he thought. Canned memory.

"In there," he said, "are movies. My whole goddamned life

since the invention of the Brownie. They probably got salt caked in them by now, but there's one in there says ELISABETH on it. You can have that, if you want it. It's from earlier, with the kid. I never did get it developed. You can have all of them."

She stared at the film box but made no move to take it. "You're talking morosely now. We've been through storms before. We'll make Cape Town."

"I don't think so."

She looked over at him and saw he was crying. "God, Harold, it'll be all right. We'll get you to a doctor."

"It ain't that. I keep thinking what the kid said about his granddad, how he was going to hell and convinced he'd never see his wife again, and I been having that same thought, I can't escape that same thought, only it's about never seeing you again. You wanting to go away. I'm afraid I won't ever see you again. It feels like drowning. I been cast out a long time. I figured it didn't matter. Till I met you it didn't matter. Now it's all I think about. Them old Greeks, you know, that's what they did. Worst punishment you could deal a man, banishment. No home. No identity anymore. Just cast out. It's fucking heartless. I want to call them on the phone and say I'm sorry sometimes. I want to beg for goddamned mercy. Beg to be let back home, ya know? If they could just see that. Don't matter what a man does, good people can pull him out. People who love him can pull him out."

She held his face in her hands. Talked to him like a boy. Like his dead mother. "I won't leave you," Beth said. "Do you see that? All the men, all the women. They all end. All the fucks, they're over. Ours never ends. Never."

"Jesus Christ–"

"Don't be sad."

"It's all so fucking lost."

She tilted her face to him then, the smile genuine warmth in a slamming creaking leaking ship somewhere two days from land. He reached into his pants then and wrenched out the sack of diamonds, the duct tape pulling at his hair, and then he pushed the bag at her. "You take these. Keep them someplace safe. They're yours." Then he lifted up as best he could to loosen the money belt and gave her that too.

"I don't want all this."

"Them rocks are currency. Get a flight to Antwerp, you'll get better money there. There's some cash too. Enough to get you there. There's more cash in the ship's safe, but I don't know if I'd try to get to that now. So take these. Just don't put them down your pants, first place Bracelin's liable to look."

He let out a forced chuckle.

She stuffed the bag down into the deep pocket of her fatigues and pressed the tape against her leg until it just clung in there, the bulge evident against her leg.

"Take these too," he said, and he set his boot knife and his boning knife on the bed.

She stared at them. "Just lie back, Harold. Conserve your energy."

"For what?" She rested her hand on his chest and patted him as he rolled over on his side. "You gotta think clearly, Bethy. Where's Maciel? Where's Bracelin? You seen him? What's he doing? You need to figure where everybody is now, that's the important thing, you need to gather everybody together."

"Leeds is in the engine room, I guess. Paynor on the bridge. I haven't seen George or Bracelin."

Snow groaned and lifted himself upright to the edge of the bed, swinging his legs out. "Help me up. Then go find Maciel and Leeds. Maciel was going for Leeds. Help me up. I gotta get up."

She looped her arm under his and he was just pulling to his feet when a knock at the door brought her head up, and she said, "Oh," and Snow thought maybe it was Maciel, that together they really could figure out some way to get off the ship finally, scooting to the Angola coast. The only problem was that voice he heard. A real voice, not the voices in his head or the whisper of the girl but the blunt baritone of Bracelin. "I figured I'd find you two fucking the dog. Not that you're fucking each other, we all know *that* ain't happening."

Beth stepped backward, her eyes casting around the room and lighting on the knives there on the bed. Bracelin's gray-black hair was pulled back out of his face and brought together in a ponytail that made him look even more sinister than usual, despite the everyday yellow rain gear. He grinned, his face pulling together.

"You need something?" Snow said from back behind her, sitting on the edge of his bunk now, holding himself there against the rocking motion. He reached for the knives, but awkwardly, and knocked them to the deck. Nobody moved.

"Matter of fact," Bracelin said, turning to Beth, "I need you for starters."

"I'm on my way back out," she said, and bent down to pick up the boning knife.

"Good idea. We're goddamned shorthanded, to say the least, and this one's pretty much worthless now." He nodded his head toward Snow. "I need all hands."

Bracelin stepped for the door and pulled it open, holding it for her to go out ahead of him. She glanced once at Snow, a dead look, like she knew this voice, had heard it first fourteen years gone when the chief engineer from a rig tender called *Dunkirk* had said, "*Ça suffit,*" and demanded that his kindness be repaid.

Snow held to the bunk. "She's with me, Brace," Snow said. "We'll turn-to now. I just had a little trouble . . . taking some medication."

"It's too late for you, Snow."

"Wait there." Snow looked at Beth. "Don't go with him, Bethy."

Bracelin looked at Snow with that dead scarred face, and Beth saw the look now too, but before she could move against the heel of the ship, Bracelin reached out and grabbed her by the arm. Her look seared into Snow, a look of familiarity; she'd been here before. He could feel her now, could put himself right there in her soft brown breast and understand a part of her he'd never quite put his heart to. "Leave her alone, Charlie. She's with me. We been through all this. She's with me."

"Fuck that. Where'd you put the rocks?" Bracelin closed the door behind him, and in the movement of the ship Beth shook herself free and reached down for the knife on the floor. As she brought it up, Bracelin's fist came down hard on her wrist and the knife clattered to the deck and slid under the bed between Snow's legs. The ship rolled, shuddering and rocking sideways as if they'd taken a rogue wave against the port side, and Beth's balance gave way. She tried in vain to wrench her arm free, but Bracelin held to her like his fist was made of stone.

Snow tried pulling himself up, saying, "Now, Charlie, come on now, Charlie"–his feet flat on the deck, not sure he *could* get up, much less be of any use once he did. Still he reached over his head and grasped the lower edge of Maciel's bunk and pulled himself to his feet. He wobbled there, steadying himself, while Bracelin pulled her closer and turned to look at Snow with his dead eyes. "Where are the rocks?" he asked again.

"Just let her go and I'll get them for you. I will. Just let her go!"

Snow's voice strained. "You can have the diamonds. I don't give a shit for any of it."

Bracelin let out a chuckle, pulled Beth close, and kissed her mouth, his thick tongue sliding between her lips.

"Ahh, goddamnit, Charlie, get off her now, I said *get off her now!*" His voice cracked with weakness and rage even as he saw Bracelin reach behind into his belt, and Snow had no sooner seen the glint of black metal than he was moving toward him, swinging his boot knife out of his belt and fumbling it, tumbling in the air, swinging with the movement of the ship. His body lunged forward and he swung his fist straight at the gun and punched it hard, splitting his own knuckle and catapulting the weapon against the desk. His momentum stalled out then, the ship rocking back the other way and Bracelin toppled toward him, and Snow yelled *"Go!"* and felt the rush of draft as Beth was gone and out the door, the two men rolling backward. He felt the full weight of Bracelin on top of him, felt the bludgeon of the man's fist against his eye, shattering the orbit. Blood pulsed and drained into his ear and mouth. Snow wrapped his legs around the mate and squeezed him, felt another blow, but this more distant, as if his face were two feet away from his brain, a distant thud that had nothing to do with the strength in his legs, drawing inward and refusing to let go even as Bracelin battered him.

"You meddlesome old fuck. What you care about these people?"

Snow felt a pointed blow to the solar plexus.

It burned into him, radiating up and out until it flooded his entire upper body. *He's stabbed me,* he thought, *the son of a bitch has stabbed me,* and through the distant burning in his chest he felt Bracelin disappear, even as the pain washed over him, and he lay still, in darkness, with the ship swirling all around under him.

THE SKELETON COAST

Snow lay on the deck in the room like he had way back in Frisco but without a mattress, thinking *what have I missed, I must have missed something godawful.* He supposed in some ways the kid was a Jonah after all. Now Snow felt he needed to say something out loud, form the words and say them, confess your sins, he said. Confess them. Straight to God, right there between you and God.

He tried to move his mouth to make the sounds, and, though he heard the words, had no idea if his ears were doing the hearing or if he could even speak now. He felt his body glow, drifting, he could ride it out here *I can ride it out here.* But then he heard that old command voice like a loudhailer on a towboat *time to turn-to, Snow, time-to turn-to!* Joaquin drifted all around him, like a swirling cloud of fire, suffocating and beautiful. The glowing heat of his voice drew the air from Snow's lungs to feed some nearby firestorm. He didn't know if he was warmed by it or in danger of being incinerated.

He only knew he had to move. He had to move now or never.

He felt that force out there now, closer than ever: some dark cascading sheet that would envelop him, Van Sickle maybe, coming for him to drag him like a shade into the gutter that ran to the Underworld. *You gotta move.*

His body was overcome then by a wracking, shivering vengeance. His head felt like a giant wood screw was being ratcheted down into it from above. In his mind he had righted himself, had leaped to his feet and run out the door, running down the passageway, running upward to the bridge–toward the wheel. He was young and strong in his wakeful dream. He had been trying to get the wheel that day in the Coral Sea when the bomb hit, had come out of the crew's mess aft with a stomach full of scrambled eggs and *look there,* so close he could have caught that bomb like a long fly ball, and when it blew him upward and he finally landed, he heaved his breakfast onto the deck while sitting in his own shit with his shoes thirty feet away and a man's shoulder on his lap.

He wondered if his life could ever have been different; if he had figured things out sooner what might have happened, how might he have lived? With that he hauled himself to his feet and pushed into the head and braced himself as best he could between bulkheads, one hand holding to the handrail by the toilet, and relieved himself into the toilet bowl, only to find his urine came out black. *Jesus,* he thought, *Jesus!* He stared at the black water in the toilet and felt surging panic.

Through the black caking of blood on his face, his left eye incapable of opening for the broken mantle of his eyebrow, he reached for the door and gave it a tug with his fingertips. The heavy spring-loaded door barely gave before it snapped back into the jamb and shut on him. He lost his balance backward, was thrown against the bulkhead, and braced himself against the map of the world with all those blue and red dots, grasping and tearing the whole thing off the wall in a single thrust as he flew backward yet again. He crawled through and past the crumpled paper and made the door, timing his rise with the lurch of the ship and holding both hands to the door handle. He jerked it open and stepped out, peering up the long dim passage toward the bridge ladder. Then he found himself lying down again. He wasn't sure how he got there, but it had to be true. A handrail led over his head and down the passageway. He reached for it, lifting himself to his knees, and in a single motion, as if snatching a barbell that was his own body, he lifted himself to his feet and wobbled there, both hands clasping the painted steel rail, and began to move. Gotta move. Gotta get to the bridge. He knew Bracelin had not wanted to kill him, simply by his being alive—after all, why bother, he was close enough to taste death all on his own.

That Snow managed to pull himself up the internal ladder was a minor miracle, and it took him the better part of ten minutes to make it. When he finally came close enough, he rocked with the movement of the ship and heaved his body onto the bridge deck and crawled the rest of the way in, looking up to see Paynor and one of the twins staring off into the swollen, wind-raked seas.

Now Paynor let out an exasperated grunt and darted to the starboard bulkhead. He spun wildly, pulled a survival kit off the console with a jerk, tearing the mounting loose and stuffing it into a nylon bag. As Paynor moved behind the wheel, beneath the chart light, he finally noticed Snow pulling himself to his feet by the lip of the chart table. "What the fuck happened to you?"

"Bracelin happened to me," said Snow, seeing everything through a kind of monocular tunnel. The ship heaved forward, and waves popped and flew over the bow, then blew on wind all the way back, raining double-time against the wheelhouse glass. "Dear God," he said.

He spied the trash can, bungeed alongside the chart table, and thought perhaps he'd throw up. His mouth flushed with fluid. He took a deep breath, felt his body relax some and the nausea pass for a moment. Then he looked out to see Maciel making his way in from the bow, wearing a rain suit, one hand sliding along the railing as he made his way to the midship square and down the stairs toward the room there.

"Listen, Snow," said Paynor, looking around as if he might be forgetting something, looking for charts on the shelves below the table. "I think it's time to get going, know what I mean?"

"Where the hell is Bracelin?"

"I haven't seen him."

"You seen anybody?"

"Not really–just Jimmy here."

"I am Danny."

The Liberian kept looking out, his brow glowing with sweat that picked up light from the control console. His eyes glowed when he finally took his eyes off the storm and saw Snow there, looking just like a man who'd recently received a beating. Danny looked back out to the storm, and the heaving foredeck. "Oh boy, that a bad one," he proclaimed, though it was uncertain just what he meant by this–the boatswain with blood still oozing from his eyebrow, or the storm outside. "Your blood black, man, you got the malaria!"

Paynor looked at him closer. "Jesus, Snow, he's right. You take any mefloquine going into W.A.?"

"I can't take that shit. Makes me crazy."

"You rather be crazy or dead? Go get some mefloquine from the damned sick bay. You look bad."

"I can't make it down there."

"I'd send Jimmy down but I need him on the wheel."

"I tell you, I am Danny," said the Liberian.

"I can take the wheel. Do you read English?" Snow asked.

"Sure. I read English. Tell him I am Danny."

"He's Danny," Snow said. "Now give me a pen."

Paynor shoved the drafting compass across to him, and Snow took it, his hands quivering badly as he opened the compass until the sharp graphite tip was as far open as he could get it. Awkwardly, through shaking broken hands and the pounding of the ship, he scrawled on a corner of the chart:

QUININE.

CHLOROQUINE.

MEFLOQUINE.

Then he tore it off and handed the yellowed corner of chart paper to the Liberian. "Bring me all these," Snow said. "Much as they have."

"Okay, bos'n."

Paynor stared at Snow's bad eye. "Why the hell did Bracelin hit you?"

" 'Cause he tried to hurt her, that's why."

Paynor took the paper from Danny's hand. "You better let me go down. I got us at this position here–" and he moved over the chart table, where he had them farther south than Snow had imagined possible.

"We're off Cape *Fria*? That's Namibia. What the hell happened to Angola?"

"We got blown past. Got blown toward the coast too. But I figure we got another fifty miles of sea room. Just keep the head up and I'll be back."

Paynor went out and down through the internal ladder while Snow stood by the chart table and Danny held to the wheel. "How's your brother doing below?" he asked.

"He okay, we no change the engine for hour or more, bos'n," said Danny.

Snow stared at the chart of the Skeleton Coast, the northern section of Namibia from here to Walvis Bay. They might make Walvis Bay, he thought, but anything in between was only sand dunes and diamond dirt. He felt the giant wood screw to his head, the voices there turning to murmurs, drowned out by pain. He tried to focus on the chart. He knew the coastline here was more variable than any chart could keep up with. There were seamounts all over, running in a diagonal away from the coast in a belt of undersea mountains called the Walvis Ridge. He read a notation from the Sailing Directions: *Warning: the coastline here is reported to be two miles west of current charts (1975).*

He looked up toward the forward windows, which from back by the chart table gave him a view of the fo'c'sle deck only. The bow lifted and slammed into a trough. He wondered about the hogging, how much worse it was now. He took the chance of letting go of the chart table and let gravity carry him to the radar scope. He checked the sweep of it–the green clutter of storm. He brought up the gain and lowered the clutter–and caught nothing but a frayed band of something about twenty miles east. Paynor couldn't be that far off his position fix; he was too good a navigator. "We got a hundred feet of water here," Snow said. "We got twenty miles of sea room, maybe. We need to put out anchors and I got no crew to do it." Snow timed his movement to the forward window, held the railing there by the radio telephone, and looked out over the whole of the deck just in time to see Bracelin come into view, bulky yellow rain suit fighting through the spray up the centerline catwalk.

"Goddamn him, goddamn him!" Snow stood as long as he could, then let himself drop to a sitting position. He sat against the bulkhead, his head knocking on the steel, which turned the wood screw into a jackhammer, pounding in and out of his brain. The swelling pulse of his headache overcame him, and he leaned over and heaved onto the deck, a bilious foamy excretion streaked with black strings of semi-coagulated blood.

"Head up, Danny boy," said Snow, trying a weak smile.

"Head up," he said, staring at the mess on the deck, then catching himself and snapping his eyes back to the gyrocompass.

Snow was sitting there for no more than three minutes before he heard a sliding sound from below, as if a giant sheet of baking trays had slid across the deck immediately below them. But this was deeper, a rumbling that came from the stern. He recognized the sound, and at the moment of backward force, he let go of the chart table and let himself be thrown aft onto the wheelhouse deck. He reached upward, put a hand to the bulkhead railing and with every last little bolt of energy he could manage lifted himself to a kneeling position, jerked himself to his feet, and wobbled there with both hands on the rail. He looked astern in time to see the covered lifeboat bobbing up a wave behind them, its orange bullet shape appearing like something out of science fiction as it rocked against the windblown crest, the inboard engine groaning as the squirrelly craft heaved over the wave and powered straight downwind toward the Skeleton Coast. He saw the thing yaw badly, turn nearly broadside to a wave, teeter on the edge and nearly roll, then right itself in the next trough and motor on away from the ship with water draining all around that hatch with the brand-new seal. Snow couldn't see anyone in the tiny angled windows at the front of the craft, but he didn't need to see, for he knew who was driving the thing, knew as certain as he knew anything that he wouldn't be getting his malaria meds now unless Danny went down to get them for him, or, worse yet, he went down on his own.

Then he refocused and saw the bridge wing, where Beth stood, shivering, gazing inward. He waved her inside and fell toward her as she passed through the door and hooked her arm up under his. "I couldn't find him. I couldn't find Leeds or Maciel."

"We gotta go down. I need meds."

They started down the external stairs, but soon it was apparent that Snow couldn't make it down in the storm. They ducked into the second-deck door, Beth helping him along. "I just wanted to thank you for what you did back there."

"Wasn't nothing to it." Snow grinned.

They worked their way down the internal stair tower to the afterdeck and around the back of the house to the side deck, where the light from the boatswain's locker cast outward, and inside they heard clattering of gear and the grunts of someone exasperated. They stepped inside to find Maciel rummaging through the cubbies, turning to see them there, his eyes showing full-blown panic. "Where the hell have you been? Have you see him? I think he got Momo. I can't find Momo."

"What about Leeds?"

"Leeds? I have no idea! Where the hell is Leeds? We need Leeds! We need *dim mak*! You think he got Leeds too? Is it possible?"

Snow found himself sitting down in a swirling puddle of water, raining in through the door. The shrieks of the wind pressed at his ears. He heard the distant groans of men, or perhaps the ship itself, wailing like a desperate human.

"Have you seen any of those ax handles? I have to find one."

Snow looked up at him, saw him dig down deep into a box of bolts like he'd find one in there, and then he caught sight of something left, a shade he thought, and Beth was rising up over him, and behind her loomed the form of Bracelin, his face all twisted up. "You looking for one of these?" he said.

And he brought the bludgeon down onto Beth.

Her reaction time was better than Snow's. She ducked and the ax handle hit her in the upper back, knocking the wind from her as she slumped forward with a grunt, and fell onto Snow. He wrapped his arms around her and turned her away, holding his hand up in case Bracelin struck again. But he was moving for George then, the kid still sifting through the cubbies looking for something, then turning with a flash of red–a small pipe wrench–that he swung in a wide sweep at Bracelin and caught him just below the left eye.

Bracelin's head whipped sideways in a snarl, then righted itself and he bull-rushed Maciel, driving his head into the kid's solar plexus and butting him straight back into the cubbies, pipe fittings crashing all around him. Bracelin let out an animal sound as the kid smashed into bolts and pipe fittings. Snow felt his legs lifting, then he was standing. Beth was reaching for an air tank. Then Snow was down again, on his ass. Then he was on his back. He saw them over his head. Maciel flailed and scratched, trying to keep Bracelin off him, trying to swing the pipe wrench again but missing. Then the kid struck him with a blow to the face and knocked him backward. Beth swung the air tank straight overhead and hit Bracelin on the back of the head with a resounding thump. Snow tried to move. Nothing on him worked. From a sitting position Bracelin drove his hand up into Beth's stomach and sent her flying backward, doubled over and gasping for air. Her voice came out airless, like those horses heaving. Snow tried to wiggle his toe. Nothing moved.

He could see everything and nothing. The first and the last. Bracelin came to his feet and took the rushing Maciel with a step to one side, lifting him and heaving him through the air. Maciel flew backward. He hit the bank of cubbies, which promptly toppled onto his back. Bracelin stepped away as the rack folded the kid in half, the compartments of pipe and nuts and bolts emptying onto his back. Bracelin turned to Beth and kicked her as hard as he could, then stepped toward Maciel and heaved the wooden rack aside with a grunt and a crash of wood and steel.

Snow looked downward to the door. He felt himself floating, bodiless. He saw Bracelin. The background of black seas, sweeping past in flashes of yellow-white waves. Bracelin descended on the kid and was about to grab him when a pink hand curled around his right eye and his head twisted back. He let out a groan, rising to a shriek as the pink gnarled fingers reached into his eye sockets, and another arm, pink and welted with the lesions of psoriasis, curved around his neck and clutched him there. Bracelin flailed, stumbling backward. He backed himself into the door frame, slamming Leeds into its edge, then falling himself, and the two of them went out the door into the wash of seas receding off the weather deck. Reeling, squirming, doing his monkey kung fu. Leper hands clasping. Maciel rose, gripping an ax handle.

Bracelin swirled and rolled trying to rid himself of Leeds, managed to claw himself to his feet bringing Leeds with him, back into the door, spinning at the doorjamb in a vain attempt to scrape Leeds off his back. The more he flailed and danced, the tighter Leeds gripped him, his legs around his waist, his arms around his neck and face. Maciel moved forward in a lurch and swung the ax handle, but Bracelin got out a hand and deflected it, the bludgeon flying out of the kid's hand and bouncing to the deck at Bracelin's feet. Leeds continued to gouge at his eyes while Maciel went for his belt knife. He snapped it open with a flick. He stepped up, casually almost, then drove the blade straight down into Bracelin's solar plexus. Bracelin erupted in blood. First it came out of the wound itself. Snow was struck by the redness of it. By the white glow of the work lights, by the hiss and rush of the storm. He remembered the moment now, on the afterdeck of the *San Luis Rey*. He remembered the strange sensation of piercing another man's skin. How easy it went in if you just gave it enough force. The kid gave it plenty of force, and Bracelin fell backward. Even then Leeds didn't let go. Maciel stood there heaving breaths, with a look of terror and bloodlust all at once, then reached down and stabbed him again. He stood there in the doorway, his eyes wild and unflinching while Bracelin started to heave up blood from his mouth. Then a wave hurled past and the kid stepped back from the crush of water through the tankerman's locker, the flushing roar of it inside. The deck had been washed clean. In a swirl of rain and wind and crashing wave, Leeds and Bracelin were gone.

Snow barely registered this. He was busy falling down a long shoot toward black space, the storm raging around him, until a distant part of him realized that both men had been washed overboard and the kid was crying over him, jumping and spinning a circle and then slumping down onto the deck of the locker and crying in great racking sobs with his head down in his hands. Beth moved for him, leaving Snow there alone in a puddle of seawater, and Snow reached out his hand to touch the kid's knee and pat it, saying it's okay, it's okay, see, there really ain't any doubt about self-defense now and he wanted to laugh but he hadn't the energy for it, and he wished he could have found time to tell the kid about his grandfather, wished he could have just said I done some bad things in my life, I killed a man once, killed more than one and maybe done worse things.

Water and waves swept the deck outside, curling around and down the drain. Snow crawled toward the opening, moving again, looking out on hands and knees to the terrible grinding sound. He could feel it out there, the cleaving of failed steel. All across the deck he saw the crack widen and the spewing of polymerizing cargoes, fanning up and out of the deck with an explosive rush. From his position on the side deck, looking forward through sheets of water draining, he saw the deck knuckle upward, the bow breaking downward until it was buried into the waves.

Snow awakened to sunlight. He heard voices around him but no engines. The sky spread over him like a warm blanket. It flooded the deck in shifting angles of the house and the pipeline, the melon-colored sky, and the feeling of being lifted, taken away by someone he couldn't see. He heard a voice, distant, echoless across the void of the post-storm sea swell, crying *Hellll*–! Snow floated toward the sound, like the pull of a song he could barely hear, and he strained forward to meet it, turned his good ear to the sound of a man yelling *Hell,* and through his numbness he felt his heart and his face flushed and hands humming. They were lifting him. Black arms at his armpits and his knees, his ass sagging before he felt nothing of his body at all, just the floating as they went over the side. Her voice was at his ear the entire way *you're going to be all right, Harold, you know, I'm not going to leave you* and all along the way the steel of the ship curled inside him. Even as they carried him he felt the ship beneath him. He had sweated on and carved rust from the hull of it for so long.

He heard that voice calling *Hell* again from out over the water, where he could see and feel a part of things even though he was facing upward and staring at sky, but he could feel the arms of his carriers working, taking one for Beth the other for Maciel or Momo or Danny, or maybe all four of them–yes, there were four sets of hands. And legs striding. Out over the sea he saw nothing but flatness and the boiling ocean, the smell of hydrogenated sulfur reeking. The ocean was boiling, in great roiling bubbles and extrusions of foam and exhalations of gas. Boiling! He himself was boiling. His brain baked by fever, infested by parasites. He could feel them in there, lunching on red blood cells and excreting the black bile of his own dying humors. He bled black, he pissed black, his waters gone to rotten mud.

The hell voice remained out there, wailing. Through the yellow-orange light he heard it. Amid a scattering of flotsam, the ship's deck pitching downward toward the swells. The water had a languid quality, lulling him. But the heat grew oppressive. A hot wind raked his skin. It must have been 120 degrees with 90 percent humidity. Only skyward brought relief. Flying over everything, as if he had bounded out and up the mast to perch himself in the crow's nest, where in old days they carried land birds and when the ship was lost they'd release the birds and follow them home through the storm. And there was the crow, lifting off, the broad reach of water toward a seamount rising in a pale rocky mass. Distant thundersqualls rose off the horizon as if the two were merged, the great vaulting columns of cloud like the smokes of the earth itself.

The water held ball-shaped fragments of white that came in sizes ranging from ping-pong balls to basketballs and larger, glommed-together bubbles of white like irregular foam balloons stretching out in a plume from the ship's middle, until his body sank into them and parted them, and he was down inside a skiff without a motor, a goddamned rowboat, seeing arms flicker and pull at the oars over his face, his body baking in the heat. He felt the occasional pause in the up and down of the waves, then a jerking, when the girl said, "Oh, Christ, and what's this?"

He could lift up and see at will. No hallucination, he could see the seamount and beyond to the white ribboned shores of the Skeleton Coast. And just shy, the call again: *Helllllll-p!*

Snow heard the cry for help and called back to it with a long internal *help!* of his own. He thrashed wildly in the bottom of the boat. The hot air hovered stagnant over his face. Then he felt a wave of strength. He grunted and tried to sit up. Maciel was there, helping his head lift up and over the gunwales of the boat. "You been out a long time," said the kid.

"I ain't been out at all."

Beth rowed through the boiling seas, toward the desolate stretch of the Namib. A hellish place. Here the sands of Africa reached out every day to claim new ground in the midst of the ocean. So rapidly was land expanding here that they once found a Spanish galleon shipwrecked amid sand a mile inland. The Namib. Where they said you could sift the sands with your fingers and find diamonds.

Then Beth's voice bent over him and the long rounded swells brought him down. "You're going to be all right?" she said. The phrase confused him. The words were a command but her voice was a question. The voice disturbed him. It sounded like his father even through the accent. Snow heard voices out past her, like a hundred boat parties out there bobbing up and down. He tried to pull a breath, the vapors of the ship heavy around his face. Then she kissed him and he thought maybe he wouldn't be able to breathe at all, that she might smother him before she knew what she'd done. He gasped inward even as he pushed at her and felt her pull away and only then could he draw a subtle breeze into his lungs, almost cool. Her face hovered over him. He could feel the air drifting through her arms and legs, accelerating around and through the filter of her body to feed him. He smelled her but he smelled fresh air too. He relaxed, his arms dropping. Her lips returned to him in a dry round kiss. Urging sweetly. When she pulled away he breathed freely.

Snow lifted, his headache thumping. The kid was rowing, tendons straining, face blank, blood on his hands. Blood on his hands and spattered on his face. Momo the cook was reading a chart. Danny perched at the bow looking out with a pair of binoculars. Maciel rowed. And rowed. The girl fed him water, warm and wet to his lips. Snow heard the voice calling, *"Hellllllllp—"*

His headache soared, whirled, spun his skull. He felt a fire in his brain that moved beyond pain as the kid rowed. As he refused to stop rowing. Snow stared from the bottom of the boat to the foreshortened legs and arms of the crew, Beth holding the cup to his lips and then hearing someone shout and turning toward the horizon and standing alongside the others. Her arm darted overhead in waves and her cries filled Snow's ears, the hoarse and uniform cries of the crew calling toward a ship emerging from the steam, bow knifing the sea. Snow and Maciel were the only two who didn't scream. They were too busy grunting. Snow thought maybe the ship was the authorities coming for him finally, and he tried to talk, but only a gurgle came out and the crew wasn't listening to him in any case. Their attention was drawn to the wicked bowsprit of a merchant ship, cleaving tropical waters toward them. Even Snow cheered then, filling his head with a throbbing pulse of pain and relief, ringing in the one ear left undamaged by war. They saw the bow sitting tall, a cargo ship light on cargoes, heaving upward as it drew closer, a man standing on the bow, a black man waving his arms furiously calling out *Ahoy* or something like it, some greeting on an open sea. Then the voices in the lifeboat fell away, deflated. "Oh, Jesus," said Maciel.

"Tell me that ain't the truth, just tell me that!" said Momo.

The bow edged toward them, with the name there, painted so brightly, the good ship SABBATH. Then he looked again and saw that they'd got the spelling all wrong, that it wasn't SABBATH at all but SABETH. Maybe some variant, he thought, or some foreign ship. Snow could see it. Painted so recently, so fresh it barely set before the storm waters blew it all away.

He kept staring. Saw the faint lettering before those left intact, a faint shadow of the rest of the name, and it hit him then, after minutes of gazing, that the name there was ELISABETH, a third of the name worn away by storm. A rust and steel ghost appearing out of the tropical mist of the horse latitudes, as if to inform them of their own death. He thought then perhaps they were all dead already. But beyond the ship's outline lay the long plume of the Namib.

A depression fell over them all. Silent, downcast mouths. Maciel rowed along the hull of the ship's forward half while they all still processed the reality of the ship's being broken in two. The man on the bow waved again, yelled again, *Ahoy,* and soon from the fo'c'sle deck they saw the Liberian named Jimmy as he shinnied down on a mooring line tied off to a deck cleat.

"Where you go, brother? Where hell you go?" said Danny. "I think sure you dead."

"Not gonna kill me," said Jimmy as he came aboard, rocking their small boat and greeting his twin with a strong embrace. Waves of laughter rolled over Snow. Ocean swells tightened and crested toward shore. Off the broken middle of the ship's forward half, more plastic balls floated, and from the broken ship he saw the exposed tanks along the midship bulkhead, sheared away cleanly in frayed ends of broken steel.

Snow heard the voice again. Calling, *Hell,* or *Help,* as if they meant the same thing. Floating in plastic. A person–Leeds now, coming to life and recognition. He floated on balls of plastic, an impromptu life raft, wearing an air pack. His pink deformed mitts stuck up over the gunwales and he hauled himself aboard with a thumping rock of the small craft. Leeds slumped to the base of the boat and tore the respirator mask free and breathed air.

The boat hunkered into the pale green water.

Snow thought out loud.

Delirium is a beautiful thing, he thought.

Who's Van Sickle? How long has he been this way?

Joaquin Maciel never killed Dutch Van!

He has been this way since we hauled him from the ship.

I killed Dutch Van! I killed Van Sickle! I beat him with the blunt end of a marlin spike and ran him through to the heart! I did it, by God, I did!

What's wrong with him?

He's got the blackwater. He's got the malaria deep in his brain.

What can we do for him?

You could pray for him.

Snow felt himself sink deeper into the bilges of the boat, the wetness at his ass. Pain from his loins rose upward until he thought he might piss fire. He had been at sea since he was five, following his father's trips around the world. The ocean never stopped, that was sure. The ocean was like the moral underground. He wished he could talk out loud. He wished his confession could be heard. A man needed that, like he needed to lay it all out there at some point. He needed a map of the world, needed to know where the limits were.

He felt the brush of sand beneath the lifeboat and then the tipping to one side, and he rolled out and onto the sand, looked up the long flat dunes north of Walvis Bay. How on earth could they have made Walvis Bay? The Namib, where Snow didn't know a soul. He had no relatives here, had never set foot here. They ran hard aground to wedge themselves on the beach north of the harbor's entrance. The sounds of German floated on the breeze: *der Ozean hat sich sie an Land erbrechen.* Maciel stood tall and wet, watching the endless sand shore. Snow wanted to reach for the kid's sleeve and pull him down, to ask him what he knew about any of this anyhow, what he knew about this German, what he knew about last rites. He felt his mouth move–or maybe not. I killed him, not your gramps; it was me.

The kid looked down at him with a confused look. Maybe sound did come out. Maybe he could hear it all. *I killed Dutch Van Sickle, and your grandfather helped me dump the body. I heaved him over the side up near Decker Island. I did it. I did it. I admit I did it.* The cadence of confession sounded like Morse code flickering in his brain. The kid held Snow's face in his hands, rough hands, swollen hands, hands with blood on them. *Why didn't you tell me?* But he expected no answer. He shook his head in pathetic commentary, eyes on eyes. *Thanks for doing it now. You have that. You have that, Harold.*

Then he moved away.

Beth's face appeared upside down over his head, replacing his image of the kid, and she peered down with moist eyes turned red by her fear of death and by chemistry, and his lungs felt the ragged bleeding from within. Now he couldn't tell her voice from his own. She pulsed inside him. Her whisper was his whisper. She pulled him, dragged him up the beach into warm dry sand, sifting through his fingers. She got him to sit up. He felt his arms hanging loose between his outstretched legs. Up the beach as far as he could see lay sand. "We made it, Harold. Goddamnit, we made it!"

Farther down he saw the bullet raft pulled up the beach, and a truck there, an official vehicle with a light bank across the top, and a black man standing by it in uniform, gazing toward him, pointing at him.

"You're going to be okay now, Harold," Beth said.

Der häßlichste Geschöpfaufstieg vom Meer.

Maciel clapped his back. Snow heard that funny little Snowman song, his long-dead mother sitting at the piano and explaining that love didn't mean giving yourself over to another, it meant finding yourself inside them. He had smirked at that; he snarled: maternal horse manure. Snow wished he had understood it. He felt the kid's hand on his face. He mumbled in a language Snow didn't recognize. He wondered if the kid was talking in tongues now. There was a time when he would have been unnerved by this, but now he felt only affection for the boy. Then he felt only humming. Snow wondered if this was God. He felt the kid's calloused hand to his forehead. His eyes stared down, black and clear. His voice came clear then too, rang low in Latin like an old chorus. Then the girl: her lips to his ear, her voice soft as a kiss. He could smell her body even as other hands hovered over him, and faces, the waving black seaweed hair of all those Hindus floating in the brown water of the Bengal with cremated mouths. They were here for him. He knew they were. *Wave them away,* she said. *Wave them away.* He wondered what that meant. Like he was supposed to understand. To wave away voices, and wet arms reaching for him, dripping silted water through their closed fists.

Snow blinked. He saw the girl's face over him. So brightly dark and round, her brow glistening with worry. He blinked rapidly in succession through caked blood and salted lids, and then the arms were gone. The black cavernous mouths were gone. Voices evaporated into stony silence, along with those unknown siblings, that lost family out there walking the waterfront for the first sight of the father home from sea. The lifeboat rocked next to him in a swirl of surf. Looking out he could see the crippled form of the stern end of *Elisabeth,* and Kairos sat there on the edge of the lifeboat dangling his legs saying *gotta redeem that steel, Snow,* then laughing in his Baptist way.

Snow wished he had people here in Namibia. What a lonely spot to die. Then again he reached for the girl and the boy, both next to him now, and Beth waved Kairos away or else brushed at a fly, he wasn't sure which. She placed an oily finger on Snow's head to test his fever, only to leave a smudge of black grease. He felt it there, dirty oil clinging to his sweated skin and then melting, starting to drip. Maciel knelt over him, leaned out over him to show his face against the sky. The kid smiled warmly, sadly even. Snow thought he heard him say something. He felt his breath, smelled chemicals. He felt the kid, holding his head in one hand, dabbing at his forehead with the other. He felt something relax inside. It came easy then, just heat surrounding him, his body encased by warm sand. Snow thought maybe it was his birthday.

ACKNOWLEDGMENTS

Profound thanks to the faculty and staff of the California Maritime Academy, in particular Bill Schmid and Dan Weinstock, master mariners, for their good company, patience at my endless questions, and technical expertise. Thanks to Dr. Mark Stinson and Dr. Jack Ellis for their thoughtful reading of the manuscript, as well as personal anecdotal information on tropical diseases in general and cerebral malaria specifically. My late mother-in-law, Morwenna Yackzan, my sister-in-law Linda Yackzan, and my wife, Dawn, all read and reread the manuscript, offering insightful commentaries. At U.C. Davis: Linda Morris and Laura Antonelli for providing space to work; Pam Houston, David Simpson, David Robertson, for the chance to teach; and Jack Hicks for his advice and encouragement. Deb and Buzz for their four years in Lagos and stories of West Africa. Mom, Dad, Auntie Bo—to all of my family for being the stable core. Humble thanks to Scott Phillips, Sean McNerney, Swan, Ron Bell, Bob Young, and Doug Masiel, in some cases for reading the manuscript in its formative stages and in all cases for their friendship and talk. Many thanks to my editor, David Ebershoff, for his scalpel-sharp blue pencil. And deepest thanks, as always, to my agent, Nicole Aragi—words fail.